Mary moved to Guernsey 1
Martins with her husband, not far from Icart Point. She often
sits on 'George's bench' when walking the coastal path.

First published in the UK by Gibson Publishing

Out of the Game
Text copyright 2012 by Mary J. Goodyear
Image copyright 2012 by Mary J. Goodyear
Cover image and photographs by Pat Wisher

ISBN 9780-9-570811-85

This is a work of fiction. All the characters and events depicted in this book are
fictional and any resemblance to real people or occurrences is entirely co-incidental.
Some locations that appear in the story are real enough, and others have been used
rather fictitiously.

To John, all the best bits, with my love.

Out of the
Game

Mary J. Goodyear

Gibson Publishing

Prologue
Small Island: Wicked World

George and Eileen Buchanan have retired to Guernsey, a granite island in the English Channel just within sight of the coast of France. It's a small island with a big personality, not the innocent idyllic setting that others have suggested but a place of strong passions - greed, lust and envy amongst them. The density of the population, sixty thousand people on a piece of land five miles by eight, is one factor in forming the island's character. So is its hard history of invasion and wartime occupation. Even the physical diversity of the place: cliffs, beaches, small fields full of crops and cows, busy thriving villages and roads dense with traffic, contributes to the sense of activity and intrigue.

If you know Guernsey, then you can skip this section. Most people don't like prologues anyway, they get impatient with information that's surplus to requirement, when all they want is to see if there's some kind of story being told about interesting or, preferably, wicked characters. For those who have never been to the island, then let's say that the following is a fairly truthful description of it overall, particularly one small corner that plays a central role. Most of the names in the book correspond to real places, which can be easily found on the map. Most of the people and their concerns are fictitious, or at least exaggerated.

This won't prevent islanders from having a guess at who they are.

We're in the South East, in the parish of St Martin. At the southern end of the South Esplanade near the capital, St. Peter Port, the main road twists and turns up a steep and darkly-wooded hill, Le Val des Terres, towards the residential area of Fort George. A smaller road forks off and curves down to sea level, where it continues for several hundred yards around a rocky promontory known as La Vallette.

Shortly after the point where the roads diverge stands a café, from the terrace of which visitors gaze out at the sweep of the bay and the tiny islands of Jethou, Herm and Sark. It's a pretty seascape of small bays and white beaches and inspires in many a longing for the sunny, simple pleasures of childhood, for times past when life was kinder.

Beyond the café the lane cuts a narrow channel through a granite outcrop, while a footpath makes a detour over the shoulder of the rock, taking walkers close to the sea's edge. There are a few benches on top of this outcrop, all of them facing out across the water. The island is small and crowded and the press of people and their mundane daily lives is sometimes overwhelming. Escape, in one form or another, becomes imperative. Some take to small boats at weekends, or fly off to the mainland; others make do with inward travel, by which they contemplate the warp and weft of their closely woven lives.

As the lane emerges from the rocky channel, on the right the hillside is covered with a tangle of trees and undergrowth. Dark evergreen oaks tower above the roadway and almost hide from view the modest entrance of the Military Museum. This runs deep underground, making use of fuel storage tunnels blasted out by the Germans during their five-year occupation in the Second World War. The museum is a refuge for holiday-makers on rainy days; they walk around silently in the subdued warmth, only half aware of the showcases of memorabilia and the background strains of Lili Marlene. Yet they seem glad to

Chapter One
Les Vardes, May, 1999

"Absence of occupation is not rest.
A mind quite vacant is a mind distressed."
'Retirement' William Cowper

"Steve, get a move on. I'm bloody frozen."

"I'll warm you up later. Now stick your chest out. That's right. Lean forward. Push them out. That's the job. Now smile. Smile! You look bored stiff."

"There's a lot say they like a girl to look bored. Turns them on. Makes them feel they're taking advantage. Anyway I am bored. What are you taking so long about?"

"Keep still. I'm trying to lose your double chin."

"I thought you liked things in pairs."

"Good good. It's better when you smile. Lifts all the droopy bits. Oi! Where you off to?"

"Had enough. I need the sun. What are we doing on this rock Steve? Why can't we go back to Sydney?"

"Come off it. You know we can't. Not for a bit."

"Why can't we go somewhere else then? What about Marbella? Where a girl can wear a dress without getting pneumonia."

"We're here because we'll be all right here. We can get on with things. Keep our heads down and no-one is going to bother us. A dozy little island, it's just what we need."

"Bloody freezing little island. I'm going outside and put the patio heaters on and have a coffee."

"What? Looking like that? You'll upset the neighbours."
"Now would I do a thing like that?"

*

Even after thirty-five years Eileen Buchanan hated the sound
of her husband with his morning toast. He always had two slices,
well-browned and laden with Keiller's Tawny. The normal
crunching was accompanied by an unnatural click coming from
his jaw-bone, which sounded like a painful rubbing together
of loose bones under a thin layer of flesh. Surely he must have
heard it himself? If not, someone should tell him. So why hadn't
she ever looked him straight in the eye and said, 'George, what
is that clicking noise that you make when you're chewing?' She
knew the answer of course. He'd be furious - and she couldn't
face it, not so early.

What she would really like to do, and after all those years she
felt she sort of deserved it, would be to look him straight in the
eye and say 'George, shut the fuck up!'

What a shock that would be. Not just the language – after all
they heard much worse than that every night on the TV – but the
bare-faced nature of it, any pretence at tact and consideration
gone, and her usual self-effacing deference blown out of the
window.

'Shut the fuck up!' Coarse but elegant, with a poetic grace,
which she recognised when she first heard it in some American
detective series. It had a musical, rhythmic brevity, something
to do with the repetition of all those 'u' sounds. The structure
was good, a concise coming together of form and function.
Linguistically it was an upgraded form of 'shut up' of course,
but not easy to parse. For example what part of speech was 'the
fuck'? A direct object of 'shut'? or a pre-head modifier of the
preposition phrase, and it was a phrase, even though it was only
one word, 'up' –

"Kkkeugh. Eeyuuugh!"

She jumped. Clearing his throat. Another annoying habit, even more distasteful than the click. Better change the subject. She leaned towards his Telegraph so as to be heard over the toast, "George? George – I must tell you. I've seen next door."

No answer from behind the paper but she knew he was listening.

"When I opened the bedroom window this morning, I heard a woman's voice and caught a glimpse of the man. Young, dark-haired, athletic-looking."

At least the chewing stopped. He lowered the paper. Over the half-glasses, recently and reluctantly required, but now used to some effect, the look was accusatory. "See any children or dogs?"

"Nope. Just the two of them. More tea?"

"Did they see you?"

"Too busy I think." A brief pause. "I was wondering whether to go over and introduce myself?" The paper went right down. That was a mistake.

"For God's sake, Eileen, don't get involved. Just leave them alone. It's just our bloody luck that Mrs. - whatever her name was - moved."

"Evans, Mrs. Evans; yes, she was nice." She hadn't moved, she'd died.

"Better still, she was inaudible. I don't care if next door are serial killers as long as whatever they do, they do it in sodding silence. All I want is peace and quiet. Not much to ask." He shook the paper and resumed his reading. "Just half a cup."

There was a brief, healing silence over the tea. He cleared his throat once more, this time in a preparatory way, "What are you up to this morning?"

His tone, indeed the very fact he'd asked her something about her intentions was conciliatory. It gave her the opportunity to present her case for an indulgent little expedition.

"I thought I'd walk down into town –it's a lovely morning - get some really good olive oil and some of that Parmesan you

7

like…" Only half true. She really wanted to buy something for herself: a cotton sweater or a pair of sandals – something made for sunshine, for being out of doors. It had been a long winter. "What about you?"

He affected a slight but visible startle reaction at the interruption. "In my study of course. I've got things to do."

Another half-truth. He would be in his study, but she knew that apart from paying a couple of bills, he had nothing to do. Nothing at all. That was the problem, for both of them.

"Won't be long." She brushed her cheek against his, immune to the lack of response, and escaped.

It really was a beautiful morning, the spring sunshine almost unnaturally bright, and the garden green and bursting with life. Below her the steep hill, stretched down to Havelet Bay and beyond that was Castle Cornet with St. Sampson's Harbour in the distance. The sea was calm and clear, with that special green-blue intensity that she had never seen in the sea round the mainland. It was good to be alive and living in Guernsey.

She glanced at the new neighbours' house as she walked past. Bigger than theirs but it didn't have the special feature, the main attraction, the one that clinched the deal, the belvedere right at the top that gave them a view of the sea. "A sea-view adds at least another £50,000 of value", the estate agent had said when they were viewing the house, "And it's not just the monetary value, it would make a lovely quiet room for reading or -", and here he had turned to Eileen with an engaging smile, "sewing."

He was right about the quiet, but wrong about the sewing; George had taken the room as his study.

All the houses along Les Vardes were large - it was a 'good' area - but they were too close together for the address to be considered smart. Location was a matter of great concern to everyone on Guernsey, incomers and locals alike. It was one of the few ways to assess wealth and social standing, clothes and cars being unreliable indicators on a small, windy island with narrow roads and nowhere much to drive. The first

question asked of new acquaintances was not the mainland question of 'what do you do?' but always 'where do you live?' meaning which parish, which road and precisely which house – the bungalow with the concrete driveway or the old granite farmhouse with the twenty vergees of land around it? Les Vardes was not a serious contender. It could hold its own in most circumstances, but not in the context of the quieter areas of St. Martin's or the modern multi-million pound mansions perched on the cliff in nearby Fort George.

They had been invited for drinks up at the Fort, when they first moved to the island nearly two years earlier, shortly after George's retirement. It had not been quite what they had expected.

"Bloody cheek." George was angry as they'd driven back at only seven fifteen to a scratch supper of cold meat and pickle at home. "All that pretence at being friendly. Only wanted to sell his bloody investment services. You see how they wanted us

9

to get out of there when he saw I wasn't interested and that we hadn't got enough cash for him to play with? Wanker."

Eileen had kept silent. She wondered if their humiliation had been her fault. When Laura Wolfson had rung her, out of the blue, welcoming her to the island and inviting them over for drinks, she'd eagerly accepted, being touched by the apparent warmth of the gesture and vaguely excited by the prospect it offered. So they would have friends in Guernsey, a social life, a bit of middle-aged fun! Perhaps this evening's drinks, she thought, would turn into dinner and the beginning of a real and lasting friendship.

But that evening, as she and Laura came back from a brief tour of the garden, and re-entered the sitting room where the men had been talking but were now silently drinking, she recognised that her vision had been naïve. The second bottle of wine had not been opened, and the sulky teenage daughter did not come out again from the kitchen with another round of canapés. Just before seven o'clock Eric Wolfson looked dramatically at his watch and reminded his wife in an overly loud voice that they shouldn't be late for their dinner date.

"We must have lunch..." he called out after George and Eileen as they drove away, the unlikely possibility of any reference to a specific day lost in the sound of churning gravel.

Since then their social life had picked up a little but it was far from the network of friends they'd had on the mainland. Eileen reluctantly decided that the locals were not easy material for close friendships. They were a tight-knit community, suspicious of newcomers, and seemingly only interested in them as prospective customers for financial services, garden landscaping, window-cleaning and the like, or as purchasers of conservatories, Jacuzzis, patio heaters, and over-priced garden ornaments. She, and George too, had expected the island to provide them with a sleepy, old-fashioned retreat. They were surprised and slightly disappointed to find the place busy and shrill with the sound of money-making. But perhaps their limited social life would change now with the new neighbours. She must find a way of introducing herself to them without making George cross.

Meanwhile today was really a glorious morning. Glorious. "The glory of the beauty of the morning" – that summed it up. Now who had written that and why, children, had he used the word 'glory'? Because he was referring to more than just physical beauty, that's the reason. 'Glory' implied transcendence, linking man to God, or if not God in an Old Testament way then at least to the pagan powers of Nature. "The cuckoo crying o'er the untouched dew..." How did it go after that? And who had written it – the name was just there but, no, it was no good, she couldn't dredge it out of her memory. Have to look it up back at home.

And the flowers! There were days when it seemed that the whole of the island was in flower; the Cliff Path, for example, in April, when wild bluebells and campion carpeted the cliffs and the air was full of - what had Betjeman called it? - "the coconut smell of the gorse", and even here, so close to town, the gardens were bursting with colour and fragrance.

In many ways the island reminded her of school days in rural Sussex, something to do with the childlike size of it as well as the unspoiled richness of the hedgerows. When she walked down the green lanes of St. Saviour, or stood looking out over the causeway to Lihou Island she remembered exactly, exactly, how it had felt to be fourteen. Every day then had been so full of promise and she had felt right at the centre of it all, specially chosen for something, selected for a miraculous transformation. Into what exactly she hadn't known, but she was sure it would be wonderful: the sky and the sea and the flowers were signs of the glories to come.

Only they hadn't come. The signs had been wrong or she had mis-read them. Over the years there had been no transformation, and no secret was ever revealed. Hers had been a common enough trajectory: school days, college, teaching English Lit.

11

at the local comprehensive, being courted by George, marriage, then Celia's birth – that was wonderful of course – then work again. She'd had thirty-three years in education; enjoyed it for the first ten and felt proud to be doing something that she'd assumed was making a difference. But later on it became less rewarding. The job itself changed, as well as the children. In the last few years she seemed to spend most of her time filling in forms after lessons and trying to impose discipline on increasingly disruptive pupils during them. She, who had always been so good with youngsters and had enjoyed their company, now longed to get away at the end of the day.

"Give it up for God's sake", George used to say at the sight of her drawn features, annoyed when yet again dinner was late. "You know you don't enjoy it and the salary's hardly worth having. If you were at home we could probably save what you make, on laundry and things. And you would have more time for the cooking. It would be much nicer for me, Ellie, having you at home all the time. Besides it's only a comprehensive."

So she left - nine years before official retirement - with a sense of something unfinished and of herself as having failed. Not that the years after work seemed any more rewarding. Looking after George and his food and his shirts was of limited appeal; it was collars and cuffs all the way to the horizon. All the way to dusty death said a small voice in her head –"And all our yesterdays have lighted fools the way to dusty death."

At least she and George were happy enough. Perhaps 'comfortable' was a better description, or 'used to each other'. At least they had been used to each other, but in recent years George had changed. Since the day he left Parson and Green, he had almost overnight evolved into something unfamiliar and unpredictable, from being a more or less reliable partner into a snappy and wily old dog that she now spent her time either placating or avoiding. The new George had many of the characteristics of the old: he had always been bossy, controlling and unthinkingly selfish, but whereas this had once been accompanied by an element of good-humoured optimism, now he was a Grumpy Old Man. Why did she put up with it? Good question. She should have stood up to him a long time ago. But it had always seemed so much easier to let him have his way. So now the relationship was fixed and brittle. She could only escape when one of them died. And if it's me that survives, she reflected, I'll be too old to enjoy my freedom. What a wimp I've been...

She actually caught a glimpse of the cyclist bearing down on her as she stepped off the kerb, a mere flash of red shirt and black helmet from the corner of her eye. She tried to stop, one foot on the pavement, one in the road, flinching from the screech of brakes and the cyclist's loud and too-late warning cry. He managed to keep his balance and speeded on, but she lost hers and fell heavily to the pavement, where she sat shocked and winded and already annoyed with herself.

"Can I help?" A woman hurried over to help and stretched out a strong young arm.

Eileen struggled to her feet with the help of the arm and started dusting herself down, but she was trembling and her wrist was grazed and bleeding. "He was going so fast."

"You were lucky he missed you. The same happened to my old Gran, just like you. They do go fast on those new bikes. Can I help you across the road?"

"I'm all right on my own, thank you."

Her legs felt unsteady as she staggered across the road, as if they belonged to somebody else, an old and doddery somebody else. She stood for a moment examining her wrist, still trembling as she picked out small pieces of embedded gravel.

It was her own fault, she should have been concentrating. But even so, that idiot cyclist had come out of nowhere! And then the way the woman had spoken to her. 'My old Gran!' And trying to help her across the road. It was so humiliating.

She moved more cautiously now down Hauteville and Cornet Street, tight-lipped and resentful, George, flowers and poetry set aside. Then at the bottom of the hill just as she was passing the town church the missing last line came into her mind, slyly and unbidden.

"I cannot bite the day to the core", she muttered triumphantly to her reflection in the mirror in the ladies' lavatory near the bus station, in between dabs at the grazes on her arm. "I cannot bite the day to the core. Edward Thomas. The Glory." This minor victory released a spark of pleasure, instantly followed by guilt. How rude she'd been. Why couldn't she have accepted the kindness instead of getting cross?

She stared at herself as dispassionately as she could and took no pleasure in what she saw: a long colourless face, tired eyes and the look of something abandoned, unfinished. She had always had a sad expression and no matter how much she tried to use make-up, her face always looked undressed – and as if she had not bothered to make an effort.

"Why don't you put on some lipstick and make something of yourself?" George used to say in the days before he gave up volunteering any comments about her appearance at all. "You look so tired."

It may have not been her fault that she was unattractive, but it definitely seemed somehow to be her responsibility. Women were expected to look appealing, it was their duty and in this she had failed. Many years earlier she had overheard George talking in a corner to a couple of his male friends at a dinner party. They had been discussing women, unaware she was standing behind them at the open doorway, with a tray of coffee. She remembered his words. She could even remember what she had been wearing that evening; a burgundy-coloured dress with a tight bodice and full skirt that flattered her slight figure. She thought she looked quite glamorous, although no-one commented. Nevertheless, it had been a happy evening, a relatively happy marriage, until that moment when she had heard George's conspiratorial but loud whisper.

"She's not what you'd call sexy, I'd be the first to admit that. But you don't need that with a wife, do you? Whole world and his dog would be sniffing round her. No-one is ever going to try it on with Eileen and that's the way I like it."

All three men laughed so loudly that she was able to turn around and go back into the kitchen unnoticed. She put the tray down very carefully and considered what she should do: walk out into the suburban night and never come back, or go back into the dining-room and pretend she had not heard.

She had weighed things up as she stared at the cooling coffee. It would be hard to start life again financially. She could manage on her own on her teacher's salary, but what about Celia? She couldn't leave her behind. No, there was no choice really. Pretence, at least for then, was the only option.

Anyway he was right. She wasn't sexy. She hadn't got whatever it was that made women desirable. She was a mousy girl who had grown up to be a mousy woman. If enough people had told her she was pretty, perhaps she would have become so. Or if only George had told her she had the kind of looks that appealed to him then she could have made more of herself. As it was, his words that night at the party had hardened her heart.

She leaned towards the mirror. Being helped across the road! But she looked every one of her fifty-nine years today in this bright light and the only reason she was not an 'Old Gran' was Celia's reluctance to settle down and produce a family. Eileen had begun to doubt she ever would, especially since the American girl who had moved in with Celia seemed to be taking up so much of her time and energy.

Feeling better for the soap and hot water, she tried smiling at her reflection as she dried her hands on a paper towel. She'd go to the delicatessen first and then look for a skirt in the little shop below Bruno's restaurant. Something in yellow. Funny that, she'd never really liked the colour when she was younger, but in recent years she found herself choosing it, first for things around the home – kettle, toaster, tablecloth – and now as a colour to wear next to her skin. She wanted now a pale yellow, with a touch of green to it; the colour of daffodils, of spring, youth and optimism. Yellow was a club and she wanted to be part of it. "Oh daffodils we weep to see thee haste away so soon...." Poetry had always been her favourite at school and still offered solace, especially when spoken aloud. "De da de da de da has yet attained his noon..."

In the mirror she saw a short heavy-built woman with a thin whey-faced girl standing close behind her. The woman, shaven-headed and with ears pierced through with many rings, looked accusingly at Eileen.

"It's all right. I just can't remember how it goes." Eileen smiled politely at her in the mirror. "It's poetry..."

"Don't you look at me like that."

Eileen fell silent.

"Kyely-Anne, come 'ere. Right now." She threw her cigarette end into the wet basin then noisily squeezed herself and the child into the cubicle and slammed and bolted the door.

Eileen stepped outside into the sunshine, wrinkling her nose against the smell of wet ash. The day was going deeply and irretrievably wrong.

*

George pulled himself awkwardly up the steep stairs to the belvedere, mug of coffee in one hand and the Guernsey Press tucked under his arm. As he stepped into the room and stood to get his breath back, he felt a momentary sense of pride at the sight of desk and chair waiting for him in the sunshine and at the warm fragrance of leather and polished wood. He set mug and newspaper down, went to the window and looked out at the view of the not-so-distant sea. The estate agent had said it added at least another hundred thousand to the value of the house. This morning the sea was deep blue and calm, framed by the Turkish oaks and the pines at the bottom of his land. At least a hundred.

He eased himself into his chair, letting out a sigh. These days he sighed every time he sat down. As if he were very weary. Or very old. Sometimes he tried not to but it seemed as natural and unstoppable as squinting in the sunshine or blinking at a flash-light. Maybe it has some Darwinian survival function, he thought, but what? It was both an irritation and some small comfort to notice that Eileen had begun doing it too, and not only when she came in from working in the garden.

He took a sip of his coffee. Mm, good. Yes, life was good. He ran through his curriculum vitae – the positive version. He'd had a happy childhood, what he could remember of it, a passable education from a (minor) public school, and a successful career, at the end of which he had received a generous golden handshake. And now he was successfully retired. Apart from the general weariness he was, as far as he could tell, in sound health and was good-looking, really, for a man his age. He'd still got his direct, challenging gaze. 'As if he knows what you're thinking' he'd overheard one of his secretaries saying; for which he'd recommended a disproportionately generous bonus that Christmas. He ran his hand over his face. The chin was not his strong point; it wasn't weak as such but he would have liked it to have had greater definition. But at least he still had a jaw-line, not like poor old Thompson, whose face had melted into his neck before he reached forty. There was enough hair to meet the Atlantic winds with confidence, and it could still be called dark - in parts. And most of his teeth, even though now they were a bit brown and gappy, were his own. He'd always been proud of his height – six foot one. Two in his formal shoes. Yes, a tall man, with strong straight legs, hint of a belly maybe, but he could cut a dash, dressing conservatively but with a flair for colour. He spoke what they used to call 'well' - 'Received English' – not that it counted for a lot these days – and he knew enough about a wine list to make choices not totally determined by price. And if he'd lost a bit of his sparkle and his winning ways with the ladies, who hadn't by sixty-three?

He owned a good house in a good area of the island and he had a plain but loyal wife and a – how should he describe Celia? – an intelligent daughter. He pictured her now, earrings swinging as she explained some detail of her job with Camden Council, and her long square-cut nails tapping in accompaniment to the points she made. Yes, she was intelligent in her modern way, although she would never have got the better of him if she'd joined his company, despite all the 'Assertiveness Training' courses he'd been on. She wouldn't have survived in the cut and thrust of a man's world like marketing. Not his little girl. Only not so little now. In the last six or seven years she had become heavy and the very short hair seemed to accentuate the fleshiness of her face. He'd made the mistake of commenting on her weight at their last encounter.

"I'm not going to take offence because what you've just said is only your point of view, George." He wished she wouldn't call him by his first name. "There's no such thing as my being 'too heavy'-" she made Boy Scout dib dib signs in the air which for a moment had George puzzled, "- period. There are no absolutes, only different points of view, all of them equally valid. I don't think I'm overweight, and really it's only my perspective that matters. I'm not here to be an object for other people. Certainly not for men, although of course for me you're not a man in that way. If I'm comfortable with being how I am, then so should you be. Things have progressed, you know, since your day."

He had considered debating the concept of progress, and its inevitable link with the ages of those debating it, but decided to leave things be. There were times when he hadn't the will to engage with her tireless energy and heavily underlined speech. Her generation was, anyway, so very different from his and Eileen's. It was hard sometimes to recognise her as their own flesh and blood. He took a big swig of his coffee, choosing to ignore the drops that spilled onto his clean blotter.

She was certainly right about things having changed since his day. But not for the better. George found himself slipping down a well-trodden incline from chirpy optimism to deep doom. Despite himself, he was opening up, yet again, the big black box marked State of the Nation. Surely it was more than just age that prompted him to think that life in modern Britain ('Post-modern' Celia would have corrected him) was all going to Hell in a hand basket?

Even in Guernsey, with its superficial air of old-fashioned charm, he could feel the cold bleak winds of change. The older citizens were a normal enough bunch but the youngsters were a shambles. It wasn't simply that they looked so unappetising, with tattoos and pierced eyebrows that made him wince with distaste, but how they behaved. They strode the narrow streets, the boys in baggy trousers with the crutches round their knees and the girls, most of them pushing prams, brazenly displaying greying brassiere straps and bulging waists. Or else they sat noisily with cans of lager on the benches near the town church, or belted round the sea front in clapped-out cars, radios blasting with whatever passed for music these days. The trouble was they had nowhere to go and nothing to do, so went round and round the island like wasps in a jam jar. Worst of all they seemed to be having such a good time. Bugger the lot of them.

Think about something else for God's sake. Your job, man, you were successful, think about what you achieved there. What did I achieve? His thoughts went back to Parson and Green and to his last years there. They weren't happy. He had been dismayed and alarmed by the new cohort of young managers. They were more confident and aggressive than he had ever been, cocky and smart-arsed, even with their superiors. They affected rough working-class accents even though some of them had been to better schools than his, and, most depressingly, spoke a marketing language he simply couldn't understand. It was the jargon of the business schools – institutions that had not existed in his day – and of journals he no longer had the time, interest or concentration to read.

In the last year at work he adopted the habit of withdrawing early from the confrontational weekly meetings with his juniors, where he felt despised and his ideas dismissed. At half past ten he would make his excuses - always related to the pressure of work - and seek the safety of his office on the seventh floor where he could lick his wounds: "Make me a cup of coffee would you Susan, there's a good girl. I've left them to it – they'll come to their senses soon enough". "Yes Mr. Buchanan, right away sir. Would you like a biscuit?" "I wouldn't mind Susan, and afterwards would you go and put a couple of quid in the meter for me – the car's just round the corner in the usual space?" "Certainly sir, my pleasure."

He often wondered how Susan got on with all the changes. He had assumed she would want to leave after the merger and the kerfuffle of restructuring, especially when she knew he'd received his early retirement package and would no longer be her boss. But no, she had decided to stay on and look after the new Marketing Director.

"Are you quite sure about staying on Susan? I can always ask around at the golf club and see if anyone's got a position to suit you?"

"I'll be fine sir and you know what they say, a change is as good as a rest. Oh sorry sir I didn't mean it to sound like that!"

"It's all right Susan I know how you meant it."

But did he? Anyway she didn't seem depressed, on the contrary, rather more than usually cheerful. He was further surprised to see, on the third day of the transition week, that she had acquired a new and rather becoming hairstyle, and was wearing red nail polish - always, in his experience, a come-on.

One week! That was all they needed of him after twenty-seven years of commitment; just five days to let the new Director know what the department had achieved under George's command, and what was planned for the next five years. He had drafted a series of presentations for that week, but the new Director – an absurdly young pipsqueak in his late thirties - wasn't interested.

"I'm not saying you've not done a good job over the years George, but I think you'll agree it's time to move on. The presentation would be yesterday's thinking. The past is dead and gone. My job is to breathe fresh air into a department that needs dragging into the 21st century. Fast Forward Change Management specialists are coming in to run a few Blue Sky creative sessions to help us all start thinking out of the box. And I've booked a couple of consumer focus groups to get it straight from the horse's mouth. It's time we connected with our customers. One-to-one marketing. Anticipate their needs." He tidied his near-empty desk then gave George a thin smile, revealing pointy but very white teeth. "I know your official leaving date is Friday but if you wanted to go early, that's fine by me. It's the new Stateside policy to let people go quietly and as soon as they have been served their notice. Easier for everyone concerned."

But George was not the sort to abandon ship just when his crew needed him most; he decided he would see his vessel – and it was still, just, his vessel – until it came into port. Meanwhile, he took his folder of acetates back to his room and filed them away, confident that he would be called upon later in the week. But the call didn't come. The new Director was too busy, poking his nose into all the departments – even ones not directly under his control –and doing something called 'data fusion' on the laptop that he carried everywhere with him. And he took lunch out every day: once with the Head of R&D, once with the Financial Director and on Thursday with the MD himself. As on each occasion he came back before two o'clock and clearly sober, George could only assume that these brown-nosing sorties amongst the Board were not a hundred percent successful.

Nevertheless, despite the upheaval, and against all the odds, there had been an upbeat mood that week in Marketing and George felt proud to be handing his baby over in such a good state of health.

Then suddenly it was Friday and his last afternoon at work. Susan stood in the doorway promptly at five thirty, ready to leave. She was smiling as she shook his hand, but he imagined he could see a certain moistness about her eyes. He kept her hand in his for a little longer than usual. She had been a good secretary.

He turned to open his briefcase, "Wait a moment Susan, I have something for you," and after a few moments struggling with the catch found what he had bought her. It was a brooch, of silver and turquoise, not very expensive but pretty enough, and he knew she'd appreciate the gesture. He'd often wondered whether she was disappointed that he'd never made a pass at her. It would be wrong to let her think he hadn't often thought about it but there had never seemed to be an appropriate occasion to say to her that although he found her very attractive, pressure of work meant there was no time to express how he felt. Work, after all, had to come first. The choice of jewellery as a gift, however, was a sign that he had always valued her as a woman and that, had circumstances been different, etc. etc.

But when he turned back, words at the ready and the little

package in his hand, she had vanished. He called out but she seemed to have left. Obviously saying goodbye had been difficult for her as well.

He cleared out the few remaining files from his desk, and put his diary, a photograph of Celia as a baby and his lucky coffee mug into his briefcase. He poured the remains of his glass of water over Planty in its pot on the windowsill. Sheila, his fifth secretary, had bought it for him and somehow it had survived for eleven years, a bit the worse for wear, mind, he thought as he tweaked off a dead leaf – you and me both, chum. Good luck. Then he pulled off the Friday, Saturday and Sunday pages from his three-year daily calendar. What was the saying for Monday? "When the going gets tough, the tough get going." How funny, that was exactly him. He'd always been prepared to roll up his sleeves and get down to hard work, face up to the problems that management sent him. Yes, 'tough' was a fair description for his work-style.

He pushed his chair neatly under his desk; tough, and well-organised. He hesitated over the engraved silver cup that had been awarded him as Best Speaker at the Conference in Norwich in 1985, but decided to leave it to the new Director. It would be salutary for him to be confronted with proof that the company had been forging ahead when he was still wet behind the ears, and a small victory for George to know that something with his name on it would still be around for posterity. There, his room was all shipshape, ready for Monday and the new man. May God Bless all who sail in her!

At a quarter to six he went out into the main office, wondering what they were giving him as a farewell do; possibly just the usual, an informal session at the local wine bar with his team. That was fine by him; no reason why he should be treated as special in any way, he'd be very happy with just a relaxed drink with his team, though they may have decided on something more substantial. The Savoy Grill wouldn't be totally out of the question given his level of seniority. Either way he expected the evening would go on for a bit, but he'd taken the precaution of coming in that day by train, and had warned Eileen he'd be home late.

There were two men in overalls outside his office door, leaning with a stagey weariness on a stack of new furniture: a massive rosewood desk with a built-in shelf for the computer, matching designer leather chair and rosewood cabinets, a huge framed map of the world, a couple of modern very abstract paintings and a glossy-leaved six foot palm tree in a brass container. For a few seconds he thought it was some kind of leaving gift and was just wondering how on earth he would get it all home, when the older of the two men gave a dramatic sigh and raised his eyebrows.

"You done?"

"Where is everyone?"

"Don't know mate, but we was just thinking you ain't never goin' to come out of there. No offence but we want to get home tonight. Can we go in now?"

He stood aside while they strode into his office, and then looked around the open-plan office. Nobody there. The department seemed empty. Where were they all? Perhaps gathered on the ground floor in the lobby ready to surprise him as he stepped out of the lift? He stood still, ears straining to hear the muffled sound of people trying to stay silent. Nothing. It was only then that a very small doubt crept into his mind, like cold water leaking out of a pipe, not yet dripping but forming a wet coating on the metal, evidence enough that something was definitely wrong. Perhaps there was nobody downstairs and no winebar session planned - informal or otherwise - no back-slapping, or shaggy dog stories, or last piece of malicious gossip. No gold watch and no chance to give the farewell speech that he'd prepared during the week. Could this be it, then? Twenty-seven years leading to this: an empty room and a silence broken only by the humming of computers left on standby and the whine of vacuum cleaners on the floor below?

So be it. He took one last look around, then walked out into the corridor and summoned the lift. At least he could take satisfaction from knowing that he had left his mark on the company, that what he had achieved wouldn't be forgotten. While he waited, the workmen joined him along with his old swivel chair, two grey metal filing cabinets, a photograph of the 1991 conference in Broadstairs and the waste bin, and set them down by the lift doors. His calendar, desk blotter and reading lamp had been dumped inside the bin. The lift came and the men carried first the chair, the cabinets, the picture and then the bin inside, and looked at George, "Going down?"

George shook his head emphatically, turned around and went back into his office. Already it looked unfamiliar. It had been cleared of his furniture, and the new stuff, shiny and confident, looked somehow very much at home. He swung the massive chair around and tentatively lowered himself into its depths; it was wonderfully comfortable. He noticed that Planty and the Norwich Conference cup had been left on the windowsill. He scooped up the cup in his empty hand and left the building by the stairs.

That evening was spent in a pub in Finsbury Square, where he sat alone smoking a couple of panatellas and trying to get drunk. After what he thought was a plausible sort of interval he picked up his briefcase and his cup and took the train home. That night he gave Susan's brooch to Eileen, saying it was a gift from his colleagues.

A week later he bought himself a gold watch and had the back engraved with his name and the dates of his working life with the company.

"What would you like as an inscription sir? There's room for up to five words – providing they're not too long."

"Don't know really. What do most people put?"

"Depends on the kind of job and – er – the level of success. 'For loyal service', that suits a more, shall we say, clerical position, or when the recipient hasn't quite fulfilled his potential.

'Always an inspiration' – that's when they don't know exactly what it was you did, but could find no reason for firing you earlier. Latin tags, of course, are still popular, even more so now that so few people understand them. 'Per ardua ad astra', for example. That can be very attractive for someone, whom everyone agrees, but nobody wants to say, never quite made the grade."

He looked at George patiently, head on one side.

"What would you suggest for someone who believed he ran a successful department but has just been shat upon from a great height?"

A pause. "I see. Well, short of 'Sod the lot of you', why not try 'Non illegitimi carborundum'? I think there's just about room for that."

"What's it mean?"

"'Don't let the bastards grind you down.'"

"Can you do it by this afternoon?"

He showed the watch to Eileen, who looked at the inscription for a long time without saying anything. Then he put it away in his sock drawer. That week he worked his way through five bottles of scotch and once found himself weeping when he thought about Shirley's plant abandoned on the windowsill and wondered if anyone would remember to water it.

After that he felt nothing. Absolutely nothing. Within three months he and Eileen had sold up and moved to Guernsey and in this new environment it was as if his work and, more disturbingly, his younger self, had never existed. In Guernsey he was, and it seemed as if he had always been, seriously middle-aged edging towards elderly. He had always been sixty something, had always had knees that cracked as he walked downstairs, and had always needed to get up in the night several times to piss.

And he had always been - how to put it - sexually challenged, of diminished drive, hormonally quiescent –oh, bugger it, impotent.

27

That had taken him by surprise. He'd not expected to carry on being able to perform with Eileen. After thirty years it would have been like incest. Anyway she hadn't seemed concerned when that part of their marriage came to an end. But he had always believed that were he given the right stimulus, a glimpse of his secretary's inner thigh or the smell of the receptionist's perfume or the sight of pert little buttocks in tight trousers, then the feelings and the capability would be there more or less as before. When he was forty he'd kept a stash of Playboy magazines in the bottom of his wardrobe for those times when he was on his own and when there was no outlet, as it were. As the years passed, he'd felt the need to move on to more explicit, more reliable material, which he'd kept locked away in an old briefcase and had still brought out from time to time, until only a few years ago. But then one day he threw them away, wrapping them in three plastic bags in case Eileen accidentally looked inside and thrusting them to the bottom of the dust bin. It was a relief of a different kind to be rid of them.

The first occasion he failed when faced with the real thing had been with number nine secretary, the one before Susan. He'd managed to get permission for her to come with him to a conference in Warwick. They had both drunk a lot and it seemed natural and fun to end up together in her bed. But Percy wouldn't perform, and no amount of joking would disguise the fact that he wouldn't even firm up. George pretended he had to get back to his room for an overseas call, but she knew and he knew that she knew. She was still giggling as he quietly closed her bedroom door. He managed to get her transferred to R&D, but to his relief she offered her resignation before Human Resources had a chance to familiarise her with the new department, and, he wholeheartedly hoped, before she'd had the chance to familiarise the rest of the staff about their boss.

After that George had been frightened of trying. Warwickshire had been six years ago and things had been more or less dormant ever since. The worst thing was not knowing if this were normal. Perhaps everyone his age felt, or rather didn't feel, that way. There was no-one he could talk to about it. Not, of course, Eileen. And his friends might ridicule him, at least behind his back even if they appeared sympathetic to his face. Definitely not the doctor; he was hopeless, even for straightforward ailments like athlete's foot and George didn't trust the sleazy-looking clinics advertised in the Sunday papers. He wished he knew someone who had tried this new Viagra tablet thing, though the cautionary stories had heard about the risk of being stuck in the same position for a couple of days did nothing to imbue a sense of confidence.

Now that he had plenty of time to think about the potential for things to go wrong he became aware of decline in other areas of his life and parts of his body: his joints ached, he needed stronger reading glasses and he often forgot why he had come into a room. Worst of all was that the world had become so much faster; everyone else seemed to talk and eat and drive at top speed. For a while he wondered why, until it occurred to him that maybe he was slowing down. For example, driving; these days he had to concentrate, where once weaving his way through the traffic had seemed an easy dance that he'd never needed to learn. Even as a pedestrian, now when he crossed a busy road, he found himself recalling what used to be printed on the back of his exercise books in primary school. "Look right, look left, then look right again, and if the way is clear, WALK across the road! Do not run!" Good advice, although he couldn't run if a ten ton truck were to bear down on him. The joints couldn't take it even if the legs could summon the speed.

What alarmed him most had been how quickly the deterioration had happened. During just two years of his retirement he had metamorphosed from hard-talking effective marketing man to pathetic old buffer.

At least this inner collapse didn't show. Last time they went back to the mainland, friends remarked on how well he looked since leaving work, "George, I don't have to ask you how things are. Channel Islands, life of leisure, sunshine – you're looking good. Just goes to show what happens when you don't have to go to work any more." To all outward appearances, George was alive and firing on all cylinders. Only he knew, and perhaps Eileen had guessed, that he was just going through the motions.

As he finished the last of his now lukewarm coffee, he recalled, against his will and with painful clarity, an incident from the previous week. He'd been driving with Eileen along Les Banques and at Halfway had hesitated briefly, surely only for a few seconds, before deciding to change lanes and turn left up Vale Road. A motor cyclist came up fast in the inside lane. George saw him, and braked, but only just in time. Both vehicles came to a standstill and the car's engine stalled. The motor-cyclist was a young kid – he couldn't have been more than sixteen – and he lifted his visor, looked menacingly at Eileen and George and shouted loud enough for anyone nearby to hear, "If you can't play the game, you dithering old git, why don't you get off the fucking pitch!"

George rested his head on his arms at the empty desk in the belvedere and gave a muffled groan.

Chapter Two
A Brief Encounter

"The glory invites me, yet it leaves me scorning
All I can ever do, all I can be…."
'The Glory' Edward Thomas

It was a dress not a skirt: a slim linen sheath in lemon yellow, sleeveless and with a kick pleat at the back.

"Do you think my arms are too old for this?" Stupid question – what could the assistant say?

"Well your arms look fine to me but if you feel a little exposed, there's a jacket that goes with it, very pretty."

And it was.

"It's on special offer: The dress is sixty-three pounds and the jacket, let's have a look, only fifty-four. That's a ten per cent reduction on both items. Our Spring Sale: a real bargain."

Eileen looked at her reflection and felt a sudden lift of the heart, a sure sign of an imminent purchase. She'd take them both.

"In fact I think I'll wear it now. I'm seeing someone for lunch. Unexpectedly. I mean I've only just heard from them. And it's such a lovely colour – and today… you know?"

The assistant gave a kind and conspiratorial smile. "I always wore my new shoes home when I was a child. Couldn't wait to enjoy them." She wrapped Eileen's old dress gently in tissue paper and put it in a carrier bag. "It is a lovely colour, especially for a day like today."

Eileen left the shop in a small daze of happiness. How could something as simple as a new dress make her feel this way? It wasn't an interesting idea or something spiritually rewarding – it was just an object, something to wear. Trivial. Nevertheless her heart welled with optimism and well-being. "Sweetly sweetly sang the kippers, in the basket with the slippers…." Or was it the other way round? "Sweetly sweetly sang the slippers?" Surely not. She'd look it up when she got home. For now she wanted to celebrate. Coffee at that place on the Victoria Pier? Yes. She'd buy a magazine, and, maybe, have piece of ginger cake with her coffee. Then go home and make a nice lunch for George. Lovely!

There was even an empty table for her outside in the sun. She sat with her drink, turning over the property pages of Country Life, letting the small bud of happiness swell up and grow inside her. Everything was for the best in the best of all possible worlds.

"Eileen? Eileen Buchanan?"

It was not so much the sound of her name as the quality of his voice – deep, friendly and oh, so familiar – that made her stomach lurch. The voice of times past; good times, very good times. She looked up. He was tall and heavy, white hair, nice smile but she couldn't see his eyes as he was wearing wrap-around sunglasses.

As she hesitated, he took off the glasses, "It is Eileen isn't it? I thought so. It's me, Doug, Doug Foster. From Greenford."

Memories flooded back at tremendous speed: the four of them having dinner at The Pheasant, driving home in Doug's open car, dancing with him at Doreen's thirtieth birthday. And that other night, 23rd October 1969, a Tuesday. The night when George was at a Conference in Harrogate.

"Doug, Doug – what a surprise – after all these years!"

He had been very persuasive: 'No one need know. George is away, and Doreen's with her Mum over in Chalfont. Besides it would be a shame to waste the tickets.'

"Can I sit down?" He nodded towards the empty chair beside

her.

"Of course." She moved her chair a little to accommodate his bulk; she'd forgotten what a heavy man he was.

It had been a wonderful evening; theatre, followed by supper then back to the Strand Palace. He'd already booked a room. "I hope you don't think I'm assuming anything. I've got to be in town early tomorrow. The company is paying. So why not come up and have a coffee and make the most of it." Was all that true or had he known that she would say yes?

Anyway, it had been one small and very easy step from the coffee to finding herself with Doug under the covers of the huge double bed, half-listening to the sounds coming up from the Strand, of the throb of diesel taxis taking couples to their homes in the suburbs. She couldn't remember much about their love-making, she felt too guilty to really enjoy it, but for many years afterwards the sound of a black cab seemed naughty and faintly erotic.

Now he was easing his bulk further into the chair and looking at her smiling. "We're on holiday, a four day cruise. It's the afternoon stopover in St. Peter's Port today."

"St. Peter Port." Her correction was automatic; it was one thing the locals were fussy about.

He had tried to reassure her when they were making love: 'Relax darling, you know George is doing the same somewhere in Harrogate. What he doesn't know won't hurt him!'

That hadn't helped much, although it was true. She thought George was having another affair with a secretary. She had suspected it after his office Christmas party when she'd come across one or two items, unsigned postcards and a silly little teddy bear, stuffed away at the back of his sock drawer.

It wasn't the actual sex with Doug that was so significant. What she remembered and valued the most were the small things, like the way he opened the car door for her and kept a protective hand on her shoulder as they walked through the London crowds. He always offered her a taste of what he was eating, whereas George told her that she had made her choice and he had made his so it was nonsense for them to try each other's food. Best of all Doug never failed to tell her she pleased him. He didn't exaggerate, didn't go beyond the realms of credibility. He'd look up when she came into a room, and say 'Nice dress' or 'That colour suits you', or when they were dancing, 'You feel just right in my arms'. He always found something good to comment on. It was such a simple recipe for pleasing a woman that she wondered why more men didn't use it.

So she'd responded in the only way any woman would: she'd fallen in love with Doug, totally and unconditionally. And here he was again, back in her life, in the flesh.

"...yeah, as I say, a stopover. We're on holiday – me, Jennifer and her sister. The girls are shopping. Bit of retail therapy. I'm just having a gander, saw you, and couldn't believe it."

Feeling a little guilty, she wondered if she would have recognised him if he hadn't spoken to her. He'd put on a lot more weight than George over the years, though he was still a handsome man: clear fine skin, very regular white teeth and big well-kept hands that he used a lot for emphasis. Now he was scrutinising her with the same intense yet loving expression as he'd worn in years gone by. Then he put on his sunglasses again.

"This sun's a bugger for your eyes. Must be the reflection off of the water."

"Jennifer?"

"Of course you haven't...Doreen and me split up, not long after you moved. We were divorced years ago."

"I'm sorry, I always liked Doreen you know."

"Yeah, me too. But it's water under the bridge, we'd been heading that way for a long time. Fancy seeing you. How long is it – thirty years? I always remember a face. I recognised you immediately. You haven't changed. You always liked yellow."

"I never wore yellow!" How typical of him to tease her. It

made her feel young again.

"Whatever. George still knocking around? Where is he? Is he well?"

"He's at home. He's fine – you know, as things go."

"You live here now? I thought you were on holiday like us. You two must have hit the big time then?" He pursed his lips as if in comic consideration of what she must be worth.

"Not really." She didn't want him to think that George had been more successful, or that they were so rich and happy that they had no place for the old days and for old friends. "They made him Marketing Director at Parson and Green, in his last year with them. I think partly because he'd been there so long. Then there was a takeover so he was given early retirement last year. So we came here."

"The lad's done well."

"What about you? Did your business work out?"

He gave a short laugh, "Which one?"

"You were importing stationery from America." She still had a set of the deckle-edged pink writing paper and envelopes he'd given her and which she had been careful not to use.

"Oh, that rubbish. That was several businesses back. No, that didn't work out. But Jen and I have a new venture now, Health Accessories."

She looked at him doubtfully.

He put his arm out on the table to show her a thin bangle. "Nine carat gold on the outside, copper next to your skin. A work of art as well as a proven - proven mind - aid against the scourge of our times."

"What, AIDS?"

"Very funny. No you silly moo - rheumatism. Selling like hot cakes."

He twisted the bracelet off and put it between them on the table. "Go on, try it, one size fits all. Just squeeze it as tight as you want."

"How do I put it on?" She laid her arm on the table, willing him to touch her.

"Just give it a good push, as the actress said."

So she had to put it on herself and then she held up her arm in front of him. The metal was still warm from his skin. He gave an appreciative nod.

"There you are. Very nice. Suits you. Good colour for your skin as well. Brings out the – paleness."

"And you say it cures rheumatism?"

"Not cures it as such but prevents it if you wear it regularly. I don't mind telling you, it's doing well. Very, very well. I'll send you the literature."

She let her arm rest there in front of them on the table, still willing him to touch her.

"Forty-nine pounds. No need to take it off; you keep it. I'll give you my address and you can send the money later."

How like Doug, hiding his generosity. But of course she wouldn't dream of him buying it for her, she'd send the money immediately. She held up her arm twisting it in the sunlight. "It's lovely. I don't know how to thank you."

"You could buy one for George as well. One size fits all. Where is he? It would be good to see him, talk about the old days."

George and Doug together? That didn't feel like a good idea. Something might get blurted out. Besides, she wanted to keep Doug for herself. He's my one folly, she thought, my one secret, my one dream come true. No I'm not going to share him with George.

"He never knew - about us. He might have suspected, of course, but I never told him."

"What do you mean?"

"You know – you and me..." She could feel herself blushing even now.

"You and me?"

"That night at the Strand Palace."

"Which night at the Strand Palace?"

"We went to the theatre, then back to the hotel."

"Oh that!" He gave her a wicked smile and a wink. "That night. Yes yes! That was quite a party. Three in a bed, eh?"

"No! Just the two of us. We went to Les Miserables. Don't you remember? George was away in Harrogate. It was wonderful."

"Ah, yes, Les Mis. Say no more. Happy days." He looked around him. "Do you have to go and get the coffee here, or do they come out and serve you?"

"You have to go and get it." Should she offer to get one for him or would that make her seem too eager?

"Would you like another?"

"Mmm, please."

"How do you take it?"

"Same as ever."

"How's that?" He sounded impatient.

"White, no sugar. Don't you remember? You used to say that real men always had black coffee and real women always white."

"That's a new one on me".

So his memory wasn't as good either. They were all getting older. She watched him walk into the café. His bottom had always been heavy, a 'love pump' he'd called it. Now it just looked fat. George had a nice bottom, like a boy's. Funny it had taken Doug so long to remember their night together. Maybe he'd felt a bit guilty about it too. He was so much like her in so many ways. Her soulmate. 'My true love has my heart and I have his...' She looked around the café, half worried that someone she knew would see them together, half wanting them to at the same time. But there was no-one she knew, just a group of walkers, obviously on holiday, and a young woman with a dog, sitting at the next door table.

He was coming back, balancing a tray with two coffees, a big slice of chocolate cake and one fork.

"Hope it's all right, I've put this on your bill. Thought we might have something proper to eat in a minute if you know a nice little place? They don't do anything here."

"You mean lunch?"

"I said I'd meet up with the girls at three. They don't want to eat –watching their weight as usual. They're doing all the jewellery shops. But we could find a bite to eat. It would be good to have company. Do you have to be anywhere?"

"No. But yes, I mean, George – George will wonder where I am. We usually have lunch at home. No, I couldn't, but thanks. I would have loved to."

"Another time then."

They drank their coffees in companionable silence. Words had always been less important to them than simply being together. She watched his fine hands as he helped himself to the cream and two sugars. He didn't offer her any of his cake. He would have done back then. He must be really hungry.

"Well if you've got to go Eileen, don't let me stop you. Look I'll give you my address".

He gave her a card from his breast pocket.

"Don't worry about the name - Edwards. That's my business name, sort of like a brand name. Just make the cheque out to Doug Edwards. Forty-nine pounds and three pounds for postage and packaging, no you can make that one pound fifty because I've given it to you here, and the only thing they'll charge me is postage for a new one to me. That's fair."

She put the card deep into the zippered compartment of her handbag.

"What about you? You won't have your bracelet for the rest of your holiday."

"Don't worry about that – I'll survive. You know me."

He made an unsuccessful effort to stand up as she prepared to leave.

"No hurry with the cheque" he said. "Later this week will do." Then he leaned forward, pulled her down to him, very lightly touched her cheek with his lips and squeezed her hand. "Don't forget the old days! What was it we used to say in the

Seventies – 'Have a nice Life'? Well you and George have a nice life and don't forget old Douggie."

She couldn't speak for the rush of emotions: nostalgia, love, regret. What an amazing and wonderful coincidence that they had met, and, she supposed, how very unlikely it was that they would ever meet again. Destiny. But at least she had his precious card.

She turned and walked quickly away, heading south along the promenade, aware all the time of eyes following her, eyes perhaps with a few tears in them like her own.

She was just past the ship's chandlers when she realised she had left the bag with her old dress in it under the table. Oh dear, she couldn't go back and get it now, not after they'd said such a romantic goodbye. She couldn't. It was only an old dress anyway. No-one else would want it, if they found it. They'd see the bag under the table and look inside, imagining they'd found something new and valuable. And instead, they'd poke around in the tissue paper and come across something crumpled and used and think it distasteful. They'd leave it there to be rejected by others in turn, or maybe throw it away in the big wheelie bin next to the café. Throw her dress away in disgust. Her dress, her faithful old friend. She stood still on the pavement, trapped by indecision. But the idea of the dress being rejected and thrown away settled it. She couldn't allow that to happen; she couldn't abandon her dress after it had served her so well. She would have to go back and retrieve it even though it felt embarrassing. Do it quickly woman, now, just get on with it. Anyway he might have left, or the bag may have already disappeared.

But the bag and Doug were still there. She could see him leaning forward, patting the dog and chatting with the young woman at the next table. As she got closer she just caught the tail end of his sentence "...mind my company, we could find a bite to eat..." The old charmer, he hadn't changed at all, he had always had a soft spot for the ladies thought Eileen with just a tiny pang of jealousy.

"Eileen – what's this? Back again like a bad penny?"

"I left my bag. Silly of me..." She laughed and quite unnecessarily pointed to the bag. "...No don't get up, I'm gone."

She had just crossed the road again when she realised that she hadn't paid the bill for the coffee and the cake. Too bad, she couldn't go back again. It would be too upsetting for them both.

What a lovely surprise to see him she told herself as she walked along the front, resisting the temptation to turn around, lovely. When I send him the money maybe I'll tell him how much he meant to me, will always mean to me. Perhaps he'll write back. She caught a glimpse of her reflection in a shop window and was glad that she had been wearing the new dress and that she hadn't lost the old.

Chapter Three
Life and Love in Camden Town

"Woe to the bloody city!
It is all full of lies and robbery; the prey departeth not."
Nahum. The Bible.

It was late afternoon on a Friday and Celia was coming home from work on the bus. She wished she could look forward to collapsing on the settee when she got indoors. There was nothing she would have enjoyed more than to open a bottle of wine and just talk office things with Margot. But instead she had to pack a bag because tomorrow morning, early, she was off to Guernsey.

The bus was stationary in heavy traffic by the edge of Regent's Park and from the hot, sweaty and irritable interior she could see glimpses of how fresh and green the trees were. Week 20, mid-May already. It had been a good year so far; she dared to say that now, when at last everything seemed to be on a firm footing. 'Everything' really meaning her and Margot.

And work of course. The battle over the last twelve years had been hard, requiring stamina and a certain amount of cunning, but she had inched up the Camden Council career ladder and, at thirty-three she, Celia Buchanan, was Head of Special Amenities, which meant forty-eight people reported to her and she had her own corner office with not just one but two windows. She was beginning to enjoy her job now that it largely consisted of meetings, preparations for meetings

41

and signing off the minutes that circulated after meetings. Even more so because, as Chairperson in most situations, she neither had to write the minutes nor send reminders around for everyone to come, nor check that there was enough paper and pencils or chairs, nor book the meeting room or get the coffee and biscuits: all this was done by somebody else's assistant. She was now free to think up more initiatives and refinements and expand her budget if she could.

She was already getting results. Take her latest initiative that wheelchair access notices be written in the twelve major languages used by the fellow citizens of Camden. That had taken only two years from inception to implementation. Tangible results, especially as she had managed to get the notices trebled in size, so they were now compliant with Disability Regulations as well as Ethnic Diversity Policy. She had a right to feel proud.

But it was the progress in her private life that had given her most pleasure. She pondered over her past existence while the bus jerked and inched its way northwards.

Her - for want of a better word - romantic life had always been a bit of a problem. For many years she realised men had been put off by her intelligence and confidence. Eileen had always warned her that 'Men don't like intelligent women' and although her mother was hopelessly wrong about most things, in this, Celia reluctantly acknowledged, she might be telling the truth. She also had to admit that Eileen was right about men and women being fundamentally different, hard though this was to reconcile with her own Marxist ideals. For starters, they communicated differently. Men, for example, didn't to and fro in their talking and create an exchange of information, but took it in turns to talk, taking little notice of what the person before had said. She'd noticed how irritable they became if somebody else starting speaking when it was still 'their turn'. Even George, her very own father, accused her of interrupting when all she was doing was adding to what he was saying:

"You can't add to what I'm saying because you don't know

what it is I want to say! You can say what you want to say when I've finished."

But she did know what he was trying to say, often enough to sit and tap her nails in frustration while he carried on until he seemed to have come to an end – a feature that wasn't always instantly recognisable. Not that the tapping nails had any impact; she was not even sure he saw them, so focused was he on his words. A woman on the other hand would have seen and recognised the body language, known that something was wrong, and would have stopped speaking immediately, even mid-sentence. Proper conversation.

She had tried an experiment at work a few weeks earlier, which proved to her beyond doubt, that men couldn't read facial expressions and therefore missed half of what was going on in their lives. One day she went into the office with a deliberately miserable face and timed how long it was before people noticed and commented on her expression. Not one man had made reference to it at all, whereas the women not only asked her what was wrong, but a couple had even offered a cup of tea and a shoulder to cry on. Case proved. Not that there should be these differences between the sexes, but there you are. Real life didn't always live up to one's ideals.

The same had been true – how she loved that past tense – of sex. She'd had no idea of what might constitute an 'average' number of partners, but felt that she had had her rightful share, although only three had lasted beyond a couple of weeks. But they had all, yes all, been unsatisfactory. The problem was selfishness; her partners had taken pains to enjoy themselves but took absolutely no interest in her feelings at all. They all seem to have read the same instruction manual: heavy-handed groping of her breasts, penetration, a minute or two of vigorous pumping, then a ten minute sleep. After the sleep they went to the bathroom to wash themselves, to get rid of her, as if what they had just done were dirty. Correction: as if where they had just been were dirty.

43

Although imperfect, men were, unfortunately, an important accessory. You were expected to have a partner. Couples only invited other couples to dinner or to the cinema or to go away on holiday together. Singles had to make their own entertainment. The pool of single people upon whom Celia relied had been gradually absorbed by coupledom. Like a game of Musical Chairs she was beginning to get left with nowhere to go, all the chairs having been taken away. The reasonable ones anyway, although there was always Gary in Technical Supplies.

"Fancy coming down to Terminal Four at the weekend?" Gary's skinny, slightly rank-smelling body hovered over her in the canteen. "They're bringing Concorde into service again. We could watch the eleven fifteen take off for New York."

"What did you say to him?" asked her friend Siobhan over a second bottle of white wine as they sat in Celia's flat.

"Said I was busy of course. I mean can you see me standing on a grass verge somewhere in West Drayton with Gormless Gary?"

"You could take a folding chair. Make a sort of picnic out of it..?"

"Thank you Siobhan!"

"Why don't you try a dating agency? You know one of those places on the internet?"

"I'm not that desperate. Besides it's dangerous. You don't know who you might be meeting."

"I think it's quite safe if you follow the rules. Meet them somewhere in public for the first time and go on from there. But don't forget your mobile in case things go wrong."

"Have you tried it yourself then?" Celia had to admit that Siobhan was hardly dating material. Plain, very plain, with the eye patch and everything.

"Actually, yes". Siobhan's good eye glittered. "Yes, I have. His name is Roger. We've been out three times. He's great. We both knew straight away. I think this could be it."

"Siobhan! How could you, how could you do this without

telling me? Find a man and not tell me? I mean…" Celia was angry at her friend's deceit but, more than that, alarmed at the prospect of being deserted.

"Thought you might feel left out. Sorry."

She did feel left out, left out and let down, big-time. The worst thing was she could do nothing about it, despite the good job and the nice little flat in Camden Town. OK she knew she was overweight, but only by a few stone, and in terms of personality she was interesting – as interesting as anyone else she knew – and she had right values. Ideologically she couldn't be faulted. It just wasn't fair.

After Siobhan's betrayal and her increasing unavailability, Celia decided to change her own routine. She started going into work early and staying on in the evening alone after everyone else had left. After all, what was there to go home to? She watched television all weekend, joined chat rooms on the internet, smoked twenty a day and woke up with some kind of hangover at least twice a week.

One Friday in February, as she faced the prospect of yet another weekend of nothingness and was opening the second bottle of wine, she stopped in mid-screw and thought again about what Siobhan had suggested. Online dating. Maybe it wasn't such a bad idea. It wouldn't do any harm to have a look. She needn't follow up on anything after all. She took the wine and her cigarettes over to her work station and Googled 'online dating London'. Wow - 238,000 results! She hadn't known there were that many people looking for love. That was encouraging. There must be someone for her amongst all those! She scrolled down the first ten, and was attracted by the Time Out site:

'Let's face it: dating in the big city is brutal business…Time Out is here to save London's singletons from a life of loneliness and hopeless alcoholism…'

They'd obviously done their market research, but a bit too extreme for me, she thought, taking a swig of the Zinfandel and lighting up. What about London Partners:

'Are you living in Central London and tired of trying to find the right person to enjoy all that life has to offer? You're only a click away from meeting new friends and, maybe, that special one!'

A little coy, not intellectual enough, not modern enough for someone like her.

'Cybersuitors.com. 'Why be alone when you can let technology work for you? Take your future into your own hands. One left click, find friends, enjoy life!'

This was more like it. She left-clicked and explored the site. It had a funky purple background and she liked the tags: 'Nirvana 2000'; 'Coolman'; 'Richard Lion Heart'; 'Thumper'; - they sounded like her sort of dudes, hip, funny, cool, not taking themselves too seriously.

She scrolled down the the Cybersuitors membership form and started to fill it in. She was honest about her 'Age and Height', had cheated - but only by two stone - about her 'Weight', and was proud to have put against 'Ethnic Origin' a big 'IRRELEVANT'. She left a blank against 'Heroes' – she was no elitist – and felt that she took the moral and intellectual high ground when she described her 'Newspaper Readership' as 'Guardian and Morning Star - online.' She gave her 'Hobbies' as 'Marx and intelligent discourse.' That last bit had probably been the hook that caught Ben because two days later she had the following mail in her inbox. 'Beano Ben, 37 years young, 5ft 8 inches, 12 stone 4, Caucasian, Guardian reader, hero - Dan Dare.' Best of all 'hobbies: computers, comics and Marx.' An interesting mix she felt, obviously intelligent, a sense of humour and the right politics. Besides, his was the only response. After a brief electronic exchange they arranged to meet the following evening, seven o'clock at The Castle in Camden High Road. Ben would be carrying a copy of the Beano. 'Camden Cyber Chick' would be wearing black. That part of things was easy as nearly all her clothes were black and then she added she would have 'significant earrings'. That summed her up all right:

modern, clear thinking, but with a touch of mystery.

It was so hard to stay focused at work on Monday. She felt fluttery and restless and was desperate to tell someone what she was doing, but infuriatingly no-one had time for a chat except Siobhan, and she was going to be the very last to know if Celia had her way. Full to bursting with excitement, she eventually bore down on one of the cleaners as she was leaving the office for home.

"I expect you're wondering why I'm leaving early tonight – must dash – I'm late for a date with my boyfriend."

"Is it you that 'ave left all dem files and t'ings on the floor?" He looked cross.

"Hmm, sorry yes it is. I haven't got time to pick them up tonight because I've got a date…"

"I 'eard you first time. T'is all right for some. Room will stay as dirt f'rall I care. And they say white folk clean! No way.'

Not a good omen. But tonight there really wasn't time to stay and explain about the repercussions of colonialism and her absolute support of negritude. She knew she shouldn't but she put her hand compassionately on his shoulder then bustled away.

Despite having a wardrobe full of loose dark garments, it proved difficult to make a final choice. She knew that with an intelligent person like Ben every garment would speak volumes. Eventually she picked out a favourite black trouser suit that had been lying at the bottom of the laundry basket. It smelled a bit stale but in terms of colour (black) and cloth (an expansive crepe) it gave off absolutely the right message of restrained sensuality.

Footwear was more of a problem. As she rejected one pair after another, she began to realise how closely shoes were linked to sex. A shoe told you all you needed to know about what someone would be like in the sack, and how hard or easy it would be to get them there. Court shoes? Boring and reluctant. Open-toed sandals? Clumsy but easy. Ankle-length boots in ginger suede? Very promising, but maybe not right for a first date. That left only her trainers; what did they say? If Ben knew his Levi-Strauss, and how to deconstruct a pair of vintage Converse 1992 cross-trainers, then he would recognise that she was playfully ironic but accessible if the vibes were right; very much like the Beano Fancier himself.

The finishing touch and reinforcement of her promise, however, would be the earrings. She hesitated between the silver Ban the Bomb classics that she had bought in the Portobello Road market many years ago and the Masai Mara beadwork clusters that a friend had brought back from Kenya. She would like to wear the Masai ones – they had always been an ice-breaker at parties – but their disadvantage, which in fact was an indication of how important it was to eliminate poverty in the developing world so the disadvantage, therefore, could also be construed as a point in their favour, was that they looked like silver but in fact were made of nickel. One night Celia had slept in her clusters and woken to find her ear-lobes red and weeping, the little holes in her skin closed with inflammation. She tried to carry on wearing them the following day, reasoning that her discomfort was probably nothing compared with the trials and tribulations of Masai women. To suffer alongside them, in time if not in place, would be to show solidarity. But the itching got so bad, and she had seen so many people recoil when she came near them at the office, that she had to spend an hour or so in the Rest Room very gently pulling them out of the festering skin. Then she ransacked the office First Aid kit and sat for the rest of the day in an aura of TCP.

But she decided the risk was worthwhile for just one evening; after all it was only for a drink and she would be home again within a few hours. If things did seem to be progressing towards supper and whatever else, then she could always slip them out once their impact had been made.

As she looked at herself in the dressing-table mirror – she had not used anything full-length since her slimmer student days –

she suddenly decided that she would wear one of each earring designs, a Ban the Bomb on her right ear and a bead cluster on the left. This would communicate her involvement with two of the biggest issues in modern life - peace and diversity - and also make her look dynamic and edgy. It only remained for her to slip her mobile in one pocket, her door keys and £30 in the other, and then walk as calmly as possible to the pub via the paper shop.

Chapter Four
A new social Life

"O for a plump fat leg of mutton
Veal, lamb, capon, pig and coney..."
'A Serving Man's Song' John Lyly.

George was roused from his desktop snooze by an unfamiliar sound – laughter. It was a woman's laugh, deep-throated, noisy with excitement, and it seemed to be coming from next door's garden. He lifted his head to confirm; the sound obligingly came again. Definitely from next door. The new neighbours were making a nuisance of themselves already. He got up stiffly and went to the window.

At first he could see nothing unusual, and then out of the corner of his eye he caught a flash of yellow, a deep vibrant colour, darker than daffodils but more yellow than oranges: a rich, thick, tropical colour, almost out of place on the island. It was a dress, worn by the woman next door. There was a glimpse of brown flesh and reddish hair, but before he could get a good look she had run, squealing, round the corner of her house, chased by a man, heavy-set but quick on his feet, who also vanished from view. Presumably he was her husband.

Well, this level of noise was definitely unacceptable; he would have to go and have a word with them. Or better still, send them a note. Maybe start it with a welcome to the area but then a few words to let them know what was expected of them in the neighbourhood. A stitch in time and all that, nipping things in the bud. He'd definitely send something if they made that sort of noise again, although he might leave it to later after a sherry and an hour's worth of the cricket. He ought to be able to get that in before Eileen came home and made lunch.

He was onto the cartoons by the time he heard the front door.

"Is that new?" He couldn't remember having seen that yellow outfit before.

"Do you like it?" She looked a bit pink round the gills – must be the hike up the hill.

"Not bad. How much was it?"

"Sixty pounds, I think."

"Well you either know or you don't know! Sixty pounds? My God, what they charge for women's clothes!"

He had to teach her a sense of proportion about money. They were all right at the moment but that was no guarantee for the future and he didn't want her to get the wrong idea. But she looked quite smart, for a change. "You can wear it to dinner tonight. It'll go with my new tie."

George had a good feeling about that evening. The Kinnock-Paceys were big on the island: he was something in finance and local government and she was one of the old Guernsey families, with a French name. Between them they had all the connections a man could want. He'd met them at a charity do and knew immediately that they were his entry into Guernsey Society.

"They're the real thing Ellie." He'd told her rubbing his hands together. "Dinner in St. Martins. We're in!"

"What should I wear? Is it formal?"

"Of course not. It's an at-home. I expect we'll be the only people there or maybe there'll just be one other couple. I tell you, he took a shine to me and it was mutual."

But now he was wondering if perhaps he should have asked how formal it would be. A dinner jacket would be over the top, but equally it would be unwise to dress down too much for a St. Martin's address. If Eileen wore her new outfit then he would wear his beige slacks, white shirt, navy blue blazer with a

51

yellow handkerchief, and the new yellow and blue tie. It looked more considered if the two of them were colour coordinated, and Eileen's background of yellow would double the impact of his choice of accessories.

Should he take something with him? A bottle of wine perhaps? That would be a generous gesture and, if he chose the wine carefully, it would give some indication of his level of familiarity with fine dining. But he knew from experience there was a dilemma here. If he took a cheap wine it would be seen, and rightfully so, as an insult. If on the other hand, he took something good, the risk was - if the Kinnock-Paceys were savvy enough - they would set it on one side, serve value-for-money plonk and George and Eileen wouldn't catch a whiff of their own superior stuff. The third alternative, to take a medium-priced bottle, was no alternative at all. It would simply look as he was worried there wouldn't be enough.

Then better take flowers. They were always well-received and at least were not socially loaded. Besides, flowers were a woman's responsibility. It was already five thirty, the flower shops in town would be closed, so Eileen had better go right now and buy some from the side of the road. It was handy that the island had a tradition of 'hedge veg', of selling local vegetables and flowers at the side of the road. If she went now they would have time to wrap them up before leaving this evening.

An hour later, he oversaw things while she wrapped a large bunch of long-stemmed Alstromeria in green tissue paper that they'd kept from last Christmas and which Eileen now ironed to look as if they'd been to the florist's.

He drove briskly and arrived at the entrance of the Kinnock-Paceys' imposing house five minutes before the appointed time of seven thirty. George insisted they sit in the parked car at the bottom of the drive for another eight minutes before approaching the house. He didn't want to appear too eager.

It was overcast and a very light drizzle had started. With no sign of life inside, nor any cars in the driveway, George looked

yet again at the address on their invitation: 'Le Hameau Farm, St. Martin' – this was definitely it.

At precisely seven thirty-two they stood together under the porch, rang the bell and waited. Two, maybe three minutes passed. They rang again, and then again, until a querulous voice cried out "All right, all right, I'm getting there as fast as I can." Footsteps and the door was opened just enough to reveal an elderly woman, in black with a maid's white cap. She peered round the door and eyed them up and down.

"Madam's got a dinner on tonight." Guernsey accent, to George's ear a cross between South African and Birmingham.

He paused a few seconds to show his displeasure, and then said in his explaining-things-to-an-idiot-voice that he used for desultory shop assistants and, occasionally, Eileen, "Thank you yes, I know that, because, you see, we're guests."

"You're too early."

The head was on the point of withdrawing when much to George's annoyance Eileen spoke quickly in her apologetic little girl voice, the one she used in almost any socially uneasy circumstance.

"Mr. Kinnock-Pacey said seven thirty?"

George snorted. The interrogatory inflection was the last straw.

"They told me eight."

"Look here, are you going to let us in or not?" George moved into the doorway.

"I'll go and ask Madame." She closed the door firmly in his face and went away.

It was beginning to get cold. They heard irritable voices from inside. Eileen, stupid muppet, hadn't worn a top-coat and she was shivering.

"Maybe we should go away and come back at eight?"

"The buggery I am. I'm going to stand on this sodding doorstep until Father Bloody Christmas comes."

"That won't be necessary." It was an unsmiling Francis Kinnock-Pacey standing at the open door, in black trousers and a dress shirt with an untied bow tie hanging round his neck.

"Sorry if you've been kept waiting. Our regular maid is away and we're having to make do. Come in."

They were led into an unheated room. "If you'd like to wait here, we'll be with you in a tick. It's Mr. and Mrs. Buchanan isn't it? I'll get Mrs. Rouget to give you a sherry."

They heard his footsteps as he trod wearily up the stone steps and then voices overhead, his voice apparently trying to calm a female voice. The maid came back and silently handed them very dry sherries, from a bottle that George recognised as having been open for some time.

"He was wearing a bow tie," said Eileen.

"I could bloody see that for myself."

"I just meant I hope we're not underdressed."

They were. Twenty minutes later two other couples arrived, the women in cocktail dresses and big jewellery, the men in dinner jackets. Then another four people came, similarly dressed.

"Oh George, how did you get it wrong?"

"I didn't get it bloody wrong. The ponce didn't say black tie. He didn't say anything. How was I supposed to know? Read the ruddy Runes?"

Marella Kinnock-Pacey took all the diversity in her stride. She wore a full-length midnight blue gown with a plunging backline, a heavy glittering bracelet and a single rope of wild pearls dotted with diamonds. She received the Alstromeria graciously from Eileen, bending her head as if to smell the scentless flowers.

"What fun, where did you find them? Thank you so much." In one move she dismissed them to the waiting Mrs. Rouget who took them away at arm's length. Other guests had brought flowers: white orchids planted in moss inside a celadon bowl, a hand-tied mass of double peonies, a huge arrangement of yellow roses and half a dozen bird-of-paradise flowers. Marella greeted each with effuse thanks and little shrill sounds of wonder. "Oh, oh you shouldn't have been so generous – these are truly wonderful, wonderful… Francis look what Reggie and Debbie have brought. Have you ever seen anything so magnificent…? "

After the flowers the first part of the evening consisted of getting to know each other over 'champagne'. George knew enough about the dinner party game to have taken the precaution of downing a double scotch before leaving the house. Two in fact. He abandoned the stale sherry on a desk in the corner on the room, and took a glass of Sekt, which stayed untouched in his hand as he circulated. Having been to a few social evenings on the island he knew what was coming, The same questions were asked of him by everyone, man and woman alike: Where do you live? Which house precisely? How long have you been in Guernsey? What line are you in?

Like a bloody court martial, thought George, and without the relief of a quick execution. But both he and Eileen had practised their responses and despatched themselves creditably. Les Vardes was a good address, Parson and Green was a publicly-quoted company and they exaggerated about how long they'd been on the island. They didn't want to be taken as socially still wet around the ears.

After the first circulation George had found two people who might be of use: one who claimed to be on the Island Development Council, which could be useful if they wanted to have a conservatory extension to the house. Another ran an offshore trust. Who knows what value that might have, thought George, but it sounded worthwhile and the fellow was wearing an impressive watch so couldn't be doing too badly. George counter traded what he had: long-term membership of the Institute of Directors, and Council Member of the Institute of Marketing - although he didn't mention that this had been in the early Seventies. It was enough for an exchange of cards. So far, so good.

He could occasionally hear Eileen at the mercy of the wives. They looked like Lunchers, women who lunched to make money, money that went to support local initiatives, such as visiting lecturers in flower arranging and other domestic arts, or money to be sent out into the wider world, such as Save the Children or the Red Cross.

George heard Marella ask Eileen. "What are you doing next Wednesday? There's a lunch at Le Fregate; on the terrace if the weather is good. It's for Albanian Orphans so you must come. Only £40."

When first invited to lunch, Eileen, in her innocence, had thought it was an invitation to an event where someone was offering hospitality. Fortunately she'd had enough cash with her to pay the £35 demanded for the new wing of the Old People's Home, but had to pay by cheque for the request for a second £35, this time for the Asthma Society, which emerged over dessert. For a while she had been pursued enthusiastically to become a core Luncher but soon learned the excuse that was always used to turn down a request: "Sorry, would have loved to, but we're off the island that week." Only once had she been caught out, when a Luncher rang on the morning of the event to check if she had really gone or was still there and available to make up the numbers. So these days she just said thank you, but no. As George had taught her, never apologise, never explain.

The first part of the evening, then, had not been a total failure. George had acquired two potentially useful business cards and Eileen - as she subsequently told him - had successfully evaded four invitations to lunch but believed she may have accepted an invitation to belong to Marella's book club. This he had heard being played out over his very dull exchange with an insurance broker.

"Do you read?" Marella's voice had a carrying quality.

"Read?" said Eileen caught off guard.

"Yes, read - you know words, books and so on?"

"Oh yes, read! I do, I do."

"Good because we're short on numbers at the moment; the Montgomerys are off for three months in their house in France. We need a replacement for our Book Club – only temporary. Until they get back"

"Replacement?"

"Oh goodness, I do hope you haven't got that illness where you have to repeat everything that is said to you. 'Eulalia' or something isn't it? Most trying."

"I think that's a town in Ibiza."

"What?"

"Santa Eulalia; we went there on holiday with Celia."

"Bourgourd? Celia Bourgourd?"

"No, Buchanan, my daughter."

"Do I know her?"

"She works for Camden Council?"

"Where? Never mind her, does Francis have your details? Excellent. I'll be in touch." And she moved on briskly. Well done Ellie, thought George proudly, impressed by her obfuscation.

Dinner itself was more challenging. They were called to the table by Mrs. Rouget and moved slowly and submissively through the double doors into the dining room. It was a small room and neither it nor the dining table was really big enough to seat twelve. Despite that, the table had been elaborately laid with several rows of silver cutlery, three very small glasses to each diner, three low table decorations of what both George and Eileen now realised were 'good quality' flowers, two candelabra (unlighted), dress plates, side plates, silver containers for ground pepper and sea salt, starched napkins, and little starched muslin holders for name cards.

Murmuring appreciation for the achievement of the table setting, the guests moved around it, peering at the curly handwriting on the name cards. Whatever disappointment might be felt on seeing that they were seated next to the dullest and most useless guest was discreetly hidden. The gentlemen, affecting a stiff and elaborate gallantry, helped the ladies to be seated. George noticed that the best-dressed couple had been placed next to the Kinnock-Paceys whilst he and Eileen were lost in the middle of the table.

The first course was soon set out on the table for guests to help themselves. Tonight there was a plate of smoked salmon, cut transparently thin and decorated with lemon cut so finely as to be impossible to squeeze. The guests were invited to 'dig in and help yourselves', but there was the usual hesitation, no-one wanting to break rank. Some looked to their hostess for permission to start, as dogs might look to their owner, but Marella was busy explaining some nicety of protocol to Mrs. Rouget and the evening was frozen on pause for several minutes while she explained the difference between when one used fish knives and when one used ordinary knives, despite the fact that one was serving fish.

"I didn't think fish knives were 'in' any more," said the best-dressed wife, hoping to bring conclusion to the exchange and draw Marella's attention back to the table and the food.

"Well maybe, and maybe not," said Marella, "but one needs at least to know the basic rules. I mean there'd be chaos otherwise." And she turned back to Mrs. Rouget.

"I say Marella -" best-dressed husband could hold back no longer, "are we supposed to be helping ourselves?"

"What? Oh yes, Martin, of course."

The gate was up, the horses hesitated and then came out at the gallop. There were ten guests and fifteen half-slices of salmon. Natural selection determined that the most powerful got two slices and the rest made do with one. George assessed the situation. The best-dresseds took the lead and got two each, so did Marella coming up very swiftly on the inside. Francis was holding back so it seemed only right, given the blazer and slacks and linen dress, that George and Eileen should hold back too. The final half slice and most of the lemon went to the man from the Island Development Council. On Guernsey, property is all.

If the losers thought they could fill up on bread and butter then there, too, they were bound for disappointment. There were fifteen half slices of thin brown bread and butter. George was glad he'd had a plateful of cheese sandwiches as well as the whisky before leaving home. He wondered how many of the others had done the same. The portly solicitor, generously offering his bread to the very plain woman next to him had probably had a three-course meal. It could only be a full stomach that also enabled the same man to raise his head above his plate, empty of all except a wafer of uneaten lemon, and, say with apparent warmth and honesty, "Marella, that was delicious."

His commendation triggered approval from other quarters: "Wonderful bread." "You must tell me where you buy this salmon." And "How do you cut it so thinly?" George turned appreciatively to the woman who made this last comment but was disappointed to see her expression was innocent of guile.

"We'll take a little rest, shall we?" Marella leaned gracefully on her elbows, allowing the table to appreciate the full glory of her bracelet. "Would anyone like more wine? I'm sure we have another bottle."

She looked disapproving when there were several affirmations, eager it would seem for the painfully acidic Chardonnay. George thought he'd earn a few brownie points as well as satisfy his own desire for honesty "Personally I couldn't take any more, thank you," and was pleased to see Marella's unsure smile as she emptied the bottle into the glass of the woman on his right.

"Darling," a reproving note from Francis, "the second bottle's not chilled. And aren't we about to have our main course? I think we've had enough."

George shot him an admiring glance; here was a man who knew what he wanted and knew how to control things, including ten thirsty guests. He might try 'the second bottle's not chilled yet' himself at home at their next dinner party. It was all too easy for this kind of evening to descend into a winefest for free-loaders.

So, no more wine then. A couple of the women, perhaps scenting potential failure of the evening's forward momentum, brightly embarked on conversations with their neighbours: "Now you must tell me again what it is that you do." Thereby a low-level and rather sulky chatter was generated and sustained for a few minutes, until the main course. Mrs. Rouget, her cap by now at a strange angle from where she had presumably been scratching her head, carried in aloft a large platter and set it down in the centre of the table. George, fortified by his cheese sandwiches, was able to look at what lay in the middle of the plate with dispassionate curiosity. It was impossible to identify it beyond being some kind of generic meat coated in a brown sauce. There was enough for one slice each, plus two spare overall. Now came two bowls of vegetables, one off-white, which George guessed to be an attempt at mashed potato, and one brownish-green, pulped, which had the smell but not the appearance of cabbage. By the time everyone had first held back, then handed everything on to everyone else before eventually helping themselves, the food was cold. But by now, anyway, the entire table seemed to have lost interest in eating, and there were no takers for either of the two slices of meat left over –George never did identify what it was - nor for the residue of undercooked potatoes or the – what turned out to be - broccoli.

Later, when a silver pot of weak coffee indicated that dinner was over, the guests were shepherded away from the table and back into the drawing room. It was time to play cards. This ensured that the hour after dinner could avoid the double pitfalls of expensive cognac and dangerous conversation. Fuelled by cheap wine and a lack of food, the play was vicious and dirty. George's cheese sandwiches still gave him a natural advantage and he played well enough to find himself against Francis in the final game. This he was careful to lose, and with it the thirty pounds in the kitty.

"Well-played Francis; you've certainly beaten me this evening." Grease, grease.

"Well at least you gave it your best! I won't say the money won't come in handy."

"It can go to the Afghan Fund. Well-played darling." Marella looked adoringly at her husband and then very pointedly, George felt, at her watch.

He checked the time more surreptitiously. It was only twenty-five minutes past nine but maybe they went early to bed. He hadn't had the conversation he wanted with Francis, but there didn't seem to be time now. Marella glanced at her watch again. It was obvious that they wanted people to go home. Hoping to accumulate more brownie points, George was the first to stand up and announce to the group at large "Well, we should be going. It's late, well past our bedtime. Thank you Marella, thank you Francis – a stunning evening."

The others looked up at him but only Marella made a move.

"Do you have to go now? We were just going to have some more drinkies and a lovely chat about mutual friends. I do hope no-one else is tired of us yet! No? Good. Well, if you two must go - let me at least show you out."

Too late to back-pedal now. They were swept along to the front door. There was just time for George to say to Marella "Thank you my dear, tell Francis I'll be in touch." And for her to reply "I'll tell him but he's awfully busy" before they found themselves back out on the doorstep. All's well that ends well thought George, but as the door was being closed he heard a great victorious roar from inside the house, like the sound of a football crowd when a goal is scored, or when the Christians have finally been dispatched by the lions. He pretended not to have heard and within seconds he and Eileen were safely in their car, bowling along in the dark towards town and Les Vardes.

"Pretty good evening," he said, as he opened the Rioja and a packet of shortbread biscuits, and the two of them settled down to watch a late night movie. "I thought it all went very well. Very well indeed. Should be useful."

Much later, after Eileen had gone up to bed, George put on his reading glasses and looked again at the invitation card. 'Eight o'clock for eight fifteen. Black tie.' It was written quite clearly. How could he have made such a basic error? Bloody dinner party, bloody St. Martins and bloody Pillock-Paceys. He tore the card into small pieces, tossed them into the loo, had a long piss over them, and then flushed it all away.

Chapter Five
Meeting Margot

"A jug of wine, a loaf of bread – and Thou
Beside me singing in the wilderness."
'The Rubaiyat of Omar Khayam' (trans) Edward Fitzgerald.

Celia, deep in the memory of her February cyber romance, only just managed to get off the bus at the right stop. At least now she was able to go over what had happened without wincing with embarrassment. Thanks to Margot.

She replayed the occasion to herself. On that evening nearly three months ago, she had ambled into The Castle at four minutes past seven – punctual, but in a relaxed kind of way. The place was quiet so she took a seat in the corner from where she could see everyone who came in and, in turn, she and her newspaper – unfortunately only the Standard – could be spotted and identified. At the bar she had a quick look around. There were two painter decorators by the look of their overalls, a small group of young clerks playing darts, several indeterminate old men dotted around the room, each nursing a last inch of beer, a youngish man in jeans and windbreaker, who looked up when Celia came in but went back to reading his magazine again, two very dark-skinned Albanian-looking men sitting at a table without drinks, a group of men in suits with briefcases who were talking loudly by the empty fireplace and a black guy with dreadlocks who was repairing the juke box. No sign of Beano Ben. This was good, very good, as it gave her time to get a drink and compose herself at one of the tables, ready to meet him and, possibly, encounter the beginning of the rest of her life.

What to drink? Wine by the glass would be undrinkable in a place like this, so it had to be a half of lager, or better still, a soft drink. The one thing I must not do is get drunk, she thought, I must stay in control, alert and fully functioning. Even Guardian readers can get over excited.

The barman, a bruiser of a Cockney, somewhere in his middle years, leaned forward with mock gallantry: "And what are you havin' my Lady? Would it be a Babycham? Cherry Brandy? Snowball?"

The cheek of the man. "Pint of Guinness! And a packet of Cheese and Onion!"

"All right, all right, keep yer 'at on. One pint of diesel coming up."

He leaned forward in a conspiratorial way as he slid the pint and the crisps across. "Think you ought to know luv, and don't take this wrong, but you've got odd earrings."

What was the point, she thought, as she walked carefully across to a little table, choosing one near the Albanians so they wouldn't feel excluded.

Forty minutes later she was nearly through the second pint and beginning not to mind that Ben had yet to arrive. He was probably held up in the traffic. In a way it was good to have an opportunity on their first meeting to show him how patient she could be, how composed and serene in the face of urban chaos. The sort of calmness a man needs at the end of a busy day. She gave a controlled malty belch as she re-read her Standard. The Guinness had been a good choice.

The workmen, the young man in jeans and the darts players had left shortly after she arrived, and the pub filled up, mostly with a younger crowd. The office workers were still there, noisier than ever and the Albanians had moved to a small table closer to hers. She smiled at them. Poor things, probably illegals; they still had not a drink between them. Maybe she should offer them one, welcome them to the land of plenty and to a fairer and more decent way of life.

Two hours, four pints, a packet of pork scratchings and a ploughman's later, she decided that something must definitely have happened to Ben. The Albanians had long gone. Her left ear was beginning to itch. It was time to go home. As she stood up, one part of her realised that perhaps she might have overdone the Guinness, although another part of her told her she felt cosy and good. As the one part moved towards the door, the other stayed behind on her chair and the bulk of her fell heavily in between, taking the small table, somebody's lager and the full ashtray with it.

Once down it seemed impossible to get up, or even turn over. She was caught in a confusing web of chair legs and briefcases, so she lay quietly amid the beer spillage and the cigarette ash and even considered staying there for a while until the dizziness passed. It was not that uncomfortable, and there were reassuring sounds of voices and laughter above. Then hands came out of nowhere, grabbed various parts of her body and pulled her reluctantly to her feet.

"Like raising the Titanic," said one man in a suit and tie, "or a beached whale, and she's not that old."

"Don't know how you tell under all that. Phew – what's that? Smells like last year's socks!"

Somehow she staggered out into the street, their laughter fading - though not quickly enough – into the distance. It was only when she was standing outside her front door, fumbling in the folds of the black crepe for the key, that she realised her mobile was missing. Bloody Albanians.

*

So that had been that with dating agencies. Then out of the blue, along came Margot.

Margot, such a lovely name. Little did Celia know that her

life would be changed irrevocably when they first met at the Demonstration Meeting in March. Celia who, as ACP District Secretary, was sitting on the podium noticed Margot as soon as she'd walked into the pre-demonstration strategy meeting. Who wouldn't have seen such a tall and graceful woman, pale-skinned and with a cloud of dark hair, picking her cat-like way through the mass of denim? She managed to make room for herself right at the front and made almost immediate eye contact with Celia. Later that evening, after the meeting had concluded, they'd sat and drunk wine in Celia's flat and talked and talked and talked: college, art, politics, careers - but not, Celia was glad to note, men. Then suddenly it was too late for Margot to catch the Tube back to Earl's Court so Celia said she must stay over, and made up a bed for her on the settee.

Celia had lain awake what seemed to be all night, maybe because of the excitement of the meeting or perhaps because of the red wine, her heart thudding with some form of expectation. They next morning they had each hurried on their way, making vague promises to get in touch. But the next time they met was also by accident. Celia had gone one Saturday to see a new installation by a young Ethiopian conceptual artist at Tate Modern. The Tate was one of her favourite places: she loved the building itself; a contrived space but somehow honest and confrontational. It gave her a sense of optimism every time she walked down the entrance ramp and was met by the bricks and concrete of the great hall. She felt in accord with the spirit of the place, absolutely non-elitist, accessible and inclusive. It was a temple – if that was the right concept in this secular context – to the sacred power of the mundane, a tribute to people who had nothing, and who knew nothing but were everything that was significant in today's world.

This Saturday it was raining heavily, and Celia felt particularly glad to be inside, moving around with others like her, ordinary decent folk, dressed in their ordinary casual clothes, united by a common love of the ordinary. For the first half hour she let herself drift around with the crowd, smiling dreamily whenever a face was turned in her direction, at one with humanity. Then she had a coffee and a Danish, wishing she could have a cigarette as well – that would make life perfect. Later, in a more or less contented frame of mind she approached the main event.

Isseka's main installation was by no means easy to interpret. The artist seemed to have taken as his theme the repudiation of tradition. All around the room were photographs of Ethiopian mountain dwellings. Not just ordinary photographs that you might see, say, in National Geographic, but something far more meaningful. For a start they were in black and white, and then Isseka – or it could have been someone in the photographic laboratory because it didn't really matter who had actually done it so potent was the idea – had scored the surface of the pictures. So now the traditional village scenes with their little thatched rondavels were barely visible. Celia understood this intuitively to mean that Western so-called progress, capitalism and the ugly emphasis on material comfort, was destroying the innate beauty of a time-honoured way of life. "So true, so true", she murmured aloud as she walked around, her understanding deepening with each distorted picture. She'd had her own fight against bourgeois values and it was uplifting to recognise the same in a like-minded person from another continent. "One world, one people..."

She had been walking the wrong way around the exhibition – not of course that there was a right and wrong in the context of art – and had been enjoying the resulting occasional physical contact with other people, when she came to the plaque describing the artist's potted history and the rationale for his vision after she'd already seen his pictures. So she was initially surprised to read:

"Isseka left Ethiopia in 1993 as a political refugee, glad to escape a regime of oppression which imposed limitations on his aesthetic development. His work is dedicated to destroying the cultural and intellectual constraints of traditional Ethiopian

67

life. In 'Death of the Village' this is expressed by abrading photographs of the traditional houses of his homeland. The original photographs are the property of National Geographic Magazine Inc. and are reproduced here with their kind permission."

After a few moments of concern she realised that his vision could be read as pre-capitalist, which illustrated an even more important and fundamental issue than respect for tradition. His was the fight of the People against the Establishment and all other forms of tyranny. He was a brother. Keep the red flag flying comrade. But didn't Ethiopia already have a Marxist regime? If so, why had he come to London? What was he escaping from? But the sign said 'oppression' so she knew that whatever it was he was protesting against, she ought to support him. She wished that he were there in person so she could shake his hand and show solidarity. Now, what else had he done?

In the centre of the room there was a large circular heap of gravel and sand. It was not contained in any way but lay on the floor in sharp contrast with the dark patina of the polished wood. Celia noticed a very strange thing. The neat edge of the gravel had remained undisturbed, despite the crowd. Almost instinctively visitors avoided stepping on it. Still fired with empathy for the artist, Celia stood looking across at the gravel until she had a sudden and profound insight. The circle that people were so deferentially walking around, and not through, represented the Establishment. The artist was sending a subtle message about the extent to which, even in industrialised nations, the status quo was reinforced by the continuing lack of vision of the proletariat. Isseka was challenging his audience to involve themselves in his struggle by destroying the circle. His work was silently pleading with them, imploring them to break out of their chains, just as he had tried to destroy the little mud huts in the photographs.

"I understand, I really do", she murmured as she hurried over to the gravel, anxious that someone else would have a similar insight and get there before her. The unbroken circle is the symbol of oppression, and the gravel represents the bedrock of humanity that binds us altogether, she thought, as she swished across the circle in her long brown skirt, scattering sand and gravel with each tread of her Freedom sandals. She didn't invite the other visitors to join her; no, let them find their own answers, but she looked up from time to time as she blurred the edges.

When the Barbadian curator came over and asked her to stop, she explained quite clearly what she was doing. But he didn't seem to understand at first. She repeated her explanation, this time using easier words and adding a West Indian lilt.

He still didn't understand, the poor fool. "I'm sorry Miss but you 'ave to get off the work of h'art right now. Them's the rules."

Soon it became an argument between the guard on the polished floor and, two yards away from him, Celia firmly planted in the sand.

"You silly man; don't you understand what it is you're supposed to be guarding? The circle is an invitation for all of us, men and women, black and white, to put aside our difficulties, break the "rules" and together shake off the capitalist yoke."

"Black and white? Black and white? That's racist talk. Racist. I'll get the Race Relations Board onto you. I know my rights. Now get off that dirt before I give you a clout."

"How dare you call me racist! I've never been so offended in my life. I've supported people like you all my life."

"There you are, 'people like me'; what's that if it's not racist? I'll have you for that."

"Don't you threaten me you little nobody. And if you dare call me racist again I'll get the whole of Camden Legal and Immigration department to send you back to Barbados."

"I'll see you in 'ell first, you evil fascist."

With that he marched off, presumably to get reinforcements, leaving Celia defiantly unmoving but in shock. She stood there for a couple of minutes until a handsome woman and her little boy stopped and watched her.

"Mummy, why is that lady standing on the sand?"

"Because she's representing the importance of the individual, of how you must be the centre of your own world." The woman was wearing a Barbour with a silk scarf tucked in the neck.

"No I'm bloody not," said Celia, inwardly cringing at the Hampstead accent. "I'm standing here as a protest against the Bourgeoisie."

"Mummy why did that lady say a naughty word? Why is she cross?"

"She's encouraging us, Timmy, not to accept anything at face value." The woman smiled confidently, her enunciation even more precise.

"Will you stop attributing motives to me that are absolutely nothing to do with the case." All the same it wasn't a bad summing up.

"Why is she dressed like that Mummy?"

By now a small group had gathered at the edge of the sand, sensing alternative entertainment. The woman from Hampstead was warming to her task: "You remember what I told you darling about not judging people by their appearance and whether or not they have nice clothes? You see what she is dressed in, an old skirt and a cheap jacket to deliberately make herself look plain? That's telling us we're supposed to look beyond the externals to whatever lies within…"

"Oh for goodness sake woman, why don't you just fuck off?"

There was a titter from the group of observers. There were now more people looking at Celia than looking at the photographs.

One woman addressed her directly in a timid voice; "Are you an Ethiopian?"

Just as Celia was wondering if this were a battle worth winning, a figure emerged from the group. It was Margot. She walked her beautiful walk right across the sand and up to Celia and before Celia could speak she kissed her full and long on the mouth. There was a collective intake of breath from the crowd and one or two embarrassed giggles. The woman from Hampstead took her son by the hand and left. Someone asked "What's the meaning of that then?" and another voice laughed and said "Nothing mate, they're just a couple of dykes."

Margot put her arm through hers and Celia, still reeling from the kiss, allowed herself to be marched off the sand and out of the room.

*

"You were marvellous, honey. As for the kiss, I just couldn't help myself. I wanted to let you know I was with you one hundred per cent."

Margot's gentle Californian accent had a slightly hypnotic effect on Celia. They were facing each other at the bar of the King's Men, thighs interlocked, drinking pints of lager looking deep into each other's eyes.

"You did understand what I was saying, didn't you? Everybody seemed so stupid this morning; I really felt that it was barely worth trying to explain things. Perhaps I shouldn't have said what I did to the guard."

"Is it true about what you said – about being able to get the Council Immigration department to send him back?"

"I'd never do that of course. It was simply to frighten him."

"But you could, right?"

"Well I couldn't personally, but I do have friends who influence that kind of thing…"

"You mean decide if people can stay or have to go back?"

"Yes I suppose so."

"Well it seemed to work; he didn't come back!"

"He's probably an illegal, poor thing."

"Shall we have another pint, or go back to your flat?"

As Celia felt the pressure of Margot's well-toned thighs against her own, she had a premonition that something very significant was about to happen. Of a sexual nature.

Her anxiety returned. For the last two years she'd been virtually celibate so it was hard to imagine what it would be like to show her body to, let alone share it with, somebody else. Especially a woman. The idea fascinated and frightened her. She had only a very hazy idea of what might be involved but was mainly concerned with how Margot would respond when she saw her body, the massive dimpled thighs and heavy breasts. She was heavier, much heavier than she wanted to be. It was superficial of her or anyone else to dwell on the fact, but it was true, she was FAT – fat. But at least she had always had regular manicures and pedicures. And her teeth were good.

When the time came, after they had left the pub arm in arm, ignoring the knowing looks of men who might otherwise have chatted them up, she found that her ambivalence had disappeared. She felt strong and beautiful and ready for whatever might happen.

It was lovely, lovelier than she had ever known. Margot seemed to understand her body so well, and what she was feeling. And afterwards, she didn't get up and dash off to the bathroom, but seemed quite content to lie there propped up in bed on one arm looking at Celia and holding her hand. Then they took a bath together, laughing and talking as they soaped each other down. She had looked at herself in the bathroom mirror as she wrapped herself in a towel and saw what love had done; it had made her beautiful, well, almost. A few days after the encounter at the Tate, Margot had moved out of her bed sit in Earl's Court and into the flat in Camden Town.

It was all so natural, that was the word, thought Celia as she stepped heavily down from the sweaty bus and made her way towards the flat, yet so hard to reconcile that naturalness with how she knew her parents would respond, were they to find out.

*

Living with someone is much more stressful than having sex with them; this Celia learned within the first week of having Margot around. She had lived on her own for nearly fifteen years and had by now her own rather distinctive lifestyle. Over the last couple of years, for example, she had been experimenting with some post-capitalist approaches to life, specifically in trying to do more for the environment. She had the basic kit: five recycling bins in the kitchen plus the three bottle crates: clear, brown and green.

She also approved of minimal packaging and bulk purchase as a way of reducing her carbon footprint and, as a result, her cupboards were full of large anonymous-looking paper bags and cardboard boxes. Non-biodegradable material simply wasn't allowed in the flat although, life not being perfect, it did creep in from time to time. Finding storage room for these extra-large packages was not the only problem; bulk supply and easily-eroded packaging eventually, as she discovered, encouraged vermin. At first it was just cockroaches, biggish, but reassuringly shiny-clean and nervous enough to run for shelter whenever she turned on the light. If she left the light on, she didn't see them and could imagine they weren't a real problem, but it was a different matter with the mice. They made themselves known in a number of ways, starting off small but building up to become a major nuisance. The first sign was chewed paper scattered around the kitchen floor, then tiny black pellets inside the cupboards, which on closer scrutiny revealed themselves as droppings, some of them still wet and smelly. Shortly afterwards she became aware of scampering sounds under the floorboards, just a few to start with but soon rising to the occasional thunder of tiny feet. Eventually the scratching, chewing and scuttling became a regular evening accompaniment as several, tens, hundreds, who knows how many mice amused themselves somewhere behind the skirting boards.

For as long as the mice themselves were invisible she felt able to ignore the problem, although the smell took some getting used to, but when she was woken one night by a chewing sound and found a mouse six inches from her face working its way through a packet of Polos that she'd left on her bedside table, she decided she must do something and the next day went to her local ironware shop.

"Traps is what you want." The shop assistant looked like a rodent himself she thought, with sharp features, soft grey-brown hair and pink-rimmed eyes. "Unless you got a hungry pussy?" His ratty eyes twinkled, "Or you can handle poison? I can give you something that would stop a herd of buffalo."

The mice were indeed readily enough baffled and despatched by the environmentally-friendly traps, although she lay awake at night dreading the small sounds of death coming from the kitchen and the task that awaited her in the morning of slipping the tiny limp bodies into the bin under the sink. But, surprisingly, the cockroaches were in an altogether different league. They were so big that initially she had hoped the mousetraps would work on them as well but they seemed to be able not only to spring the traps but to walk away with the cheese. She couldn't bring herself to step on them and she had resisted using chemical poisons, so what to do? The problem had been ongoing, until Margot's first evening of residency.

"My God, sweet Jesus, will you look at this?"

There was the sound of stamping feet.

"Celia this goddam place is infested. Have you seen them? There are hundreds of them!"

"I've seen a few but, um, I didn't think there were that many."

"Sweetie the place is alive with them. Give me some money and I'll go down to the corner shop and get some bug killer."

She had come back with huge violent-looking aerosol cans.

"You're not going to use that are you? It's poison."

"You're damn right it is. If you don't like the smell, walk around the block or something."

At the weekend Margot asked for more money and came home with a large number of kitchen containers in environmentally unsound white polythene, and quite triumphantly threw away all the bags and boxes. So that was that.

Things had also changed in the office after Margot's arrival, changed in a curious but positive way. The other girls started paying her complements about her earrings and nail polish. They invited her to join them at lunch, where they asked her opinion about boyfriends. It's as if I've suddenly been allowed to join some club thought Celia. I've become a member of something. I'm on the inside, part of it all, whatever it is. Even the men dropped into her office for a chat, laughed at her jokes and sometimes included her when they went off to the pub for a drink before going home. It's as if I've been dead and have come alive again, she thought as her boss went up to the bar to buy them both a drink. She had never been so happy. How easy life had become: work, play, sex, it was all so very simple when you loved someone and knew you were loved in return, mind, heart, body and soul. Yes, soul. Celia had been an atheist for as long as she could remember and had never really considered whether she had a soul before. It had been almost a point of honour to deny the possibility of there being anything more to life than the here and now. Ideas of immortality, after all, were just a prop to support the feeble-minded, and she refused to give them serious consideration. Now, as she made the bed – their bed –or sorted the washing into loads, or read the labels at Sainsbury's she was filled with a sense of mystery as to how such mundane tasks had become so numinous.

She still hadn't told George and Eileen. She'd said that she had a new American flatmate but had let them think that this was in order to share the cost of the mortgage. But everything she wrote in her occasional letters to them, and everything she said in her weekly telephone conversation, was about Margot. They must, surely, have noticed?

Now in the flat, as she packed her overnight bag with clean underwear and a couple of changes of clothes, she listened while Margot suggested she tell her parents about the relationship so that all of them could live their lives with total honesty.

"The sooner you tell them, the sooner they'll get used to the idea and not disinherit you."

"Disinherit? But they're not ill."

"You never know. They're both getting to that sort of age."

"Anyway I don't think they have that much money. Maybe coming up to a million absolute total I suppose…"

"Pounds? Well that may not sound a lot to you but it sure rings a few bells with me. You should take care with money like that."

"That's counting the house and everything. But I don't know if there will be much left for me later on – if they die."

"When, honey, when."

"I hear what you say Margot and I do want them to know, but it isn't easy."

"Yes, it is," said Margot, "when we've got each other, everything's easy."

True.

Chapter Six
When love walks in

"When Love walks in and takes you for a spin,
Oh ! La la la, c'est magnifique!"
'C'est Magnifique' Cole Porter

George said he would pick Celia up from the airport while Eileen stayed at home and prepared lunch. It was another hot day and if Eileen wanted to go to the trouble then George agreed that, yes, they could have lunch out in the garden, for the first time that year.

The drive to the airport was slightly marred by his having to take the car up on the kerb twice, to make room for a bus and a lorry, a manoeuvre that always seemed to scrape the hub cap. He was also closely followed for much of the way by a youngster on a motorbike, a silly little fool who revved the engine in a show of pretend frustration every time the traffic slowed down or stopped at traffic lights. Even with the windows closed, the noise was dreadful. The road was too narrow for the boy to overtake but when it widened out George held a position firmly in the middle and blocked him successfully all the way to the airport. Finally, just as he saw and heard the rider getting ready to overtake, he put on his indicator and turned hard into the airport approach road. There was an angry squawk of a horn as the rider braked: a small victory, but barely compensation for the irritation.

The plane from Gatwick was late so he amused himself by

walking round the little airport building. He went into the shop and bought The Economist and a packet of Extra Strong Mints, then he looked at the flower stall, the photo kiosk, the box with coins and foreign money in it for the Lifeboat Fund, the machine that would print your own business card for one pound and, finally, he picked up some pamphlets about Guernsey from the Tourist Board desk. It was the first time Celia had been to the island so she would probably appreciate some local information. Especially if she and Eileen went out sightseeing.

He hoped they would. He and Eileen were used to being on their own and it had been a long time since Celia had been a member of the household. She no longer fitted in as she used to but had developed her own way of living and her own habits. At thirty-three that was not surprising.

She smoked, for one thing. George used to smoke but gave it up in 1982 and now he couldn't bear the smell of it in the house. He must remember this weekend to ask Eileen to ask Celia to confine her smoking to her bedroom or out in the garden.

She was also someone who took up a lot of space, always right there with you, not only filling the landscape with her tobacco, endless cups of coffee and her bags and jackets strewn around the place, but also filling the air with her voice. Like many of her generation she spoke Estuary English and its nasal, uneducated drone was a source of displeasure to George in particular who had, after all, paid for her to go to a reasonable public school and get a decent accent. Eileen seemed to cope with the voice more easily but then she was rather soft when it came to Celia. Moreover, the years with the Council had given Celia an additional language, an overlay of phrases and vocabulary redolent of bureaucracy and the culture of complaint. Her speech was peppered with words that through repetition had lost their meaning: 'diversity', 'remit', 'robust', 'enabled', 'empowered', 'reciprocity', 'process', 'vibrant' and George's pet hate, 'accessible.' There were times when she was in full flood, describing this or that incident in her office, her head wagging confidently, her eyes looking concerned behind the thick lenses and her long-nailed fingers tapping non-existent ash off yet another cigarette – when he just had to walk away.

"Passengers from the delayed flight BE 913 from London Gatwick will be coming through Arrivals Gate Number Two." George moved over towards the little group of meeters and greeters at Arrivals. It was the usual assortment: travel agents meeting early holiday makers, taxi drivers come to pick up this or that insurance consultant and drive them into town, and people like himself who had come to collect friends and relatives. He stood watching the doorway, wondering if, when she appeared, he should hug her and give her a kiss on the cheek. These days one had to be so careful about who you could touch and where, even with family. It sometimes seemed as if bodies had become a social disease.

He watched the doors with concentration, worrying that perhaps he might not even recognise his own flesh and blood – not that it had been so long since he'd seen her but there was something about looking for people you knew well in a crowd, they looked different, often not at all like their normal selves – when he was startled to feel a light but confident touch on his shoulder.

"Excuse me, you dropped this, love."

He turned. She was holding out a Tourist Board leaflet that must have fallen from his hand.

"What? Oh, oh, thank you. Thank you very much." He couldn't say more, he was too busy looking, and listening to the reverberations going on inside him. Something was happening, something that shook him to his core. There was music playing, and it was familiar music. It was the song of youth: of warm hair, smooth skin and bright eyes. It was a song of lust: those slim ankles, that tiny waist, those jutting breasts. It was a song of mystery - the deep soft voice, that scent of more than flowers. It was a song that George had not heard for a very long time indeed and which he had not actually sung for even longer.

"Don't I know you?" She tossed her auburn hair and pouted as best she could with her wide, full-lipped mouth. "You live next door, don't you? I think I've seen you in the garden. Am I right?"

"What, Les Vardes?" he managed to ask, his voice struggling with a dry mouth and a swollen tongue.

"That's right. We've not been in long."

George's heart leapt. Oh Joy. Oh thank you God. This improbably wonderful vision lived next door. She ate, drank and slept every day a mere thirty yards away from him. "Did I hear you out in the garden, yesterday? Wasn't sure but I thought I could hear someone laughing? Such a happy sound."

"Gloria likes a laugh all right. That's me, Gloria. And Steve - that's my husband, well, partner actually."

Gloria in excelsis deo. What an unbelievable stroke of good fortune.

"Gloria. Gloria. What a beautiful name. And Stephen too, of course. Very good for a man." He stood there smiling and nodding.

"Shall we get together? Have a drinkie or two? Steve and me and you and – have you got a wife? Or perhaps you're a bachelor? Gentleman living on his own?"

"No, I have a wife. Eileen, that's her name." What an old-fashioned fuddy-duddy name it sounded today. "We've been married - a long time. George and Eileen Buchanan. "

"Are you on for it then George? A little of what you fancy?"

"Most definitely."

"I'll ring you. Now - must go and see a man about a dog."

He watched her backside as she moved forward to greet some foreign-looking man coming in from Customs. What a looker.

"George, George, I'm here." And there was Celia, to his surprise and relief, looking much thinner and quite happy for a change. And she was wearing a normal pair of trousers, not a long skirt or the dreaded dungarees. Yes, there was his little girl. He reached his arms around her and gave her an extra long hug.

And she hugged him back.

"Welcome to Guernsey. We're going to have a lovely time."

*

This was what made life worth living, the three of them sitting around the table in the garden under the sunshade, finishing off a good meal with Dorset Blue Vinney and the last few inches of Fleurie. This was La Dolce Vita, La Vie en Rose, the Good Life that they had hoped for. And Celia looked so much better than she had done last time, and seemed relaxed, less worried. And George, bless him, was coping magnificently, listening to Celia talk about the office, even asking questions. He really wasn't a bad old stick. Of course the sun helped; it did bring out the best in people.

"What are you two thinking of doing now? Off for a bit of sight-seeing?" George looked at his watch and then up at the sky as if making professional calculations of both the time and the weather.

"Aren't you coming with us?" It would be so nice for the three of them to stay like this for the whole weekend, close and self-contained like a family should be.

"No, old girl. Got things to do. I'll see you when you get back. Don't forget we're going out for supper this evening." He carried a couple of plates into the house as his contribution towards clearing the table, and then they heard him climbing up the stairs to the belvedere.

"What's George going to do?"

"Oh I don't know, settling some bills I expect. He keeps himself busy. I'll just put these things in the dishwasher, now don't move, you just sit there and finish your cigarette."

Moments later Celia stood at the back door. "Is that his study right at the top? Where the window is sort of set into a tower?"

"Yes. It's a belvedere."

"He's at the window, looking through binoculars."

"Bird watching I expect."

*

Eileen parked the car at the Doyle Monument and she and Celia set out along the Jerbourg coastal path. Perhaps it was all for the good that the two of them were alone. We can talk more easily, she thought.

"That's Sark over there and the little bit that slopes down and up towards the right is called La Coupee. The island on the left is Herm, and next to it Jethou and right over there, on the horizon, is Jersey."

Just for a second she felt proud of living on the island. Perhaps she and George would be able to settle down here and properly call it home. Of course it felt like home right now simply because Celia was there. She, more than anything, or anywhere,

or anyone, was what rooted Eileen in the world. There's my future, my reason for being, she thought as she walked behind Celia on the narrow footpath along the cliff towards Fermain.

"What's it like living on an island? It seems so small."

"Sometimes it feels as if we're under a magnifying glass, and sometimes it's like looking the wrong way through a telescope. I mean either everything seems much too big or else it's tiny and very far away. Like Alice in Wonderland."

"Sounds unreal."

"I expect I'll get used to it, later on."

But even after nearly two years on Guernsey, Eileen still felt ambivalent about the place. It was at least safe and secure and, at times like these when the sun was shining and the sea was cornflower blue, it was beautiful. On other days, and not only when the winds blew in with rain from the Atlantic, there was an air of melancholy and menace about the place. What had seemed pretty became trivial, what had felt cosy seemed barren and mean. On those days the only solution was to dig deep into one's own resources. When they were emptied, it was time to escape, one way or another.

They sat down on a patch of short grass, looking out over Marble Bay. A light breeze blew in from a turquoise sea. Perfect.

"There's something I want to tell you, Eileen. It's about Margot and me." Celia started shredding a piece of grass between her fingers. "We're really close, you know?"

Eileen felt the ground shift. Or was it just a cloud suddenly blocking the sun? "What do you mean, dear?" she said, more for time than information.

"You know, she and I – we're an item...."

She'd heard the term before but only in relation to boys with their girlfriends. What could Celia mean?

"What does that mean?"

Celia looked up with an expression that Eileen hadn't seen since she caught her in the larder as a ten year old finishing off the Christmas cake.

"It means we - we get on well together. Just that really."

"You must bring her over some time."

They fell silent again, and sat there a bit longer looking out to sea. I used to have strong attachments at her age, thought Eileen. It's nothing serious.

Chapter Seven
Dinner with Steve and Gloria

"They are not long, the days of wine and roses."
'Vitae Summa Brevis'
Ernest Dowson

After scanning next door's garden George sat down at his desk and reflected on what had happened to him that morning. There was no doubt something had happened. He had not only seen this woman – Gloria – he had felt her in every cell, corpuscle and follicle of his body. As he tried to recall the precise shape of her face and the colour of her eyes – grey or green? – he was aware of a stirring in his groin. By God he wanted her. As a man wants a woman. So, he wasn't dead, there was life in the old dog yet. Several times he got up and looked out of the open window but next door's garden was disappointingly empty. A new torture seemed to be in store for him. Just as he was beginning to feel alive again, the object of his desire was not – what was that damn word - accessible! 'Never the time, the place and the loved one', he said to himself as he went to the window again and pressed his loins firmly and hopefully against the windowsill, willing her to make an appearance. He only just heard the door bell. There, it rang again and quite persistently. Could Eileen and Celia be back from their walk already and maybe forgotten their key? They'd forget their own heads if they weren't attached. Hold on, hold on, he was coming as quickly as his knees would allow. It rang a third time.

Why were they so impatient? They must know he'd be up in his study. Then, he had a sudden revelation; it must be Gloria! He'd willed her to come and she had.

"I'm on my way!" he shouted, "Hang on." He jumped the last three steps, feeling only a twinge of pain in his knee, ran along the hall, and flung the door open.

Two women stood in the porch, neither of them Gloria by a long chalk. Both middle-aged, not that their age was of any consequence to him, and dressed like something out of a low budget wartime movie: long skirts, short-sleeved blouses, gloves, ankle socks and sandals. One tall, one short. What were they? Social workers? The local W.I.? They both gave him radiant smiles, a frightening development, which he found himself obliged to return.

"Good afternoon, I hope we haven't called at an inconvenient time?" said the short one.

"Not at all."

"So many people out enjoying themselves. We're lucky to find you in."

"Have you come to see Celia?"

"No it's your good self we've come to see. To tell you about the forgiveness of Christ. We are all sinners, sometimes in deed but sometimes only in thought. Don't you agree?"

"Well, I…"

"It isn't just the big sins – murder and adultery – that God cares about…"

"Adultery?"

"…but small things, like being critical of a loved one, or of turning away from a soul in need."

"Look it's awfully good of you to come here but I don't really think I've got anything to say about these things."

"Perhaps it makes you uneasy to talk about God?"

"Well, it's not that – I can see why you're doing this…"

"I knew you must be an understanding person from the moment we turned into your gateway. Didn't I say, Maureen, that this was a house of love? Do you have children?"

"Well, just one…"

"Then you'll know the love of God. Boy or girl?"

"Actually a girl, but…"

"That's nice isn't it, Maureen? The love a man feels for his daughter is so pure. I know you agree with me, I can see it in your eyes."

"Now, look, I don't think…"

Maureen reached into her carrier bag and brought out a handful of leaflets.

"We have some literature here, about people who are not as lucky as your daughter, and how the love of God has transformed their lives. I know you'd like to read it."

She proffered the leaflets but George kept his hands firmly at his side.

"Only forty pence each…." The gloved hand moved closer towards him. He recoiled slightly. The hand had a disembodied look, as if it were some kind of prosthesis - like the one in Moonraker, or was it Goldfinger?

"George! Coo-eee…"

They all turned to see Gloria walking down the drive. She was in pink from top to toe: pink scarf in her hair, pink high heels, short shorts and a bright, tight clinging top - she really did have magnificent breasts. The two women were still smiling. Gloria took off her sunglasses and gave them a frosty stare.

"Hello, what's happening here? Am I interrupting something?"

"These ladies are from the Church."

"Jehovah's Witnesses are we? I don't think we need any of those shenanigans. Excuse us ladies, that's all for today. I need to talk to George. Yes, thank you very much. Goodbye, goodbye." She fluttered her hands in the general direction of the front gate.

The women recognised a superior force. "God bless you and watch over you," they said in unison and turned to go.

She watched until they were half way down the drive and

almost out of earshot, "Silly cows. You don't want to listen to all that stuff, life's too short."

George liked a woman who spoke her mind, it saved a lot of time.

"Look, I won't stop. Just come to ask you over for drinks this evening."

"We're going out to dinner."

"What time?"

"Eight at Nello's"

"All right then, come over at half six."

"Our daughter Celia's staying with us."

"The more the merrier. It's informal so don't bother to dress. Ha ha, listen to me! You'll think the worst!"

"I look forward to that - not the clothes bit of course. I mean - wonderful, we'll be there."

She took herself off down the drive. George stood at the door in case she turned around to wave. She didn't, but the back view made it worth staying there until she'd gone from sight. An awful excitement rose up in him at the prospect of going into Gloria's house, even with the family along. But what should he say to Eileen?

*

"So I said we'd be there at half past six."

"But I thought you didn't want to get involved, and that they probably weren't our type?"

"Felt quite sorry for them, being new and all that. Anyway this isn't 'getting involved'. We're only going for a drink for Pete's sake."

"I had thought Les Vardes was an elitist sort of enclave." said Celia, "There's obviously a bit more inclusiveness than I expected. Do we have to change or can I go like this?"

"Glad rags I think, don't you? It's a big house." They must make a good impression.

At six thirty-five the three of them, now dressed for dinner, stood on the front porch of Steve and Gloria's house. George had taken longer to dress than the women. He had laid out a number of potential outfits on the bed, then held each one up against him and regarded the effect in the long mirror: dark blue blazer with a blue and green striped shirt; beige linen jacket with cream shirt; then, in desperation, dark blue jeans and short-sleeved sky blue stripes from M&S. He was well aware that the choice could determine the course of his relationship with Gloria. He was in no doubt that there would be a relationship: they were destined for each other, it was Fate. He knew that - but did she? That was the question, and that was why his decision was so crucial. How he appeared to her tonight could make or break what might be his last chance of happiness as a man.

Twenty past six. He heard first Celia and then Eileen go downstairs. Deciding that discretion was the better part of valour, he climbed into the blazer ensemble: conservative but classy. A safe bet.

He instantly regretted it when he saw what must be Steve at his front door, wearing baggy surfer shorts, a dazzling white t-shirt and flip-flops. More disturbing than his clothes was the underlying muscularity of his walnut brown body. He vibrated with power. Even the thick black hair looked as if every curl had been individually teased out and then charged full of electricity. To George's annoyance Steve was undeniably young and looked undeniably and depressingly virile.

"Hi there. George and Eileen isn't it? Good to meet you." He extended a strong hand, "And you must be Celia, is it? Wonderful. Welcome to our modest abode."

Unlike Gloria, whose voice intimated origins near Essex, Steve had an Australian accent. George thought that his tan couldn't have been acquired from English summers. There was also a not-quite-British look to the interior of the house as well. The hallway was a spectacular mix of beige and cream, silk tapestries on the wall, marble floor, a big chandelier and a huge painting of a lubricious-looking nude. George was careful to give it only a quick glance but would have liked to have stood and stared. The face was a lot like Gloria; he couldn't say for the rest.

"The wow factor I think you'll agree," said Steve, "follow me."

He led the way, walking in the manner of cowboys in the movies with a rolling, slightly bow-legged gait, as if his balls were hurting. Maybe it was the flip-flops.

"We're out on the patio. We're having a barbie tonight. Shame you couldn't join us. Yeah. We like a barbie, don't we Glor?"

The patio had been 'done over' since Mrs. Evan's days, too much to be in good taste thought George, but it was certainly impressive. A wide expanse of stone terracing, lamp-posts around the edge and a wrought iron wheelbarrow planted with flowers. There was a comfortable-looking arrangement of chairs - not like the Buchanan's wooden garden furniture but some kind of synthetic basket weave, which George had rejected when he'd come across it at the garden centre as much too expensive - a large drinks trolley and two patio heaters going full blast even though the evening was warm. The place smelled of money.

Glor had changed out of her shorts into some kind of what George could only think of as lounging pyjamas. They were in a swirly pattern of pink and orange, not really to his taste but they close-fit to the body and the bodice was cut nicely low. Her breasts, apparently totally self-supported, swayed with every movement. They definitely were to his taste. He fought hard not to look down at them as she leaned forward and pressed a glass into his hand, but failed.

"Now get your hand round that. It's a Gloria special – I won't tell you the recipe even if you got down on bended knee, and I expect you'll do that before we're finished." She parted her big fleshy lips and laughed and the breasts joggled accompaniment. "Cheers!"

The Buchanans sipped politely; they were not a family for mixed drinks, but it tasted good and, George thought, not too strong.

"So tell me about yourselves." Steve was sprawled in one of the chairs, a big circular job with dark brown cushioning. He lay back with thighs apart, muscles or bulges in every department, the Alpha male in his lair.

"Not a lot to say really," said George, crossing his legs despite himself, "I used to be Marketing Manager – well, as good as Marketing Director in terms of the scope and responsibility of my job – thirty-five years for Parson and Green."

"Oh yeah?" Steve seemed suitably impressed.

"Do you know them?"

"Not really, no. What are they? Undertakers."

George gave a short sharp laugh, "Hah! You're not far wrong there. Many a true word spoken in jest! They would have been the death of me if I'd chosen to stay there any longer. They were a good company before the merger, but it changed, it all changed. Too big."

"Yeah, ain't that the problem with business these days? Best keep it small and then you can control it."

"That's it exactly. When it gets too big there's nobody knows any more what needs to be done or how to do it. It's all systems, delegation down to the level of incompetence and then finally get the consultants in to clear up the mess and skim off a chunk of the profits. Nobody seems to do a real day's work any more."

"A bit of hard graft? Know what you mean. Anyone for a top-up?"

"Why not? I'd like a drop more of Gloria's special brew." George found himself warming to Steve. He looked unpromising but was turning out to be a bit of a rough diamond.

"Good, good. What about the ladies?"

"Oh no, I couldn't, thank you." Eileen put her hand over the top of her glass. She was looking a little flushed already.

But Celia nodded and held out her glass.

"I just love your earrings." Gloria leaned forward and touched the silver hoops hanging from Celia's ears. "They're beautiful, really make a statement. And they look so good with that shirt."

Celia seemed pleased. She was looking quite passable this evening thought George. She was wearing some kind of silvery silk top and managed to look bulky but smart. But the earrings looked like cheap hippie rubbish. Still, it was kind of Gloria to be complimentary.

"They're hand-made by the women's craft guild of Pondicherri. The guild is an association to help the local women become empowered. The association guarantees that they get paid a proper percentage of the final wholesale price. It's a Fair Trade initiative so I give them support."

"I'm all for women getting their fair share." Gloria smiled at Celia and winked.

George was surprised to see Celia blush, and even more surprised when she laughed out loud. It must be the drink he thought, trying not to look at Gloria's nipples which were standing out like little thimbles through the swirly thin material. Was she or was she not wearing a brassiere? Either possibility gave him very positive food for thought and he sat back in his garden chair enjoying it all. This was what he had hoped to find in Guernsey, sunshine, a relaxed drink or two, and, most important of all attractive, vital new friends, people who had seen a bit of the world and who could give him something to think about. Everyone this evening seemed so at home with each other, and the drink was going down very pleasantly indeed. Yes, he could take a lot more of this and of them, Gloria and even Steve.

"So what are you two in?" Celia asked the question that George had felt he couldn't.

Gloria looked at Steve, and Steve looked at Gloria before he answered, "A bit of this and a bit of that. Wheeling, dealing…"

"…but never stealing," smiled Gloria.

"Import export?" asked George helpfully.

"No, no, more like distribution, e-commerce, that sort of thing. We run a lot of it from home."

"You're a dot com?" George had always despised anything to do with computers, having successfully fought off having to use them at work. Even when one had been issued to him and set up on his desk he'd had it moved to a side table and resolutely refused to turn it on for the seven months it was there. Now that he was no longer expected to get involved he found himself much more tolerant.

"Kind of – yeah, that's right. Yeah, we have a lot of fingers in a lot of pies."

Gloria gave her deep-throated laugh, the one George had heard from the belvedere. This time the sound filled him with desire.

"Do you work as well, Gloria?" asked Eileen.

Gloria immediately fell silent, put her head on one side and then looked Eileen straight in the eye: "I do what I can to support Steve. I think that's a woman's job: make the home comfortable, keep the garden looking nice and be there, really be there for them. Do you know what I mean?"

"I think you're right; though it's probably not fashionable to say so. I have always put George and Celia first."

Gloria reached forward to touch Eileen's hand: "It doesn't take much to see what a good job you've made of looking after them. And from what I can see of your garden it looks as if you're a real old-fashioned homebody."

"Do you enjoy gardening then?" asked Eileen in a slightly frigid voice tinged with disbelief, one that George knew well.

"Mother Nature is my second name." Gloria smiled broadly, seemingly unmoved by Eileen's tight expression.

"Really? You don't look as if you do much digging, not with those nails?"

"Perhaps I should say I love looking at gardens, but I'm hopeless at making things grow. Well, most things!" And here Gloria giggled and put her hand with their long scarlet nails

93

on Steve's thigh. George found himself laughing too, for no good reason except to keep the party happy and, besides, it was warm and they seemed to have finished a whole jug of Gloria's special.

"My goodness. Look at the time. We should be gone." George struggled unsuccessfully to get out of his low chair. He fell back once and then twice. It seemed so natural for Gloria to stand in front of him, her breasts almost grazing his forehead, before she took his hands firmly in hers and then leaned back and pulled him up, that he didn't feel ashamed. Not at all. Especially as she hadn't let go of his hands but was still standing there smiling in his face. Yes, her eyes were green. Green with honey-coloured flecks in them.

"Well Buchanans you'd better be off." Gloria loosed his hands, turned round playfully and to George's surprise and disappointment gave Steve the kiss that he'd hoped to receive himself.

George drove quickly down the hill into town. They were nearly a quarter of an hour late. There wasn't space to park outside the restaurant so he set the women down while he drove on to the big car park by the ferry terminus. He walked back past the harbour, glad to be alone for a few minutes. It was a mild and cloudless evening, the sea was calm and he was wonderfully full of joy and expectation. Gloria had held his hands and looked deep into his eyes. He knew that she knew what he felt for her. And he knew that she felt the same. Her kiss with Steve had just been displacement activity; he recognised that now. He stumbled as he crossed the road and tried to convert the loss of balance into a heavy-footed jog, ignoring the look of concern from a passing taxi-driver. Look out world, here I come.

*

No-one mentioned the drinks party during the first part of the meal; all of them, if they did but know it, for the same reason – Gloria. Eileen's thoughts were dark. Something had been going on back there that she didn't like. It wasn't simply that Gloria had been flirting with George and he, vain old fool, had responded to her like a dog to bone. No, what she felt uneasy about was the way that Gloria had flirted with all three of them, played with them, and told each one in the crudest possible manner what they wanted to hear. She may have wanted to present herself as a rough-edged and straightforward woman, but Eileen thought she recognised something much more manipulative and dangerous behind that façade.

"When shall we ask them back?" asked George scraping at the remains of his chocolate mousse. "I feel we should. They were very hospitable."

"I'm not sure they're our type of people."

"Oh Eileen!" this from Celia, flushed in the face after half a bottle of Amarone, "'Our type' – you're so out of touch. We live in a pluralist society: race, class, nationality, age, gender, it's all so irrelevant now. We're all as good as each other."

"It isn't a matter of who's better than whom..." Eileen wasn't prepared this time to cede her viewpoint, even to Celia. She didn't approve of Gloria or Steve, and, besides, she was beginning to get a headache. "It's whether we've got anything in common. And I don't think we have."

"There's humanity. You have that in common with them." Celia looked solemn behind her spectacles.

"And they're our neighbours Ellie – isn't that enough for you?"

"No it isn't. Just because they're human beings and live next to us isn't enough. It might be when you're young but not when you get to my age. I want people who understand what I know and how I feel. People who have lived the same sort of life as I have, who have read the same books, know the same poetry. Who have the same values. And there isn't anybody like that in my life here, nobody at all. I'm all alone and people like Steve and Gloria - coarse and illiterate - make me feel it even worse."

Her head was beginning to throb now and she could feel herself coming close to tears. How maudlin; she shouldn't have had the red wine on top of Gloria's Special.

"It's no good. I don't want to spoil your coffee. I want to be alone. Give me the keys and I'll go and wait for you in the car."

She stood up abruptly, ignoring their surprised faces and left the restaurant. But it was Saturday night and the usual cavalcade of cars was racing round and round the perimeter of the car park, then up and down the front. It was the youth of Guernsey, more than a little drunk and drugged, going nowhere fast. The streams of cars passed too thick and fast for her to cross the road in safety. Youngsters hung out of the windows and shouted and swore as they passed. She had no idea why the authorities didn't stop this nonsense. Everybody knew it happened every weekend. Nobody cares, that's why, she thought. Then it was suddenly all too much and she stood alone on the edge of the kerb and cried like a lost child.

*

They were all late down the following morning, and Eileen noticed that breakfast was a muted affair, the conversation confined to the weather and the quality of her homemade marmalade. Had she ruined everybody's weekend? Perhaps it had been wrong to say what she had thought about Steve and Gloria. Certainly to cry in public. Pathetic. It must have been that wretched drink; although it hadn't tasted strong.

She waited until George disappeared upstairs with his coffee and the Sunday papers, then said to Celia, "Let's go to the Sculpture Park."

The Park was a soothing place and they could get a cup of tea there and have a chat. It was an easy walk away and, as if by agreement, both Celia and Eileen talked about safe and inconsequential topics as they strolled along the wide grass verge of Fort Road. By the time they turned into the gravelled drive of Sausmarez Manor and the Sculpture Park Eileen was beginning to feel more relaxed. This mood increased when it was obvious that Celia enjoyed rambling along the little paths through the rhododendrons and camellias, coming across the various sculptures that had been placed half-hidden in the trees.

They were having a cup of tea and Celia, cigarette in hand, indicated the tables set out near the little pond, the ducks preening themselves on the grass and the flowers in the garden surrounding the old manor house.

"You know you are very privileged to be here Eileen. When I think of the way some of my clients live in Camden Town, let alone Kings Cross, it seems incredible that you and George should be enjoying all this. Life's not fair."

"Your father has worked hard all his life – I mean his retirement money didn't just fall into his lap. That doesn't mean I don't appreciate what we have here. Of course I do. Especially when you're here and we can come on little outings like this."

"Doesn't George ever go out for a walk?"

"Sometimes. Well, no, not often. We have our own lives, our own ways of going on. Most people do after they've been married for some time. You establish a routine. You'll see one day."

Celia was looking pretty today. She did have good skin; that was always an advantage for a woman, and she kept her hands nicely. Eileen could see herself in the way Celia stood and how she put her head on one side when she was thinking, and in her fine, pale hair.

"What are you staring at?"

"I was thinking how well you looked. Much better than when we last saw you. You must be eating well, stopped all that alfalfa business."

"Wheat juice Eileen, full of anti-oxidants."

"Whatever it was, you looked very pale on it."

"If I'm pale it's living in London that does it, and having a hectic job." Celia put her head on one side, "I'm trying to lead a more balanced life now."

"You still seem to be working as hard."

"Yes, but it's different now that I have someone to come home to."

"Who's that?"

"Margot, of course."

"Doesn't she live her own life?"

Celia breathed in deeply, and then stubbed out her cigarette until it was reduced to fragments.

"We're living together Eileen. Sharing our lives. In every respect."

Eileen's fingers tightened around her tea cup, which she held in front of her with both hands. A small mewing sound escaped her lips, but she could find no words.

"I'm gay, Eileen."

"What?"

"Gay. Lesbian."

"I know what the word means."

"Sorry if it's a shock."

It was more than a shock. It changed the world. Eileen needed time to work this out. Her first feeling was an immediate sense of denial. Celia was normal, there had never been anything wrong with her, apart from her weight, so how could she be – gay? And what did this mean anyway? The second feeling was of repulsion. She had only the murkiest of ideas about what lesbians did together, and she didn't want to know more. It seemed not only distasteful but faintly ludicrous, the idea of two women trying to do what a man and woman did. The third feeling was too overwhelming to absorb properly. If Celia stayed with this Margot creature then there would be no husband, no children, no succession. Celia's future and her own, and George's of course, would just come to an end, dissolve into nothing. It was the end of the road for all of them.

"You're not cross are you?"

"No, no, of course not, just surprised. And disappointed I suppose."

"You'll feel differently when you see her. We've been so happy. It's made all the difference in the world."

It's true that you look happy at last thought Eileen and some part of her managed to say out loud "I'm glad you told me and I'm glad that you're happy."

"I was thinking of telling George..."

"No! Don't do that, not yet. He's got so many things on his mind at the moment. I don't think he'd take it too well. We'll tell him later."

"You don't know how much better I feel. Telling you I mean. I feel so relieved, I don't know why but I didn't expect you to be so, so modern."

Eileen looked at her watch and then stood up. "Let's go home to Daddy. If we walk back along the Cliff path from Fermain we should still have plenty of time for lunch. What time did you say your plane left?"

Later that day, as she was getting ready for bed - in the spare room as she couldn't face being close to George with this terrible secret in her head - Eileen went over and over what Celia had told her. It was nothing short of a disaster. She might be able to cope with it in time herself but how was she ever going to tell George? He would be devastated by the news. He might even turn against Celia. Her only hope was that this might be some sort of stage that Celia would eventually grow out of, or that in time Margot and all her subversive attractions would lose interest in Celia and go away, disappear. That way George need never know and life could go back to normal.

Chapter Eight
George meets the Vikings

"A man who has no office to go to – I don't care who he is
- is a trial of which you can have no conception."
'The Irrational Knot' George Bernard Shaw.

Friday: five thirty in the morning. George lay awake and restless. Eileen was still asleep so he couldn't disturb her by reading, but in the end a full bladder drove him from bed. Once out, he decided he might as well get up for good. He carefully extracted his chinos from the trouser press where he'd left them the night before, picked out some underwear and a clean short-sleeved shirt from the drawer and crept out of the room to the bathroom. This was the fourth night in a row that he'd slept badly. Not that it had seemed to make much difference to how he felt during the daytime; the worst thing was lying there in the half-light, unable to put on the light in case it disturbed Eileen, and yet totally unable to go back to sleep. Either it was because it was summer or maybe, God forbid, yet another symptom of the onset of old age, a new torture for his sunset years. Downstairs he made himself a coffee. He was bored. The paper wouldn't be delivered until after eight and there was only some rubbish for farmers on the radio. Why not go for a walk and see what the world was up to?

It was a modest, quiet sort of morning. Still too early for there to be many cars, but as he walked towards Fort George he passed a couple of people walking their dogs. Maybe he should get a dog; that would force him to go out and get some exercise.

He'd think about it. Fort George itself seemed dead. No dog-walkers, no cars in the driveways, no sounds of life at all from any direction. Still it was pleasant enough to walk along the empty roads and look in at the big houses with their manicured gardens and close-cut hedges. He walked along the Corniche to the Fort itself. It was surprisingly warm although the sky was grey and the horizon misty; he couldn't even see Sark.

He started down steps at Terre Point, which led to La Valette but halfway had to stop to rest and rub his knees - they were aching already. He took the opportunity to lean on the ivy-clad wall looking down over Havelet Bay. The tide was in and the sea bathing pools were nearly full.

"Excuse me! Morning!"

A tall man, about his age, dressed in shorts and holding a rolled-up towel under his arm, was jogging down the steps towards him. George stood to one side to let him pass, "Good morning", turned to watch him go and a minute later saw him reach the road, from where he jogged into the building at the entrance to the main pool. A car drove up, and then another. The two drivers got out, acknowledged each other and they also went into the building. He heard laughter, looked at his watch; it was only twenty past six, what could they be up to at this time of the day? He felt a pang of envy as he carried on down the steps. Here were men who had something to get out of bed for.

He spent a few minutes exploring the foreshore beside the main pool, poking round a cave he found in the rocks and pretending to be interested in whatever the tide was bringing in. Minutes later he'd climbed up through the railings and was standing on the rough concrete, around the main pool. He leant casually back against the rail and looked around him. There was no sign of the men so he looked out to sea and waited. The far edge of the pool was now submerged, fused with the sea. The stillness of the water reminded him of childhood holidays, when the days stretched to the horizon and he felt he had all the time in the world. But now behind him he heard the men talking and joking as they came out of the changing room.

"Good morning again. Thinking of joining us?"

It was the man who had passed him on the steps. George could tell now that he must be at least seventy, but was still a good figure of a man, tall and straight and with plenty of greying hair. But his age showed in the tanned weather-beaten skin and his pale and rheumy blue eyes, which looked as if they'd seen too much. He briefly adjusted his goggles, pulled them firmly over his eyes, and without waiting for George's answer, slipped over the edge in a graceful dive.

The other men had come out. There were four of them standing on the concrete, all putting on goggles and one of them a bathing cap.

"What are you doing?"

"Now there's a question and a half! What does it look like Pal? We're going to swim. In t'water of course." The speaker was a thickset man of about sixty with a rubbery expressive face and a stagey Yorkshire accent. "We are Guernsey's only synchronised swimming association for the senile. You can join us if you like. You look old enough."

"Don't mind Donald, he was dragged up in Sheffield so he's got no manners." This was from a small thin man wearing a red baseball cap. He was probably only a few years younger than George but his slight build and the red cap gave an initial impression of youth. His voice was light but his hands were square and rough-looking and his small grey eyes looked sharp.

"Watch it you!" Donald made a mock rugby pass and then leapt into the water with a loud splash and came to the surface with a shout.

"By 'eck it's better out than in. Coom on in, the water's bloomin' luvly - freeze your balls off if you 'ad any."

He set off for the further end of the pool in a fast choppy crawl and the two other men went into the water after him, and gave chase. The small thin man said "We're the Vikings. It's a swimming club. Men only, and we're all pushing the years a bit, sixty-something going on thirty." He took off his cap, threw it on a bench and walked down the steps into the water. "I'd better get in now before they pull me in. I like to take it slow especially when it's bloody freezing. Arrgh, Jesus."

George watched them as they laughed and cavorted and swam around like kids. The sun had broken through the early morning cloud and the sea-water suddenly sparkled as it slapped around the basin. He bent to feel the water with his hand. My God it was cold. Yet they seemed to be enjoying it. He was envious.

Twenty minutes later he strolled over to them as they sat on the concrete benches drying off in the sun. The thin man, wrapped in a towel and with his cap back on his head, offered George a cup of tea from a flask.

"Sit down, have a cup of tea. The name's Ray."

"George. How long has the club been going, then?"

"Andrew there," said Ray, nodding in the direction of the

older man, "is the founder member; he got it going about ten years ago when he'd just retired from the navy. I joined a year ago. Don joined just before me. And Kevin over there, he's been around for about five years. Bill only joined last year. All in pretty much the same circumstances you know: retirement, getting bored, sitting around too much."

"Weren't getting' it enoof." Don was passing round the biscuits.

"Now Don's fighting them off." Bill seemed to be the youngest, a fair haired man with a pleasant open face.

"You don't look old enough to be retired."

"Well there it is! That's the benefit of being a Viking. He's been rejoovenated!"

"Not retirement, more like redundancy," said Bill, "Company on the mainland. Golden handshake just enough to make it worth to come over here. But money or not it still gets to you. I was beginning to take to the drink a bit more than I should -"

" 'Bit more'! Bloody 'eck, it were like watching a camel come out of desert."

"– there just didn't seem anything to do here. It's not only the island -" Bill looked serious as he towelled his hair "- if you've worked hard all your life, you know, been active, given up most of your time to work, you feel it when it's all gone..."

"The time to feel it is when you're standing in the bus queue – you know liked pressed up to the woman in front."

"...The first month or so it's like a very, very long weekend. You do all the things you were longing to do when you were working: you get up late, you spend all day reading the newspaper or watching the cricket. Or drinking. Or thinking about the next meal. Then when that gets boring you start ringing your old colleagues to see if there's anyone to talk to, or if anyone wants to go for a drink after work. But they're all getting on with it and haven't got any time. And there's a new girl on the switchboard and she doesn't know who the hell you are...and you realise you've become a nobody, a nothing. So what's left of all those years?"

"Bloody nowt. What Bill says is true. Though I'm loathe to admit it seeing as 'ow he talks rubbish most of the time. In my own case I were top of the R&D department, agro-chemicals: knew me stuff, did my job, made them money. I chose, chose mind, to take early retirement because I could see bloody writing on wall. I were too good for them. I knew that. They were havin' to pay me too much money because I were too good. Found out they were angling to get some thirty year old in as department head – thirty, would you believe – and give me some back room two day a week consultancy. I told them where they could stuff it. Up where the sun don't shine. I went early and we moved here. And just like he says, bugger all to do except go shopping and get under the wife's feet. So when Andrew here said come and be a Viking, I thought why the bugger not? Nothing to lose and mebbe something to gain."

"How often do you meet?"

"Twice a week, Tuesdays and Fridays, summer and winter," Ray turned his cap back to front. "If you don't see the improvement within two months, you get your money back! We meet one hour after dawn..."

"She's usually got herself going by the time we get here-"

"-into the water, cup of tea if you've remembered your flask, bit of chat and then home. We don't talk about work or anything serious and it's first names only. It's your home away from home. You feel better for it."

George watched them as they collected their things and went their separate ways, Andrew loping off towards the steps, the others driving back along La Vallette. George refused the offer of a ride up the hill from Ray but he couldn't face the steps either. He decided to walk back home the longer but more gentle route via the Havelet. He had something to think about and it was a good something. He'd found out that he wasn't alone; there were other men like him, who knew what it was to be retired, who understood how he felt, and, more to the point, who had found a remedy.

His envy was reshaping itself into a resolution. He would join them. He would come down to the bathing pool twice a week an hour after dawn. He would bring his swimming gear, a flask of tea and biscuits. He'd swim up and down in the cold water, come rain or shine and talk and laugh about it afterwards. He would feel like a man again, he would become a Viking.

*

"You're up early." Eileen was reading his paper over the remains of breakfast. She was looking glum.

"Woke up early, so I took a constitutional."

"My tooth's hurting, the big molar that I had filled last time we were in London."

"Oh yes," He couldn't remember but was inclined to be sympathetic this morning. "Do you think you ought to see someone about it?"

"I could try and find someone on the island but I think I'd rather go back to David."

"What, go to London?"

"If I can make an appointment, yes. Do you think I'm being too extravagant? I could go just for the day, catch the seven fifteen, come back in the late afternoon."

Eileen out of the way for a day, though usually inconvenient, suddenly seemed quite an attractive proposition. It would be even more attractive, he thought, if she stayed away overnight. George pictured himself alone in the house, sitting at the desk late into the evening, planning a new life.

"You could stay over and make it a bit more of a trip. I expect Celia's got room."

"Yes I could." Her face brightened. "It depends on whether David can see me or not. I'll ring and see if he can give me an appointment after the weekend. But sure you don't mind?"

"Of course not."

Usually George did mind having his routine disturbed but not just now. He needed time on his own. He had to work out a strategy for making the most of the two big opportunities that had come his way, getting back into the world of men, and the much more frightening prospect of re-establishing his sex-life. But where there was a will there was a way. The Vikings and Gloria were going to be his salvation.

Chapter Nine
Ambitions and Aspirations

"While the cat's away, the mice will play…"

It still felt strange to Celia to hear the radio on when she let herself into the flat after work. There had not been time that day to buy food for supper but perhaps Margot had been out to the shops; after all she was not working at the moment. But a quick look in the kitchen told her that no, yet again, there was nothing. It was the television she could hear, not the radio. Margot was watching it as she lay on the settee, in jeans and her oldest t-shirt, a half-empty glass of wine on the table beside her.

"Oh Margot – I thought you were going to get something for us to eat…"

Margot sprang up from the settee and put her hand lightly and teasingly across Celia's mouth. "Hush, sweetheart. You know I would have done that and more, but I had absolutely no money left. Not one cent. So I had to wait for you. We'll eat out tonight and tomorrow I'll go to the bank and get some cash. OK?"

She took her hand away. Celia wasn't sure what she wanted to say.

"Is that OK?" Margot was looking at her from under raised eyebrows. She really had a lovely face.

"Sorry, it's been a pig of a day."

"Come on, sit down, have a sip of my wine – nope, sorry,

the bottle's empty. We'll have to get some more on the way to supper."

"Eileen rang. She wants to come and stay on Monday night. She's got to go to the dentist or something."

Margot frowned, "Doesn't she know I live here now? There's not a lot of room for three."

"Of course she knows you're here."

"You have told her about us, right? I mean like everything?"

"Of course. It took a bit of time but she's fine about it. Really, quite happy. We'll make up a bed for her on the settee."

"I didn't think the first time we'd meet would be in such intimate surroundings."

"Don't worry. I know you and she will really get on; it'll all work out." They had to like each other. Margot was her future.

"Well if you're sure..." Margot put on her naughty girl look, then grinned, "It's Friday night. Let's go eat somewhere special. You deserve it and I'm hungry!"

She really was irresistible.

*

The weather turned hotter. Eileen, full of paracetamol so that her toothache was now a dim sensation in the background, spent much of the weekend in the garden. It was a source of great pleasure and a sort of a retreat, especially when George was irritable. Not that he was at the moment, on the contrary he was unusually quiet and preoccupied. Like today, for example, when he'd taken himself off to his study with a plate of biscuits and cheese and said she was not to bother cooking anything because he didn't want any lunch. So she had eaten a yoghurt and a nectarine, then put on her gardening gloves and gone outside.

The garden wasn't huge but big enough to keep her occupied throughout the year and now, in June, it was filled with an array of old-fashioned flowers: roses, peonies, fritillaries and hollyhocks. Eileen moved slowly amongst them, dead-heading, staking up those plants that couldn't lift their heads and pulling out the chickweed. Sometimes the garden felt too big a responsibility, as if she'd been left a brood of beautiful children who needed looking after and nurturing. But today it was easy work.

Watering was one of the tasks she most enjoyed. It was barely a task really, a bit how she fancied fishing must be, a way of doing something and nothing simultaneously. She directed the hose towards the peonies watching the water soaking into the earth, imagining the plants' gratitude and relief. One is nearer God's heart in a garden than anywhere else on earth. A cliché, but like all clichés, so true.

Her thoughts turned, as they usually did, back to George. He had definitely been different these last few days. He'd kept himself to himself and even when he was in the same room she'd hardly noticed him. She wasn't yet sure which she preferred: the familiar irritable George huffing and puffing and generally finding fault with everything, or this new man with his abstracted expression, who seemed content to do nothing but sit for hours in his room. Perhaps he was only now getting used to his new unemployed status. Maybe this was how he was going to be from here on in.

If so, this would certainly make life easier, but, at the same time, also more difficult. George in his old mood took up most of her waking hours, but if, now, she were to have more time to herself then she'd have decisions to make, namely what on earth she wanted to do with her life – or what remained of it. For many years she had thought about trying to write something – poetry, short stories, even a novel. There hadn't seemed time while George was at work but shortly after they had come to Guernsey she sat down one day at the kitchen table with a sheaf of A4, and with a good clean-running biro written 'Chapter One' on the top sheet. She underlined the words carefully with a ruler, and then sat looking at the paper until George came down from his study and asked what was for lunch.

It was not an auspicious start. Then she remembered what she had heard on a programme on Radio Four, that the first paragraph of a book or story was often the most difficult to write. So the following day she'd started halfway down the page with "Dear Connie". Her intention, vague, and with only feelings rather than ideas to give it substance, was to tell a story based on the correspondence between an older woman and a young girl, a series of exchanges which would illustrate how different generations manage to relate to each other despite the many differences in their personal circumstances and changes in the world at large. Nothing too highbrow, Mrs. Gaskell rather than, say, George Eliot.

Starting halfway down the page certainly worked, because after 'Dear Connie', she found the sentences just flowed, so much so she could hardly write fast enough to keep up with her thoughts. Two hours later she stopped for a rest and looked triumphantly at sixteen pages of neat small handwriting. She'd written one complete chapter, well almost complete, apart from the first paragraph, which she could see now might take the form of a prologue, which would be useful for setting readers on the right track. Sighing contentedly, she made a coffee and started to read what had come out of her pen.

She had realised while she was writing that all was not quite as planned, that the story about the wisdom passed one through the generations had twisted a bit in the telling. But the reality of what she was now reading was from a completely different world. The characters she was creating – or did they already exist somewhere just waiting to be brought to life on the page? - were living with a passion and a vulgarity that she herself had never known. Where had it all come from? And why was it coming in such floods of words, many of them quite unspeakable? It all seemed so unpleasant and aberrant that she hid the manuscript in the broom cupboard in an old biscuit tin. Better that George didn't know she had thoughts like that.

Nevertheless she couldn't help feeling excited and impressed by the energy that had pushed the pen, energy obviously just waiting for the opportunity to express itself, and a few days later she retrieved the manuscript, reinstated it on the kitchen table and set to again. The rush of ideas and dialogue came just as before and over the next three months she spent a few hours every week writing, getting rid of the story that had taken up residence inside her. There had been no question about characterisation, plot or dialogue for the first few chapters; the story just seemed to tell itself. It was all so wonderfully easy. Then one day she took up her biro, the fourth one she'd used, all of them the same kind for luck, and found her mind empty; the characters and their lives must have moved on; she could no longer see or hear them, there was nothing. The paper stayed blank. After several weeks of this emptiness, of sitting dutifully in front of the paper waiting in vain for all that exotic life to come back to her, she admitted defeat, wrapped the half-finished manuscript in an old nightdress and put it away in her bottom drawer. Something exciting and thrilling had come into her life and then suddenly left; her initial sense of shame at the outpouring was now joined by a deep regret for its having passed on. The manuscript and her short-lived glimpse of a much larger life would have to stay a secret. Like her feelings for Doug, she reflected.

"I'm not effing going to!"

The voice was just the other side of the hedge. Gloria.

"You sort it out some other way, you bastard. And don't tell me to shush – they can't bloody hear and I don't give a fuck, ow!..."

There was the sound of a scuffle, footsteps on gravel, then a door slamming followed by silence.

The flowers and the garden and Eileen standing there with the hose and her memories of unfinished dreams suddenly seemed like foolish remnants of an innocent and long-lost world. She remained stock still, watching the water bend the head of a magnificent peony, and wishing with all her heart that Gloria and Steve had never moved in next door.

*

It was early Monday morning. George took Eileen to the airport for nine o'clock and then drove into town. He needed to get himself kitted out for the Viking Club: new bathing trunks, a pair of shorts and a zippered windproof jacket.

He tried Marks and Spencer's but soon decided that the situation demanded something more stylish. The sailing shop down on the front was expensive but had good French-made stuff in rich, strong colours. An hour later he emerged having bought a pair of navy blue cotton bathing trunks, white shorts and a red sailing jacket with blue trim. And new plimsolls. Well apparently they weren't plimsolls but trainers; it seemed that plimsolls, or tennis shoes if you were thinking fancy, didn't exist any more. Their place had been taken by running shoes, jogging shoes, cross trainers, athletics shoes and God knows what else. Despite the fact they all looked identical – clumsy multi-coloured boats – each one had innumerable features and benefits. Selling a pair of what used to be simple canvas shoes now required extensive knowledge of foot anatomy as well as the processes and history of shoe manufacturing. The salesman had been very fussy about fitting them and when they eventually found a pair that was acceptable to both of them he was alarmed to find they cost ninety-five pounds. He was even more disturbed by the total bill, which was just under three hundred. Not to worry. It's worth every penny, he thought, if it's going to help me become a new man.

In the newsagents he bought a copy of Country Life, The Spectator, Healthy Living, and then with a casual gesture picked up a copy of Esquire: let the market researchers try and profile him with that lot.

He broke his shorts in that afternoon. He wanted to make sure that they were not too obviously new when he wore them to the Vikings tomorrow. Besides, his legs needed a bit of sun. He'd been disturbed to see how pale and unattractive they'd looked in the dressing room mirror when they'd always been one of his better features.

He sat on the sun lounger for half an hour leafing through Healthy Living before deciding to fetch a bottle of wine, a glass and Esquire from the house. That was more like it. He read until the sun moved round the corner of the house and the bottle needed renewing. As he went into the house he paused to look at himself in the drawing room mirror. Not a pretty sight. Both his face and the front of his legs were an angry red. It'll calm down by tomorrow, but it wasn't a good start. Then he heard the doorbell. Oh no, not the Jehovah's Witnesses again.

"You!"

"Yes, me." Gloria was in a white floaty dress of very fine cotton, almost transparent. Her breasts were bundled together under the thin material, which forced them to the top like drowning men coming up for air.

"Glad you're in, I need a screw…"

Did she realise what she had just said?

"…a corkscrew. Ours has broken, just when we were getting ready to have a drink. So I said to Steve, hold on, Sunny Jim will have one."

"Hah, yes, of course I do. It's on the back patio. I was having a drink. Eileen's away." Why on earth had he said that? She might think it some kind of invitation.

"I take it that's some kind of invitation?"

"You what?"

"An invitation to have a drink."

He hesitated on the threshold to the patio. This was too good to be true.

"You said you were having a drink so I thought you were inviting me to have some." She made a pretence of looking exasperated, then smiled. "I like the shorts. You've got good

115

legs for a man your age."

"Would you like some?"

"Wine do you mean? I'd better not. His Lordship is sitting there with an unopened bottle so I'd best get back."

"But you've only just come."

"I can come again. I'll bring the corkscrew back later on. As long as you won't need it before then."

I need it right now thought George, pleased to feel himself stirring in his new shorts. "It's all right I've got a spare."

"Wish all men could say that! See you later, and I'll bring something with me for those legs." She reached out to put a cool hand on his thigh; he shifted his weight uncomfortably. "You're really hot."

Did she know what she was saying? The possibility that perhaps she did not, made him feel both guilty and yet more lustful. He stepped back to escape her enquiring hand.

"Tender is it? I've got something to sort that out. Instant relief, trust me."

She turned and marched through the house. George followed her to the front door, looking out nervously in case anyone passing in the street saw him in his shorts, watched her walk up the drive and then closed the door. God Almighty! Things were all happening so much faster than he could have hoped. She was coming back later! But did she mean what she appeared to mean? Was Gloria, well, a woman of her word? He had never been a gambling man and life in recent years had predisposed him even more strongly to play it safe. But somehow he felt his luck might be on the turn. After all, she had hinted at some possibilities at their last meeting hadn't she? What eventually tipped the balance was the reality of the Vikings. Whatever did or did not happen this evening, tomorrow morning, one hour after dawn, he was going to meet the challenge and have the consolation of being accepted into a new and exciting clan, of becoming a man amongst men again. Besides, he comforted himself, even if Gloria and I don't hit it off, Esquire will still be available. At that moment the phone rang.

Chapter Ten
Eileen & Margot & George & Ray

"World is crazier and more of it than
we think, incorrigibly plural"
'Snow' Louis Macneice

"It's me." Eileen spoke quietly; the girls were in the bathroom getting ready to go out to eat, but all the same she didn't want them to overhear. It hadn't been a totally successful evening so far. "Just ringing to see how you are."

George sounded cheerful, probably he'd had a glass or two. "I'm fine Ellie. Had quite a busy day but going to sit down and have something to eat in a moment."

"Don't forget there's a quiche in the fridge. Or eggs and bacon, or lasagne and there's all sorts in the freezer, Chicken Tikka, lamb chops, breaded cod, chips …" It was important that he put something in his stomach other than wine.

"Don't worry, I can find something. Are you all right?"

"The filling had half come out; he's put in a new one and said it should last a few more years."

"The filling – ah yes, good show. And how's my little girl?"

"Sends her love. They're taking me out to a Thai restaurant."

"Who's 'they'?"

"Celia and her flat-mate Margot."

"What's she like?"

"Very pretty. Got hair like your cousin Louise. They seem to be getting on together well. Really well…"

She half hoped he would pick up the clue in her voice and start asking some real questions, but no. Maybe better that way, she didn't have time to explain the situation now.

"Good, good. Well I won't delay you, give Celia my love and I'll see you tomorrow at the airport."

"You needn't bother to come and pick me up."

"Don't worry, I'll be there."

*

Eileen had arrived at the flat before Celia got home from work. Margot had been there to let her in. There was a slightly awkward moment at the door as each scrutinised the other, before a polite exchange of names and Margot's invitation to come in and take a seat while she hung up Eileen's coat. Eileen avoided the settee and sat on a small armchair next to a heap of magazines.

"Would you like a cup of tea?"

Eileen said yes, largely so that she could spend time on her own while Margot was in the kitchen. Maybe Celia would come home before it got embarrassing. But within a few minutes she and Margot sat facing each other over two mugs of Earl Grey and a plate of digestive biscuits.

"It's nice to meet you. Celia has told me so much about you." No, that didn't seem quite right. "She's been so happy since she's known you."

"I am really happy to have met her Mrs. Buchanan; she's a wonderful person, warm and generous..."

This was new; Eileen had never thought of her daughter as particularly warm and generous. Intelligent, yes, forthright, assertive, honest - definitely, but 'warm'? Maybe Margot brought out that side of her. Or did 'warm' mean something else in this context? She tried to imagine the two of them together physically; it was all so unlikely, and strange, and, and hideous.

"...and of course she speaks her mind, which is what attracted me to her in the first place. And she really knows what she's doing with her career. I guess you're really proud of her."

"I am. We both are. She's very close to her father you know." Do I mean that threateningly Eileen wondered, as in 'if you don't leave my daughter alone, George will come and beat you up'?

"I had the impression that you were the dominant one in her life."

"She does take after me a lot I suppose."

"I meant in terms of influence and control. Probably not so much now you're living on the island. You and Celia certainly don't look alike physically."

"You don't think so?"

"Even allowing for the difference in age."

The little madam!

"What about your parents Margot, do you keep in touch with them, let them know what you're, er, doing...?"

"I have a very loving and close relationship with my mother. She's wonderful. She's a doctor but that's only part of it. She sculpts and writes as well; she's just written a cookbook based on the native ingredients in the Sierra Nevada."

"You mean things like bears' paws in honey?"

"What? Nooo!" Margot gave a low chiding laugh while simultaneously giving Eileen a sharp look that made her seem a lot older than thirty-something. "Her book is all about berries and 'erbs. She's really in touch with nature, and she's very beautiful. People can hardly believe she's old enough to have a grown up daughter. You should meet her. You'd love her. Everyone does."

"I expect she looks forward to you going back."

"I have no plans to leave Mrs. Buchanan. Not for as long as I can be with Celia."

Eileen took a sip of tea and tried another tack: "What do you do, for work I mean?"

"Right at the moment I'm between jobs. But I have a number

of work-related skills: production assistant in a recording studio, modelling - mainly for catalogues - photographer's assistant... all kinds of things, mostly creative."

"When did you last work?"

"Do you mean when was I last employed?"

"Exactly that. Or maybe you aren't allowed to work in this country? Do you have a work permit? Hope that's not a rude question." It was rude but Eileen didn't care if it were to protect her baby.

"I've applied for one."

"So, presumably, you haven't been receiving a regular salary over here?"

"Well, goodness me," Margot looked into the depth of her tea as if searching for the facts. "I get the odd little job that pays cash, but I..."

"Isn't that against the law?"

"Everyone does it you know."

"That's as maybe. So how do you live? It must be difficult to pay your share of things?"

"Well, Mrs. Buchanan - Eileen, I just try to get by..."

"Knowing Celia I'm sure she's doing her best to help you?"

"I hope you don't think that's what I meant when I said she was generous. If either of us were in need then the other would...er...this is very much a fifty fifty relationship."

"What's your contribution?" Eileen surprised even herself by this question and was relieved at that moment to hear Celia's key in the door. Meanwhile Margot went into the kitchen and only came back some time later.

The next hour was spent mostly listening to Celia talk about her day at work, and then it was time to get ready for the Thai restaurant. Eileen was still shaken by her conversation with Margot. She was up to no good, no matter how happy Celia might seem. The woman was an unscrupulous, slippery character, and obviously a sponger. Something must be done to get rid of her. At least when she phoned George, things at home sounded steady and normal as ever.

*

George was in a state of panic. How best to prepare for seducing Gloria? He must get himself ready but first he should make the house look welcoming, create a little love nest. Flowers, that's what the place needed.

He found Eileen's secateurs and went into the garden to find flowers that would create the right mood of lust and carnality. He found the very thing: big heavy pink blossoms that were already drooping under their own weight. He snipped them off and set them in a vase and put in the sitting room. The room itself was already tidy enough but he collected the remaining sections of the Sunday papers that were still lying around waiting to be read and removed Eileen's gardening gloves that had been left on the coffee table. Then he took the two photographs that were on the mantelpiece – one of Celia on her graduation day, the other of himself and Eileen on holiday in Italy – and put them away in a drawer. Face down.

Upstairs he pondered over which bedroom, if such became a possibility, to use? Obviously not the marital room, and the bed in the spare room used for visitors was hard and uncomfortable. The middle room was best; Eileen retreated to it occasionally when she needed to have sleep uninterrupted by his night-time trips to the lavatory. In fact she used it most of the time now. The room was neat and pretty and, most importantly, the bed was big and just the right consistency. He tested the springing with his hand: restrained resilience. That's what mature lovers need he thought, bounce is for beginners. Should he change the sheets? Ideally, yes, but practically no. He didn't know which ones fitted this bed and he hadn't got time to experiment now. If things happened, then they would have to happen on, rather than in, bed. At least it was warm enough and if they need to get between the sheets afterwards then by that stage no-one would mind if they weren't freshly laundered. He turned back the cover and had a sniff. They'd do. Then he closed the curtains. It was nine o'clock and only beginning to get dark but Eileen's room overlooked Steve and Gloria's house.

In the shower he was extra careful to ensure that all his nooks and crannies were clean and afterwards he made generous use of Eileen's talcum powder. He found the eau de cologne he'd been given two years ago for Christmas and patted it round his jaw and neck, wincing as it met his sunburned skin, then dabbed some very gingerly round his genitals. Did he have time to trim the hairs in his nostrils? Actually they weren't in his nostrils any more, although that was still their starting point. Over the last ten years they had started to grow further and further out of his nose, only temporarily inhibited by their monthly trim. He found Eileen's curving nail scissors, and holding up his nose with his left hand snipped away with his right. The right nostril was easy, but he had trouble with the left. There was one particularly resourceful hair that had kept very close to the entrance early on in its life but had started working its way across his face and was now at least half an inch long. He had tried tweaking it out by hand while he was watching television, but it proved cunning and recalcitrant. After one prolonged and unsuccessful session he began to have a kind of respect for it. After all, the hair was part of him and he had to admire its, and thereby his, tenacity and vitality. You should get out more George, he thought, giving a quick snip with the scissors and flinching at the pain. He'd missed the hair again but nicked the skin. He tore off a piece of lavatory paper and held it to his nose to staunch the blood, and when it had calmed down he left a little piece of paper sticking to the wound to keep it closed. He decided to abandon the trimming, although in a perfect world he would have liked to have tidied up his ears as well, but Steve was a hairy sort of man so maybe she wouldn't mind, might even prefer it that way.

What to wear? Should he change into slacks and his Polo

short-sleeved shirt? No, wait, she was coming back with the sunburn cream so his legs should be available for her soothing ministrations. Besides, it shouldn't look as if he had made too much effort, that he had any ideas. Anyway, shorts would be easier to get out of. It was half past seven, she could be here any minute. He didn't have time to tidy up the bathroom. It would have to wait until later.

Downstairs he opened another bottle of wine, a good Californian Zinfandel, potent but easy-drinking stuff that should get them quickly in the mood. What next? Music, of course. He put a stack of CDs in the player; there wasn't time to make an intelligent selection and, besides, he'd left his reading glasses upstairs, so whatever music came on would have to do. He switched on the reading light and half closed the curtains, leaving the French windows invitingly open. The evening was warm and encouraging, full of earthy smells from the garden. The strains of Vivaldi's Spring settled easily on the air. He sat enthroned on the settee with his magazines, trying to relax. He poured himself a glass of wine and leafed through Country Life, though without his reading glasses he was only able to read the headlines and see the larger pictures. It was nearly nine o'clock and she still hadn't arrived. He got up and went to the front door and looked out, just in case by some chance she'd been ringing the doorbell and was standing on the front porch waiting for him to answer. Nobody there.

Back on his settee he decided he was as ready for her as he ever would be; he poured himself another glass of wine, opened another magazine and closed his eyes, imagining what her breasts would look like when at last he saw them. In his mind's eye he viewed them from every angle and began to feel their warmth and weight in his hand. Mmmm...

*

The next moment he awoke to the sound of snoring and, could

that be, Christmas carols from Kings College? He opened dry gritty eyes and saw that it was almost light. The sitting room curtains were blowing gently in the breeze and he could clearly see a patch of pale grey sky, early morning sky. He examined his watch at arm's length: five forty-five? And he was downstairs and still in his clothes? Oh no, on a night when he should have been seducing Gloria, he'd not even got to first base. For that you have to stay awake you silly old fool. He'd fallen asleep – shit, shit, shit. He was struggling to get out of the settee when he saw the tube of cream, and then the corkscrew. And then he saw something written in black felt-tip on the page of the magazine he'd been looking at when he fell asleep, Esquire of course. He struggled out of the chair, lurched up the stairs and retrieved his reading glasses from the bathroom. Downstairs again he could read what had been scrawled across the bare bottom of Miss Cheeky from Leighton Buzzard – "Sleeping Beauty, thanks for the c. screw, hope the cream works, G."

She must have come in while he was asleep. Probably through the French window. She would have rung the bell and then come round the back of the house when she didn't get an answer. Dear God, what would she have seen? Him slumped asleep on the settee, no doubt snoring, Miss Cheeky on his lap, a piece of white lavatory paper stuck to his nose and Away in a Manger going at it in the background. Sod it.

He trailed into the kitchen to put the kettle on; might as well have a cup of tea before going up to the warmth of his bed and catching another two or three hours. But hold on, it was Tuesday. He had another date, this time with the Vikings, which meant he had to be down at the pools one bloody hour after dawn. He stood by the sink with the kettle in his hand, filling it from the tap while he pondered on what to do. He wanted very much indeed to have a cup of tea and go back to his bed. The idea of taking off his clothes and sinking himself into cold salt water seemed insane. He was a man in his sixties, at a time in his life when the body was already beginning to look for the exit sign, so surely it wasn't a sensible thing to do, let alone desirable? But then what about Gloria, the pursuit of a healthier lifestyle and a younger, fully-restored vitality? If he gave up at the first fence he'd never be able to enter the race again. If he didn't go down to the pools this morning and become a Viking, he knew there was no hope. The water overflowed the kettle and splashed onto the floor. He ought to mop it up, but too bad, it was nearly six; there wasn't time for tea and barely enough to have a shower and collect his new bathing gear. On the way out he winced at the brave strong colours of his jacket, which now seemed to have been chosen in a different and happier era, and bundled everything into the car. It was twenty-five past the hour as he started down the hill, still blinking and yawning.

Andrew was already in the water, swimming with long easy strokes up and down the length of the pool.

"He does long distance," said Ray, "in the sea. Goes right out into the shipping lanes."

"Isn't that dangerous?"

"Sure. By the way, you've got a price tag hanging off your costume."

"Have you come to be one of the lads then?" Don walked up to him and slapped him on the back. "I hope they told you that there was an initiation ceremony? Though by the look of those legs you've been through it already!"

The water seemed deadly cold today. The thermometer indicated sixteen degrees, but what was that in old money? It was too early in the day to work it out so let's just say 'cold', brass monkey cold. He joined Ray on the steps and they inched their way down. How long was it since he had last been in the sea; four years? Five? Probably on their last trip to the Mediterranean? No it had been in a heated pool in Tunisia. Now as the water crept up his legs and then his torso he felt an unfamiliar and malevolent chill invade his body, working its way easily through the loose flesh towards the ageing vulnerable bones. He wasn't sure it was wise to continue but it was too late to turn back now. Ray was already properly in and had begun a slow but quite graceful breaststroke. George committed the last bit of himself quickly, pained and angry at the assault of the cold water over his shoulders and around his ears.

He came up spluttering and swearing, then launched himself down the pool with a wild backstroke, kicking his legs vigorously to counteract the cold. At the far end he managed to turn around in quite a seaworthy manner. It was not a proper underwater turn but he felt it should look slick enough to anyone watching. Andrew came and swam backstroke alongside and they did another four lengths, not racing but at a fair speed. Then Don fetched a water polo ball from the changing room and they spent another ten minutes throwing and catching; this was easy in the shallows but hard work at the deep end, where the waves of the incoming tide broke hard on the concrete and rushed into the pool. Twice George found himself thrown back against the pool wall on the backwash. Despite the cold and discomfort he began to loosen up and after the ball game felt more in his element. He swam a little way underwater, then climbed out and dived in again from the edge. He stood on his hands and walked along the bottom and then he did his dead man's float. By now he wasn't fighting the water and the cold but sort of joining in with it. He did a somersault and then another, then sprang above the surface, spouting water like a youngster, jumping, jumping, jumping – just like being fourteen again when the school holidays had started and the prospect of six weeks seemed like a lifetime. This was wonderful. He wanted to stay in the pool for ever, especially as strangely it wasn't even cold any more. The others had finished but he swam another length, and then on the return, quite suddenly, knew he must get out, and straight away. He splashed over to the steps, worried that all the feeling seemed to have gone from his legs, and his hands were fumbling to hold onto the metal balustrade as he hauled himself out. He staggered over to the changing room, grabbed his towel, wrapped it round his shoulders and stood with the others outside in the sunshine, shaking and juddering uncontrollably. He started rubbing himself down hard but this didn't seem to make any difference to his pale, stiff, numb limbs. His blood, if he still had any, had retreated to some furthest corner of his body.

"You've overdone it; take this, it'll warm you up."

It was Ray with his flask of tea again. George took the plastic mug with trembling hand, spilling, but not feeling, some of the hot tea over his skin. As he drank, he found it did help, but he still wished he'd brought something warmer to wear than his shorts. He put all his clothes on, shorts, shirt and jacket, but continued to shiver as they sat together on the bench. The promise of sun had not been realised and clouds had rolled in from the South West.

"How do you manage in the winter?" He could barely get his words out.

"Everyone but Don has a wet suit, you know a half suit, just leaves your legs bare. Don's got enough subcutaneous fat to keep warm without."

"Fat, my arse, you Southern pansies. Real men don't take no notice of the cold."

"No brain, no pain is it?" said Bill.

George was grateful for the movement that was involved in laughing and kept it going for as long as he could without appearing half-crazed. Andrew also seemed impervious to the cold. He'd come in from the pool but was just standing there, the water streaming from his body, making no attempt to dry himself. "You'll get used to it. But you've got to do it regularly to benefit. It helps if you don't take a shower before you come, that way you keep the layer of natural oil on your skin from overnight. And you don't want to stay in too long, not to start with."

He went into the changing room and came back with a half bottle of rum.

"Time to welcome George, a fellow Viking. As allowed the

Eileen & Margot & George & Ray

Senior Service we can toast him sitting down."

The bottle was passed down the line and they all took a slug after raising the bottle to George, "To a fellow Viking."

The rum burned first his throat and then his stomach. He was grateful for both. Never had alcohol tasted so benevolent. As the warmth spread through his body, he began to feel restored. Moreover the disappointment of the previous evening was rapidly and rightfully shrinking in the context of this big simple world of friendship and innocent pleasure. After all what were women and their complexities, compared with the honest companionship of good men? The bottle went down the line again.

"Why is it called The Vikings?"

"Because of the rape and pillage on alternate Fridays. Chance'ud be a fine thing. Lads, I'm off. Thanks for the drink, Andrew. See you Friday, same time, same place."

It had started to rain. This time it was Ray who hadn't brought his car and he accepted George's offer of a lift. George felt proud and pleased to be able to do something as simple and satisfying as drive a new friend home.

*

"Come in for a coffee?" Ray lived in town, in a small house perched on the hill at the top of Paris Street.

George followed him into what must be his study. There was a big bay window overlooking the harbour, a wall of shelving overflowing with books, a large telescope on a stand, pointing towards Castle Cornet and a desk with a computer and monitor to one side of the window bay.

"Do you use one of those?" George indicated the computer as Ray came in with a tray of coffee. "I never saw the point of them frankly."

"I'm only self-taught but yeah, I use it increasingly. Got to have one these days, just to keep up, and for work."

"What do you do?"

"Do you want the long or the short version?" Ray poured the coffee out carefully and set a cup down in front of George. "A long time ago I qualified as a marine engineer. Specialised in oil rigs. Spent a lot of time working overseas: Nigeria, Bahrain, Malaysia, China. I had a good job and it paid well. When I retired, I wanted to keep my offshore tax status so I came here. Been here nearly six years."

"Do you like it?"

"Yeah, well enough. It's a mix of good and bad like any other. Financially it's good. And it's secure. I mean where else can you leave your house unlocked and still expect to find it untouched when you get back home at the end of the day? Like everyone else I get pissed off with it being so small, and crowded. And it's not well-governed – there's a lot that irritates me about the place. But then that would probably be true of anywhere."

"How do you spend your time?"

"Keep myself busy. The Devil really does find work for idle hands. I should know. I had just retired when I came here. I had time on my hands and nothing specifically to do and no-one to do it with. I used to walk around town buying things I didn't want, went to the pub every evening, watched a lot of videos during the night…"

"What changed that?"

"I had a nervous breakdown."

It was not an answer George had expected or wanted to hear.

"One day I just flipped. Couldn't face going out or seeing anybody so I just sat here, crying most of the time. It was the contrast. I'd always been busy, working in dangerous environments, always with a crew of men – tough characters they were too – and then suddenly I was here, on my own and living a girl's life."

"What happened?" George was horrified at the prospect of a perfectly normal looking man not being able to cope with retirement. After all he had not found things easy himself but he couldn't imagine it would defeat him entirely. He was embarrassed on Ray's behalf to be hearing the story of his weakness, not that Ray seemed at all disturbed.

"I went to the doctor, got some medication, felt better. But I knew there was no future in that. Didn't want to keep on the damn stuff for ever, so weaned myself off it."

"I've never had to have anything like that. Not even a sleeping tablet."

"I sat down and thought about what had happened to me, and how life doesn't prepare you for retirement. If you were to say to someone in full-time work that being retired is like falling off a cliff, they'd think you were mad. But that's what it is, a slow free-fall into nothingness. And they never tell you this. If you read advice about retirement it's all about pensions and money and health. It's made out as a small world of small details; what kind of marmalade you're going to buy, or whether you're going to take a walk before or after supper. But it's a bloody huge world, and it hurts a lot. And you keep asking yourself totally unanswerable questions."

George was silent, looking down at his hands still clutching the empty cup for the remnants of warmth, and matching Ray's words against images of his own life: the ignoble last weeks at work, his lack of purpose, the unstoppable decline of the body, and above all his sense of losing ground, of being replaced, of feeling already dead.

Ray carried on talking as if he knew about George and his life, "So I thought I've been through this terrible period in my life and I've come out more or less upright but I've still got nothing to do. Why not do what many others have done before me and make my life experience the raw ingredients for the next stage? So I went into coaching, to help people with their personal development."

George had come across coaching before, at work. One of his young brand managers had discussed with him the idea of getting team-building professionals in to help the brand managers work together more effectively. The whole concept seemed unnecessary to him, just one of these trendy ideas that companies turned to when they couldn't think of how else to spend their pre-tax profit. He was certainly not going to get involved with it himself; he was the boss, not part of a team, and although it made good business sense to let the lads have a bit of fun, it would be suicide, from the point of view of maintaining authority, for him to be part of it.

"Yes we used to do that at my old company."

"So you know what's involved then."

"Mmm-er yes, broadly speaking, though I wasn't in the front line myself."

"You'll know then that it's mostly about the basic techniques of learning to listen to people, and help them set goals and work out how they can solve their own problems."

"Listening to people? That doesn't sound too difficult."

"You'd be surprised. Most people don't listen, they're too concerned with what they want to say themselves."

George hoped he looked as if he were listening hard. "Do you go into companies here on the island?"

"It's all private stuff, not corporate – and I counsel them over the 'phone."

George nodded as if in agreement and understanding but he was wondering how a man like Ray, someone who had had a nervous breakdown for heaven's sake, could do anything to help other people, and not even face to face.

"What sort of people do you 'counsel'?"

"Mostly retirement age. What to do when you step off the conveyor belt of school, college, work, and have to start making real choices. In many ways retirement is the first time ever in your life when you ask yourself what do I really want to do in the time that is left to me?" Ray smiled at George, "Maybe you'd be interested in a session or two?"

"Good God, no." It was a revelation to hear his problem identified and described, something he would bring out later to examine in greater detail, but he still couldn't imagine a few exchanges with Ray would provide any answers. "Nothing personal of course but, I mean, you know things are OK at the moment."

"Are you going to come to the Vikings again?"

"I need to get fit – don't do as much as I should. Until a year or so ago you see I was holding down a top management job, busy as hell one week and then the next I was walking away, with a bundle of cash but sweet F.A. to do. It would be all too easy for me to sit around being idle. Not so bad for me wife of course; she's got me and the house to look after."

"You don't share the housework then?"

"Good heavens, no, that's always been her responsibility. I wouldn't know what to do. I'd only get in her way."

"So she'll only retire when you kick the bucket?"

George laughed. "A woman's work is never done. Anyway she enjoys it. It's natural for them isn't it?"

"You should hear the complaints I get from a couple of my lady clients. They're expected to keep on just as before only in retirement it's worse because he's there, moaning about being bored, asking what's for lunch and then what's for supper, and where his shirt is…"

"I'm lucky with my wife; she's always enjoyed looking after me. Anyway I give her a lot of freedom."

"It's yours to give is it?"

"What?"

"I envy you. It sounds as if you've got yourself sorted out with a good woman. Congratulations. I wish I had."

George suddenly felt uneasy; maybe the Vikings, an all-male group, were not quite what they seemed.

"You never met anyone, you know, permanent?"

"I've had lots of women. There's a lot of sex out there, even for a middle-aged man. Especially for a middle-aged man; we're nicer than the young ones, more patient. But marriage? Tried it once a long time ago. Didn't work. Wasn't cut out for it

133

then. A few years ago there was a Chinese girl…"

"Chinese?" A few exotic images flashed through George's head.

"Beautiful little thing, tiny, like a bird. She thought I was a giant of a man, you know what I mean. She was always happy, always very affectionate. But she wanted to party all the time and I was just beginning to slow down and look for a quiet life. I was fifty, she was twenty. Just a kid! So we split. I've been more or less on my own ever since."

"Still, twenty, pretty good. And Chinese."

"I know what you're thinking – Oriental girl, Shanghai Grip – everyone thinks the same. Mind you, she certainly knew what she was doing in that department. Happy days. Do you fancy some bacon and eggs? I'm going to make some for myself."

"Terrific, thanks." George was longing to tell Ray about Gloria. "I like my women well built up top. Like the woman who lives next door. She has a great body."

"Fancy her do you?"

"Beautiful tits. Beautiful."

"One egg or two?"

After breakfast they sat for a bit over more coffee. George had at last thawed out and he was feeling good to be in Ray's house talking about retirement and women and life in general. They had a lot in common, surprisingly.

"What do you use the telescope for?"

"I like watching people, boats, the traffic. Take a look if you like."

George spent the next five minutes scrutinising the harbour and the boats. It was strong enough to see the houses on the western coast of Sark, a helicopter landing on Jethou, even individual sheep on Brechou. And that tiny dot coming in from the North East he could see was a plane coming in to land. Marvellous, even from here he could make out the tail-fin of a Flybe. Plane? My God, Eileen!

"I have to dash. Just remembered my wife's plane is due in at ten and I said I'd meet her. What time is it? Quarter to? I'll never make it. Thanks for breakfast – see you Friday."

He drove through the centre of town, up Fountain Street, round the back of St. Martins and onto the airport road. It was still raining and the roads were busy and by the time he had parked the car and jogged along to the arrivals area of the airport it was just after ten.

After a quarter of an hour's wait he had to admit that either she had not been on the plane – which was most unlikely - or she had taken a taxi home. Too bad he hadn't had time to tidy up the house a bit, but it couldn't be helped. He was just swinging the car round the corner into Les Vardes when he remembered he'd left the copy of Esquire with Gloria's message in it on the kitchen table.

Chapter Eleven
Connecting

"I have a gentle cock, croweth me day
He doth me risen early my matins to say."
'I have a Gentle Cock' Anon.

Eileen did not sleep well on Celia's settee, although the evening had gone better than might have been expected. The strong clear flavours of Tom Yum Gai had created a mood of entente, as good food often does, and the three of them had been so taken up with the business of eating that there was little time for any meaningful conversation until the meal was nearly over. Eileen had also taken the precaution of seating herself alongside Margot at the table so that the focus of attention was on Celia seated opposite them, who was, as usual, in a talkative mood.

She watched her daughter with a mixture of pride and frustration, pride at the confident out-spilling of ideas, frustration at the thought of her vulnerability to Margot. She still didn't understand the dynamics of their relationship but there was something wrong. Why should the glamorous Margot be interested, sexually or otherwise, in Celia, who, it had to be admitted had never really made the best of herself and although possessing a lively personality was, conventionally speaking, plain and overweight? Was it simply that Margot was attracted to the security of having found someone who adored her? A somebody who had a flat and a regular income? Maybe.

"Eileen you must do something about George. You're both retired you know, it's not just him, and yet he seems to expect you to do everything for him. Classic chauvinism, it really is."

"Oh he's not too bad these days. He cooked breakfast the other weekend and he usually comes to help with the shopping. It's difficult for him you know after the position he held at work."

"There you go again, always defending him. Have you talked to him about buying a computer? No, I thought not."

"You know he's always been against them. And I'm still not sure what we'd use it for."

"Writing letters, sending emails, surfing the web, buying stuff, books, connecting – you'll see…"

"It all sounds as if there's so much to learn; you have to remember your father and I are older now, we don't absorb information so quickly."

"You'll get left behind if you don't. Won't she Margot? Once you have one it will become absolutely part of your life and you'll wonder why you didn't do it earlier. Trust me."

Celia's words struck deep. They were getting left behind. Life was like a relay race and it felt these days as if she and George had run their course and handed over the baton, while all the excitement had run on ahead and was rapidly getting out of reach. She put forward one last obstacle:

"It's not that I'm against it. It's your father who doesn't want one in the house."

"It doesn't have to be in his room. You could put it in one of the bedrooms; create a little work station for yourself."

Eileen had a sudden vision of herself sitting in her bedroom at her own computer. While George watched what he wanted on the television – mostly sport and crime movies – she could be in front of her own screen doing what she wanted, in privacy and without interruption or criticism. Maybe with a computer she would be part of things, a bit more connected, as they say. Perhaps with the computer she could, at last, finish the book.

"I'll think about it."

"Don't just say that Eileen, do it. We'll keep reminding you, won't we Margot?"

"I'm not going to bully your mother into doing something she doesn't want to." Margot turned and gave Eileen a ghost of a smile. "When you're older I guess you go for the quiet life."

That settled it. She would buy one.

Perhaps it was this resolution, made so one-sidedly – after all she still had to find a way to persuade George - together with the coffee that kept her awake that night. But she was also aware as she twisted and turned that she was listening for any strange and unacceptable sounds that might come from the room where her daughter was sleeping with her lover. She eventually drifted off into dreams peopled by technicians in white coats, and it seemed only a few minutes later that Celia woke her.

The plane landed ahead of scheduled arrival time and she was first through arrivals with just hand luggage. It was only a quarter to ten. There was no sign of George. He'd probably forgotten. If she hurried over to the taxi rank now she'd get one before the rush.

Twenty minutes later she was home. She half expected he would come to the door when he heard the taxi on the drive, but everything was quiet. The car wasn't there, yet the light was on in the porch, and also upstairs. What was wrong? Where was he? She hurried to unlock the door. The house was silent.

"George, George, I'm back." Still silence. "Coo-ee."

She took her bag upstairs. The bed was unmade and the floor in the shower was still wet. He must have been in a hurry because his towel had been thrown down on the bed instead of neatly folded on the rail as he usually left it, and there was a mess of talcum powder on the floor in the bathroom, and a bottle of his aftershave on the side of the basin. He never wore aftershave, not in the daytime. Uneasily she went downstairs. The sitting room was empty but the lights were on and the French windows were open. The cushions on the settee were rumpled and there was a near empty bottle of wine and an empty glass on the table. And a half used tube of Aftersun cream – not a brand she had ever bought. Curiouser and curiouser. As she turned to go into the kitchen she caught sight of the vase of peonies. Oh no! She looked outside at the garden to confirm that they were indeed her beloved blooms. How could he! She had staked and watered and nurtured them all spring. How dare he cut them and bring them into the house? What had he been thinking of? Then she noticed the photograph of Celia was missing, and the one of her and George on their trip to Verona.

When she went into the kitchen she became certain that something very odd had been happening. Health News and some girly magazine were on the table. The latter was open at a picture of a girl, naked except for a thong – Miss Cheeky. Someone had written a message written across her bottom. Eileen pulled reading glasses out of her handbag and read it.

What did it mean? Why Sleeping Beauty? And what kind of a screw would be called a 'c'? And who was 'G'? Her heart was pounding with anger though she didn't exactly know why she felt cross. At that moment she heard the car on the drive, so she closed the magazine and left it on the table. She decided to stay silent and just see what George had to say.

He burst into the kitchen wearing new clothes: white shorts, big new plimsolls and a bright red yachting jacket. He hadn't shaved, his legs were sunburnt and his hair was sticking up as if he'd been walking in a force ten gale. She looked at him and waited for an explanation.

*

George had thought through his strategy on the drive back from the airport. Everything to do with the Vikings was an OK area. Eileen might be pleased that he was intending to take some exercise; she was always nagging him to go for a walk. Breakfast with Ray was also legitimate. They could even have him over one day for dinner or something and then she could see for herself. But the Miss Cheeky message in the magazine was a different kettle of fish, and he needed to be creative to explain it. Eileen would be a bit surprised and disapproving that he'd bought the magazine to start with. So, OK, Steve had brought it round with a couple of others, man to man. Esquire and Health News were both Steve-type reading, even Eileen would acknowledge that. And if they saw Steve in the near future, George would ask him to keep shtum, explain that he didn't want Eileen to know he liked looking at the odd bit of soft porn.

As he came into the kitchen he saw with relief that the magazine was closed anyway.

"Must have missed you by a whisker," he leaned over and kissed her on the cheek. "You were probably climbing into a taxi just as I was parking the car. I thought we'd agreed you were going to wait for me?" Rule number one, attack was always the best defence.

"I did."

"But not long enough – what a shame. Anyway, did the trip go well?"

"What's happened?"

"What do you mean? I was parking the car -," and here he spoke very slowly and pseudo-patiently as if barely containing justifiable anger "- and you must have been getting into the taxi just as I was coming back to find you. But you're here and so am I, so everything is all right."

"No, I mean the French windows. You left them wide open. Anybody could have come in."

He'd forgotten all about the windows; they had been open all morning and indeed all night. "I was in a hurry to leave for the airport. Anyway nobody's going to break in, not in broad daylight. Not in Guernsey. "

"Is this yours?" Her hand was resting on the magazine.

"In a manner of speaking. Steve popped over last night. He'd

140

finished with it and thought I might like it – I suppose it's what men like him enjoy."

"Steve came over? Just to give you a magazine he'd finished?"

"Yes." The hesitation was minimal. "No, he came to see if we wanted to have supper with them - tonight. Then he said would I like a few magazines that he'd finished with and was going to chuck."

"So what did you say, about supper?"

"That I'd check with you. I know you're not very keen on the idea."

"I'm not. Did you pick those peonies?"

"Peonies?"

"The flowers in the sitting room."

"Is that what they're called? I – er – put them there to – er - make the room look nice." Rule number two, always stick as close to the truth as possible. "For you, to welcome you home." Rule number three, don't be afraid to use a bit of emotional blackmail to throw them off the scent.

"George, you know that I hate flowers being cut from the garden; it's taken all my time to grow them and then you just snip them off and stuff them in a vase."

"Not 'stuff', Ellie. I think they look lovely, don't you? I only cut them because the stems had gone; it was really windy last night. So I thought I ought to rescue them. I thought you'd be glad."

He knew he was too old for his naughty boy look but the sad look with the direct gaze was still reliable. He gave her his sad look.

"Well, yes, they do look nice. It's just that I expected to see them in the garden."

She was weakening. Time to reinforce that with a little generosity.

"Sorry."

That seemed to do the trick.

Only a few moments later however, Eileen renewed the

attack. She was on strong form today.

"Where is Celia's photo, the one in the silver frame that we keep in the sitting room?"

He assumed his quizzical look which bought him a little time, "Which one?"

"You know, your favourite one, in the silver frame, on the table by your armchair. Next to the one of us in Verona."

Yesterday's discretion was in danger of becoming today's fatal oversight. "They're still there, surely?" He asked in a perplexed voice as he strode into the sitting room. "Oh no, that's right. I put them in the drawer when I was cleaning the table top."

"Cleaning?"

"Spilled some wine. Put the photos away for safe keeping. Knew you'd be furious if I broke them." Attack, attack, and now ease off. "Ready for a cup of tea? I'll put the kettle on."

Minutes later as they sat together in the kitchen he decided everything was back in control and that he could strengthen his position. "You haven't commented on the shorts yet. You'll be pleased with me. I made a decision to get fit, do some more exercise. This morning I went for a swim down at the bathing pools in La Vallette, which is why I was late to the airport."

"The bathing pools? What made you think of that?"

"A group of men get together there twice a week early morning. They're all retired, my sort of age. I thought I'd join them."

"What do they do?"

"Swim, have a chat and a cup of tea. That's it."

A slight hesitation, then she said "Good. Good that you're doing something new I mean, because I've decided to do something new as well," and now she looked at him defiantly, "I'm going to buy a computer."

George looked at her with a mixture of irritation and respect. "If you really want to...."

"You need not get involved. It can go in my bedroom. It won't be in your way."

Eileen with a new source of power was one thing, but Eileen keeping it to herself was altogether different. Who knows, perhaps at some time in the future George would want to play with it too. He attempted a voice of reason and authority. "We should give some serious thought about where it goes; it needs a special socket. It might be better to put it on the ground floor somewhere, perhaps the dining room."

Eileen hesitated, a fatal weakness.

"You decide which computer you want Ellie and I'll find the best spot to put it."

"But I want a little work station. Of my own." She was asking not telling. Advantage George.

"We'll set it up on a desk with a proper office chair and everything. I know what's needed just leave it to me."

"And I want to go on the Internet."

"We'll see." George needed time to think about this.

"No it's what I want. I'm going to get connected."

George was silenced. Deuce.

"Was that your sun cream I found in the sitting room?" Advantage Eileen.

But the next shot was easy.

"I thought it was yours Ellie. I found it under the settee. It could do with a Hoover under there, by the way. Next time you're cleaning."

Game set and match he thought as he went upstairs to shower and change.

*

He looked down at his body as he stood in the stream of blessedly hot water. Was it his imagination or did he already look leaner and meaner? The front of his legs had already turned brownish and if he sucked his belly in he could see his feet. Not bad. It wouldn't take him long to be ready for Gloria, but what and when should the next move be?

143

Wrapped in his towel he stood at the window which looked down over Steve and Gloria's drive at the front of their house. There was a white car with a blue light on the top. It was a police car for Heaven's sake! Parked right outside their front door! Now what was all that about? What could they have been up to? He carried on drying himself, every so often returning to look out of the window. A couple of minutes later two policemen emerged from the house followed by Steve. They stood talking a while, and seemed convivial enough. Then the constables touched their caps, got into their car and drove off down the hill in the direction of town. Steve stood on his doorstep and George stood back and looked from behind the curtain. He didn't want to be caught snooping. Besides he was already feeling guilty about his intentions with Gloria.

Chapter Twelve
Love letters

"The stait of man dois change and vary,
Now sound, now seik, now blyth, now sary."
' Timor Mortis conturbat me' William Dunbar

The next morning he woke late. He had a headache, a sore throat and every joint in his body was shouting for attention. It must have been the cold water; Ray was right, he'd stayed in too long. What a fool.

"Here's some tea. And the papers." Eileen put the Telegraph and the Guernsey Press beside him on the bed. "You were still sleeping so heavily, and snoring, at eight that I thought I'd leave you to it."

"I feel terrible. Think I've got flu'. Have you got anything for it?"

She brought him some extra strength Aspro and a glass of water.

"It's probably the swimming. It's still early in the season. Why don't you stay in bed for a bit? I've got to go into town, but there's no reason why you shouldn't stay here until you feel like getting up. I'll be back by one."

She seemed sympathetic but in a brisk and superficial way, as if it suited her for him to stay in bed. What was she up to he wondered as he picked up the newspapers, but he was too tired to give it much thought. He looked at the headlines. The Telegraph carried articles about corruption in the Home Office, record levels of illiteracy in England, another influx of illegal economic immigrants and the results of a public survey that revealed that 90% of the public under the age of twenty-five had never heard of Winston Churchill. The Guernsey Press reported robberies up twenty per cent from the previous year, a record number of vehicles on Guernsey's streets and the details of a dawn raid on a house in St Sampson in a search for drugs and pornographic videos. It was too depressing to read any further. He laid them aside and turned his head to look out of the windows. The sky was grey and the trees were waving around in the strong winds. For God's sake it was June! This was supposed to be summer.

He lay back on the pillow, glad that he wasn't walking down the steps into the water at La Vallette. He just couldn't imagine what it would be like swimming there in the Guernsey winter, wet suits or not. He and Eileen had come to the island expecting a French sort of climate, something warmer and gentler than the weather on the mainland. They had been surprised then, by the gale force winds in winter and the fog that rolled in from the sea at any time of the year bringing down the temperatures and closing the airport. As if to sustain the illusion that the place was blessed by a milder climate, local people continually protested the warmth of their winters and the length of their summers, and, as personal proof, Guerns of all ages changed into short sleeved shirts and shorts at the spring solstice, and stayed in them until November, apparently impervious to the weather. They'd probably die young as a result, he thought.

They were in a similar state of denial about their surroundings; the island was beautiful in parts but they'd allowed too much development of the wrong kind: flimsy bungalows that were poorly built and damp-looking and set down cheek by jowl amongst ugly retail parks and acres of decaying greenhouses. He couldn't understand why so many householders had been allowed to create junk yards in full view of the public. He'd stopped and counted seventeen old cars in the garden of one bungalow, nestling like some modern sculpture in a heap of rusting barbed wire, brambles and remnants of industrial-strength blue polythene.

He lay there quietly fuming, planning how he would change things if they would only let him take charge, when he heard the front door bell.

I can't even be ill in peace, he said to himself, willing whoever it was to go away. But, no, the bell rang again. Perhaps it's the police. Maybe they are working their way along the road about some problem or another and were at Steve's yesterday and here today. Better see who it is. Holding a handkerchief in one hand as justification for still being in his pyjamas and leaning heavily on the banisters, he stumbled downstairs. "I'm coming, I'm coming" he shouted irritably, exaggerating the nasal quality of his voice.

She was standing there in a mackintosh of a pale, slightly shiny material, white high heels and a chiffon headscarf. Gloria. She looked annoyed, as well.

"Are you going to let me in or do I have to creep round to the back door again?"

He stood back and she strode across the threshold, taking off the head scarf and shaking out her hair.

"I've got a cold."

"I can hear that, and see it. You look awful, your eyes have gone all piggy."

He looked at himself in the hall mirror. It was true, he did look a bit seedy.

"I don't feel well. I was in bed when you rang."

"I didn't think the outfit was Savile Row. Is Eileen out?"

"She's gone shopping I think. She said she'd be back by one."

Gloria glanced at her watch. "I could do with a coffee to start off with."

What do you mean, he thought, 'to start off with'? But he took her through to the kitchen without asking. How did she manage to look so sexy even in a raincoat?

"I've been thinking about you Gloria."

"And what have you been thinking?"

"That you're a bloody gorgeous woman. And I'd like to run my hands all over you."

"Like a pianist fingering the keys?"

"You know what I mean."

"All right, why don't you?"

"What now?" He hadn't even cleaned his teeth.

"I've seen the way you've been looking at me. And I don't mind, I like a man with a bit of class. Steve's busy and Eileen's out. And it's raining." She stood up and loosened the belt of her coat.

George sat anxiously looking on as she pulled her coat open. It was all happening so quickly again. This wasn't quite how he'd planned things. Not so fast, and not in the kitchen, though Eileen had left it neat and tidy.

"Do you want coffee with milk?"

"Sssh!"

Under the coat all she had on was her underwear. But it was not underwear as we know it, Jim. This was lingerie, naughty stuff, an arrangement of lace and feathers: a brassiere that barely seemed big enough to contain its load, a suspender belt straining to hold up the fine stockings and a piece of red lace that looked like panties in the front but as she turned seemed to disappear up between her buttocks. Just like Miss Cheeky.

"Wow!" He felt like a seven year old who had just been given a train set and a box of Mars bars. Except he wasn't a child, he was a fully grown man, ready, willing and, he hoped, able. He just wished he didn't feel so muggy; he wanted to commit this all to memory. She really did have a wonderful body and that red outfit looked like something from one of those cabaret shows that the marketing department went to at their conferences.

"You can touch if you like." Gloria came and stood next to him, her breasts at his eye level. He tentatively reached out his hand and caressed her waist, her skin was warm and slightly oily. He ran his trembling hand over the lace over her breasts and felt their weight.

"All my own work." She said from somewhere above his head.

"Hm?"

He closed his eyes and ran his hand down her slim waist and rounded hips. Hers was an old fashioned body, full of curves and caves: Paradise.

Before he had fully contented himself with exploring her she lowered herself astride his lap. He wanted to kiss her but she lifted her face away from his, and, instead, in a surprising move, slipped her hand through his pyjama flies. He stopped breathing; things had leaped ahead and he wasn't sure if it were for the best. Her hand started to move around his body, and his anxiety returned a hundredfold. What if he couldn't respond? But her fingers were warm and soft, and excitingly different from his own, and the suspense of it all was gradually remedied by the sureness of her touch. He began to feel as if he had started flying towards something, a sort of free-wheeling down a hill, gathering power and speed, and all with so little effort: a wonderful sensation that he had almost forgotten. He opened his eyes to enjoy her enjoyment but she seemed to be in a trance, not looking at him at all but at a point over his shoulder in the direction of the wall clock. If they just went on long enough he might be able - but to his disappointment, and yet also to his relief, she suddenly stopped.

"That's all we've got time for today. The girl's got to go."

"Oh no, not yet?" He was sure he could maybe manage it if he had a rest though was rather glad he didn't have to prove it. One step at a time.

"You're all right aren't you? Apart from having a feather stuck to your face." She brushed it off.

"Can't you stay Gloria? There's so much I want to say. And you haven't had your coffee yet."

"Haven't got time for a chat this morning. Steve be will ready for his lunch and we don't want him to suspect anything."

Sensible girl. Of course they must be careful.

"I will see you again won't I?"

"Only if you want to."

"Of course I do. We must."

"That suits me. I like a bit of fun. Next time we could do more, maybe the full works. Have you ever tried Viagra? You can have a good time on that."

"Viagra? Where can we go?" He was desperately trying to think of a safe and private place they could use for further experiments. He could try to book a hotel for a few hours, but that would be fatal; might as well take out a full display ad in The Guernsey Press.

"We can find somewhere if you don't mind doing it in some strange places. It's summer; we could find a place outdoors."

"Whatever you suggest." Anywhere would do for him, even Forest Stores on a Saturday morning if need be.

"I'll think about it and let you know. Make you an offer you can't refuse. We could use Perry's Guide. You've got one haven't you? Tell you what, I'll ring you and give you a page number, a letter and a square, and a time. That'll be where we meet. If Eileen's in the room when I call you can just pretend it was a wrong number, or one of those arseholes who tell you you've won a holiday in bloody Miami. Just say 'yes' if you can make it and 'no thank you' if you can't. Have you got that?"

"Use Perry's. A map reference. Say yes if I can and no thank you if I can't. Clever woman."

"Something I picked up in the Girl Guides."

"Were you really..?"

"Don't be daft. Just a manner of speaking."

"What if Eileen answers the phone?"

"I'll put the phone down. And try again later. Now I must scarper Lover-Boy. I'll let myself out."

George went upstairs, climbed into bed and promptly fell into a deep and dreamless sleep. He woke two hours later feeling very much better.

*

"There you see," said Eileen, "I was right. Just those few hours in bed have made all the difference. I'll put on some soup later for lunch."

"Mmm, that would be lovely." He nestled down in bed his bright eyes peeping over the bedclothes.

He wasn't such a bad old tyrant she thought, quite endearing at times.

As she went downstairs she heard the sound of mail being pushed through the letterbox; two bills, a couple of bits of junk mail for George and a letter, with a handwritten envelope, addressed to her. The writing was vaguely familiar. She took everything into the kitchen, left the letters on George's side of the table, apart from the handwritten one. Now whose writing was that? Some part of her subconscious must have recognised it because as she looked at the strong sloping hand she felt a tinge of excitement. She held back from reading it immediately; she wanted the surroundings and the moment to be just right. First she would make a cup of coffee, get a chocolate biscuit, sit down, put her feet up and give herself up to it, give it one hundred per cent of her attention. She opened it carefully; this was what she hoped it was, what she had begun to think would never come, a letter from Doug.

She had sent him his cheque for the bracelet a few days after they'd met in town and although she told herself she shouldn't, she couldn't resist enclosing a little note with her address at the top. After an hour of false starts she eventually wrote a letter that she felt steered a sensible course between friendship and desire.

"Dear Doug,

What a treat it was to see you again last week; you haven't changed very much, still the same lovely man as when we

151

*were close so many years ago. I feel you should know that my
feelings for you haven't changed either; I will always think of
you with great affection, especially when I look at my bracelet
– I'm wearing it now.*

*I appreciate that our lives have taken separate paths and that
there is no real reason to keep in touch, but if, occasionally,
(the addition of the commas somehow made it more poignant)
you feel like writing, I would always be more than thrilled* (she
hoped he would be sensitive to the fact that 'thrilled' carried a
touch of sexual or at least sensual excitement which words like
'delighted' or 'pleased' did not) *to hear from you."*

Writing this had been easy, but the sign off had required more
thought. The ending of a letter always told the full story, no matter
what had been written in the body. If she put 'love, Eileen', for
example, that might seem a little too eager, especially with the
formality of the full 'Eileen': he would know she was making a
definite overture. 'Love, Ellie' on the other hand, seemed girlish
and insincere. 'Lots of love' was what people dashed off, often
quite indiscriminately to friends and lovers alike, when they
wanted themselves to be seen as lovable in a general sort of
way. 'Best regards' was too dry, ditto 'Best wishes'. 'Warmest
wishes' sounded emotionally constipated; as if the writer just
couldn't bring themselves to say 'love'. 'All the best' was what
a senior executive would write to a junior executive, friendly
but a little on the formal side and patronising. 'Thinking of
you' was mawkish, 'Affectionately' too much like a spinster
aunt and 'Love and kisses' – although this in fact was what
Eileen would have most liked to have put - was dangerously
uncontrolled and verging onto the desperate.

'Yours, ever' slipped into her mind as she struggled with
the problem and struck her as a good candidate. 'Yours, ever':
sincere, constant and ever so slightly ambiguous. Perfect.

"Yours, ever,

Eileen."

In the weeks that followed she had given up any idea that

he would write back, and had become annoyed at herself for letting him know how she felt, for revealing her vulnerability. She thought she'd been foolish to hope that her feelings were reciprocated, but obviously she had been wrong. Their love had been real and was still alive and here was the proof. She took a sip of coffee and read:

"Dear Eileen,

Thanx for the check. You never said if you wanted another bracelet for George. Let me know and I'll post one off.

It was nice to meet you again; clever of me to recognise you but I've always been good with faces even after they've changed a bit. Sorry George wasn't there I would have enjoyed seeing him – maybe next time.

I hope you don't mind me being cheeky but dont ask and you dont get –things are hard at the moment, they'll improve no doubt but cash flow right at the moment is nil. Could you see yourself to a loan of say £100? Sorry to ask but George was a good friend and it looks like you two are making out all right. I can let you have 2% below bank rate. You can send the check to the same name and address as before.

Ignore this letter if it's not on.

Doug."

She put the letter back in its envelope and slipped it in her pocket. "Nice to meet you again…" She would go through it again later and think about what he really meant. Lots of men found it difficult to express their feelings, especially in writing.

Back to her real life; George needed soup. She bent down to get a saucepan out of the cupboard and caught sight of something bright, a red feather, on the kitchen floor. Now where on earth had that come from?

Chapter Thirteen
A June Wedding

"Things fall apart: the centre cannot hold
Mere anarchy is loosed upon the world."
'The Second Coming' W. B. Yeats

Margot was conditioning her hair. She had used real henna mixed with some kind of mud, and the process had taken most of Sunday morning. Now, with her head wrapped in a towel turban, she was sitting cross–legged on the settee watching television and massaging her insteps.

Celia was on the Internet at her computer in the alcove. She had been trying to find out more on the latest EU Directives about access for the mobility-challenged in public buildings, but the noise of the game show and the excitement she felt within her made it difficult to concentrate. Tomorrow would be a very special day for her and Margot.

She looked back over their relationship. They had lived together for nearly twelve weeks, and most of that had been in harmony, although Celia had to admit, if pushed, that it was largely because she always gave way whenever there was friction. Margot had an elfin, almost ethereal beauty, but was surprisingly wilful and readily lost her temper. Sometimes, maybe most times, this was done deliberately. This Celia could forgive and forget, but much more of a problem – one that was growing but had not yet been fully discussed – was the fact that Margot was still out of work and, as she had no work permit, was not eligible for unemployment benefit. Whatever small amount of money she had when she first met Celia had long since gone and right from the start she refused to get casual labour for cash on the black market.

"I mean, honey, can you see me washing floors? I should be working in a studio, either in front of a camera or behind it. It'll all be sorted when the permit comes through. We just have to be patient for a couple more weeks. Two more weeks, that's all."

"If you get your right to stay in the country."

"I thought you were going to be able to look into that for me? Tell me how to make the right sort of appeal to the authorities that would help me stay here. To be with you. Isn't that what your department does?"

"Not my department, no. I know a few people who would be in a position to help but it wouldn't be right to ask them. I couldn't make a personal request, ask them to bend the rules for you as a special case."

"You could if you loved me…."

"You know I love you Margot."

"Why don't you help me then?"

The two weeks stretched to three and four, and then six, and there was still no guarantee of any permit in the foreseeable future. Celia's salary was having to stretch to two, and Margot didn't like cheap. But cheap was all they could afford these days and Celia was finding it difficult to know how to economise further. They had virtually stopped eating out and Margot had been forced to spend at least part of her day buying the ingredients for their increasingly simple meals at home.

Celia had found a certain satisfaction in their newly impoverished state; she liked to think it had brought them closer together and created a different, more homely, intimacy. She didn't mind the monotony of omelette, spaghetti, casseroles, salad: the very prosaic nature of their meals made them seem like any newly married couple finding it difficult to make ends meet.

"Now that would be a solution, if we could get married," said Margot "If we were married I would have the right to live and work here. That would be the perfect solution."

It would be the perfect solution from Celia's point of view as well. However much she despaired of Margot's laziness, she did love her. Their sex life had quietened down, considerably. It's bound to, thought Celia, still surprised and grateful that there was any activity at all. She comforted herself that relationships are about much more than sex and she felt privileged just to have Margot and her beauty under her roof. Margot living with her had been like seeing an exotic bird flying overhead out of reach, and then finding it had come back and was making its nest in your garden. Margot was a fabulous creature and Celia never tired of observing her.

Then one evening Margot had come home looking very excited.

"Now I want you to sit down and listen carefully to this my darling. I've just been down to Rosario's Bar to see if any of the crowd were there and I started talking to this guy..."

"Which guy?" Celia felt a pang of anxiety. Both she and Margot were aware that the other had had relationships with men but all that, they agreed, was in the past and over with.

"Don't get worked up, he's gay, really cross-the-line gay. I only spoke to him because he had a great pair of jeans – fantastic cut and I said how much I liked the jeans and we got talking..."

Celia still felt uneasy. The sudden possibility of Margot preferring a man had made her stomach lurch and she could barely hear about the rest of the encounter.

"...partner is Brazilian and can't get a permit. And he said what we have been saying, wouldn't it be great if only we could be married. That would solve the problem for both of us - and of course be a lovely thing in itself – and he came up with this truly great idea. He said why don't we get married."

"Who?" Celia's stomach was still floating around, unsettled.

"All four of us. The two Brits - you and Andy - get married to me and the Brazilian guy – I forget his name. As Andy's wife I get citizenship, and the same for the Brazilian with you."

"I get married to the Brazilian and you get married to Andy? Would we all live together? I can't see that working."

"No stupid, we don't all live together. The marriage is just for the documentation. After the ceremony we go our separate ways, Andy and the Brazilian, you and me."

"You might fall in love with Andy."

"Oh my God, how many times do I have to tell you, I couldn't fall in love with Andy, he's gay. Anyway I'm not your 'fall in love' type of person."

"You do love me though, don't you?" Celia had never dared ask before.

Margot leaned forward across the table and put her hand over Celia's as an answer. "It's a great idea isn't it? It will solve all our problems. I'll be able to get a proper job, get some decent clothes, start to live again instead of dragging along like we're doing on tea and baked beans. Living as a poor person is no fun."

"But getting married seems, I mean, it's a real commitment." Celia was thinking about Eileen and George. They had been married for about forty years and yet she was sure they didn't love each other in the way that she and Margot did. It must have taken real commitment for them to stay together, almost a sense of duty, but duty to whom and for what reason she couldn't say.

"Don't be so old fashioned. Marriage is just a legal contrivance, created by the authorities to keep us all in our boxes. It's relationships that require commitment. Marriage is just a civic act. Really, Celia!" She tossed her hair back, a sign of imminent sulking. "OK? That's settled then. Now give me five pounds and I'll go get us something to celebrate with."

Tomorrow they were to be married.

Celia had bought a smart new dress and jacket and Margot looked out an old retro-style velvet trouser suit that she hadn't worn in a long time. The weddings were booked at Camden

Registrar's office: Andy and Margot for eleven thirty and Celia and Vittorio at eleven forty-five.

The plan was to have lunch afterwards together, wish each other well and then say goodbye. All that would have really changed would be that Margot and Vittorio would have the right of abode, and be able to sign on for benefits.

But Celia still felt fluttery and uncertain. She couldn't dismiss the idea of marriage as an act sanctifying a relationship, in a civic, legal and emotional sense. Before the law tomorrow she would be stating her lifelong commitment to Margot, even if only indirectly, and despite the fact it looked as if she were promising eternal love to a Brazilian exotic dancer of indeterminate gender. The exoticism was also a source of anxiety. She had been alarmed when they met as a foursome and she saw Vittorio in a dress and high heels, and hoped that he would tone things down at the registrar's office.

"I am a bride" she said to herself, and despite the circumstances of the wedding, and despite ten years of immersion in prosaic work with the local council, the word evoked a long chain of associations for her, both romantic and strangely spiritual. Images intruded themselves into the details on screen of EU-determined ramp size and pitch for wheelchair access to public buildings. To be a bride was, first and foremost, to be beautiful, the epitome of a beauty compounded of youth, innocence, love and optimism. It is the beauty of living things on the verge of ripeness, which age and experience have not yet soured. It is the beauty at the very heart of romantic love, where there is good fortune, eternal hope and happy endings. It is the beauty of the senses, of flowers and white veils, and of an allotted hour when a woman knows she is truly loved by her partner and admired and cherished by the larger community. Even with her heavy body and thick glasses, Celia had always secretly longed for this.

She struggled for days with the question of whether she should tell George and Eileen. After all this was the only wedding that she would have and that they could go to as parents of the bride, and they still had time, even now, to get on a plane and come over for it.

Her parents, she knew, longed for her to be married, to be a traditional bride carrying roses, walking up the aisle with a good man. But there was the problem: a good man. Vittorio could hardly be called a man, and 'good' didn't come into it. It was probably better that they knew nothing.

"Margot, have you told your parents about tomorrow?"

"As in 'have I invited them to come over for it'? Are you kidding?"

"I mean have you told them you're getting married?" After all, in a way, the marriage was a confirmation of the permanence of their relationship and Celia wasn't sure as yet if Margot had told her parents that she was, well – 'spoken for'.

"No way, Jose. They'd hit the ceiling if they saw those freaks. How many times do I have to tell you that it's not a real marriage? It's just a practical thing that we're doing. A means to an end." She looked approvingly at her feet, then turned angrily, "Don't you dare tell me you've asked your mother?"

"Of course not. I was only thinking that if it were a real wedding then it would be nice to have her there. And George…"

"Honey - and I'm saying this for the last time - this ain't no real wedding! This is about you and me fixing my work permit. Nothing to do with brides and confetti. More like a party. There you go, think of it as a party."

"I suppose you're right." Celia sighed and then tried to concentrate again on her screen. Anyway parties could be fun.

The day dawned on a grey morning with a strong easterly wind blowing dust and litter along the pavements of Camden High Road. The girls picked their way carefully along the crowded street, Celia feeling chilly in her cotton suit.

Her first thought when she saw the grooms getting out of the taxi was that she was glad that Eileen and George were not there. Andy was fairly conservatively dressed in a suit of beige linen, the jacket of which had, presumably, been intentionally cut to drape loosely round his thin frame, but which had the effect of making him look as if he had borrowed his father's clothes. Vittorio, meanwhile, looked like he was dressed for some kind of beach party, in low-slung bell-bottom trousers and a cropped maroon jacket that revealed a brown waist brimming over the waistband. He had a silver ring in his belly button, and wore two studs in his left eyebrow and another through his tongue.

"Don't fancy yours" said Margot in a stage whisper, and Celia had to laugh. At least he was wearing trousers, although as he got close she could see he was also wearing eye shadow and mascara and both men smelled strongly of Poison.

Worse still, although Celia should have been prepared for it really, was that the men were high. They even looked stoned for heaven's sake, could barely keep their balance and kept hanging on to each other and giggling. They did straighten up for the actual ceremonies but both fumbled over their signatures and Vittorio took an embarrassingly long time to say his name.

The Registrar had seen it all before - or if not exactly this than something very similar - and managed to be patient and courteous. All the same, when Celia's turn came, she suddenly felt ashamed. This was not how she had hoped her wedding would be. (She had learned by now not to refer to it openly as a wedding, but still felt it was the nearest she would ever come to having one). It wasn't just the sham marriage she felt ashamed of; there was something else, something about the basis of her relationship with Margot that didn't seem right in this context. Theirs had been a private decision, made knowingly against the normal expectations of what might be called the natural course of life, and the contrariness of it was uncomfortably revealed today, in this room dedicated to the approval - if only in a legal sense - of society. More than ever before, she felt a sense of being excluded, and this time not because of how she looked or for any accident of nature but by her own determining and will. She had decided to swim against the stream, rather than play the game according to the rules. Tears of regret welled in her eyes, but she kept very still and eventually they dried where they were, so nobody saw.

Afterwards, as they gathered on the pavement outside, Vittorio and Andy kissed each other with prolonged relish. Celia looked hopefully towards Margot, but she was checking her watch and then, after a curt "See you guys," she strode off. Celia bustled along behind her. Perhaps they were off to celebrate in a nice restaurant. But no, Margot had been heading for the pub. As they sat at the bar drinking beer with vodka chasers Celia reflected on how much of an anticlimax it had all seemed, more like a funeral than a wedding. As Margot had said, it was just a means to an end, an end that Celia, increasingly, was unsure of.

Chapter Fourteen
The Summer Solstice – Ray's Story

"I am the master of my fate
I am the captain of my soul."
W.E. *Henley*

The twenty-first of June dawned fine and dry in Guernsey, a soft mist clearing away from the sea as the day's heat strengthened. This was the summer solstice, the point in the year when the chilly north comes closest to the sun and when life can be lived as it should be, full-bloodedly, without inhibitions and to the hilt. It's a time for adventures, for daring and for love.

Yet as Eileen parked her car at the Adult Education Computer centre, she felt a nervous anxiety at the prospect of learning a new task in a new environment. Would she be able to cope? She'd been a willing pupil but not particularly gifted, except perhaps in literature where she always got good marks, especially for poetry. But school was a long way behind her and she wondered, at fifty-nine, how readily she could learn a new skill?

Certainly a new skill was needed. She and George had bought a computer and it had been installed in the house the previous week, and although the young lad who set it up had gone through everything with her, once he had left the house Eileen felt totally lost.

"Don't expect me to help," said George as he walked past her and up the stairs, leaving the words 'I told you so' unspoken, but heavy in the air.

The classroom at the centre was not laid out like a schoolroom but sectioned off into three rows of small work stations. There were half a dozen people there already, mostly women, and all of them much younger than her. The receptionist directed her to an empty desk, showed her how to turn the computer on to the audio programme she needed, handed her a pair of headphones and told to follow directions she would hear. She was to ask the 'teacher' – a bored-looking man who most of the time, rather anachronistically thought Eileen, sat at the front reading a novel - whenever she had a problem.

There was a sign on the pegboard in front of her which said in big capitals:

"DON'T EAT OR DRINK WHILE USING THE COMPUTER
MOBILE PHONES TO BE SWITCHED OFF
ABSOLUTELY NO SMOKING
DO NOT TURN OFF THE POWER."

She'd no sooner read this when she heard a mobile ring from under the desk next to hers. Her neighbour on the left, a young woman in smart office clothes put down her sandwich and cup of coffee, took off her earphones, rummaged in her bag, retrieved a phone and started talking animatedly and at full volume. Her gaze was directed at Eileen but apparently did not notice her as she carried on chatting. Thank God George was not here; mobile phones were his bete noir, or rather one of his betes noir. 'Why do they think we want to hear about their insignificant lives? Why do they have to shout? Why can't they exist for a moment in the here and now?' All perfectly valid questions, but of course unanswerable. This was just the way of the modern world and it's a braver person than I, thought Eileen, who would dare to tackle someone about it, ask them to turn their phone off or simply speak more quietly. Even girls these days could turn nasty she thought.

She put on the headphones to seek refuge in the voice of the instructor but how to call the voice that of a teacher with any sense of conviction? She sounded like a seventeen year old brought in from the streets and forced at knife point to speak into a microphone. The mangled vowels and missing consonants were painful enough, but worse still was her apparent lack of understanding of the text or even the underlying structure of language. The words clustered together in randomised clots. What were they teaching them these days in school? Eileen gritted her teeth and tried to be as open minded and obedient to her task as she could. It's only because you're tense, because you're worried that you won't be able to do it, she told herself. Try, try and try again.

After an hour of stumbling through the basics, constantly interrupted by her neighbour with the mobile, she went out into the hallway and looked for the Ladies Room. She didn't want the loo she just wanted to lean – aah, that felt better - lean up against the wall and ease the ache in her back. It must have been the crouching position over the keyboard that was the trouble. Now a rinse of the hands and some cool water on the face and she was ready to go back in.

A man had taken the vacant seat on her right. Thin, small, balding. Maybe a couple of years younger than her. He looked up briefly and smiled; he had a severe face but a bright-eyed intelligent look. She was glad to see that he was only on Tape Three, not much more advanced than herself.

The next quarter of an hour went well and she began to feel she was making progress.

"Excuse me," the man leaned across in front of her, so close she could smell his aftershave. He addressed the office girl, "Would you turn off your mobile please. Like the instructions say." He was polite, but the tone of the voice implied an order rather than a request. The girl looked sulky for a second but switched off the phone and put it back in her bag.

"Thank you. Now we can hear ourselves think." He leaned back and winked at Eileen.

He was right; it was much easier to concentrate. Eileen grew more confident until right at the end of the tape. Then she obviously made some kind of a mistake, because a series of boxes came up on the screen, the last one telling her she had executed an illegal procedure.

"Oh gosh. I think I've broken it! Help, what do I do?"

Bright Eyes took off his headphones and smiled encouragingly, "It's all right, you just haven't closed the file down in the right order. Just left click that red square at the top right of each box one after another. That's right – keep on going. Now click 'Close', then 'Exit' to get out of the file. There you are." A slight North Country accent but she couldn't place him. "This your first time?"

"Never touched one before. I'm terrified of doing something wrong."

"No, you'll be all right. You'll soon overtake me; you know how to type properly. I only hunt and peck. Three finger job."

"I feel really daft."

"I feel really thirsty. Want a cup of tea in the canteen down the corridor?"

"I, er – well, why not?" She needed a reward.

He bought tea and fruit cake for two, putting cups and plates on the same tray, then took her to a table and set things out so they could sit facing each other. He's quite homely she thought, kinder than he looks.

"So tell me all about yourself. Why are you learning the computer?"

"At this stage in my life do you mean?"

"Ay, if you want to look at it that way."

"I've been feeling sort of past it recently, too old, if you like, to try new things." Silence. "Felt I was getting left behind." Still no response. "Got quite sensitive about it."

"In what way?"

She hesitated, she hadn't told anyone about the incident with the cyclist. "The other day I fell over in the street and grazed my arm and a young woman came and helped me up, and I'm afraid I was really quite rude to her."

"Shock, do you think?"

"Maybe, yes. But what upset me was when she said her grandmother had done the same thing." Silence. "She obviously thought I was old enough to be her grandmother!"

"Are you?"

"I suppose I am. But I really resented the fact she said it."

"What's wrong with being a grandmother?"

"I don't know; it seems so old, really old. Not just middle-aged but past it."

"Past what?"

"It. Life. Everything! She was saying I was someone who was no longer part of it all."

"Maybe she just thought you were old enough to be her grandmother."

Now it was Eileen's turn to stay silent.

"Age is what it is – you can't change that. You're the age of her grandmother; that may be the truth factually. But to see that as a veiled insult about whether you're past it or not, whatever we agree that means, may just be your interpretation. Do you have grandchildren?"

"I have a grown up daughter but she's not married."

"If she had children maybe you'd be proud to be identified as a grandmother."

"Are you a psychologist or something?"

"I've listened to a lot of people talking about their lives. Men and women have different problems as they age but it all adds up to the same thing. A slow, panicky sense of loss and decline, of being left behind, abandoned. I'm going through it myself so I understand."

To her surprise Eileen found she wanted to tell him more. Even about the most private things. So, as they sat over the empty cups and crumbs, she talked first about Margot, then very discreetly, because after all she didn't want to be a traitor especially as one day he could possibly meet George, she told him about George's irritability and depression, and even a little about herself and her childhood dreams that had never been realised. He sat and listened, occasionally asking for clarification, but otherwise he just let her go on uninterrupted until she stopped, suddenly aware of the time.

"I'm so sorry. I must be boring you to death. And I don't even know your name. Mine's Eileen. And thanks for listening."

"Don't apologise. You talk with honesty, not many people do that. And you have a nice voice Eileen, very easy on the ear. Glad to have met you. The name's Ray." He reached his hand out to her; it was small and rough, but nicely warm.

She drove home in jubilant mood. This had been a good morning; she had learned at least something about how to use a computer and she'd made a friend, a man at that, and someone who thought she had a nice voice.

*

Ray came back from the computer class and went straight to his room overlooking the sea. He sat at his telescope and swung it slowly around, taking in White Rock pier, Castle Cornet, Havelet Bay and the bathing pools beyond. He found and focused on a solitary angler leaning on the railings. From this distance he felt sympathy for the anonymous figure standing purposively looking out to sea, trying to catch what he could more easily buy, filling a lonely weekday with an unquestioned ritual. Ray knew what this solitary existence was like and he was tired of it. More importantly he was beginning to be afraid of it. He had this picture of himself at, say, seventy-five as a smaller, drier version of himself, struggling with the requirements of daily life, both bored and increasingly confused: a figure of pathos, a lonely old codger. Like lots of lonely old codgers he'd met in his time, all unable to connect, even with each other. He could so easily end up how he had started off in life, unloved, unwanted and ignored.

It fucking won't happen he said to himself. I know what I want and I'm going to get it. There's nothing and no-one to stop me. So what did he want, Ray Meldon, self-made man? Quite simply, roots. Roots in a nice little community with someone to keep him company, give him optimism about the future and to look after him in his old age. A bit of connection and security to make up for all the early years.

Even back in the Forties, when most people had little, he had less than any child could reasonably expect. There had been no money, no security and certainly no love. From that

unpromising beginning he'd had to make his life inch by inch, week by week, penny by penny, using the talents he'd been born with: a quick brain and great reserves of energy. It took an accidental encounter with a dog to teach him how to succeed.

The lesson came while he was still at St Aubyn's orphanage. He had been a small baby, the unwanted product of a brutish man and his undernourished niece, and he grew to be a small child, an easy target. The other children had teased, taunted and tortured him in the way that only children can, without real malice but with no concern either, for the outcome of their

actions. So he became a loner, forming temporary alliances that were easily destroyed by jealousy, envy and fear.

Until the age of eleven his response to the bullying was to cry, even while he carried on trying to fight back, his small fists flailing as the bigger boys held him at arm's length. His tears came from anger as much as fear but he was branded as a cry baby and picked on all the more.

Then one day something happened out in the yard that changed him forever.

He'd heard a lot of shouting outside one summer's day and went to see what was happening. It was a puppy, a black and tan-coloured mongrel, dirty and very thin. One of the boys was poking it with a stick, laughing to see the dog wobble and fall over. It tried to escape but other boys joined in kicking the dog when it tried to escape. Ray watched from outside the circle. He had no particular feeling for animals, no more than for any living creature, but there was something about this creature's behaviour that interested and moved him. It was small like him and being bullied by his enemies but the dog never gave in. However often he fell over or was temporarily stunned by a kick to the head he carried on snapping at the hands. It just never gave up.

The boys would probably have kicked the dog to death, in part just to finish what they had started, but the bell called them to supper. Hunger and fear of Father Jonas won and they ran off leaving the dog inert but conscious. Ray stayed to watch the puppy as it eventually managed to stand up and limp off, squeezing under the chestnut paling into the grass of the old bomb site next door.

That evening Ray managed to save some of his meat at supper and, wrapping it in a page from an old copy of The Eagle, he crept out of the building while the rest of the boys went to play table tennis. He found a gap in the fence and eventually found the puppy asleep, sheltering under a piece of corrugated iron. It woke when it heard or felt his footsteps and snarled weakly, revealing a couple of broken teeth. Ray crouched down some distance away, aware that he would not be allowed to get close. He set the paper with the meat inside as close as the dog would let him, then walked a few yards away. When he looked back he was pleased to see the dog sniffing at the paper.

He smuggled food to the dog this way every day for nearly five weeks and liked to think that it was growing fatter, more solid-looking. It never allowed itself to be touched but in the third week it let him stand by while it gulped down the better part of a slice of meat pie. Ray gave him a name – Joey – and fancied that the dog trusted him, recognised him as a friend and protector.

Then one day one of the boys saw Ray squeezing through the gap and reported it to one of the Fathers. The boy was rewarded with double helpings of pudding that night at supper, but Ray was given four lashes with the strap, and kept indoors after five o'clock for a fortnight. When he next had the chance to get through the fence there was no trace of the dog apart from a slight impression of his body in the sand under the metal sheeting. Joey had gone.

The incident stayed in his mind. He recognised that there was something important about it and something particularly important for him. It had shown a different way to be, even in a world as pointless and indifferent as St Aubyn's. It changed him. The next time Alfie, one of his worst tormentors, started a fight Ray made a promise to himself. Whatever happened he would not give up. So he carried on fighting through all the pain and bruising, the swollen eye and broken nose, until Alfie stood back, waving his arms as if to ward off any further blows and declared the fight was finished. But Ray decided otherwise and had lurched forward, blood coursing down his face from his nose, and managed to throw a punch on Alfie's jaw that knocked him out. The boy slumped to the ground. Even that didn't stop Ray, who now leapt on his senseless opponent, punching at the body left and right over and over again. He was eventually pulled back by Father Thomas and no amount of saying that he had been picked on, that Alfie had swung the first few punches, and that he, Ray, was only defending himself, could save him from the priest's tight-mouthed fury:

"You feckless miserable scoundrel – Mother of God that such wickedness exists! You will do what I say Raymond do you hear me, or I'll make sure you never do anything again."

Ray was dragged into the study where he was given the strap twenty times until his hand was bloody and throbbing, although he managed to stay dry-eyed throughout, saved from disgrace by the adrenalin still racing round his body. Later he stood trembling in the sick room while Matron cleaned him up. She stuffed cotton wool roughly up his nose to stop the bleeding, put Golden ointment on his eye and then bandaged his hand in a not unkindly way.

"So Raymond you're growing into a man are you?" She took him by the shoulders and bent down to look him full in the eye. "Good lad. Maybe I shouldn't say this but I'm glad you're looking after yourself because there's no-one else but you can do that. You're on your own in this life. And if you want something then you'll have to get it for yourself. It's a terrible truth but that's how it is."

She reached up and, a rare treat, picked out a toffee from the big tin on the top shelf, the unfamiliar honeyed pleasure of which helped reinforce her words, printing them deep into his brain.

Alfie had regained consciousness within a few minutes of being knocked out and was declared fit and fine the following day, but neither he nor any of the other boys ever picked on Ray again.

He had learned the two most important lessons of his life because of Joey. The first was never ever give up and the second, which was much more profound, was that he had to make his own life. Whatever happened would only ever happen if he made it so. There was to be no parental guidance, no steering by an interested mentor, no lucky stroke of fortune, no deus ex machina and nothing in effect that would create his future. He was on his own.

Forty years later he was a rich man, having worked his way from labouring on the docks to being an engineer, and eventually joint owner of an oil rig in Hong Kong. His money bought him a fine house in Midlevel and the daughter of an expat lawyer as his wife. There was a live-in housekeeper, a maid, a driver, two Porsches, a Rolls Royce Silver Shadow and a Gold Star bike. He was a member of The China Club and the Yacht Club and drank champagne at the bar of the Mandarin. He was so rarely at home that after a few years, and before there were children, his wife left him. A succession of younger women, ex-pats and locals, replaced her without any noticeable change to his equilibrium.

He was fifty, a dangerous age for a man, when one morning, a morning not obviously different from any that had preceded it, he realised that either he or the world around him had changed. All that he'd been and done seemed to have soured. He was bored with it all, the money, his possessions, his whole way of life. It had lost its magic.

Once he realised that the magic was not coming back he was eager to see it all go. He went on a selling spree, not for the money but to be rid of things and make more space in his life. First his collection of jade, then the massive mahogany furniture from Malaysia, the Chinese temple dogs, the ivory elephants and ancient porcelain plates – it all went with accelerating speed and no second thought. At the last he sold the house itself, regretting only the loss of the huge picture windows with their view of the harbour.

He moved into a small apartment built over a massage parlour in Kowloon, living cheaply like a local. It was here to the accompaniment of the sounds of happy life rising up through the floorboards, that he spent his money and time on the acquisition of knowledge: astronomy, Enlightenment literature, Greek architecture, early Japanese porcelain, Asian herbal medicine - whatever caught his eye or took his fancy. When he finally came across Maslow in a weighty psychology volume he at once recognised the pattern his life had taken and the progress that he had made. He had achieved a state of 'Self-Actualisation', of determining for himself, rather than have it defined by others, what it was in life that held meaning and significance. By his own efforts he had become the Master of his Fate.

One day a few years later he had another change of heart. The book-littered flat in Kowloon, the shrill-voiced girls below, the smell of pork fat in the air and the cats fighting over the scraps from the café next door all seemed like somebody else's life. It wasn't home. He didn't belong. He knew he had to leave, and within a month, taking his money but little else, he moved to London and from there to the Channel Islands.

In Guernsey's grey and insular Atlantic climate he experienced real loneliness. For the first three months he spoke only to shopkeepers, barmen and the builders who came to lay carpets and to take out the bath and install a huge shower. Where making money had been easy he now realised he was less successful at relationships, the people side of things. After the breakdown that followed several months of isolation, he did what had always worked for him before. He learned how to make friends. Other people did it naturally but if he had to proceed step by step, so be it. Anything would be better than staring into the void every day.

One day he heard the plumber stop work on the new shower to answer his mobile. There followed a strange one-sided conversation which went on for so long that he knew it couldn't be a request to fix a leak.

"I see. So how do you feel about it? Yes. Yes. Yes. Linda you told me that he's been taking advantage of you before? And you'd decided that this wasn't good and you wanted to change the pattern. Yes, yes. I see. Do you want to change things? OK what will you do? No I can't make your mind up for you. You decide and then you do. Remember it's in your hands. I'll be here any time you want me." Eventually the man put his mobile away. "Sorry about that, mate, it's a client. I'll work a bit extra this afternoon to make up for it."

"What the hell was that?"

"It's something called coaching. Helping people become successful at doing things they want but don't think they can. I've done two courses. Got a diploma and going to start my own business. It will fit in quite well with this for as long as necessary but I'd like to do the coaching full time – there's more money in it. And it's easy once you've learned a few tricks."

"Like what?"

"Listening to people, mostly. Being non-judgmental. That sort of thing. Helps you understand people and get your own way."

A year and a couple of correspondence courses later, Ray had acquired an understanding of the principles involved and was pleased to see an improvement in his social life as well as a few hours' profitable work a week to pass the time. He sometimes doubted that he actually liked people any the better for understanding them, but he knew he could now at least simulate intimacy, and convincingly too.

He put away the telescope, stood up and stretched. He had the skills to connect, but now he needed someone to connect with. Maybe today he'd found that someone in – what was her name – Eileen, the woman at the college.

She was the kind of person he could tolerate: unassuming, unobtrusive and, above all, easy to manage. I could do with her, someone for the next ten or twenty years, whatever time is left he thought. She was older than his usual type so he wasn't sure of what the sex side would be like, but he wasn't fussy. Anyway that had become less important. He didn't need it in quite the same way. And to be honest it was quite a relief to be free from all that pursuing and wooing. Of course she was married, but her husband sounded like a bit of loose change. He ought to be able to break that up. Besides, he said to himself as he went into the kitchen to make a bacon sandwich, I like a challenge. Yeah, I can get her if I try hard enough and long enough.

Chapter Fifteen
Summer solstice – George and the request

"All things that love the sun are out of doors."
'Resolution and Independence' William Wordsworth

With Eileen in town at her computer class, George had the house to himself; he could have taken the paper out onto the terrace and sat in the sun to read but he didn't want to be out of earshot of the phone. It was over a week since his encounter with Gloria in the kitchen; she must, surely, contact him soon.

It was tricky staying alert for the phone when Eileen was around. On the few occasions when it had rung he had nearly fallen over himself to get to it first, all the time rehearsing what it was he had to say and what he should be listening for. On one occasion Eileen got there before him, George having failed to get round the dining room table in time. He collided painfully with the corner of the table and could feel a bruise in the making on his hip bone, which only added to his sense of panic and frustration. The call was a short one but it sounded as if Eileen knew the caller.

"Who was that?" He couldn't prevent a note of anxiety from entering his voice, and he couldn't help but see that Eileen had noticed.

"The hairdresser's. They want to change my appointment time. Why, what's the matter?"

"What's the matter? You're the matter. You don't usually

bother with the phone and now all of a sudden you seem to be in a rush to get to it before me. You could see I was preparing to answer it and you just pushed ahead as if I didn't exist."

"Sorry. I didn't know you were expecting a call."

"Of course I'm not expecting a call. Why should I be expecting a call? It's nothing to do with that. It's to do with you. The way you are. Oh forget it!"

He strode off purposively, ending up near the phone in the kitchen. But if Eileen had been suspicious of his behaviour and really, why should she be, she didn't show it, and he was further pleased to see that over the next couple of days she left him to answer when it rang.

Today, with Eileen safely out of the way, his anxiety was not about who would pick it up, but simply whether it would ring in the first place. He tried to distract himself with other things but couldn't settle to anything but waiting.

Another problem of course was how to keep himself available for Gloria. He'd barely left the house over the last few days. He hadn't gone with Eileen for their weekly shop or volunteered to go to the Vehicle Registration office to renew the tax disk for the car - a task that he had always seen as the man's duty, involving as it did their means of transport and the local authorities. It was a different matter concerning the Vikings of course. Tomorrow was their Friday meeting and he'd be there come what may. He'd lost another couple of pounds over the last week and wanted to keep up the momentum. Anyway Gloria wasn't the type of girl to make contact before eight or to suggest an early morning session.

Aah, the telephone! At last! He hurried to the receiver and then waited three seconds, breathing out slowly to calm himself and steady his voice.

"Yes, George Buchanan speaking."

"Is Roland there?" A man's voice, trembling and hoarse: an old man who probably didn't make many calls.

"I think you must have the wrong number. There is no Roland

here."

"Well he said this number."

"Which number?"

"The one you answered."

"Which number did you dial?"

"Eh?"

"Look this is 234105. Which number did you want?"

"I want to speak to Roland."

This was taking valuable phone time. Gloria might be trying to get through to him at this very moment.

"I'm sorry but Roland doesn't live here."

"Has he left then?"

"He doesn't live here. He never has. You've got the wrong number."

"Roland Davies. Guernsey 234105. Tell him it's important."

"He doesn't live here. You've got the wrong number."

George slammed the receiver down as best he could with these new plastic jobs. Old fool.

A minute late it rang again.

"234105. George Buchanan here."

"It is the right number, I've just looked it up."

"Well I'm sorry, but if Roland Davies lived here once he doesn't now. Please stop ringing this number."

"It's the number I've been given."

"Look I'm a doctor and this is an emergency line. Just get off and stay off."

"Sorry Doctor, only this is an emergency. Doris has died. She died last Tuesday. I said I'd let Roland know because he's got some money coming to him."

"Well you can send it here if you like as long as you get off the phone."

"Is he there then? I've got an address."

"No, no that was a joke. I didn't mean it. He's not here."

The voice sounded aggrieved, "I don't think it's right that a doctor should be making jokes at somebody's expense.

Especially as I am a bereaved. And a pensioner. It's not right. I only asked a civil question."

"Will you get off the bloody telephone!" George slammed the phone down again.

It rang again thirty seconds later. Whoever the old fool was, he didn't give up easily. George decided to settle things once and for all by giving him something to think about. He would try his famous imitation of a dog barking. He could do it very loudly and, everyone said, very realistically. At the fourth ring he picked up the receiver, put it close to his mouth and barked as loud as he could. Maybe it sounded more terrier than Rotweiller, but was convincing enough.

There was a brief silence.

"Is this an inconvenient time, Lover Boy?"

"Gloria!"

"Thought it was bloody Crufts for the moment. Quite a turn on to hear you all worked up. Are you alone?"

"I was making that noise because some fool keeps ringing me…"

"Of course you were. Do it myself sometimes. Now, are you alone or is the whole pack there?"

"Yes, but she might be back at any minute."

"Can you make this evening? Nine thirty. Page 30 B5. The Car Park."

"Yes, yes! This evening. 30 B5. I'll be there."

Even as he said this he was aware that he'd need an excuse to give to Eileen, but he'd work that out later. Love will find a way. He heard a click as Gloria put the phone down. Maybe Steve was around. He wrote the map reference down on a Post-it pad kept near the telephone, and carefully peeled the top page off and put it in his breast pocket. Next to his heart. Now where was page 30? He knew their house was on page 25, but that was all. Where was the Perry's Guide? He rummaged around unsuccessfully for a few minutes in the kitchen then remembered Eileen had taken the Guide with her to find the

Adult Education centre. He'd have to wait until she got back. Damn. Never mind; he could fill the shining hour by trimming his ears.

In the bathroom mirror he could see that the renaissance of his sexual life had transformed him. He looked brighter of eye, fitter, and several years younger. And the tension of the last two weeks, of not knowing when Gloria might ring, had effectively put him off his food. His belly was definitely on the retreat. He had just finished trimming the hair in one ear when he heard the doorbell. As he walked down the stairs he recognised Steve's broad outline through the frosted glass panel in the front door. He stopped halfway down. What on earth could he want? Had he been listening in when Gloria rang? Did he hear about the assignation? Did he know? Dear God, pleaded George silently, as he opened the door with fumbling fingers, I'll do anything you say as long as he doesn't know.

"Steve, what a pleasure." His voice broke on the last word so he turned it into the more prolonged noise of clearing his throat.

"Hiya mate. What are you up to?" Steve stood foursquare on the doorstep, in a tracksuit, no doubt ready for action. "Well, can I come in?"

George backed nervously into the hall, wondering how, if it came to fisticuffs, he would defend himself. There was an umbrella in the cupboard under the stairs but it would take time to get it out and he'd have to open the cupboard door first. He edged towards the kitchen.

"Actually I've come to ask you a favour." Was that a veiled threat, as in, keep off my wife or I'll thrash you within an inch of your life?

"Sure, sure." George found he had backed himself up against the wall, "Whatever you want."

"Careful, you don't know what it is yet." Steve moved closer and put a big hand on George's shoulder. "Is it too early for a beer?"

"What?"

"Don't make me spell it out. Makes me feel like an alkie!" His smile revealed a lot of teeth.

"A beer? Why not? Come on in." George exhaled in a funny way - half laugh, half whimper - then led him into the kitchen, took two cans of beer from the fridge and handed one to Steve, who opened it and took a swig straight from the can.

"It's like this. We've just had a load of stuff come through, recording equipment and blank videos and DVDs, that kinda stuff, and we're out of space. So I wondered - actually it was Gloria who suggested it -…"

George struggled with a mouthful of Carlsberg, managed to get it down and gave a loud belch.

"…steady! As I say, - whether we could use one of your garages? Just temporary like."

"No problem, Steve, no problem." Thank you God. "One of them is completely empty, we never use it. Plenty of space there and it's got a lock if you want it."

"Well I shouldn't think there's any need for that, not here. But hey, you never know. That's grand mate, thanks a lot."

"When do you want to move the stuff in? I'll get Eileen to sweep it out for you."

"No need to disturb the little lady. Everything is double-wrapped; a bit of dust won't make any difference. No difference at all. If it's all the same with you, now would be good for me."

"Now? OK. That's fine. Would you like some help?" George would have hoisted the stuff up the stairs into his study if Steve had wanted,

"That's uncommonly kind of you. I won't say no." Steve poured most of the rest of the beer down his throat while George poured most of his down his shirt and had to grab a kitchen towel on the way out.

The boxes were in a big pile outside next door's back door, spilling out onto the patio where so long ago the Buchanans had got drunk on Gloria's specials. George was relieved to see that there was no sign of her in person. He estimated there were maybe a hundred boxes, each of them about the size of a small tea chest, all regular in shape and well-wrapped. He picked one up; it was surprisingly heavy. Without his glasses he couldn't read the label but the marks looked foreign. Anyway this was no time to ask questions; Steve was already loading a trolley and George went off to fetch his wheelbarrow.

The next hour an a half was spent going backwards and forwards shifting the boxes between the two houses and stacking them neatly in the garage. It was hard work and the midday sun was hot. George, who felt obliged to at least try and keep up with Steve, was soon sweating profusely.

Eileen drove in at the front gate just after they'd stacked them all and locked the door. George felt weak. He hadn't done so much physical work since they'd last been on camping holiday in France, which must have been when Celia was about ten and he was in his forties. He leant against the garage door breathing heavily.

Steve wiped his hands on his tracksuit before shaking Eileen's hand and giving her a peck on the cheek.

"Good to see you Eileen. Your hubby's just been helping me here with a problem. Ace stuff. He'll need a rest after all that. Got to go now. Thanks a million mate. And I'll take the key if that's all right?"

George handed Steve the key even as he wondered if this was a good idea. "Anytime you need help." But really the key was a small price to pay for his life and limb. "Anytime. Only too happy."

"What was that all about?" asked Eileen as they sat over quiche and a salad in the kitchen. "What is it exactly, in the garage?"

"Blank videos, that's all. Something to do with his business. Anyway enough of that – how did this morning go?" On to automatic pilot as Eileen chatted on while he made plans for the evening.

As soon after lunch as seemed natural he went out to the car and sat in the driver's seat studying Perry's Guide. Page 30, square B5 - the car park at Icart Point. He had been to Icart once when he and Eileen had first come to the island. They had decided it would be good exercise to walk the Coastal Path from east to west in easy three mile stages once a week. They would take a car to a point along the route, walk one and a half miles in one direction and then double back to the car. Next week they would drive and park a bit further up the coast, and repeat the exercise until they reached Portelet Harbour in the far South West.

For their first walk they had started at the Aquarium and skirted Fort George, then taken the wooded path along the coast, past the Ozanne Steps towards Fermain Bay. The plan was to have a cup of tea in the Fermain café before turning round and walking back to their starting point. It had looked like an easy walk on paper, but they'd not appreciated how closely the path adhered to the contours of the cliffs. After forty minutes of climbing up and down a seemingly endless succession of steps they were still only halfway to Fermain and George's knees were threatening to give out. They carried on until they reached a bench, set back from the path and sheltered amongst the blackthorn trees. George had sat down heavily and announced that he would sit and look at the view and that Eileen could walk on and pick him up on the way back.

Two weeks later he had reluctantly agreed to tackle the next stage, from Fermain Bay to the kiosk in the car park at Jerbourg Point. The problem this time was his ankle and he walked the entire way, but slowly and complainingly about five yards behind Eileen. A month later she had suggested the fairly easy stage from Jerbourg to Moulin Huet and back. It happened to be pleasantly sunny but cool that day and the going underfoot was dry, and while George couldn't say that he enjoyed the process, he let the event pass without comment. It was two months later before Eileen could finally persuade him to walk Stage Four: Moulin Huet to Icart Point. The day had started fair but soon it was raining and their discomfort was made worse by a keen south westerly wind. They trudged on silently up and down great terraces of steps, occasionally acknowledging other walkers, German tourists in hard weather hiking equipment, or locals, as ever in shorts and sandals, walking their dogs. When they had thawed out over tea and fruit cake at the Icart café George declared Eileen could do as she pleased but he was not going to walk back. He had then rung for a taxi to take them both back to the car and that was the end of the Coastal Walk programme.

Now as he looked at the map, he couldn't imagine how he and Gloria were going to make themselves comfortable either in a car park or at the café. It would be getting dark by nine thirty and the tea room would be closed. At least the day was warm and dry. All the same he decided to take his new sailing jacket.

A more pressing preoccupation was to find an excuse that he could give Eileen for going out so late. Usually by nine thirty they had had supper and would be finishing off the wine in front of the television. Regardless of what they were watching it was one of the most convivial times of the day, the time when they felt most at peace with each other and with life in general. What possible justification could he find that would make it seem natural for him to leave her at that time and go out into the night? If he said he was off for a walk, she would be very suspicious, and more than likely want to come too.

She would also think it unnatural if he said he was off for a drink. They rarely went to the pubs in Guernsey, which, contrary to their expectations turned out to be like their mainland counterparts, full of youngsters competing to see who could get the most drunk.

Perhaps he could engineer some kind of a row and then storm out of the house as if angry. But supposing she refused to take offence or to get upset? So often these days she said yes dear and then just ignored him; it had been many years since real emotions had come into their arguments. Besides, it didn't seem fair to leave Eileen miserable as well as alone, when he was going out to have a good time with another woman. Not quite cricket.

Then the solution came: the Vikings. He'd pretend that one of the Vikings had asked him to go round for some reason or another; perhaps they wanted to discuss a problem or borrow a video or plan some swimming event, or a charity – yes that was it –discuss a sponsored swim for charity. The Vikings were planning to run a sponsored swim down at the pools and we're going to have a meeting at Ray's house this evening, late, to organise it. Voila! Problem solved. It would be easy enough in a few weeks' time to pretend that the sponsored swim had taken place. Eileen would never know.

*

As she cleared up the dishes after lunch Eileen was thinking about Steve storing his packages in their garage. It seemed an innocent enough request on the face of it, but she was inclined to expect the worst of him and Gloria, even though as neighbours she recognised the importance of cooperation and good manners. Had she been correct in seeing a slight hesitation when George handed over the key to the garage? If so, perhaps he had forgotten that there was a spare key in the drawer in the sideboard in the dining room. For the time being she would keep this information to herself.

Meanwhile, she wanted to have some time on her own to think about all that was happening. Most of all, to her surprise, she wanted to think about Ray.

So with gloves and small fork she set out for the bottom of their little garden, a place where George rarely ventured. It was her favourite spot because, although the sun left it early in the day, it was not overlooked. Here she could be in her own world and have her own thoughts without fear of interruption.

Today the garden smelled of turned earth and things growing, a lush pagan fragrance. Today, she reflected, was June 21st, the summer solstice. This had always been a special day for her, when the sun reaches its northernmost destination and hangs perfectly still in the heavens before starting its return journey. She saw it as time stopping for a fraction of a second like the interval between heartbeats. Should the world go back to what is known and certain, or venture forward to other, less predictable futures? The solstice is a time between times, and offers the careful observer a split second of limitless possibilities.

She knelt down and bent over the beds of hellebore, working silently and seriously as if in supplication to some Arcadian god. The sounds and senses of the place surrounded and immersed her. She took off her gloves to feel the soil, warm and soft and smelling of spice; it reminded her of childhood, of the weeks before Christmas and the little carton that her mother took down from the cabinet when she made the cake. How carefully from year to year she had measured that half teaspoon of brown dust, as if it had magical properties and the power to transform.

The world had seemed solid then, rooted and unchanging. Now, fifty years later, it all seemed insubstantial, the garden where she knelt, the island in its ocean, the ocean in the world and the world just a blue ball spinning unsupported in the sky.

Did she still have decisions to be made? It seemed unlikely. Her own life's solstice had passed many years back. I'd be about late October now she thought. Not a bad month, but not much to look forward to.

Yes there is. She could hear Ray's voice. It all depends on how you look at it; the dying of the year or the season of mists and mellow fruitfulness. You've your life in front of you; make of it what you want. No-one else can live it but you. It's up to you to enjoy these years. Don't wait for someone else to tell you how.

It's true she had been waiting – all her life really – for some outside sign to instruct her when and how to start living. Now Ray was suggesting she make her own way. It was up to her. He

187

was right, she knew. How strange that she had spoken so openly to him that morning. In just half an hour she had told him more about how she felt, how she really felt than she had told George in thirty-six years of marriage. She didn't reject speculating that if those had been thirty-six years with Ray, things and she herself, might be very different.

As she carried on working, the process gradually took away all thoughts of who she was, or what she might have been. Here and now pressed in about her. She was becoming this weed, that flower, even the black beetle scurrying to hide under a pebble, until she was both gardener and garden.

Chapter Sixteen
Summer Solstice – Celia and Helena

"Now is this song both sung and past
My lute, be still, for I have done."
'To His Lute' Sir Thomas Wyatt

"It's the longest day today. How shall we celebrate?" Celia was eating toast while watching Margot zip up a pair of skinny jeans.

"How do I look?" Margot had an interview today with a production company. Jeans and an expensive white linen shirt would send out the right message of creativity and attention to detail.

"Wonderful. Wish I could wear jeans like that."

"You could if you weren't always eating."

That was the second time this week Margot had mentioned her weight. She must know how hurtful it was. And she was slimmer, she was. Everyone had said so at the office.

Two weeks had passed since the weddings and Celia had been worried to notice that instead of the longed-for sense of permanence there had, instead, been a perceptible decline in her relationship with Margot. The 'honeymoon' had never happened. On the contrary, they had virtually no physical contact. In fact Margot seemed to be avoiding it. For the last three nights she had made up a bed on the settee, claiming that she was anxious about the job interview and that her restlessness might disturb Celia. Celia's protests, that she didn't mind at all and would rather have Margot by her side than be alone, fell on deaf ears.

Margot also seemed to spend more time out these days and was often not at home for their frugal meals of pasta. Celia sat disconsolately on her own, watching television and eating and drinking for two. There was the occasional fleeting moment when things seemed to be getting back to how they were, when they laughed together or Margot hugged her, but that first intimacy had gone. They were just two separate people again, living separate lives. Celia became frightened of the future, not just of the upheaval that seemed imminent but of the long and probably empty years to follow.

"Margot shall we go for a walk in the park this evening and then treat ourselves to a meal out? Or maybe go and see Jenny?"

"I don't know what I'll be doing. I'll call you at work."

But she didn't call and she wasn't at home when Celia got back. Neither had she done the shopping, so Celia made cheese on toast and then sat at the window looking over the gardens at the back of the block. It was a warm evening and there were at least another three hours of light. She suddenly longed to be out on this, the longest day of the year. Why not go out on her own into the park? She used to go there a lot before Margot moved in. She'd leave a note, then if Margot got back early she could come and look for her.

She put on an old pair of trainers, left a note on the kitchen table and slipped out onto the busy street.

The traffic was heavy that evening and so were the crowds on the pavements. Everyone seemed to have company and all of them looked as if they had somewhere to go. Celia felt increasingly aimless. She was glad to walk into the relative tranquillity of the park where the trees and the flowerbeds provided her with a legitimate reason for her presence. She was taking a walk, a reasonable enough excuse for being a woman on her own and not an indication that she was some kind of misfit in the process of being abandoned and placed beyond the pale. She spent the next half an hour strolling on the grass and looking at the ducks on the lake. She even sat down on the grass for a while and leaned against a tree, reassured to see other solitary people walking in the evening sun. Perhaps life on her own again would be possible if the worst came to the worst and she and Margot separated.

This prospect had her on her feet again, this time restlessly walking round the Inner Circle, head down examining the toes of her trainers, all the time fighting to control her runaway thoughts. She only realised she was standing outside the Open Air Theatre when she found herself part of a crowd. A performance of A Midsummer Night's Dream was due to start at eight o'clock. There was a 'Sold Out Tonight' notice across the poster. The audience was collecting outside the entrance and Celia mingled with them, envying their sense of excitement and anticipation.

"Are you buying or selling?" he was thirty-something with glasses, unruly dark hair and was sort of jigging on the spot with energy.

"What?" Celia felt a sense of affrontery rising up within her.

"Tickets! Are you buying or selling? I've got some for tonight's performance. Only a tenner. Interested?"

"What are they charging at the box office then?"

"Six fifty." He had an engaging smile.

"I think that's really despicable, making money without working for it. It's just profiteering."

"I agree. It's not what I would choose, but I don't have a choice. I'm going to the anti-capitalist meeting in Seattle this autumn and I need the air fare." He hesitated, and gave a sly smile, "Unless you feel like helping me with that directly. Sort of like sponsorship?"

"As a Marxist I totally approve of what you're going to be doing there. I'd like to go myself in fact. But I don't have the money to sponsor you…"

"All the best people are poor, comrade," he smiled again,

shifting eagerly from one foot to another, "You want the ticket then?"

"I don't even want..." she hesitated, what else had she to do that evening? There would not be a better proposition. And he seemed a nice guy. "All right I will – seeing as it's going to a good cause."

"Just the one?"

Celia looked around just in case by some miracle she could see Margot running along the path to join her, "Yeah."

She gave him two fivers, then pushed her purse back deep into the recesses of her Guatemalan sisal bag. "Good luck with Seattle."

He'd already disappeared into the crowd.

Ticket in hand she joined the throng of people moving slowly into the auditorium, looking for their seats. She found hers on the end of a row and near the back; not the best position for seeing all the action. She didn't mind as it gave her a chance to experience the play as a social event as well as a drama. Already seated in the next seat was an old woman, possibly in her late seventies, a little bent over but with bright brown eyes and smooth skin. She appeared to be on her own as well. She looked benignly as Celia sat down and went back to reading her programme.

The Dream had been the only Shakespeare play that Celia had studied at school. Deconstructionist analysis had penetrated even the conservative environment of her private school and the play had been introduced as an example of the canon of Western Literature, an elitist and now demoted list of 'higher cultural artefacts' instated and revered by mainly Anglo-Saxon men. Her English teacher had helped the pupils tear the play apart, line by line, character by character. They were to note the class consciousness and disparity of power revealed in the language spoken, first by the members of the Fairy Court and then by the so-called 'ordinary people', the mechanicals such as Bottom and Peter Quince. The relationship between Titania and Oberon was subjected to an analysis based on feminism, and the relationship between Titania and Bottom as the Ass was briefly referred to in the context of bestiality. The presence of Puck and the four fairies was seen as evidence of the author's possible paedophiliac leanings and his known homosexuality.

The adolescent Celia hadn't heard any of this. She was absorbed by one single theme - romantic love and the idea that it can exist at first sight, that it transcends all physical inferiority. Obediently she wrote out the theories and literary references from Foucault, Derrida and Lyotard, but her own interpretation, which after all she had been told was as valid as any other, was that love, illusory or not, was all powerful and pervasive. As indeed it was proving to be in real life, the grown up Celia thought to herself, comforted by the realisation that she could still enjoy irony.

"So sorry." Her neighbour was reaching down by Celia's feet. "I've dropped my programme and I think it went under your seat. I wonder if you could..."

"I'll get it." Celia had to stand up and lift the seat before she could find it and hand it over.

"I'm so sorry for making you move. Thank you. You're very kind." The old lady hesitated. "It's always been my favourite of the comedies. So romantic."

Exactly so. And what a beautiful voice she had: old fashioned, clear and well-modulated, a product of education and training.

"You sound like an actress yourself."

"Funny you should say that. I used to enjoy the stage but only as an amateur. I acted quite a lot during the war. For ENSA. Entertaining the troops you know. It was mostly light stuff: Noel Coward, Binky Beaumont...But occasionally we'd put on a Shakespeare. I was always surprised how popular it was with the soldiers. It's not easy to listen to. But there, they sat absolutely still and quiet, taking it all in."

"Were you ever in The Dream?"

"Indeed I was. I played Helena. Which I thought back then

was rather appropriate because that's my real name. Helena. I even fell in love with my Lysander. But his real name was David. He was twenty-five years old. So handsome. Yes, David." She was silent for a few moments. "Terrible business war. He used to call it The Great Game. As if it were a particularly strenuous form of tennis."

"Did he – were you...?"

"Married? No, although we were engaged. People got engaged in those days. He was killed in the last month of the War. I cried for weeks and, I suppose, never got over it. He was so beautiful, you see. There was no-one else for me."

"Sorry, I didn't mean to bring back memories."

"I'm glad to be reminded of David my dear. Not many people are interested in listening, not to an old woman."

"You're not old."

"Oh but I am. I'm eighty-one on Sunday. Eighty-one! It seems incredible to me. It has all passed by so quickly – life I mean. This evening is my birthday treat to myself."

The house lights dimmed and the play started. It was an unremarkable enough production, but the warmth of the air and the diffused light of the setting sun gave the evening a lustre and lyricism that carried Celia and her neighbour into another world. Even the noise of the traffic and the sight of the jet streams in the sky overhead couldn't break the enchantment. At one point – when Helena was alone on the stage with Lysander – Celia leaned over and put her hand on her neighbour's arm, in recognition of a special moment and in remembrance of the long-dead handsome David.

At the interval Celia escorted Helena to the bar and on impulse bought half a bottle of champagne. They drank to birthdays, to lovers and to the second half of the performance. Helena talked a little about her past job as a secretary at the University and her mostly solitary life in a tiny flat in Belsize Park owned by the Women's Secretarial and Clerical Housing Association. She managed, she said, although she found that life in London was getting more difficult. She had been wondering about whether to move in with her friend Amy in her bungalow on the coast in Hampshire. The house had two bedrooms and two bathrooms so the women could be relatively independent, but at the same time they would still have each other for company.

"As you get older life gets so lonely and everything begins to lose its meaning. It all seems to drop away, like leaves from a tree. There's a great temptation to live in the past, it's so much more comfortable. But one must look forward. My dear mother used to say that to me, so I try, you know."

But her friend in Milford-on-Sea had recently gone into hospital and she didn't know when or even if she would be able to come back to live at home again.

"I'd like to come and visit you," said Celia, "I don't live very far away, just off Camden High Road." She could see they could be friends. It would be nice to have someone older to talk to, someone who also knew what it was like to be lonely.

"I would love that my dear. It would give me something to look forward to."

"Perhaps I could come on Sunday. Your birthday. We could celebrate."

It seemed natural to Celia to sit close to her new friend for the second half of the performance and slip her hand around her arm. They occasionally nudged each other over some small incident on the stage, when Peasebottom got his lines wrong or Bottom did some funny business with his ass's head or when the lighting effects were particularly beautiful against the night sky. Then Helena's arm didn't respond to Celia's squeeze and Celia looked sideways and saw that she was sleeping, her head fallen forward on her chest. It was probably the heat and the champagne.

She still hadn't woken up when the play ended. Celia gently disengaged her hand in order to applaud. All in all it had been a magical performance, she was so glad she'd come. The actors took their final curtain call and the audience was standing up and getting ready for going. Helena was still sleeping. Celia gently shook her arm and then again more firmly. But as people pushed past them to catch trains and buses home she was alarmed to see her slump over to one side and stay there, leaning with her head almost touching the arm between the seats. After the last of the audience had moved from their row Celia straightened her up and looked closely at her face. Her eyes were shut but her mouth gaped open a little. Her face had become foxy-looking, the bones suddenly sharp under the waxen skin. There was a profound stillness about her, and an atmosphere of total absence. It was then Celia realised that she was dead.

It must have happened in the last act, sometime during the play within the play. For a moment it seemed vitally important to Celia, although she had no idea why, to find out precisely which words had been the last that Helena had heard. Of course, that was impossible. Anyway what did it matter now?

What to do? Was it embarrassment that prevented her from asking for help from one of the people hurrying out of the theatre, or a sense that such a move would be inappropriate? It somehow seemed more dignified to pretend that she and Helena were sitting there in order to avoid the crowds and were waiting to make their exit in their own time. Celia found a piece of paper in her bag as a sort of displacement activity and wrote down 'Helena' and 'David' then 'Women's Secretarial and Clerical Housing Association' and then 'Amy?' Milford' and 'Hampshire'. Then she rang Margot on her mobile.

"Hi there." Margot sounded in good spirits and maybe a little inebriated.

"Margot it's me. Something terrible has happened."

"Oh hello 'me'. Where are you?"

"I'm at Regents Park Open Air Theatre. I came to a performance and the woman next to me has – well I'm not sure but I think she's dead." She stopped, the emotion of it all suddenly constricting her throat.

"Are you kidding me?" Margot gave an uncertain little laugh.

"What do you mean dead?"

"We got talking. She's quite old. I thought she was asleep but now she won't wake up."

"Doesn't she have anyone with her?"

"No, only me. I don't know what to do."

"You don't have to do anything. Just go tell the man at the gate. Then come home; I've got news."

"I can't leave her Margot. Not on her own here."

"For God's sake Celia this is not your problem. You only just met there right? So it's not your responsibility. Now just go tell the doorman; he'll know what to do."

"OK. I'll try. See you soon."

She put her things away in her bag and stood up slowly. The movement disturbed Helena and she slumped sideways. Celia reached down and gently pulled her upright again. The body felt warm and light and empty, like that of a bird. It would be sensible, as Margot said, to leave, but she just couldn't. So she sat down again and waited by Helena's side, propping her up until the St. John's Ambulance man came to find out why they were still there in the empty theatre.

"Are you a relative?" He was a big man, kind and courteous, with an open face. Helena would have liked him.

"No, we only met this evening. I was sitting next to her and we got talking. Then she..."

"Don't worry love, leave it to me. This kind of thing does happen; it's why we're here. We'll look after her. Let's see if she's got any form of identification."

"I could come with you."

"No need love. We'll get a doctor and after he has confirmed death by natural causes we'll take her on to the morgue. When I find an address book I'll be able to notify her closest relative, if there is one."

"What happens if there isn't? Shall I come with her to the morgue?"

"Don't you worry, we'll sort things out. You'd better give me

197

your name and telephone number just in case we need to get in touch. Then you get yourself home and have a nice cup of tea or something stronger if you will. You've done all you can."

As Celia left the theatre she turned for a last look and saw him politely looking through Helena's handbag as two men with a stretcher arrived. She wasn't sure why she wanted to keep contact with the dead woman but for some reason it seemed so important to tell somebody somewhere who knew Helena and cared about her, how she had spent her last hours and how she was happy when she died.

She walked home in a daze.

"Well I know you've had a shock and everything but you've got to admit, it's not a bad way to go." Margot gave her brightest smile, "Now for the good news. I've got the job. They loved me, I could tell. I can start at the beginning of July. Isn't that wonderful?"

At the end of the longest day of the year Celia lay in bed on her own, smoking. Was it a good way to go? She didn't want to die alone in a theatre with no-one but a friend of two hours' acquaintance; a friend who had not even had the loyalty to see her safely home.

Chapter Seventeen

Summer Solstice – George and Eileen find Love

"My love is like a red red rose that's newly sprung in June."
'A Red Red Rose' R. Burns.

As the evening progressed George was pleased to see that the weather was still warm and dry. Now that the time of the rendezvous was close, he'd become strangely calm and determined.

"Can't remember whether I told you Ellie but, er, I've got to go out later. The Vikings are having a meeting."

"What, down at the pools?"

"No, at Andrew's house. They're arranging some sort of sponsored swim and I said I'd go along to discuss it. Can't let them down as a new boy."

"Where is it?"

"St. Martin's. Said I'd be there shortly after nine. I'll be back before eleven I would imagine, but don't wait up for me. You never know, it may go on a bit."

"That's fine, I thought I'd go out for a walk anyway; it's the longest day and I don't like to miss that."

George had a sudden vision of Eileen happening upon him and Gloria; Icart was a fair walk but not too far for Eileen when she was in the mood.

"Where are you thinking of going?"

"Don't know really – probably over Fort George way."

He gave an inward sigh of relief. "Well, be careful. You never know who might be out there."

"Mmm, true."

Just after nine, George, discreetly tidied up and smelling - subtly he hoped - of cologne, got into the car. 30 B5 here I come, he said to himself, surprised that his hands and legs were trembling with excitement. He opened the window wide so he could breathe in the summer evening better. He felt good. Life had purpose and movement again and he was at the centre of it. He was in a mood to drive quickly, and made a rather daring move at the first roundabout that left the driver of a Ford Escort shaking his fist. Then he overtook a motor cyclist along Fort Road and gunned his engine when they were both at the traffic lights at the Jerbourg Road junction. He even made a false start, as if the lights had changed, and laughed when he saw in the rear view mirror the motor cyclist lurching forward a few yards, then having to brake again. That's what old gits could do when they tried.

As he cruised into the village of St Martin looking for La Route des Coutures, the traffic was pressing him from behind and what few road signs there were couldn't be read in the evening light. He caught himself wishing Eileen were there to help him navigate. Damn – there it was! He'd overshot his road. He'd try the next left and then take a right. When he passed the British Legion hall for a third time he knew something had gone wrong again. How could so small an island be so baffling and have so many roads and so many places? Even the places had places, each with several completely different names. He struck out again and found himself on a painfully narrow road which performed a few right-angle turns before coming to a dead end at a hotel right on the cliff. Nice location but not the one he wanted right now. Guernsey was winning again. He'd have to do what he hated and would do only if absolutely necessary: ask someone the way. As he turned the car around and retraced his route he soon came across a someone, an old geezer walking his old geezer-type dog. Looked like locals. He was bound to know the way.

"Excuse me, am I on the right road for Icart Point?"

"Eeecarr!"

"What?"

"Eeecarr Point. You're at the Fosse here. Out of your way altogether."

"Isn't it round here somewhere?"

"Long way. You want to go back to Les Dooves and turn left. Don't go right or you'll find yourself in Moulan Wet. Don't go down to Saints Bay, and don't go down Route de Saints. And keep away from Marettes otherwise you'll end up in the Villiette! Just keep straight on."

"Thank you, thank you." Clear as mud.

"What you going to be doing on the Point eh?"

"Er, watching the sunset actually." None of your business you prurient rustic fool.

"Is it? You'll see a lot of sunset there. Other things too if you keep your eyes open. Chirri."

George drove away, towards whatever Les Dooves was, baffled.

When eventually, to his surprise, he came to the junction of Icart Road and Rue des Marettes and saw from the map that he was properly on his way, he sat for a couple of minutes trying to restore a sense of equilibrium. By now his heart was thumping with a mixture of anxiety and anticipation at the prospect of seeing Gloria. It was never a good idea to let a woman see that she has that kind of power over you, so he forced himself to think of some of the more boring aspects of his job at Parson and Green in order to calm down: market research presentations for example, the ones that were all pie charts and diagrams with arrows, while academic types said 'On the one hand, but on the other hand...' as they carefully avoided conclusions. Thinking about all that seemed to do the trick, he was soon approaching the car park at Icart, feeling mature and in control, and exactly six minutes before the appointed time.

The tea room had long since closed and there was only one other car parked at the front, overlooking the sea. Was it Gloria's? It looked like her car but it was empty. Maybe she'd already got out and was looking for a place where they could sit down. He drove up and parked alongside but realised it wasn't hers. What now? Should he wait inside or outside the car? He sat for a while, then decided it would look more natural on an evening like this, and avoid the possibility of looking over-eager, if he sat on the bench near the edge of the cliff. From there he would be able to see Gloria approaching and he would appear to her quite relaxed, sitting on the brow of the cliff with the sea behind him, like any innocent man enjoying the evening air.

He'd forgotten how beautiful the headland was. He'd not been in the right mood before when he had walked there with Eileen but now, with the promise of Gloria on her way and with the sun setting over the sea, the golden light making rocks and water rich with colour, he felt it really was rather special. They'd made a good decision when they decided to come to the island. It wasn't just the tax; they had found a lovely place to make their home, small but with everything a man could wish for. Everything. Looking at the huge sweep of the bay it was even hard to think of the island as small and crowded. This evening, for example, he was absolutely on his own, apart from a couple of figures he could see on a far distant part of the coastal path.

He heard before he saw Gloria's car approach. He knew it was her, he could see the gold of her hair. He looked at his watch, she was only a quarter of an hour late, they still had plenty of time. And perhaps it was safer now that the sun had disappeared and it was getting dark. She parked the car briskly at the back near the path into the tea room. As she stepped out he could see she was wearing those red pedal-pusher things and white shoes. He stood up ready to wave, anticipating the feel of her skin and the warmth of those brown hands but she didn't turn

round. Instead she pulled what looked like a rug out of the car, slammed the door then slipped through a gap in the hydrangeas towards the tea room. Better join her. He walked quickly across car park and then padded as silently as he could along the path, intent on creeping up on her and giving her a happy surprise.

He remembered that the tea room had tables and chairs outside, set in a series of small interconnected outdoor 'rooms' created in the middle of dense bushes of hydrangeas. This arrangement provided a degree of privacy, and the bushes helped protect against the prevailing southwest wind. But now it was dark in amongst the shrubbery and the layout wasn't clear. George had to feel his way along until his eyes grew accustomed to the lack of light and he saw her standing by one of the empty tables. He crept silently towards her, his hand outstretched to grasp her backside...

"Don't even think about it!" She didn't sound a happy bunny.

How had she heard him? Even he couldn't hear his own footsteps. Was he was getting deaf, as Eileen kept telling him when he turned up the volume on the television?

"Oh don't look such an old misery. I was only teasing."

She gave him a brief peck on the cheek and didn't struggle too much when he held her to him and kissed her properly and with passion.

"Easy, tiger." She pulled herself free and looked at him, "Now, you've got lipstick all over you and I'd only just put it on."

"You don't know how long I've been waiting to do that." So much for keeping cool and in control he thought. It couldn't be helped.

"Well we haven't got all night. Let's go onto the grass at the back."

He followed her through a sort of tunnel cut through the bushes until they emerged into a small grassy clearing. It was sloping very gently towards the sea but was hidden from the coastal path by a low thick hedge of hawthorn. Behind them the empty tea house and the little garden enclosures were obscured by the hydrangeas. There was no-one to see them or hear them.

"No friends or relations on weekend vacations," sang George.

"What's that?" Gloria asked suspiciously.

"A room with a view and you and no-one to worry us, no-one to hurry us through this dream come true…" He'd several times been told he had a pleasant singing voice. "We've got a room with a view all right. Come here you beautiful woman."

He made a lunge for her but she slipped past him laughing.

"OK lover boy, the show's about to begin. Get your kit off and sit down here while I get ready."

"Are you sure no-one will come?"

"What idiot's likely to be walking round these cliffs in the dark? Go on, live a little."

She spread the rug on the ground and then disappeared behind the bushes.

Ready for what, he thought? He was glad to climb out of his hot jacket and take off shirt and trousers, which he folded up and laid neatly on top of his shoes and socks. Then he lowered himself carefully onto the rug. It was a pleasant sensation as the grass underneath was thick and soft. He lay flat on his back looking up at the darkening sky and thought what a curious thing life is. Just over a year ago I was sitting in an office, with fifteen people reporting to me, spending my waking hours thinking about analgesics and antacids, and here I am today, lying naked on the grass on a cliff top, ten o'clock at night waiting for Gloria to give me a good time. If only they could see me now! Especially that little fool Mitchell whom he always suspected had been laughing at him behind his back. Who has the last laugh now Mitchell, who...

"Ta-ra!" His machinations were halted by the sight of Gloria, a dim figure emerging from behind the hydrangea. He couldn't make out what she was wearing but she had started to hum - "De daa daa dum, de daa daa dum, dum dum dum dum de-daa daa daa daa, de-DUM, de-DUM..." 'The Stripper.' He recognised it from Conference days. As she moved to the music he could just about make out her silhouette against the sky. Then a light came on; she had brought a torch with her which she used to reveal her body one part at a time. First of all a strong brown thigh, then darkness. Now she was facing away from George and shining the torch down her back. She was naked and her body was golden and gleaming in the light. She looked wonderful he thought, and strange, not like an ordinary woman at all but like some kind of high priestess dancing before the gods. He propped himself up on one arm watching her with admiration and a growing desire. Then, the bit he liked best, she shone the light on her breasts which swung above him like huge and irresistible fruit.

She put the torch down, sat beside him on the blanket and felt for him with her hand. He found to his joy that he was ready for her.

"Are you prepared?"

"I'll say." With every fibre of his being.

"I can't feel it."

"What?" This was worrying.

"Have you got a rubber on?"

"What?"

"Which part of the word 'rubber' do you not understand?"

"What?"

"Gawd will you stop saying 'what' like that. Have you or have you not got a rubber on? No? I thought not. Luckily I've brought one with me. It's in my pocket. I'll get it. Amuse yourself for a bit."

She came back, opened the packet and helped him roll it on. "I'm good at remembering a man's size. There, fits a treat."

*

Afterwards George lay back on the rug, eyes closed, heart racing, trying to get his breath back. He was undeniably tired and yet more alive than he had been for what he must now acknowledge were years of dormancy. What he'd just experienced was some sort of emotional, spiritual – what was the right word, existential experience. An epiphany. Yes, that was it! He had been granted a glimpse not simply of Paradise – after all you could get that with a good bottle of Bordeaux – but of an understanding of life's purpose. For the first time he understood himself and the path his life had taken, a path that seemed to have led gradually but inexorably to this moment in place and time. Here and now was the reason for his existence, here and now…

He looked at his watch. Had it only taken seven minutes? Even so it was long enough for the night to have turned chilly and he could feel the grass getting dewy. Reluctantly he started to put on his clothes. Gloria meanwhile had already dressed and was standing by his side ready to go.

"Do you love me Gloria? Because I love you."

She was silent for a second. "Like the man said, 'depends what you mean by love'." She chucked the condom into the hedge, a gesture that gave George a small pang of regret.

"Well it's us, being here, feeling as we do. In our own special world." He'd never spoken like this before and wondered whether perhaps he had gone too far, shown his hand too early, as it were. Nevertheless, what he said had been, was now and would always be, absolutely true.

She shivered and began to rub her bare arms. "Maybe. Now I ought to get back or Steve will think I'm out on the game."

George enfolded her in his new French jacket, his arms round her waist, his face buried in her hair. They were facing the darkness of the sea but the sky was still light above them and the calm air was charged with some indefinable sense of magic. I have never ever been as happy as I am now, he thought, but did not dare to say.

She struggled free and the moment passed.

They made their way back through the bushes into the car park, but as George turned to her, at the door of her car, to try for one last embrace, he were dazzled by headlights from the car parked next to his. He shielded his eyes and the lights were dipped, but to his horror the car came closer and stopped right next to them, the engine still running. George couldn't see who was inside but he then he heard a vaguely familiar female voice.

"I said it was you, didn't I Maureen? Isn't it a beautiful evening for a walk? I can see that you and your wife have been doing the same as we have. God gives his Blessing to the Righteous and to the Sinner alike. We'll be coming to see you next week. Expect us any time – there's so much to talk about."

*

Eileen slipped into her walking shoes shortly after George drove off to his meeting with the Vikings. It was still light enough to see the way across the meadow by the Val des Terres. Instead of turning up into Fort George she decided to go down the footpath and the steps towards the swimming pools. It was a perfect summer evening. She looked around and breathed in deeply. There was a heavy fragrance of freshly-cut grass, which brought back memories of her parents' garden on a summer's day and the whirr and clattering retreat of their old push mower, of herself lying with friends on the school playing fields between lessons, and of clumsy tennis games with an early boyfriend at

the local club. Such happy times.

And I'm happy now she thought, on this evening, to be here, walking across a meadow towards the sea. She followed the path past a small car park and viewing terrace, down through the trees to the steps at Clarence Battery. There she stood at the top for a moment to appreciate the view of the pools, the lighthouse jetty and the water of Havelet Bay, turquoise and silver in the twilight and reflecting a nearly full moon in its smooth surface.

"For lo, the level lake and the long glories of the winter moon…" Only it was the sea and very definitely not winter.

As she made her way down the steps her skirt billowed out around her with the warm air rising from the road. She wasn't so much as walking but floating down, gracefully and without effort, light and carefree as a young girl. She and everything around her was beautiful. Everything, she thought, except the pools, with their uncompromising and severe lines. Nevertheless she climbed the steps to the small terrace of the café built over the changing rooms, sat down on a plastic chair and leaned forward against the wall, enjoying the stone's warmth from the day's sun. By now the growing darkness softened the harsh edges of the pool leading the eye out across dark water.

There was an unexpected muted, oily-sounding splash from below, a 'plop' as if a large fish had lifted out of the water and then slipped back in. Someone, she could see it was a man, had just dived quietly into the pool. He sliced through the water in a leisurely, easy crawl barely breaking the surface of the water. If I could swim properly, she thought, that's exactly how I'd like to do it, at one with the elements, a link between water and sky. Chin on hands, she carried on watching him. After a few minutes the swimmer turned over onto his back and floated to the side, pulled himself up the steps, took off his goggles and shook his head. There was something about the small neatness of the man and of the way he moved, quick but graceful, that even in the dusk she recognised. She leaned cautiously over the parapet to get a better view. As she had thought, it was Ray, her new friend from the computer class. At that same moment he looked up and in her direction. Eileen sat back from the parapet, observer embarrassed at being observed. Her first instinct was to wonder if she could make her escape without being seen, it would be awful if he realised that she had been watching him; even worse, she reflected, if he had already recognised her and were then to see her run away.

The dilemma was an old one. This was how she had always

been, anxious about being seen, of being recognised, and having her motives and feelings not only visible but understood. Highly strung, her mother had said in her defence, allowing Eileen to hide behind her skirts, or to stay on the landing when there were guests for tea, an excuse she'd accepted as part of who she was, a shy girl who was allowed to watch rather than join in.

But today was the summer equinox, the time of revelation, transformation and change. Perhaps it was the strange qualities of this evening that allowed some inner voice – a new inner voice, one she had not heard before – to tell Eileen Buchanan not to retreat but to move forward, be seen and play whatever part was demanded. So she leaned forward and peered over the edge. He was still looking up.

"Eileen? I thought it was you! What are you doing here?"

"Taking a walk. Enjoying the evening."

He shook his head again as if trying to get the water out of his ears.

"Don't run away. I'm going to get some clothes on. Be with you in a minute."

Her first feeling was of triumph. Eileen, the shy and retiring introvert, had said yes to whatever might follow. A second sensation - experienced deep in her gut - was that she was fifteen again and Ray the boy next door. Her heart quickened, her stomach fluttered and she couldn't stop smiling.

"Out on a walk, on your own?" He sat down beside her.

"It's a beautiful evening."

"Yeah, that's why I came for a swim. I usually come in the morning."

"And it's the longest day."

"Ah yes, the twenty-first. All downhill from here on in then!"

"Mmm, a bit like that. I always try to celebrate it somehow."

"I've got just the very thing." He took a small bottle of cognac out of his kit bag and poured a tot into the cap and handed it to her. "Here's to the longest day", then took a swig from the bottle while she sipped at the full cap, "and here's to us."

"To us?" Oh goodness, she could feel herself blushing, thank heaven it was getting dark.

"We're friends, aren't we?"

"It's easy to be with you Ray, I don't know why."

"Chemistry, Eileen. We're on the same wavelength."

"Physics then as well?"

"Bad girl! No second helpings for you". He laughed and took another mouthful from the bottle. "You know very well what I mean. We understand each other. That's just the way it is. We're a good fit."

They sat together in peaceful silence as the sky and the sea grew dark and purple in the warm air. The lights of Herm and of more distant Sark were twinkling away on the horizon. Perhaps, she thought, there are couples over there at this moment sitting side by side looking out towards Guernsey, towards the pools and towards Ray and Eileen.

When they eventually stood up to go their separate ways home she wasn't sure what she wanted to have happen next. Ray smiled as if he knew how she felt and leaned forward, kissing her on the cheek, a little awkwardly but lingering long enough for her to smell the salt from the sea on his skin.

"We'll be seeing each other then, down at the computer centre? Now take care of yourself and don't speak to any strange men or I'll be jealous."

At the precise moment he said this, in the Regent's Park theatre Celia had linked arms with her new friend, and George was lying like a god on the grass at Icart Point. The magic of the longest day had touched them all; the world had stopped in its tracks. Who was to say that new and wonderful things would not happen?

Eileen, at least, walked back up the Havelet, with a joyful heart.

Chapter Eighteen
Friday June 22nd

"And calmly as if indifferent quite,
you would close your terms here,
up and be gone." 'The Going' T. Hardy

At a quarter to six the next morning George swung his legs over the side of the bed and, after two attempts got to his feet, and lurched stiffly towards the bathroom. That grass must have been damper than he'd thought. Would he be making additional trouble for himself by spending another session in the the pools this morning? Probably, but now he was up he might as well get on with it. Besides it was a matter of principle; when the going gets tough the tough go swimming. He looked at himself in the mirror. His clear adulterous eyes stared back. He definitely looked younger, shame he could hardly walk.

He found his swimsuit and towel in the airing cupboard, put on his sailing jacket and quietly closed the front door so as not to wake Eileen.

Nature rewarded his self discipline with a perfect morning. The sun was well up and he could already feel its heat. There was no wind and the sea was flat calm. He took the car down the Havelet and along La Vallette.

"Thought you'd given up on us. Thought mebbe we weren't good enough for you." Don had already changed and was putting on his goggles.

"I had things to do," said George smugly, turning to go into the changing room.

"I wonder what that could have been? Whatever it was, by the state of that jacket, it must have involved a lot of lying around in the grass. By 'eck look at the fellow, he's bloody blushing like a girl."

George started brushing off the grass from the back of his jacket.

"Give him a break, Don, you're only jealous."

"You're right there, I am. Someone do a forensic on that jacket and find out where the bugger's been. Might still be some left over. No wonder he's walking funny."

"I'm stiff, that's all."

"Bloody boasting again." Don jumped into the water, and the others soon followed.

"So what have you been up to then?" Ray asked later, when the swimming was done and the others had left.

"Nothing," said George too quickly, with a sideways look.

"Managed to seduce the woman next door yet?"

"What?"

"The one you said had beautiful knockers."

"Did I?"

"Yes, you did, last time we met. You said you liked a woman with a lot on top, like the woman next door."

"Oh her!" George hesitated. He longed to be able to talk about Gloria. Half the pleasure of all his office affairs had been when they became common knowledge around the department. There was a change in the way the men spoke to him and how they looked at him: amused, envious, respectful. Wouldn't Ray be surprised if he knew, and wouldn't he be jealous if he saw Gloria? Maybe when their relationship had settled down into something more permanent he could mention it in casual conversation - 'My girl friend says this' or 'Oh there's a friend of mine over there, come and say hello...' He imagined Gloria in her yellow dress meeting him at the pool and the stir it would cause when the men realised that she had come for him. But of course that wouldn't be a wise move. Guernsey was a small island with a joyfully inquisitive population. It was better to at least try and keep things quiet.

"No, nothing's happened. It was only wishful thinking. What about you?"

"Funnily enough I've met someone since I last saw you." Ray gave a sly smile.

"Good God. You haven't found a Chinese girl here?"

"No. She's as English as they come. About my age, too. Nice looking but nothing fancy. Quiet, thoughtful type. There's just something about her. I feel good when I'm with her."

"You mean she turns you on?"

"I feel at home with her. It's a good feeling. Natural."

"Amazing how some bodies have just what it takes."

"I'm not really talking bodies. I've not even touched her like that."

"You mean just looking is enough?" George pictured Gloria's golden breasts. "I can understand that."

"Yes, in a way."

"Married?"

"Yes but not particularly happily. It's the old story, he's got too used to her and she feels neglected."

"Have you seen him?"

"No. She was alone when I met her. She's in my class at the college."

"Any sign she feels the same way about you?"

"I'm not sure. I hope so."

"What do you intend doing?"

"Bide my time. Wait and see."

George looked at Ray's small frame, his sparse grey hair and the dragon tattoo on his forearm. The woman, whoever she was, might be plain and middle-aged but what, he wondered, would she ever see in a man like Ray? Andrew was more the sort of man a woman prefers; he was older but he still looked good in his clothes and had an authoritative air, the sort who opened car doors and knew which wine to choose. Women liked that. No, whoever it was that Ray fancied, she was unlikely to reciprocate.

"Where's Andrew by the way?"

"We probably won't see him until next week. His wife died three years ago at this time. Cancer. He was very upset. Don't think he can face seeing people what with it being the anniversary. It was the same last year."

The thought of Andrew and his wife stayed on George's mind as he finished dressing. Some people said cancer could be brought on by depression or from feeling unloved and neglected. He had a sudden urge to get back home and make sure Eileen was all right. He drove briskly up the hill, glad that he still had a wife, and looking forward to his breakfast.

*

Eileen had heard George close the front door quietly followed by the sound of the car as he drove down to the pools. She had been half awake for some time, mulling over the events of the previous evening specifically when Ray had made what was almost a declaration of love. She lay there savouring the notion. After all these years someone had expressed interest in her. That someone was a nice intelligent and perceptive man, who'd probably had many lovers, but nevertheless saw something special in her. She turned the idea around in her mind very cautiously. She'd thought it would never happen again, that she was finished with all that. What did she mean by 'all that'? Not sex, well maybe sex but not just sex; other things like intimacy, partnership, true friendship, romance. To be in a relationship meant being part of things again, part of the energy that made poets write their poetry and artists paint their masterpieces, part of the energy that made the world go round.

Of course Ray could have just have been sweet-talking, or even under the influence of the cognac. Or perhaps the both of them had come under the spell of the evening's warmth and the fact it was longest day. Whatever it was, just for now she was going to enjoy the feeling of being properly alive again, of being in touch. She lay on her back in the middle of the bed looking up at the patterns made by the early sunlight on the ceiling.

Later, as she stepped into her bath she assessed herself swiftly and dispassionately. Her romantic life, surely, was over. She could not imagine that her body invited an embrace, let alone had the power to excite a man. Year by year she'd noted the loss of her appeal, as her waist thickened and the flesh grew slack, until she realised she could walk in public totally unwatched. It's true what they say, she thought; after a certain age women become invisible. Maybe Ray just had something platonic in mind; a close friendship centred on what might have been. In a way that would be easier, and maybe sufficient. She lay back in the hot water and had just closed her eyes when she heard the sound of cars and a screech of tyres. Surely that couldn't be George back so early? There were car doors slamming and the crunch of shoes on gravel, then voices, male and loud. She hurriedly got out of the bath, wrapped a towel around her and went to the window. There were two police cars on the drive in front of Steve and Gloria's house. A couple of policemen were going around to the back of the building, while the others stood at the front door. She heard Steve's voice and then she saw the men enter the house. Something was definitely wrong.

Twenty minutes later, dressed and downstairs, she peered out of the front window; the police were still there. It must be something serious. As she went into the kitchen to make breakfast she was relieved to hear the front door being closed and George's footsteps in the hall. She hurried to meet him.

"George something odd is happening next door. There were five policemen – they came about twenty minutes ago – and surrounded the house, and they're still there. Two of them went round to cover the back door, as if they expected Steve and

218

Gloria to make a run for it."

George stood transfixed at the threshold but, before he could reply, there was the sound first of the doorbell and then an urgent knocking at the door.

"Leave this to me Ellie." George said as he went to the front door. "I'll deal with them. You stay out of it."

Eileen did as he said, but stationed herself next to the open door of the kitchen and watched and listened. She caught a glimpse of the Constable, a heavily set man in his fifties. He had a blank expression in his eyes, no doubt acquired through long practice at being inscrutable. By contrast his hair, thick and blonde and lively, sprang out from under the rim of his cap like an errant halo. He stepped towards the threshold as if expecting to be asked inside, "Sorry to bother you at this hour sir, but I'd like to ask you a few questions."

Instead of inviting him in George walked out onto the porch, half closing the door behind him. Eileen had to move into the hall and stand listening by the foot of the stairs to catch what they were saying. She heard George say, "No, they're very quiet...good neighbours." Then the Constable asked a question, of which she only heard fragments, which sounded like "possibility...asked you to store stolen goods...shed or garage?" to which George answered with "Good Heavens no." Then the Constable said something else ending with "Thank you, sorry to disturb..." at which point she slipped back into the kitchen. She heard the front door shut and then there was George, looking troubled and pale.

"What did they want?"

"Nothing much. Just whether we'd heard anything suspicious in the neighbourhood."

"Suspicious in what way?"

"Unusual noises or comings and goings..."

"Why were they interested in next door?"

"I don't know if they were particularly."

"But I saw them. Two of their men went round to the back

door while the others went to the front. That's not normal is it?"

"I don't know, do I? Maybe they haven't paid their taxes or something. It could be a million things." George sighed irritably to show that the matter was closed. "Anyway it's nothing to do with us. I'm going upstairs to change. I'll have my breakfast when I come down."

Eileen looked out of the window in the hall and after a few minutes saw the police drive away down the hill. George hadn't told the truth, either to the Constable or to her. Why? Could he be protecting Steve in some way? If so, why would he be doing that? What was in their garage anyway? She hurried into the dining room and opened the drawer. The second key was still there. She took it and hid it in the inner pocket of her handbag. She would look in the garage for herself at the very first opportunity.

*

Celia slept fitfully and on her own. She had half expected to have nightmares about death and decay but when she eventually awoke at seven thirty, she could not remember having dreamed at all. It was a sunny morning and she could hear Margot on the telephone in the sitting room, where obviously she had spent the night. Who could she be talking to so early and with such animation? She was still talking when Celia emerged from the bedroom dressed and ready for work.

"Must go now." Margot put down the phone and smiled at Celia. She was wearing her striped blue and white nightshirt, her hair fluffed out and her face shiny and happy. "Hi honey. Did you sleep well?"

Celia wanted to ask her what was going wrong between them but now was not the time; she was chairing the monthly cross-departmental meeting at nine and she hadn't read the minutes from the last meeting yet. She perched awkwardly on the arm of the settee.

She took a deep breath, "Margot, can we please talk sometime?"

Margot's eyes widened, but whether in real or mock surprise Celia was not sure. "But we talk all the time, hon. That's what I've always valued about our being together."

"No, I mean talk about us."

To Celia's surprise and relief Margot's face relaxed and looked serious. She nodded her head slowly. "Sure, we can do that. Whenever you say so, I'll be ready to talk about whatever it is you want to talk about."

"Oh Margot, you don't know how relieved I am to hear that."

Margot stood up and again to Celia's surprise, put her arms around her and gave her a little hug.

"I know you had a terrible shock yesterday with that woman in the theatre. But don't let it get to you. You'll be fine, just fine."

Celia felt herself on the point of getting weepy, so disentangled herself and wiped her eyes. "Thanks for that. I must go now; this meeting is absolutely key. See you this evening. I'll be home as soon as I can. I'll get supper, something really nice and we'll sit and talk."

"You get off now for your meeting," said Margot, and then, with unusual intensity, "take care, be brave." She blew a kiss.

In her office, preparing for the meeting and feeling more positive, Celia began to think about what she should do about last night. She had been wondering if she should try and find where Helena's body had been taken, and see if there was anything she could do to help tidy up her affairs. Margot's unexpected display of affection strengthened her resolve.

She bluffed her way through the cross-departmental meeting by making constant referrals to past clauses in past minutes which needed resolution before they could proceed. It was a tactic that she had often observed others using and despised them for it, but today it was necessary. When she was not pointing out, metaphorically and literally some abstruse legal point or potential procedural difficulty, her eloquent fingers jabbing the air with emphasis, she sat back, as if listening to the counter arguments as they shot around the table, but in reality remembering how Helena's dead weight had been no weight at all.

When at last the meeting was over and the members of the sub-committee on Ethnic Minority Women's Self-Help Group started to collect outside the door, Celia bustled out, ignoring invitations to wander over to the canteen and carry on talking about the morning's unresolved issues.

During the coffee break that morning she had rung the St. John's Ambulance local office and found that Mr. Burrows the kindly faced man who had rescued her from a night spent in the stalls, had called an ambulance and accompanied Helena's body to the mortuary at King's Cross. He thought they were still trying to trace any relatives. Celia decided she would go to King's Cross herself on the way home.

The woman in the gloomy reception area of the mortuary was appropriately sallow-faced and painfully thin, as well as unhelpful. No, Celia could not see the dead woman or access her file, unless she had proof of relationship to the deceased. Celia was relieved. She really hadn't wanted to view the body and could barely contemplate the atmosphere she expected to encounter in the mortuary itself. Death had not been part of her life so far. It would be so much more comfortable to walk away. Anyway, rules are rules. Then she remembered Helena's face as she sipped her glass of champagne during the interval and her words, "This is the first time I've had champagne in a very long time". She thought about how she herself had been looking forward to seeing Helena again at the weekend, of looking after her, of buying her the occasional treat and offering a measure of protection. That was the nub of it; Helena would have been someone to love and Celia was not ready for her to disappear so soon after coming into her life. She needed to find out whether there was someone who would want to share Helena's death with her, and here and now at the mortuary was her only chance.

"Be brave", she said to herself and thought about the warmth of Margot's embrace that morning. She didn't have to accept the status quo. She was strong. She wouldn't be defeated.

"I'm with the Council myself actually. Celia Buchanan, Head of the Department for Amenities for the Disabled. I work with John Nicholson and Freddy Truscott – if you've heard of them. And Ken of course from time to time."

Celia put her card on the desk and the receptionist studied it carefully with obvious respect, and then gave a wan smile.

"Sorry about the rules here. It sometimes feels as if we're completely cut off from the outside world. It's like everything exciting is happening elsewhere."

"You ought to think about moving across sometime; it's quite easy if you know the right people."

"I've often thought I'd like a job in a room with a window."

"I'm sure that's possible. Give me your name and if you're wanting to make some sort of career change, just let me know. There's a number of positions that you might find interesting. You can contact me any time."

The sallow face lightened a little. "That's very kind of you Ms Buchanan. Look, seeing as how you're a senior colleague, if you want to, go in for a few minutes.... If anyone asks I'll say you're her niece."

"That is kind of you. I won't be long."

"Don't you want my details?"

"Er, why don't you write them out and I'll pick them up on the way out?"

The man in charge, a grey-faced Scot in a grubby white coat, led her into a big cold room, which was well lit and silent. When the moment came, Celia turned down the offer to view the body. After all, what was there but an empty shell? She did ask if she could access the locker containing Helena's belongings. The Scot went elsewhere leaving her while she gently searched among the woollen coat and the scarf, still with a few silver

223

hairs clinging to them, and found the handbag. It was an old fashioned bag of soft black leather with a metal clasp and as she opened it there was a delicate lavender fragrance that Celia thought she could identify as Mitsouko. Inside, amongst handkerchiefs, ticket stubs, a receipt, comb, powder compact and a half-finished roll of peppermints, she found what she had hoped would be there, a small leather-covered address book.

The book had obviously been in use for many years. The cover had a soft silky patina and it was nearly full, the pages covered with a precise cursive hand. As Celia turned the fragile pages, she noticed that most of the entries had been altered, sometimes several times, and many were scored through. She soon realised each entry was a record of life unfolding, from youth through to maturity's prime, then to widowhood, from there to decline and dependency and eventually to being crossed out, to having no address at all.

Thus, 'Maureen Noble, 27 Kensington Church Street, London W8' expanded into 'Mr. and Mrs. J. Amhurst, Pauline and Jeremy, 'Hunters Moon', Beaulieu Road, Brockenhurst, Hants', then dwindled to 'Mrs. M. Amhurst, Flat 4, Bedford Close, Lyndhurst, Hants SO4 3JB', and in a slightly shaky hand was reduced to 'Maureen, c/o Forest Residential Home, Lyndhurst, SO4 3RD', and was finally crossed through with two wavering lines.

Most of the few remaining intact addresses were functional: the doctor's surgery, the dentist, a grocer's shop that delivered, the oil suppliers, the University Women's Association Trust. These were the remnants of Helena's world. One single exception, not yet scored through was 'Amy Randall, 'Island View', Keyhaven Road, Milford-on-Sea, Hants.' Celia wrote down address and telephone number, carefully replaced the book and closed the bag.

"If no-one comes forward to claim the contents of the locker, do you want us to contact you?"

She nodded and filled in the form. She would like to have

224

the scarf with the sad stray hairs, and the handbag with its aura of Guerlain. Then, somehow relieved and re-energised and just about remembering to take the card from the receptionist on her way out, she emerged into the light of day.

On her way home, she stopped at the delicatessen and bought smoked fish, Lebanese salads, pitta bread and some American-style cheesecake. At the off licence she chose two bottles of Sauvignon Blanc and a tin of mixed nuts. Stopping every now and again to set her bags down and ease her fingers she made her way home slowly but contentedly. Good living was the best revenge.

It took but half a minute, once she had crossed the threshold, to realise that something terrible had happened.

The shock came in waves. The first impact made her set down the bags with a thump. Margot's coats and Celia's raincoat and umbrella were missing from the rack in the tiny hall. The telephone directory had been left open on the little table alongside an empty paper bag and the remains of a sandwich. The telephone itself was missing.

The next shock was in the kitchen. There was washing up left in the sink and the door of the dryer was open as if someone, presumably Margot, had just removed a load of laundry. An empty cardboard box and several plastic bags from the local supermarket were littering the floor. Celia's new radio had gone together with the emergency cash tin they kept on the top shelf. Gone, too, were her best big plates, nearly all the cutlery, the wine glasses, the carving knives in their block and the corkscrew.

The settee in the sitting room was still made up as a bed, with the sheets in a tangle and the pillow on the floor but the handsome tartan blanket bought at a sale in Liberty's was not there. There were big gaps in the bookshelves: dictionaries, the Times World Atlas, a Thesaurus and the Book of Quotations had gone. So too had the computer and printer, two new boxes of floppy discs and an untouched box of paper. The television and the Victorian bronze statue they had bought together at Camden Lock with Celia's money had also gone.

The scene in the bedroom was the same. Her sheets, the new ones she had bought to celebrate Margot's moving in, had been taken from the bed, together with the two new down pillows and the duvet. Margot's cupboard was bare apart from a few pieces of old and dirty underwear that had been left on the floor. Celia opened her own wardrobe; the clothes had been disturbed but nothing appeared to have been taken. Then she realised that her favourite grey silk kurta wasn't there, neither were her two pashmina shawls. The drawer in her bedside table was partly open; her favourite earrings were missing; so too the gold bangle and the garnet brooch that had belonged to her grandmother.

The bathroom was still warm and smelled of Margot's perfume. She must have left the flat only an hour or two earlier. The doors of the bathroom cabinets were open and all her cosmetics had gone. The bottles and tubes that littered the top of the vanity unit belonged to Celia. There was a rim of scum round the bath and a few long black hairs were blocking the plug hole. The plug itself was not there.

Margot, her glorious, exotic bird, had flown the nest.

Celia spent the evening listening to her old crackly radio and working her way through every bit of the food and wine she had bought for their romantic supper. If she was going to be alone in the universe then she might as well be as big as the universe. At the end, as she sat back amongst the crumbs and the odd wine stain, she felt a growing sense of resentment and for the first time allowed her misgivings about their relationship to surface and find words. If Margot had sometimes appeared to be selfish and scheming that's because she was - a selfish scheming greedy cheating bitch. So bugger Margot. Bugger love. Celia Buchanan hated the world and everyone in it and she would never be fooled by anyone ever again. From this moment she would dedicate herself to Camden Council and her career and to becoming the embodiment of Ms Hatchet-Face, Rosa Klebb, Cruella de Ville – the Woman from Hell.

The tears came later, firstly when she lay down in her bed, newly made up with the old sheets and blankets that Eileen and George had given her for college, and again the next morning, when she stepped out of the shower and was startled to see, in Margot's handwriting, the words 'Have a nice life!' revealed in the steamy mirror.

Chapter Nineteen
Saturday June 30th

"Life is just one damned thing after another."
Frank Ward O'Malley

On Saturday afternoon Eileen stood with hand outstretched; the telephone had rung once, and then was silent. George must have picked it up in the next room. Why was he so eager to answer the phone these days? She was tempted to lift the receiver and find out who it was, but thought better of it. It seemed a cheap thing to do and, besides, George would be angry if he heard her. He had been especially irritable and impatient over the past few days; she'd been glad to spend time at her computer class or get out into the garden and be away from him.

She had still not been able to explore the contents of the garage; it was tricky with George lurking around the house all the time. There was no way she could raise the subject and talk openly about it with him; some divide had been created whereby he needed to lie to her. If she wanted to find out what was behind the lie she would have to work it out for herself. All of this just when she thought the need for subterfuge had long passed.

Her mood lifted at the thought of Celia's arrival. She had rung the evening before, sounding depressed and, it must be said, as if she'd had a drink or two. Could she come over this weekend for a couple of days? Of course, said Eileen, surprised and delighted, whenever you can get a flight. It was always wonderful to see Celia, but right now she also welcomed her as a source of moral support.

*

"Fourteen Four C. The bird hide. Six thirty tonight."

"Where have you been? I thought you'd never ring – I've been waiting - I mean yes, yes! Fourteen Four C. Six thirty. Bird Hide?"

She'd put the phone down. He'd said 'yes' but had no idea there was a bird hide on the island, let alone its location. He got the map, now kept in the kitchen where once it had been in the car. Indeed, on page fourteen, in square 4C, there was a tiny bird symbol on the edge of what seemed to be a small nature reserve off Rue d'Enfer in Castel parish. That must be it. It was only as he put the map in the car that he remembered that Celia's plane was due to land at eight o'clock. Whatever he and Gloria managed to get up to in the bird hide they'd have to be damn quick about it. Not a problem from his point of view.

Despite some relief from hearing from her at last, George did not feel any easier in himself. Ever since his encounter with the constable on Friday morning he'd been in a state of high anxiety. He had lied when they asked him if he had been approached by his neighbour to store anything for him. He'd not dared to tell the truth, and the reason for that was because he was sleeping with his neighbour's wife. If Steve found out then George had no doubt that he would be in very real trouble. Steve was not only physically powerful, he obviously had some sort of criminal tendencies, and therefore, presumably, was capable of professionally punitive behaviour. The word 'kneecaps' came to mind.

What the hell had he been given to keep in the garage? How he wished that he had never said yes and that he hadn't given

Steve the key. He didn't dare ask for it back. He couldn't talk to Eileen about it because she would ask why he didn't go to the police. For the time being all he could do was pretend that it wasn't happening. But however much his mind told him to forget the incident, his body was working to a different, more troubled agenda. He couldn't sleep properly and when he was awake he couldn't concentrate. All the time he seemed to be waiting for the telephone, or the knock on the door or the sound of cars on gravel. The benefits acquired from his new healthy regime were rapidly dissipating: he was feeling more tired and had acquired an irritating new symptom, a nervous twitch of his left eyelid that gave him an air of perpetual conspiracy. Equally worrying was the realisation that he wasn't sure he could cope with seeing Gloria again, not in that sort of way. The police business had produced a nasty effect on his libido in so far as over the last few days it had completely disappeared.

Things had seemed so innocent to start with; just a little indulgence, a little foolishness with another man's wife, but now he could feel himself getting deeper into the mire. He sat in this troubled state in his study for another couple of hours until six o'clock.

"Got to pop down to see Andrew about this sponsored swim event so I'll pick up Celia on the way back. That will give you a chance to get on with supper."

He could tell that Eileen was disappointed – she liked going to airport herself and waiting for Celia – but needs must when the devil drives, he thought as he sped down Victoria Road to the Grange. He then drove up towards Castel church crossroads, went straight over at the lights and at the bottom of Rue de Preel turned left towards Kings Mills. He slowed down so as to find the narrow entrance of Rue d'Enfer. As he did, he heard motorbikes coming up fast behind him. There were three youngsters all with L-plates, revving their engines and sounding their horns as if to speed him up. The high granite walls magnified the sound and George drove with gritted teeth,

trying to find his turning. Shut up you little bastards he mouthed at them in his rear view mirror, before suddenly seeing his road and slamming on the brakes. The boy leading the trio only just managed to avoid running into the back of the car but veered across the road and up onto the pavement. The boy at the back, who braked too late and too hard, skidded and collided with the wall but managed to stay upright. George didn't have time to see what happened to the third rider but swung the car round the corner and drove smartly down the hill, not bothering to conceal his smile. That'd teach 'em.

The bird hide was about four hundred yards down, and a few yards from the road, half hidden in a corner thick with trees and hedges. There were two parking spaces and both were empty. George swung his car to a standstill with a flourish and looked at his watch. Five minutes early. He stepped out of the car to have a look around. The hide, a small wooden shed, painted in blotches of green and brown camouflage, was surrounded by long grass and tucked half behind a low hedge of hawthorns. Very discreet. He found the door, drew the bolt and stepped inside. There was a bolt on the inside as well, which he slid it across experimentally; they could use this to keep themselves nicely private.

There were two viewing windows opposite the door and a thin hard bench beneath them. He sat down in front of one of the windows and opened the hatch. The nature reserve was a boggy-looking field surrounded by trees, enclosing a small pond. There were a few birds on the water, nothing very colourful or interesting as far as he could tell. He fastened the hatch into the open position and sat watching for several minutes, wondering at the motivation of birdwatchers. The bench was uncomfortable and he couldn't think how Gloria had expected they would get up to anything, let alone enjoy themselves. Maybe all she wanted to do was talk; tell him what Steve was up to and why the police had come on the scene. He was just thinking she was late again when he heard a car stop and park alongside his. His heart beat faster, despite himself. There was a scrabbling noise as she tried to open the door; he leapt up and unbolted it.

"Hold on sweetheart, I'm ready for you."

A tall thin man in an anorak, festooned with birding equipment, stood at the threshold.

"Sorry, I thought it was – er – someone else." George tried to show his displeasure, willing the man to go away.

"Sorry, I didn't know it was locked." The figure, unfazed by George's grimace continued to stand at the threshold. "Can I come in?"

"What? Well, I'm going to be here for a bit. And then my friend will be here soon." He realised his voice sounded petulant and unconvincing.

"There's room isn't there? For three I mean?" He peered over

George's shoulder indicating with a nod of his head the benches that would take at least four people.

"It'll be a bit squashed," said George severely.

But the man was inside, and getting organised. He put his tripod down, struggled out of his anorak and sat on one end of the bench, setting out his binoculars, telescope, notepad and pencil and a loosely wrapped packet of what smelt like cheese and pickle sandwiches in front of him on the narrow ledge.

"What have you seen so far?" Then without waiting for a reply. "I've just had a dotterel down at Lihou."

"Have you now? That's good. Yes, jolly good."

"I'll give you the coordinates if you're interested. There'll still be time to catch it later this evening." He leaned forward looking out of the hatch. "I see the herons are still here."

Damn, thought George, where is she?

"Forgotten your gear? You can use these if you like." He offered George the binoculars, who decided there was nothing for it but to settle down and watch a pair of herons as they went about their domestic duties on the lake. Twenty minutes before Celia's plane was due to land he decided that Gloria was not coming. He said goodbye to the man in the anorak, returned the hope that they would meet again, then drove back up to Kings Mills. He turned left up Rue du Compte and took the cross-country route to the airport. He was struck by the absurdity of what he had just done – spent an hour in a shed waiting for a woman who never turned up, even if she had a good reason. It was not what a man of his age should be doing and for the first time since he met Gloria that time at the airport it crossed his mind that maybe he was losing interest in the whole affair.

One of the bad things about growing older is performance failure, he said to himself as he parked the car and walked towards arrivals, but, on the other hand, one of the good things is lack of desire. Although he would be eternally grateful to Gloria for the interest she had aroused and revived in him, he wasn't sure how much longer he wanted things between them to go on. It was such hard work, not just the sex itself, but all the subterfuge that went with it. And uncomfortable! His bottom was still numb from this afternoon's wooden bench.

Celia's plane was delayed. He sat down in a corner of the airport, well away from the other people waiting, grateful for half an hour of uninterrupted nothingness and a relatively comfortable chair.

*

Eileen was preparing sea bass for the oven. If there was one good thing about Guernsey it was the fish. This one was a beauty, plump and fresh, its eyes still bright and the scales silvery black. She filled the stiff body with chopped fennel, ginger and lemon and then wrapped it in buttered foil. She scraped new potatoes, peeled carrots and shelled fresh peas. Then she made the salad: early tomatoes, olives and fresh basil and, separately, a bowl of rocket, avocado and walnuts. She was just in the middle of making the dressing when she heard the doorbell.

Two middle-aged women stood at the front door dressed in a strangely dated fashion: flowery summer frocks and what looked like home-knitted cardigans. Their thin legs were bare and both wore sandals and white ankle socks. They had eager faces, more like elderly girls than women, as if they had never left school, but had been stranded for fifty years in the Upper Sixth by some administrative oversight. One stood smiling, a small leather document folder clutched under her arm. The other was burying her face into the roses climbing the trellis to the porch. They brought with them an air of innocence, sanctity and, Eileen thought, just a hint of menace.

"Oh hello, good afternoon. Such beautiful flowers. I always say don't I, Maureen, that where there are flowers there is love. Now, my dear, you are not who we were expecting. We were expecting a man, weren't we Maureen?"

"My husband is out." Eileen felt uneasy. "Who shall I say

called?"

"I'm not sure we have the right house. The gentlemen we want was with his wife and I don't think it was you. No, you're definitely not his wife. Icart Point last Thursday evening? We'd been for a walk on the Coastal path – it was such a lovely evening – and he and his wife had been doing the same. We told him we'd pop in and see him. We must have the wrong house don't you think so Maureen?"

"I remember our man is called George." Maureen said with a proprietorial air. "Do you know if there is a 'George' living in this road?"

"My husband is George."

"But you don't look like his wife. His wife had red hair, didn't she Maureen? We both…" She stopped with her hand to her mouth. "Oh I hope I'm not saying something I shouldn't. Oh dear, I do apologise if I've…." She trailed away uncertainly.

"Why do you want to see him?"

Maureen rummaged in her bag and pulled out her pamphlets. "We've brought him some reading matter. We promised we would. It's all about the love of God and the forgiveness of sins."

Afterwards Eileen closed the door and stood very still in the hall, clutching the pamphlets. Thursday night had been the longest day, the night when George said he was seeing the swimming club members about the sponsored swim. The women claimed to have seen him on Icart Point that evening with someone they had assumed was his wife, a woman with red hair. It seemed unlikely but I could only mean one thing – he was up to his old tricks. Was that possible? Here on the island?

She went back into the kitchen. Yes, she decided, it was. All the strange happenings of the last few weeks fell into place; the mysterious telephone calls, the new clothes, the irritability. She should have recognised the signs, but it had been some years since the last time. She had thought he was over that type of thing now.

But who was the mystery woman? They hardly knew anyone who could be described as desirable, let alone a siren with red hair. A second later the answer came to her with absolute certainty; of course, who else but Gloria!

She sat down and let the idea sink in. It was obvious that Gloria had sex appeal and that she was well aware of the impact she made. Eileen had not forgotten that first evening, when they all had drinks together: Gloria's clothes, her inappropriate laughter, the way she found an excuse to touch people, to stroke them physically and emotionally. George was middle-aged, vain and vulnerable and he had time on his hands, lots of it. He would be so easy to seduce, even for someone with fewer charms than Gloria.

Why on earth would Gloria be interested in George? That was much more difficult to understand. George had some money but he was not what you could call wealthy, not in the context of Guernsey. Steve could surely match him in that area, and was young enough to have a future, to make himself even wealthier. Could it be simply a matter of lust? Perhaps with Gloria, George was an impassioned and skilled lover. Eileen considered this for a moment, trying to imagine the same George who had difficulty getting out of a low chair transformed into a sexual athlete.

Maybe Gloria was bored with Steve and just wanted to try her hand, as it were, with someone within easy reach. Perhaps it gave her a sense of power to have another man become besotted with her. George was still handsome in his way and relatively well-preserved for his age, but even so...

What should she do? If she confronted him, that could just drive the affair underground and, possibly, give it an extra spice and excitement. It might be better just to leave it to run to its natural conclusion as she had done so many times before. One of them, surely, would sometime soon decide that it was over? Unless of course it was true love; an absurd idea but the world was full of absurdities. She tentatively explored the scenario of coming home from shopping, say, or from her computer class, to find George packed and ready to leave for a new life with Gloria.

Leaving her alone. What would that be like, living alone, really for the first time in her life? Her first thought was – not all bad. She had always put George and Celia's comfort before her own, and it was only now that she realised that she had been waiting subconsciously for some sort of sign from them that they were aware of this and knew that it was basically unfair. She had vaguely expected that the one way flow of altruism would some day be reversed, that the wind would change and it would suddenly be her turn. But recently she realised that what she thought had been her gift to them had been assumed by them to be their right. Over the years they had grown into being the two alpha members of the family and she had become a fixture at the bottom of the pile, the daily help, cook and chief bottle washer, the all purpose drudge. She could now see that they would never voluntarily change: and why would they want to?

So living alone would bring new freedoms and the possibility of, at last, compensation for some of those sacrifices. Things would be different without George. She could keep whatever hours she wanted, watch documentaries instead of crime series on the television, have the outside slice of the roast, the cream on top of the milk, the best chair in the sitting room and talk on the telephone for as long as she liked without feeling guilty. She could even turn his study in the belvedere into her own sewing room.

Getting her fair share would be one thing, but Eileen was conscious that underlying the concern about her position in the pecking order was a more fundamental anxiety, the fear of there being no order at all. Perhaps she needed to be one of a group, whatever her position within it. She needed the security, both physical and psychological of being with people. Mankind, after all, was a social animal and total isolation was not an option.

She wasn't sure she could even survive on her own: create a new routine, keep their friends, and find something meaningful to do. Housework only made sense when there was someone else to enjoy and judge the results. Why cook and clean for yourself? She imagined the house piled high with unpaid bills and unwashed dishes from which she'd eaten sandwiches and Chicken Tikka from M&S. And how would people treat her, as a woman on her own, a woman of a certain age, a mousy woman of no particular talent and with no particular interests beyond poetry and the garden? Life was a lonely business at the best of times.

Then she thought of Ray. He would have some answers, know what she ought to do. She wished he was here in the kitchen to talk to her right now. He would probably caution her to let the affair run its course, but meanwhile keep an eye open for problems and developments. Go with the flow. Yes, that's what she would do. Just take things as they come. George and Celia would soon be back. She put the sea bass into the oven, finished making the salad dressing and put a bottle of Viognier in the refrigerator. The Watchtower and the other pamphlets were still on the table; she scooped them up and pushed them deep into the rubbish bin.

*

George was also thinking about Gloria's motives as he sat watching the door to the arrivals hall. What did she want from him? More importantly, and here he forced himself to ask the unthinkable question, one that he had hoped he could ignore, just why had she encouraged him? What was there about him now at this stage in his life that could interest a beautiful, ripe, young, well, relatively young, woman like Gloria? His hour in the bird hide, half listening to facts about oyster catchers and dotterels had given him the opportunity to review his situation in a new light. In a way, looking through the viewing hatch in the side of a shed at creatures going through their Darwinian paces had made it easier to clarify his own situation. Female dotterels accepted the attention of male dotterels because they wanted to make fertile eggs and they chose the biggest and the strongest male they could find. George was pretty sure Gloria did not want him to fertilise her eggs and he certainly wasn't the biggest, most powerful male in the flock. In fact if it came to flight or fight, between the two of them, George had to admit that in either mode the odds probably favoured Gloria. So what the hell was she up to? Maybe he should ask her next time they met; if we meet again, he thought gloomily.

He was almost relieved to see Celia coming through from customs, despite the fact that she looked particularly unattractive, with her face free from make up, and her hair both short and greasily unkempt. Moreover, she was today wearing her dungarees. He smiled jovially nonetheless and reached out to her and was surprised and foolishly pleased by the intensity with which she clung to him.

Chapter Twenty
A Meeting with Amy Randall

"Ripeness is all: her in her cooling planet
Revere: do not presume to think her wasted."
'To an Old Lady' William Empson

It was Sunday morning. George took the Telegraph and his second cup of coffee up to the Belvedere, leaving Eileen and Celia sitting over the remains of breakfast. It was too early for female company. Later he could cope with their jumbled conversation, too fast and constantly interrupting each other, but right now he couldn't face it. He needed some space and silence in which to think more about his future with Gloria. Anyway, he said to himself, they probably want to talk about women's things and won't want me around. That was certainly true of the previous evening. Eileen had given all her attention to Celia and had hardly addressed him all night, even later when they were alone in their bedroom. She went through her nightly routine in total silence and only said goodnight as she left him to go and sleep in the spare bedroom. She must have something on her mind he thought. Haven't we all?

"I'll be in my study if anyone needs me," he said in their general direction, but neither of them looked up as he left the room.

*

Eileen was studying Celia's mournful face and clothes, which were always a good sign of the woman within. Today she was wearing loose black trousers and an old t-shirt that strained across her bosom. She had regressed towards her lumpy, unloved look. The situation with Margot must have deteriorated, though try as she may Eileen could still not believe that Celia loved Margot in the way that a woman loves a man, romantically as well as sexually. So far Celia had not even mentioned Margot, in itself unusual, perhaps indicating that things were not going well.

The previous evening, with the three of them together, there had been no discussion of personal matters either. They all had their reasons. So their conversation had strolled around generalities: the weather, current affairs and the doings of mutual friends and relatives. Just before ten o'clock, when most neutral topics had been visited, revisited and exhausted, George turned on the television. Pretending to watch the news gave them the chance to be together but, simultaneously, to retreat into their own personal worlds. But now, in the sociable atmosphere of a Sunday morning there was no excuse for staying silent.

"How's everything going in London?"

Eileen tried to sound neutral but there was a note of concern in her voice that she knew Celia would recognise and which would put her in a defensive mood. She had always been an independent creature even as a little girl, hating to be seen as needing help or sympathy.

Celia gave a slightly theatrical sigh, "We're really busy for the rest of this month. I've got the full responsibility of monitoring the proposals for expanding the wheelchair and handicapped access signage system to public buildings. It's essential this initiative is coordinated with Wandsworth Council and eventually Westminster, although to get them to cooperate on anything is a struggle, especially if it requires using some of their sacred budget. I'm going to have my work cut out trying to ensure synchrony amongst all the different fiefdoms, not just for now but to take us through to the next couple of quarters. You see, people don't appreciate that we're dealing with an ongoing process, not a single act. We have to agree the terms of reference and the terms of engagement, as it were, and then establish a good working dialogue, all of which is going to be my responsibility. The buck very definitely stops with me."

"I do hope you're not working too hard." Eileen had given Celia space to talk but had neither understood nor retained a word of what had been said, only seen the strain and shadows in her daughter's face.

"Oh Eileen I do know how to pace myself."

"All the same you look tired. More tea?" Then, said as lightly as she could as she poured them both a third cup, "How's Margot?"

"Actually, things aren't too good right at the moment. There's been a lot happening." Celia put down her cup very precisely, took off her glasses and meticulously wiped the steam from the lenses, her large eyes suspiciously moist as well. Eileen knew better than to pursue the topic, but a spark of hope glimmered within her that the relationship with Margot might be crumbling, and that Celia would now find herself a nice man and become a normal daughter again.

*

Celia couldn't talk about Margot. It was all too humiliating and painful. She had considered telling her parents about the incident with Helena, and about her trip to see Amy Randall, Helena's friend. George and Eileen might feel reassured by both of these that there were things happening in her life beyond the relationship with Margot. However, by the end of Saturday evening she still hadn't mentioned either, perhaps because she knew both encounters had been significant and she needed more time to digest them herself.

Helena's death had shocked her. It had shaken the foundations of her world, a world that hitherto she hadn't known was shakeable. It was the first time she had come face to face with the power of death, and of what that power means in its totality.

She had been more or less prepared for the sudden discontinuity of life as we know and expect it to be. There was a time-thin but irrevocable boundary between the Helena who excitedly sipped her champagne and recalled David for one last time, and the small, still bundle of air and old clothes that stayed perched on the seat only an hour later. That disparity was what Celia would have expected of death had she ever given it much thought.

Yet she was surprised and disturbed by the fact that it had happened without her awareness. She had not known that death could be so subtle. How could a life end – a long life and not uneventful – without giving any outward sign? How could she herself have sat enjoying the play when, alongside her, eighty years were folding up and going home? All those years – the parties, flirtations, friends, meals, books, walks in the park, catching the bus to work, the daily combing of hair and remembering to take a handkerchief – all this doing and getting and spending had vanished as silently and finally as a snowflake melts into grass, or as seawater, on a wave's retreat, soaks into the sand.

The really alarming aspect of it all, the one still churning around, largely in her unconscious mind, was that all this life lived, this slowly-woven web of reflexes, thoughts and desires had gone, in its entirety and for ever. Death didn't just destroy the here and now; it erased the past as well as denied the future. There was very little left of Helena and her life, but it was shocking to realise that soon it would be as if she never existed.

Worst of all Celia realised that Helena's lost existence was, had been and always would be, absolutely, of no consequence whatsoever to the world at large. Any more than when Margot walked out of my life, she thought, when their months together had vanished and the love that she thought they shared proved to have no substance at all. Who was there to say it had ever mattered?

The meeting with Amy Randall had also taken Celia by surprise, as much by the way that it happened as by what took place during their hours together. The opportunity to see her seemed to have come about by chance and by what was initially an inconvenience. When she tried to book her travel to Guernsey all the flights from Gatwick were fully booked. However, there were seats available on the Saturday flight from Southampton. She decided to take an early train from Waterloo, and spend a few hours looking around Southampton before catching the flight in the late afternoon. She could look around the Titanic museum, and maybe have lunch on the Marina. It will be my little treat she thought as she sat alone in the still half-empty flat on the Friday before she left. It would also solve the problem of what to do at the weekend because she had nothing to do and no-one to see. She had considered ringing her friends Jenny and Alison but couldn't bear the questions they were bound to ask and the answers she had to give. For the time being she wanted to keep the pain and ignominy of Margot's departure all to herself. Unusually for her she wanted to be alone or in the reassuring, undemanding company of George and Eileen.

That Friday evening the flat felt dead and empty, and so did she. Who was Celia sitting with a book on her knee and a glass of wine on the table? A thirty-four year old council worker? A graduate in sociology from Brighton Uni? A lesbian who had just 'come out'? A fat girl with clear skin and nice teeth? With no-one to answer these questions she was just a name listening to life going on outside, unable even to concentrate on her book. At least tomorrow I'll be with George and Eileen, in their sanctuary on Guernsey she thought. Tomorrow I can be their daughter. That's an easy role to play.

Is this how it is when you're old, she pondered, on the outside of the world, sitting, doing nothing, waiting for nothing, while all around real people are planning, connecting, being alive? This must have been how Helena felt once her youth had gone, and she was no longer needed at work, no longer of any value to anyone except her one surviving friend down on the south coast.

Celia had always felt sorry for the old people whose deaths were occasionally a topic for discussion at council meetings, pensioners who had died in their third or twenty-third floor flats, unseen, unheard and uncomforted, with the milk collecting on the doorstep and the television still on at full volume. Sorry, but mystified as to how they had ended up so isolated. She had always assumed they were one-off eccentrics who had made a lifestyle choice, but now she suspected that this process of decay was perfectly normal and that most people grew lonely because their lives simply disintegrated. Friends and family died or moved away and replacing them became more difficult as resources, energy and interest in life dwindled. Hard to believe that the ability to make friends was simply a stage in life, but perhaps it was as transitory as wanting to play hopscotch or liking pop music. Was it possible to outgrow the desire as well as the ability to connect, to no longer want be part of whoever had laughingly called it the family of man?

That hadn't seemed to be true of Helena had it? She had been alive and in touch. She had still been in the game, playing her part. Until the moment she died, sitting next to me in the theatre thought Celia, as she filed her nails for the second time that evening.

She wondered who would tell Amy Randall about Helena; perhaps no-one. Mrs. Randall would wait and wait, then maybe months later ring Helena's number and get no answer and never know why. She, Celia, was probably the only person who was aware of their friendship and who was in a position to tell her. I should write her a letter she thought, explaining what had happened. It was the least she could do. She found the slip of paper in her bag with Amy's address: Keyhaven Road, Milford-on-Sea, Hampshire She looked for it on an old road map. There it was, not far from Southampton, twenty-something miles at most. But wait, instead of writing a letter she could go to Milford-on-Sea tomorrow morning. She could stay on the train past Southampton, and go on down to the coast. The nearest station seemed to be a place called New Milton. From there she could find a bus to Keyhaven Road, find Mrs. Randall, tell her about Helena, and offer what sympathy she could. It would probably be more interesting anyway to be by the sea than spend the time in Southampton. Yes, a brilliant idea.

The train journey the next morning gave her a welcome sense of purpose. She was going somewhere and she had someone to see and a message to deliver. She settled herself comfortably in the window seat and watched first the suburbs of south London and then the countryside of Berkshire and Hampshire flashing by in a slipstream of red brick houses, back gardens in full flower and, eventually, open fields in their brightest green of the year.

The countryside was at its best, the trees in full fresh leaf; haymaking was nearly over and the wheat was ripening in the fields. Even the embankments were thick with uncut grass and colourful invasions of marguerites and lupins. At Winchester station as the train slowly pulled away she saw three children standing on top of the embankment waving to the train. Her first reaction was to draw back from the window, reminded of recent stories about kids throwing stones at passing trains, but these seemed to be real children, a little girl in a gingham dress and two even smaller boys in shorts, jumping up and down, waving because they were happy. She waved back, tentatively at first and then more vigorously, leaning right up against the window eager that they should see her, that their innocence should be rewarded. It was a good omen.

Ten minutes after Southampton Central they passed the docks and came to the boundaries of the New Forest. Oak and beech trees towered above the track and in between the stands of woodland Celia caught glimpses of open heath, grazing cattle and the bright acid yellow of gorse in bloom. The train stopped again at Lyndhurst Road, then Brockenhurst, and soon after paused for several minutes at a small station called Sway. She sat in the sunshine looking at the buddleia and the marguerites forcing their way up through the cracked concrete. 'No-one left and no-one came on the bare platform' said Celia to herself, remembering a poem that Eileen used to read to her when she was little.

At New Milton she hoisted her rucksack on her shoulder, stepped down heavily from the train and made her way towards the gate into the station yard. She headed towards the taxi rank but saw other passengers, slimmer and faster, take the two cars that had been waiting. So be it. She would have to stand and wait on the hot tarmac; not a problem. She set down her bag in a territorial manner at what she thought would soon be the front of a queue but after several minutes realised that nobody else was going to join her. So she relaxed, lit a cigarette and looked around her. The place had a small town feel, just enough traffic and bustle for there to be a sense of life but the tubs of flowers on the platform and a vague smell of sea brought an air of holidays and time out.

Then, as she watched the shoppers walking past the station driveway, she realised that it wasn't a holiday town, more a place of retreat and retirement. Most of the passers-by were of an age, somewhere in their sixties and seventies that is rightfully described as 'elderly'. There was a preponderance of women, still young enough to be dressed in floral frocks and cardigans, but old enough to need their wide cushioned shoes and wheeled tartan shopping bags. Some had graduated onto walking sticks, used jauntily, defiantly, like Alpine staffs, as if carried for style as much as support. They walked by slowly, occasionally in couples but mostly alone. Yet there was uniformity in the cheap cotton pull-on hats, the short wispy white hair and their smooth, untroubled faces.

They looked like mothers and grandmothers and aunties of the old fashioned kind thought Celia: never forgetting birthdays, always making cakes and summertime jam. They probably still enjoyed their gardens and were still able to walk down the road to the sea with their best friend – soon, inevitably, to be their only friend – for an ice cream at the kiosk. Every so often, less frequently as each year passed, they would make the trip to Bournemouth, for the theatre, or to enjoy the lights, or simply go for a day's shopping, catching a late, but not the last, train home.

They had learned to ignore the fact that their once strict domestic routines, the cast-iron inherited ideas about how life should be lived, were adapted to fit their diminishing strength and concern. Allowances were made for the fact that the sheets were left on the bed for three weeks, then six, then eight – 'it's only me and I'm clean'– and they had learned not to mind that each solitary meal, eaten from a favourite plate on a tray in front of the television, was either cheese and pickle, a nice bit of ham, or fish fingers and tomato ketchup. They accepted without complaint that there would come, one late summer day, a time to wipe the blades of the lawnmower, squeeze a little oil on the moving parts as once long ago their fathers had shown them, cover the machine with a cloth, pat it and then lock it away for good in the car-less garage.

They also tried to hide from the decline they could see so very clearly in the world around them, by turning away from the news, all of it bad and so depressing, and by keeping the front door bolted, even on a summer's day. They rarely answered the bell without anxiety, as all unexpected events now were unhappy ones, and the sound of the telephone turned up to its loudest volume but still not quite loud enough, filled them with dread and resignation.

Oh God, will I be one of these, thought Celia, a soft-faced old woman walking down Station Road with a basket on wheels, visiting the library and spending an hour in the stationer's choosing a birthday card? Lying in bed at night waiting for the sound of predatory footsteps on the gravel or the sudden squeeze of an unreliable heart? She was relieved when her cascade of gloomy thoughts was interrupted by an empty taxi drawing up alongside.

They stopped at a florist's shop on the way to Keyhaven; it would be nice to take Mrs. Randall some flowers, especially if she were newly out of hospital. It was an old fashioned shop, smelling of polished wood and freesias. Celia padded her way carefully round the buckets full of hothouse flowers; what to buy for an old lady? Certainly not red roses, and freesias were more for a bride. Violets would be good but there were none at this time of the year. What about lilies, big creamy-white ones with strong profiles and a bold scent; they were what Celia might choose for a girl friend or for herself, but somehow they were not right for a frail old lady living on her own, too stark and self-confident. Mrs. Randall would probably prefer some colour, flowers to brighten up her life not to make a lifestyle statement. She picked out dark blue irises and scarlet carnations.

"What a lovely smell, it must be brilliant working here." Celia said to the grey-haired assistant who was wrapping the flowers in soft purple tissue paper and tying them with a shiny scarlet ribbon.

"You'd think so wouldn't you?" The woman looked up with an automatic smile. "But after a couple of hours you can't smell them any more, except for the lilies, and they always remind me of death."

Death. Exactly so. Chastened by this response Celia climbed back into the taxi and sat quietly while they drove on through town, past a stationer's, a cake shop, an old fashioned ironmonger's with buckets and stepladders spilling out onto the wide pavement, gentlemen's outfitters with tweed jackets in the window, the Post Office and the supermarket, where, outside, a group of teenagers lounged on benches, bored with the peace and tranquillity.

It was the sort of place that Celia, too, had long thought boring: middle England at its most parochial and monocultural. Surely nothing could be worse than to live out one's life in such a small-minded and non-inclusive environment? Today, as they passed the photographer's studio, the pub with the beer barrels for tables in the garden and the sprinkling of small houses with their neat small gardens, it didn't feel too bad. In fact it was all quite comfortable and comforting, the sort of place where Helena perhaps would have been happy to live out her years.

Now they had left the town and were speeding past fields and copses, a golf course, farmland and an oak-lined road signposted 'Angel Lane'; an unremarkable landscape, but today on this warm blue morning it seemed idyllic. Just before Milford the road went close to the cliff-top and there was her first sight of the sea; the Solent, blue-grey and flat calm, rimmed by a heat haze.

"Can't see the island. Sign of good weather." The driver caught her eye in the rear view mirror and nodded towards the horizon, where Celia could only just see the outline of the Isle of Wight. She felt a small spurt of optimism; the trip was going well and the driver knew Keyhaven Road. It was narrow, more of a lane really, and led from the village green down towards the marshes and the sea. He drove slowly until she spotted 'Island View'. It was in a pleasant sunny location but she could see at first glance that it was the house of an old person, of someone too tired or poor or indifferent to renew the paint and prune the roses. This must be the right place.

Now that the search was over, she felt awkward. What was she doing coming unannounced to visit a friend of a woman she had hardly known? To offer comfort, she reminded herself. But what if Mrs. Randall wasn't at home, or didn't answer? Or didn't want to see Celia and be comforted? Then I'll leave the flowers with a note, and walk back into the village, thought Celia, get a newspaper, something to eat and find a place to sit until it's time to go back to the airport. Even so, she asked the driver to stop just beyond the house so she would have time to compose herself before she got to the door.

As she walked up the unweeded drive, a black and white cat

uncurled itself from the porch and came to greet her with lifted tail and soundless open mouth. She bent down to stroke it, and it followed her back to the front door where she rang the bell and waited.

There were sounds from the road, a motor mower in a nearby garden and an angry sounding bee in the roses but from inside, only silence. She leaned forward, trying to see through the frosted glass of the front door, and was just wondering whether to lift the flap on the letter box and peer inside when the door was suddenly opened. In front of her stood a short, heavy-bosomed woman, with bushy grey hair, dyed brown with silver roots. There was a strong beak of a nose, small shrewd eyes behind tortoiseshell glasses and heavily-powdered cheeks. Her mouth had been very approximately touched with a dark purple lipstick. Despite the heat she wore a beige twin set and a shapeless colourless tweed skirt. The garments were well-worn and stained. Her legs, surprisingly slim and elegant in fine stockings, ended in thick winter slippers edged with nylon fur.

"Mumpty." The woman leaned down stiffly and the cat ran forward, avoided her outstretched hand, and disappeared into the house. "Where did you find him? Little beggar's been out all night. It's the heat I suppose."

"Mmm, I didn't find him. He was here on the door step."

"Well, thank you anyway."

"I've come to see Amy Randall."

"You're looking at her right now. I am she." The eyes beaded behind the thick glasses. "Do I know you? You're not from Social Services are you?"

"No I'm not. My name's Celia Buchanan. I've come about Helena."

"Helena who? Do you mean…?"

"Your friend, Helena…" Celia swallowed, unable to continue.

"What about her? Is she coming down? Is she here?" her eyes scanned the drive over Celia's shoulder.

"No, she's, er, I found your address in her book. I came to tell you that she's…whooer, she's…" Celia took a deep breath but it didn't help. She's…she's er passed…whoo…", she looked at Amy Randall, her throat thickening, eyes full of tears, and managed to say "…away. Sorry."

"Oh my dear, how ghastly. When did it happen? Look you'd better come in." She led the way into the dusty hall, across parquet flooring and through to a drawing room untidy with magazines and newspapers. Celia sat down on a faded chintz settee, fighting back the tears, while the cat which had jumped up onto her lap, started kneading her dungarees.

"What a shock. Dear Helena. I knew her heart was a bit dicky but it's always a surprise, isn't it? Death I mean. I can see you've been affected as well. Understandably. You're young. I'll go and get us a drink. It's nearly twelve, though what the difference that makes I don't know I'm sure. I drink whenever I feel like it now."

She came back pushing a squeaky trolley on which were a bottle of scotch, two tumblers, a small jug of water and a box of cigarettes. She took the cigarettes, offered them to Celia, took one herself and lit them both with a porcelain table-lighter. She inhaled deeply, poured them each a generous slug of whisky, added a little water and sat in a cloud of smoke "Tell me all about it."

Celia felt better after a sip of scotch and with a cigarette in her hand. She told Amy about the theatre and A Midsummer Night's Dream and finding that Helena had died.

"Poor old thing. I was very fond of her." Amy topped up her drink. "And poor you for being there. It must have been a dreadful shock. Did she tell you that we had been talking about her moving down here and sharing this place with me?"

"She said you'd been in hospital and that she could only move in after the convalescence. In fact I was worried you might still be in hospital."

"Hmm, yes, well, I'm afraid that was a bit of a porkie pie. Haven't been in hospital and wouldn't ever go into one not for a King's ransom. Going to die in my own bed. Anyway, I don't need a hospital, touch wood: fit as a horse, strong as a fiddle, thanks to thirty a day and the odd dram. Hope you won't be shocked but you look the no-nonsense type so I won't give you any. The truth is I'm too ancient to live with anyone, even an old friend like Helena. She was a great gal in her time, loved her dearly, best mate. But it wouldn't have worked, two women in the same house. When you're older you don't want people, you see? Done with all that. And they're done with you."

"She seemed very fond of you."

"Well she wouldn't have been if she'd lived here. Better for her to have stayed in London and kept her illusions. That's the way we remained friends. When you're older, you see, you need your own company and your own space. There's a lot to think about: past times, good memories, regrets. It sort of plays on in your head endlessly, all the things you've done and the people you've met…Nothing else outside that world seems quite as interesting, except for the odd drinkie and ciggies of course. And Mumpty when he's good. Just a fact of life. It was lovely to see her when she came down for holidays, we had some good times. But you know, even with Helena, after she left, I was always glad to have the house to myself again. There, you think I'm a selfish old trout don't you?"

"Not at all…"

"Well you should because I am. And I'm not ashamed of it because that's how God – not that I believe in Him anyway but that's another topic altogether – made me. Made all of us. You're still too young to understand this; it wouldn't be right if you did at your age, but you must believe me when I tell you that when you get older, when you get old, as I am, you don't want people, not like you did before. Not their noisy living presence around you making demands of your time and your energy – you have so little of either anyway. No, you want to be alone. You can do what you like when you like and if you feel the need for company there's books and the Home Service and the telephone if you're really desperate. And there's always Mumpty if you want to hang on to something warm. Is he bothering you? I can see he's begun to dribble. He thinks you're his mother. Ready for another drink? Better still, why don't we walk down to The Gun and get something to drink and eat? I'll need my walking stick, but we can take our time. I'd better get my outdoor shoes on and a sun hat."

An hour later, after a slow walk down between the fields leading to the salt marshes and the Yacht Club, they were sitting in the back garden of The Gun, Amy with another scotch, Celia with a pint of lager.

"Here's to my best friend. God Bless her. I'll miss her terribly of course. But it's not a bad way to go."

"Funny, that's what my friend said. My flatmate. Correction, my ex-flatmate."

"So you found it difficult to share your home as well?"

Then Celia found herself telling Amy about Margot, about how beautiful she was, how they thought they loved each other, then all about the weddings and even her disappearance, though she didn't mention what Margot had stolen, nor the message on the bathroom mirror; those details were too shameful for anyone to know about. Amy listened carefully, nodding her head from time to time, but waiting until Celia had finished before offering any comment.

"So she only wanted you for the Right to Work permit, was that it?"

"No! No, I don't think so..." But Celia let the awful idea trickle through her mind as she replayed the various stages of their relationship. In the early days it had been love, definitely. Definitely. It wouldn't have felt so wonderful if it weren't. And Margot had been as much in love as Celia – hadn't she? She couldn't have planned it all just to get the permit, could she? But there was no denying that things had gone cold. The honeymoon didn't materialise and in fact Margot never touched Celia after the weddings, except to kiss her, as it turned out, to say goodbye. Perhaps Amy was right.

Celia toyed with her glass of lager, turning it round and round, wondering as ever why the liquid inside stayed stationary.

"I never understood why she wanted me. Maybe you're right. Maybe that's all I was to her."

"I wouldn't waste any more time thinking about her. She was obviously attractive to look at but handsome is as handsome does. And from that point of view she sounds quite repellent and didn't deserve you. Chalk it up to experience and start looking for someone else. That's what I would do. Would have done."

"I don't think I'll ever find anyone who means so much to me."

"Yes you will. At your age the world is full of people looking for people. Nature's way. Later it's a different matter, of course. But at your age it's inevitable. Biology is not easily thwarted." She leaned forward and looked at Celia with a sudden intensity. "Now listen to me on this one. Whatever you do don't stay on the sidelines of life. You must join in, do you hear me, otherwise you'll regret it one day and that's the worst thing that can happen to you."

"Were you ever married?"

"I was, if you can call it a marriage." She took a long drag on her cigarette, holding the smoke in her lungs before exhaling with a little sigh. "For eight years. Mummy picked him out for me. I was twenty-five and getting a bit too long in the tooth to stay single. Jimmy was from a good family – that's how we called it then – solicitors. But it was an absolute disaster. He was a bore, both in and out of bed. Well we gave up sex after the first year. Then at thirty-two I had an affair out of sheer desperation; I wanted a bit of life before it got too late. He found out and divorced me on grounds of adultery; it was a great scandal in those days to get divorced, let alone for the woman to be the guilty party. No-one would look at me again from the point of view of marriage – damaged goods you see. But I had a lot of 'offers' on the side. I suppose they thought I was up for it and might know what I was doing, and I've always had a good figure, so I stayed cheerful enough. Besides I had my work and do you know I grew to love coming back to my little flat in Victoria and being able to do what I liked with no-one to answer for."

"What happened to him?"

"Who, Jimmy? I found out he was a bit of a bounder. All the time we'd been married he'd been having an affair. She was spoken for as well but when her husband died at least Jimmy did the decent thing and made it legal. But all that time he'd been having this affair it was no wonder he didn't have anything left for me!" Her laugh was thickened and prolonged by a smoker's cough. When it was over she looked ironically at Celia through the lenses.

"Never tried it with a woman though. We didn't know it was an option in those days, but it might have been better. Couldn't have been any worse." She gave her choking laugh again.

Later that afternoon, as she sat in the Departure Lounge, Celia reflected on the afternoon's adventure. What had she learned from an old woman in a dusty bungalow by the marshes? Whatever it was, she recognised that instead of consoling Amy she had herself been strengthened and given hope, by the whisky and the cigarettes and the slow walk back from the pub punctuated by wheezy laughter. It was only as she was boarding the plane that she realised she was still carrying the red and blue bouquet.

Chapter Twenty-One
Contents

"What's done cannot be undone. To bed, to bed, to bed."
'Macbeth'   W. Shakespeare

Mother and daughter stayed silent as they washed up the Sunday breakfast plates after George had gone upstairs. Celia had just recalled that today would have been Helena's birthday.

"What's wrong with George? He seems really on edge. It's not me, is it?"

"I hadn't wanted to say anything, especially as it seems you've things on your mind at the moment. And I expect you'll think we've gone daft in our old age and I'm sure it isn't anything really...but then again it might be..."

"Eileen for heaven's sake ..."

"All right, I'll tell you. Steve, you know, from next door, asked George if he could store some stuff in one of our garages. We never use it so George said yes. So he and Steve packed it with boxes and then locked the door and Steve kept the key. We thought no more about it until the police came twice to Steve's house, and just before you arrived yesterday they came round here and asked us if we had noticed anything unusual going on next door. Or if we were storing anything for him."

"Oh my God. What do you think it is – drugs?"

"According to George, Steve said something about blank videos or DVDs."

"Can't think the police would be interested in those. Anyway why doesn't George have a look and see what it is?"

"Steve's got the key."

"Ask for it back."

"In theory he could…"

"So why doesn't he?"

"It's a bit more complicated than that. I overheard George tell the police that no, he wasn't storing anything for Steve. He lied for some reason. As if he wants to go along with Steve or protect him."

"Did you ask him why?"

"No, he lied to me as well. He doesn't know I overheard him. He seems very concerned not to talk about it, sort of brushes over it in the way that he does when he's hiding something."

"What on earth can he be hiding at his age? Do you know?"

Eileen took a deep breath, "I think I do. And why he wants to keep Steve happy."

"He admires him in some way? Or owes him money?"

"Nothing like that. Well, all right. I think he's having a thing with Gloria, and he doesn't want Steve to find out, so he's just going along with whatever Steve asks him to do."

"Oh Mum! A thing with Gloria? Her of all people! I mean, how obvious can you get?" Celia could hardly believe that George had it in him to be having a 'thing', unless that meant he was having a bit of slap and tickle. But surely at his age he wasn't capable of the full Monty? What on earth was happening to her parents? They were supposed to be solid pillars of the community, people she could rely on and anticipate.

"I'm not absolutely sure, but it all adds up…"

"Oh, yuck! What are you going to do?"

"What can I do? Leave them to it I suppose."

"Aren't you angry?"

"Not really. He's trying to be discreet, keeping it a secret from me as best he can. I love your father but not in that way. I don't feel for anyone in that way. You don't when you're older."

"What made you suspicious?" said Celia, hoping she wouldn't hear any more about her parents' obviously dysfunctional sex life.

"Somebody had seen them together on the cliff, on an evening when he said he was round at his swimming club. But there were other signs; he has been behaving a bit oddly for some time. I guessed something was up."

"Does he know what's in the garage?"

"I don't think so. Steve locked the door you see, and took the key. But I think your father's forgotten something. There's a second key, in the drawer of the sideboard."

"So come on, let's take a look."

"Yes but only when he's out of the way. The next time I know he'll be out for certain is Tuesday morning, when he goes to his swimming club."

"What is this swimming club thing?"

"They call themselves the Vikings. A group of men he swims with, twice a week at the outdoor pools, very early in the morning. In all weathers."

Grief! What happened to people as they got older?

*

Upstairs in the belvedere George reacted with surprisingly agility at the sound of the telephone, and picked it up before the second ring.

"Twenty-one G3, near the edge of the reservoir. Ten pm tonight."

"Where were you yesterday? I waited as long as I could in that bloody bird hide, until some berk of a birdwatcher came in and carried on babbling about dotterels and God knows what else."

George could almost swear that he heard Gloria laugh. Or

was it a cough? "Are you going to give me an answer?"

"Ssh! Not over the phone Lover Boy. Remember what we said."

There was a muffled sound as if she were covering the handset, then "Now, ten o'clock or not? The choice is yours."

"Where was it again?"

"Twenty-one G3 – there's a new parking space off the road near the reservoir."

"All right but…" The line went silent.

He sat looking at the coordinates that he'd noted on the yellow post-it, wondering what excuse he could give to Eileen and Celia for going out so late. He'd have to see what opportunities presented themselves. It would have been easier in a way to say 'no' to Gloria, and put a stop to all the anxiety. But he argued he needed to find out why the constables were interested in Steve and what the hell he'd got stacked in the garage. That wasn't the whole truth of course. He would find a way to go to the reservoir this evening because he felt something for Gloria, something he'd never really known before, an infatuation that was very much like love, was love, proper love, deep and passionate and true. Wild horses couldn't keep him away from his rendezvous at the reservoir.

*

The day passed slowly and he watched the clock like a hungry animal waiting for its supper. He couldn't read his paper, couldn't concentrate on anything. He refused the option of a morning walk and fled to his study immediately after lunch. He could almost feel his blood pressure rising.

His suggestion, made just before a quarter to ten, that he would take the car for a run as it didn't seem to be firing properly, was accepted without much comment. Eileen and Celia seemed to accept it as a perfectly normal idea. Which of course it was, he reminded himself.

"How long will you be?" Eileen was even smiling at him.

"As long as it takes me to get her onto the coast road, try and keep her above fifty for a spell and give her a good blast through the pipes." Celia was smiling too. What had he said that had pleased them? "See you in an hour or so."

The car started perfectly but he let it die, as if there were some problem with the ignition. When he started it again, he revved the engine several times before moving off.

He had tried to memorise the route but struggled with the Guernsey names -Ruettes Brayes, Vauquiedor, Route St Andre, along Bouillon Road, past the entrance to the Little Chapel, right into Route des Houguets, along Les Buttes, past St. Saviour's church and the rectory, then left just before Mont Varouf School to ease down the hill towards the reservoir.

It was dark by now and he needed full headlights along the

narrow country road, the car brushing the long grass of the banks that rose up high above him. The road came close to the reservoir and on the left there was the parking space. Nobody there. He backed into it carefully, leaving room for her car alongside his. He wound down the window and tried to relax. The engine made little crackling noises as it cooled. Five to ten. She'd probably be late again. It was the nature of the beast. Like Marilyn Monroe. Joan Crawford, Ava Gardner - didn't they all used to be late as well? A woman's prerogative. Like changing their minds. Or not turning up at all. He looked at his watch again but it still showed the same time. It wasn't quite dark and for some reason he found that heartening. The air was cool and smelled of grass and marshy plants and he could hear the sound of birds on the reservoir. He felt their relationship seemed to be approaching some sort of decision point, and, as the man, it was up to him this evening to propose what they did next, in a calm and adult fashion. All the same his ears were straining to catch the sound of her car and his heart was thumping uncontrollably.

*

Celia stood at the window watching George as he disappeared down the drive, while Eileen went to fetch the key and a torch. The weekend was turning into a soap opera; the sort you don't want to watch but do anyway. It was not what she had come home for, to see her father drive off to a liaison with his lover and have Eileen creeping around her own garage with a torch.

"Don't put the light on, Steve might see us."

Floor to ceiling was stacked with big, regular-shaped boxes wrapped in thick brown paper. Eileen's voice was low and urgent, "We'd better hurry in case he really is only checking out the engine."

Celia took the torch and shone it over the neat piles, "What did he say they were?"

"Something about blank videos."

"These are addressed to Steven Levinsky in Brighton, but they've been stuck over something else, shall I have a look?"

But Eileen had already started tearing one of the boxes open, pulling ineffectually at the thick brown masking tape.

"There's another label underneath – to someone in Brussels. Here, let me, my nails are tougher than yours. You hold the torch."

Celia clawed at the tape and managed, eventually, to tear off enough to be able to open the box and peer inside. It was tightly packed with video tapes, each sealed in cellophane. She had prised one of them out. Eileen shone the light on it while they both tried to read the label.

"Three's a Crowd." What do you think that means?" Celia turned the box over but there was no other information. "It looks as if they're pre-recorded, not empty at all. Let's try another one."

But before they could start on another parcel, they heard footsteps on gravel: light but hurried. They froze, and Eileen switched off the torch. A car door was opened, and then slammed shut. An engine started and the car drove off. It was next door. Gloria by the sound of it.

Celia extracted another two and read the labels, "'The Happiest Days of your Life.' And this one's 'Boys Extreme Party" – they sound like TV programmes. Shall we try them on the video before George comes back?"

"I don't know if that's wise." Eileen sounded worried.

"We'll never get to the bottom of this unless we do." said Celia and marched off into the house with the three tapes leaving Eileen to lock the garage door again.

"Which one first" said Celia kneeling in front of the TV –"'Happiest Days'?"

"If you like." said Eileen uneasily from settee.

The tape quality was poor as if many copies had been made of the original. First came the title 'Happiest Days – a Storia Production', a long blank bit and then in full colour a mock-up of a rather old fashioned school room, with wooden desks and chairs, and maps on the wall and a blackboard. A female voiceover, young and breathy but with a strong London accent said "School days can be the happiest days in your life. Especially if your school friends are full of fun."

A young woman came on camera; somewhere in her twenties, although it was hard to tell because she was wearing a school uniform of short gymslip, blouse and tie, had her hair in plaits and was sucking a lollipop.

The voiceover continued "When little girls are good they are very very good", and here the camera zoomed in onto the woman's lips as she sucked at the lolly, "but when they are bad they must be spanked!" The woman winked, turned round and bent over. No knickers.

"Porn!" Celia grabbed her mother's arm and fell backwards against the settee laughing. "Pornography. In Guernsey! Who'd have believed it?"

The voiceover carried on describing the likes and dislikes of little girls. Then another 'schoolgirl' in plaits appeared. She was wearing a gymslip and cardigan.

"Look, isn't that Gloria!" said Celia. "It is, I swear it. Look at the eyes. And she's wearing the same rings. It is her. Oh my God, what a laugh!"

They watched her as she went through her paces, which involved a lot of posturing and striking poses. Then, miming that she was feeling the heat, took off her cardigan. The skimpy gymslip top flattened her breasts until they bulged out at the side; the result was both erotic and absurd.

"She must have had implants?" Celia thought Eileen's voice had an element of envy.

"Bound to have done. They look very odd." Celia surreptitiously felt her own soft, low-slung bosom.

As if to prove their point Gloria now removed the top of her gymslip, as if it had been too constraining, and her breasts sprang out and up. They were awarded a close-up.

"Oh my goodness," murmured Eileen "I think we've had enough of that."

"Let's try "Three's a Crowd" said Celia, in an upbeat voice. The tapes were a relief after her fears about drugs and gun-running, and somehow, the idea that her father was having an affair with a floozy rather than someone more serious made it all a bit of a laugh.

It was Gloria again, this time on a huge bed with two men, neither of them Steve, although it would be hard to recognise anyone from the camera angles.

Eileen scrambled to her feet. "The stupid man – what has he got us into? It's horrible. Celia, turn it off quickly and put the wretched things back in the garage."

Celia stopped the machine and took out the tape.

"Do you think George knows about her? About what she does, I mean?" Celia was very rapidly reassessing her image of George. The world was performing one of its seismic shifts again.

Eileen shook her head. "He's always been such a careful man, fussy. Clean underwear and fresh shirt every day. I mean… He doesn't know about this…I'm sure. He might be stupid but he's not…like this…"

"What about 'Boys' Extreme Party'?"

"I don't want to see any more. I'm going to bed. You do what you like but take them back to the garage when you've finished and lock the door. He mustn't know we've been poking around."

Curiosity, so the psychologists say, is the strongest human drive after the basic ones of food and sex. It was this instinct, rather than any real desire to see the contents of the third video, that prompted Celia to take it out of its box and slip it into the machine. But she only ran it for less than a minute before turning it off. This one was most definitely not a joke.

As she sat there shocked by what she had just seen she heard the front door open and close. George! He mustn't know that they'd been prying. She pushed the first two tapes under the settee but didn't have time to take 'Extreme Party' out of the machine; she would have to leave it there and just hope and pray that he didn't want to play a video that evening. Quickly she found Channel Four on the TV; Sylvester Stallone was crouching in a cave, hunting-knife at the ready, just as George put his head round the door. He looked normal enough except for his eyes; the pupils were enlarged, and had a wild expression, as if he's on drugs she thought, which seemed highly unlikely. But he'd been up to something, that was for sure. She turned her face away from him in case he could read on it the disgust and horror generated by her glimpse of the contents of the third tape.

"Where's your mother?"

"She's gone to bed."

"Fancy a drink?"

"It's a bit late."

"Think of it as a nightcap."

He went into the kitchen and came back with two glasses and his bottle of Glenmorangie. He poured them both a treble and then sat down heavily next to Celia. He smelled of the outdoors and of something more; the sort of acrid smell like the atmosphere in a pub when things get violent, or when some of the worst juvenile offenders were brought into a courtroom. It was the smell of adrenalin.

"How's the car?"

"The car? The car's fine." He looked bemused and then frowned, "Ah, much better. Only I didn't go to the West Coast, I went up to L'Ancresse," and here he looked at her intently as if to impress the information into her brain, "Do you remember we went for a walk there once by the Golf Course and stopped and had lunch at Le Chouet, right up on the north western tip of the island?"

She couldn't recall having been there, but nodded uncertainly.

"What's on the box?" He stared unseeing at the television.

"Nothing much, I was just thinking of going up to bed."

"Shame. I thought we might sit up for a bit, have a chat. Is that Stallone?" He poured himself another whisky.

After sipping her drink for another few minutes, by which point in time he appeared to have become absorbed by the film, she went upstairs to bed. She could not bring herself to give him the usual goodnight peck on the cheek, but he appeared neither to notice nor care.

Chapter Twenty–Two
A Terrible Accident

"Oh the mind, mind has mountains; cliffs of fall
Frightful, sheer, no man fathomed."
' *No Worst , there is None*' *G. Manley Hopkins*

He was not aware that Celia had left the room; his head was busy and growing busier with the night's events, which he could replay at his leisure now he was safely at home and alone.

First the encounter with Gloria. He had not had long to wait by the reservoir before she joined him. She looked very pretty, in a sweater and slacks of some lavender colour: gentle and feminine.

"Sorry to be late." She opened the passenger door and got in beside him, "It was hard to get away. Steve was on the que vive."

"Where did you tell him you were going?"

She gave him a sardonic look then turned her face towards the windscreen and the darkening sky. "What I always tell him, that I'm coming to meet you for a bit of hanky panky."

He cleared his throat. "I waited for an hour in that bird hide, but you didn't come."

"That, as they say, was unavoidable." Her voice didn't encourage further questions. Then she turned to look at him and in the dim light he saw her smile. "If you were a sensible and carried a mobile I could have let you know. But I'm really sorry."

The sincerity and tenderness in her voice went straight to his heart.

"I'm a silly old dinosaur, I know. I don't know why you put up with me." Then he lifted her hand and pressed it to her lips, a gallant gesture that seemed to surprise them both. "I would always forgive you, no matter what", he said thickly.

"So, how have you been?" She withdrew her hand from his, but gently, and opened the window wider. "I need a smoke, do you mind? I'll blow out through the window."

He watched her while she opened her bag, and had to fumble to find her cigarettes and lighter. Just like all the women he had ever known he thought tenderly. It had been his intention to start that evening by confronting her about the police, but right at that moment, in the mood they were in, it seemed inappropriate.

"We've been having a few problems with the police. I think they came over to see you didn't they?" she lit a cigarette and drew on it deeply.

"Yes, yes they did." He was surprised by her honesty, her straightforwardness.

She exhaled through the open window, then turned back to him, her eyes still narrowed against the smoke, "I expect they wanted to know if you were keeping any stuff for us. Was that it?"

"I told them no."

"Well, who was a naughty boy then?" She laughed, "That was good of you, and foolish too." She removed what might have been an imaginary fleck of tobacco from her lower lip. "How do you know Steve hasn't asked you to store a few hundredweight of Class A drugs in there?"

"I trust Steve." That wasn't quite true. But he wanted to trust Steve.

"You haven't looked then?" She regarded her nails as if to find more stray shreds of tobacco.

"I can't, the door's locked and Steve's got the only key."

"So you would have looked, would you, if you'd got a spare?" She blew a perfect smoke ring out through the window, where it hovered intact for a few seconds in the still air.

What game was she playing?

"If I had, would I have been surprised?"

"It's only videos, like he said, but Guernsey Customs are claiming that we owe them excise duty for the stuff we brought in last month and they've been creating a right stink about checking through all our stock. Eager to lay their hands on some money."

"Have you been slipping some stuff in then?"

"Nothing you could put your finger on. It's all negotiable on this island, that's what Steve says. Anyway he's got them off our backs. Said we should get ourselves a good local lawyer, someone who can beat them at their own game."

"I can recommend someone if you like." George felt a load lifted from his shoulders. So he hadn't compromised himself with the police, and Steve and Gloria weren't up to anything really illegal. Nothing terrible was going on. Everything was all right.

"Steve will be in touch if we need to. But thanks anyway for lying."

"It wasn't really a lie."

But Gloria was adamant. "It was, most definitely. You lied to the police to save us. That's a crime. Come on now don't sell yourself short."

"Yes I suppose if I were telling the truth now I would have to confess that I did lie to the police, because I am storing stuff for Steve."

"There you are." She flicked her cigarette out of the window with a strangely triumphant gesture. "You lied to the police on our behalf and just because you and I are having an affair, you didn't need to go to those lengths. But you did. So thank you."

"You don't have to thank me for anything. If I lied to the police it's because I love you." George edged towards her and laid his right hand on her breast. She let him slip his hand beneath her jumper and as he fondled her he felt himself brimming with happiness and desire. Desire, yes, the urge had come back! He had wanted to talk to Gloria about the other thing, what she really felt about him, but right now it seemed so obvious that his feelings for her were returned that the question could wait a bit. Besides, he loved her enough for the both of them. There were questions to be answered and decisions to be made, he knew that, but they would have to wait until he had finished.

"Could we, er, find somewhere, you know, to..."

"Not in these clothes I can't, not on the ground. Anyway I've got to go."

"Surely we can do something?" His need for her was urgent and uncomfortable, but she had snapped her bag shut, opened the door and was already out of the car. "When shall we meet again?"

"Soon. It all depends."

"On what? On what Gloria?" But his question was lost in the sound of the engine. She blew him a kiss and drove up the hill towards St. Saviour's church.

Shifting uncomfortably in the car George pondered over the ache in his groin. They really must find a place where they could relax and do things properly. He could arrange an overnight trip to London and find a nice little hotel if she could get away, and of course, if it suited her. She seemed to enjoy the furtive nature of their meetings so he might just have to make do with what he got here on the island. But tonight hadn't been enough and he felt cheated. He slammed the car into reverse and backed out into the little lane completely blocking it. The engine died. Irritated he tried turning the key in the ignition, but caught his fingers in the key ring and instead of turning the key he pulled it out, and heard it drop into the foot well. Damn and blast it! Almost immediately he saw the single headlight of a motor bike in his rear view mirror; the rider came up behind him and stopped, unable to get round him on the narrow road.

"Hold on, hold on" George shouted through the open window as he scrabbled on the floor for the key. But the rider, a young guy by what George could see of him sounded his horn and revved his engine in a derisory display of impatience.

"Stupid bastard" shouted George, doubting that he could be heard above the noise and getting angrier by the second, his arteries swelling. The harsh noise of the engine seemed to be amplified by the narrowness of the lane and he felt as though his head would burst. At last he found the key and got it into the ignition and started the car. He drove up the hill, the motor bike close behind him, its headlight on full beam, dazzling George whenever he tried to look in his mirror.

"Fuck off!" George shouted but of course the cyclist couldn't hear, not with his helmet on. So he gave a V sign out of the window, which the rider must have seen because he rode towards George's flank and shone his headlight directly into the wing mirror. George covered the mirror with his hand but now the rider was playing some sort of game. First he cut his light altogether then put it on again as soon as George took his hand away. Although George drove as fast as he could with one hand on the wheel and the other being taken on and off the mirror, the bike easily kept pace with him in the narrow lane, and the rider carried on playing his silly game.

Then George remembered they were coming up to a fast bit of the road, at the end of which there was a very sharp turn; the lane went right, while straight ahead was a tractor entrance into a field. He had a moment of inspiration. I'll teach the little sod a lesson he thought, we'll see who wants to play silly buggers. As he approached the corner, and just before he made the sharp turn, he switched off all his lights. At that crucial moment the bike rider's light was off too, and both vehicles were plunged into sudden darkness. George successfully swept round the corner clipping the verge, but the motor cycle seemed to go straight on towards the field, as he'd hoped it would.

He slowed down and looked in his rear view mirror. The lane was empty.

He considered driving on, but some part of him, his conscience or curiosity or maybe just sheer tidy-mindedness, decided he should check on the situation. Not to offer any help, but just to make sure that the bastard had got what he deserved. The road was wider here so he pulled the car over into the grass, leaving room for another car to pass, not that there was likely to be anyone out in this part of the island at night.

He stepped out of the car and stood still. He could hear the bike's engine still running. Funny, why didn't the boy turn it off? Maybe he'd fallen and was trapped underneath. George felt a wild and satisfying sense of revenge. So much the better. He stalked silently along the verge until he came to the opening to the field. It was too dark to see anything but he could definitely hear the engine strumming gently to itself. There was no sound from the rider; perhaps he had fallen off and been stunned in the fall. George stepped forward to find out but was stopped by something firm across his stomach. He jumped back immediately, his heart racing. Reaching out in front of him his hand closed around a single strand of wire, barbed wire - thick and taut. He felt along its length carefully. Someone had stretched it right across the opening, to keep people out or cattle in. The bike must have gone underneath. He stooped stiffly under the wire himself and walked slowly towards the engine sound, but halfway he became cautious and stopped. The rider might be standing there, silent in the darkness, waiting for George to get closer in order to attack. George was under no illusions; even a determined fifteen year old could outfight him these days. Better not to put himself in danger. Neither did he feel it was his business to find out if there were any injuries, although the longer he stood there the more likely it seemed that there must be injuries, possibly serious ones at that. The engine was still throbbing, but beyond that absolute silence and – or was he imagining it - a faint and familiar smell which for the moment he couldn't identify. It was a disturbing smell and he turned away. Discretion is the better part of valour, old boy, he said to himself, leave well alone. You did what you set out to do, something has happened which is not your fault, now turn around, go home and read about it in tomorrow's Guernsey Press.

Calmly he walked away from whatever might have happened. It was the most sensible thing to do. But as he stood on the edge of the field his hands started shaking. Then the rest of him was shaking too, a shuddering sensation that came up and out in the form of a loud grunting sigh, followed by a deep intake of breath. He held the breath for a long time, feeling the air trapped in his chest, his whole torso braced against the inevitable. Then it came rumbling and gurgling, pushing up through his throat, creating a tunnel from his belly to his mouth until it exploded into the night air. Laughter. Very long and very loud laughter.

He was shocked by the sound. He hadn't made the laugh; it had happened to him. He couldn't stop it. He was a passive agent for the sound, like a host or victim, and the more he tried to suppress it, the stronger its force. The sound of the laughter exploded round the little valley, a big happy sound, the sound of the winner, of victory and triumph.

Every now and then the laughter would ease up a bit and for a few minutes he'd start thinking seriously about what he should do. Then a big choking explosion would rise up in him and he was lost again, mouth open, tears streaming down his face, doubled over with the pain of it. Gradually the bouts of laughter diminished and the intervals between them lengthened. He had to think seriously and now about what to do. The first thing was to consider if he had left any traces that could be identified. Was it possible to take fingerprints from the barbed wire? He must clean it down. He pulled up some grass from the verge and wiped the wire as best he could. Now he must calm down, get home and just hope that nobody had heard him.

As he stepped into the road, he saw the headlights of a car in the distance, but rapidly approaching. He just had time to stumble back into the field and crouch behind the bushes, before what looked like a Range Rover went past him and on round the corner. The driver would be sure to see the Fiesta but would they be able to identify the make and the colour, or, God forbid, read the registration plate?

He heard the Range Rover brake a little, no doubt as it squeezed past his car, but it didn't stop. He peered through the bushes to see the tail lights disappear safely over the hill. Then with calm efficient movements he walked to his car, got in and drove away speedily, making as little noise as possible. As soon as he turned onto the main road he relaxed. Nobody had seen what had happened nor how it happened, and nobody would be able to trace it to him. He was in the clear.

But as he drove on home anxiety grew. His first thought was that he should he go back and check what had happened. He could use the car headlights to see what was in the field and what had happened to the driver. Or if not that he should at least call an ambulance to the scene, anonymously of course. But can't they trace calls? If so, inevitably there would be questions about how exactly the accident had happened, and why he had taken that route, and what he had been doing by the reservoir in the first place. No, he couldn't do that. A terrible sense of guilt was growing within him. Something bad had happened, maybe something extremely bad, and it could be construed as his fault.

He tried to remember the system they used at Parson and Green for evaluating complex marketing environments. Before trying to assess it in a holistic way, break down the situation from the very beginning into its constituent parts, and then build up the total picture from there. So, what was the beginning of tonight's situation? Forget Gloria, although in a way her refusal to do anything tonight had set things off on a wrong footing. Technically speaking, the beginning was when he was being harassed while looking for the key in the foot well. Question one: did he regret getting angry with the motor cyclist? Answer, no. He couldn't help how he had felt and in a similar circumstance the same would probably happen again. Question two: did he regret turning off his lights with the intention of making the motor cyclist have an accident? Not at all; it was the other guy who had started it all; he was merely trying to stop him and teach him a lesson. Question three: did he feel sad about the possibility that he'd caused an injury? Answer, um, no. How could you be sad about someone you didn't know, especially as they'd chosen deliberately to play dangerous games. Perhaps he ought to, but in reality he didn't. Not really.

No doubt about it, Parson and Green had some good systems.

Now the last question, the one that always hit the jackpot and really sorted the sheep from the goats.

Question - whatever number it was - did he regret that he, George, who had always thought of himself as a civilised man, didn't care about whether another human being had been injured because of him? Answer, right now what he felt about himself was, was –it was pride. Yes, that was how he felt, not proud because he didn't care, but proud for being honest about not caring. Honesty, it could be argued, is a more admirable virtue than compassion. After all there's nothing you can do about how you feel, that's at the level of instinct, but you can control what you say about a situation, whether or not you tell the truth about your feelings. It's the sign of a proper man, he thought, as he drove on across the island to his home and family, to be honest and not regret those sentiments he didn't feel.

To thine own self be true – wise words. I might like to have concern over what has just happened but I, George Buchanan, don't feel any concern. Frankly my dear I don't give a damn. In fact I've never felt better in my life. I feel – what is that word that Celia was always wanking on about – empowered, that's it! I got my own back, well and truly. Silly young prick, two, bumbling old git, ten!

He took the corner into Les Vardes with all his old finesse and flair.

*

Eileen had taken a deep and very hot bath to make herself sleepy but was now lying, still awake, in the small spare bedroom. Even after the bath she didn't feel properly clean. She would never feel clean again and all because of her stupid, stupid husband. She heard his car, and that was the sound of him coming into the hall. Some minutes passed and she had almost drifted off to sleep when she heard Celia coming slowly up the stairs. More time passed. She could hear the television still on downstairs; he must have fallen asleep on the settee, as he often did. Usually she went down and turned it off, but not tonight. She was not going into their bedroom, not tonight, or any night. What a fool he'd been, getting mixed up with people like that. Now she had the problem of what to say to him about the videos? He'd have to know about them sometime.

What would Ray do in a situation like this? She wished he were there, just to talk to.

*

Celia sat at the open window of her bedroom, smoking. She watched the smoke as it rose, a thin pale thread spiralling up into the night air, at first clearly defined and then curling and blurring and eventually merging with the darkness. What a rotten world it was when even her parents seemed to have been touched by evil. What should be her role in all this? She had always prided herself on her decision-making but tonight was beyond her. Small things first; that mindset always helped in a crisis. She must remember tomorrow to take the third video out of the machine and put all three tapes back into the garage and lock the door. After that she didn't know. How could her father be such a poor judge of character, she thought, then blushed in the darkness: like father like daughter. I wonder what Amy Randall would say.

*

George sat watching, but not seeing, the late night movie. He had been the hero of his own movie that evening and it was a lot more exciting than anything simulated on the box. He longed to tell someone about it, but there was only one person in his life who would understand and he couldn't ring her at this time of night. He carried on drinking the whisky until at last he fell asleep, curled up like a baby on the settee.

Around half past two he woke up, turned off the TV and hauled himself upstairs to bed. Their bedroom was empty; Eileen must be in the spare room. Good, he needed the place to himself tonight. He pulled off his shoes and trousers, then fell across the bed diagonally on his back, arms outstretched, and was soon deeply and peacefully asleep.

Chapter Twenty-Three
What Next?

Aye, now the plot thickens very much upon us."
'The Rehearsal'   George Villiers.

Eileen woke early, with a brain fully alert and running at top speed. Six thirty and it was light; she knew she wouldn't be able to go back to sleep. There was too much to think about; anyway she'd probably had six hours - that would have to be enough.

Celia was already down in the kitchen, sitting in her pyjamas with a mug of tea in front of her. There was no sign or sound from George. Even so they kept their voices low.

"I've put the tapes back and put the key in the drawer."

"Well done. What time did George get back last night?"

"About eleven thirty. He was in an odd sort of mood."

"What do you mean?"

"Looked a bit shocked. And he wanted me to have a drinking session with him and watch a movie on TV."

"Did you see any of that third tape?"

"Yes." Celia hesitated, "Yes I did, enough of it to know what it was like. George came home in the middle of it. I just had time to switch it off."

"So, what was it like?" said Eileen, who had been thinking that the school days tape wasn't so bad, quite funny really. They called it 'soft porn' didn't they? A lot of men liked that kind of thing and it was pretty harmless after all.

"Oh Mum it was awful. Different sort of thing altogether. Young boys."

Eileen pulled a face and sat down awkwardly. This was different. No wonder the police were interested.

"I would have known, wouldn't I if he'd ever been that way inclined? I'm sure I would have known."

"Eileen! What are you saying? George isn't like that. Don't be daft. I bet he has absolutely no idea what's on those tapes."

"No, of course, you're right. What shall we do?"

"I think first we tell George what's on the tapes. And then we've got to go to the police and tell them what we know, give them all the evidence we've got."

"Not yet. Not until I've discussed it with George; he's the one who has to sort things out with Steve. I don't want to put him in any danger."

"There was a website address on the last tape; if we could get into that maybe we'd know who makes this stuff and how Steve and Gloria are involved in it. It would give us more of a case against them."

"We could do that now, if you like. George wouldn't know what you were doing."

"The trouble is if the police come round to check up on you they could look at the history of the all the websites you've visited. You wouldn't want them to find this."

Eileen thought for a moment, "They go online and surf the web at my computer class. We could go there. I'm supposed to have a session this morning anyway."

*

George eventually came downstairs at nine thirty. He'd had a good night's deep and dreamless sleep, uninterrupted by any need to go to the bathroom. Memories of the events of the previous evening came back to him when he finally opened his eyes at eight thirty. His recollections had a slight worrying edge to them but were suffused overall with a childish sense of triumph, of his having prevailed in some way.

He sugared his coffee, buttered his toast and propped the Telegraph against the marmalade pot with his usual anticipatory sense of pleasure and only gradually became aware that the women were unusually quiet. Eileen was standing doing something to the dishes in the sink and Celia was silently standing at the French windows blowing smoke outside into the garden.

"Got any plans for today?" He carried on crunching as he spoke but kept his head down in the newspaper. Last night's event had lost most of its impact but he feared his face might tell another story, and that Eileen and Celia would intuitively know that he'd been up to something. He needed time on his own to talk to Gloria, tell her about his idea of a weekend in London, and maybe about what happened with the bike and the field and everything.

"We thought we'd both go to the college for my computer session, in a moment. You don't mind, do you? We'll be back before lunch."

He couldn't have organised things better himself. "Good idea, good idea. But why don't you stay and have some lunch in town? Have a nice piece of fish at Bruno's? You'd enjoy that."

"If you don't mind?"

"Not at all, I've got plenty to do in my study. And I can always make myself a sandwich."

*

They sat together expectantly in front of one of the college computers. Celia got the Storia website up on the screen. It seemed innocent enough, purporting to buy and sell regular videos and DVDs.

"Look you've got to put in a membership number and password. I expect that's to get through to the other stuff. Password, six digits. They could be letters or words."

"Something obscene I suppose?"

"Not necessarily. It could be an innocent sort of name."

"Six digits. What about 'Gloria?'

"Could try." Celia keyed it in. "Password Not Acceptable".

"Hello ladies. Sorry, didn't mean to startle you."

"Ray! Ray what a surprise!" How wonderful he was there. Eileen would have liked to have reached out and grabbed his hand but she wasn't sure how he'd react. Or what Celia would think.

"This is my daughter, Celia Buchanan. She's staying for a few days."

"Nice to meet you. What are you two up to, a bit of surfing?"

They looked at each other.

"Have I asked something I shouldn't?"

Eileen looked at him in desperation. She wanted to tell him and get his opinion but she didn't know where to start. He leaned forward, as if sensing her ambivalence "Do you want me to leave you to get on with it? I won't be offended if you say yes?"

"Don't go." Eileen was sure about this. "I'd like to ask your advice. We need your help. But we can't talk here."

"OK. Why don't we go and have a coffee."

They established themselves at a quiet corner table in the canteen and Ray went off to buy the coffee. Eileen watched him as he wove his way back towards them between the tables. Today he seemed older and somehow physically insignificant, except for his manner which was poised and confident.

She spoke slowly and carefully, making decisions along the way as to how much to tell him. She didn't want him to know about the affair.

"So let me just see if I've got this clear. You've got a load of boxes locked up in your garage, which your husband agreed to store for your neighbour. You've looked at some of these and have found out that they're pornographic, some of it soft but there's other stuff which is extreme. The constables are chasing the neighbour about something, but for some reason your husband has lied to them and denied that he's storing anything?"

"Yes, that's about it."

"So why not simply tell your husband what you've found? Surely he wouldn't want to store them in those circumstances?"

"I can't do that. He must have his reasons for lying."

"What reasons? Either he knows what the stuff is and therefore is involved in some way," he was watching Eileen's expression "and I can tell from your face that you think this isn't the case. Or he doesn't know what's on the tapes but feels obliged to keep quiet for the sake of your neighbour. Is that likely?"

Eileen shrugged uneasily.

"If so, you need to find out what hold this man has on your husband and what he's likely to do. If he's dealing in this kind of material he's likely to be dangerous; there's a lot at stake if he's found out."

"I didn't tell you everything." Eileen realised that she would have to let him know more. "My husband didn't tell me that he had lied to the constables; he sort of fobbed me off that they were just making a general enquiry. But I overheard them."

"Why would he lie to you?"

"The same reason why he's protecting our neighbour; he's having an affair with the wife and is frightened that he'll be found out, both by him and by me. So I think he's keeping quiet about the tapes, to protect himself from being beaten up - or whatever jealous husbands do."

"I see. Difficult situation. There are two issues: the videos and the affair. Do you want to tackle him on both of those?"

Eileen thought for a moment, then sighed, "I don't need to discuss with him about what he is or is not doing with this woman. It will all probably die down on its own anyway, but I do need to tell him about the videos. We must get rid of that stuff; if the police do a search and find it, then we'll be implicated. Besides I just want it off our property."

"What do you think, Celia?"

"It's up to Eileen really. I mean I've met the neighbours and they're gross: she's all boobs and bangles, but Steve, well I can imagine he would be violent. He's the one to be wary of. He looks the part; he's huge."

"You don't want to be too sure about that." Ray exchanged a look with Eileen, "Sometimes it's the little ones you have to watch."

Eileen placed her hand fleetingly on his arm, "I doubt that."

"How do you think your husband will react, when you tell him?"

"George will worry about what Steve might do if he realises we know about the tapes."

"Is your husband George Buchanan?"

"Yes, why, have you met him?"

Ray hesitated. "Does he do a lot of deep sea fishing? Shares a launch called 'Eventide', with Joe Leroy? No? I must be thinking of someone else then. Sorry." He gave Eileen a curious smile, as if he had a secret, a good one, which some day he might share with her. "It sounds to me that you've got some thinking to do. I can't tell you what to do but honesty is usually the best and easiest policy. Look, I'll leave you to it, I have to go now."

"You've helped a lot Ray. Just by listening."

"If there's anything you want to talk about, Eileen, or if you feel you're in any kind of danger, ring me. I mean that. Anytime. Day or night. Here's my card. Good to meet you Celia. Look after your mother won't you – she's a very special lady." He took the baseball cap from his pocket and stuck it firmly on his head, then strode off to his car with a quick jaunty walk.

"What an odd bloke. 'Day or night'... Eileen, you're blushing!"

"Nonsense! Don't be daft." All the same she laughed, high and apologetically, like a young girl, "Come on, let's go and find something to eat." She pushed the card deep into her bag. The situation seemed more hopeful again.

*

After they had left the house, George sat for a few minutes more, staring at his paper and reading it aloud to get the information in and keep any negative memories out. He was working up the courage to phone Gloria, and decided that if Steve answered he'd just put the receiver down. He climbed up the stairs to his study, sat down at his desk, took a deep breath and punched in the number.

"Hello there?"

It was Steve. George dropped the receiver onto the base in a combination of guilt and, yes, fear. He stared at the 'phone, anxious that Steve might find out who rang and call back. He must think of a reason why he rang and then why he had put the phone down. His mind chased along unsuccessfully, considering one excuse after another. But there was no call back and gradually as the minutes passed he found himself relaxing. He'd try again later. He sat down and carried on reading the paper for another twenty minutes.

What was this on page five? "Ninety year old mugged in her own home by fifteen year old youth." There was the usual close-up of the victim; the face could have been male or female it was so bruised and battered and the eyes – nearly closed to slits – looked confused and defiant. If anything vindicated the hate he felt it was articles like this. He'd like to stand the youth that did this up against a wall and shoot him. Just as he was picturing the scene in his mind and the gun being placed in his hand, the telephone rang. He jumped and picked it up, "Yes!"

It was Gloria. "Was that you rang just now? Steve said it was a wrong number or something and I said to myself I bet that's Georgie Porgie."

"Can I see you, today? Now?"

"What about?"

"Nothing. Everything. I want to tell you an idea I've got,

about us -"

No response.

"- and what happened last night on the way home."

"What was that?" She sounded wary.

"An accident. I can't tell you on the phone. I could be in big trouble."

Again no immediate response, but it sounded as if she had put her hand over the mouthpiece. There were a few muffled sounds and then, "Tell you what, Steve's just on his way out. Got to see a man about a dog. He'll be gone for a couple of hours. Why don't you toddle on round here?"

"What right now?"

"Give us ten minutes. Then come on over." Silence. She'd put the phone down.

George contemplated the situation. He was now committed to telling her something big had happened but what precisely? There were several possible versions, each involving different levels of guilt. He could tell her that he'd seen a bike come off the road and driven on when perhaps he should have stopped to help. Or that he'd had a tussle with a driver who almost forced him off the road and then had some kind of accident? Or version three, that in anger he had forced a boy to fall off his bike, possibly badly injuring him. That was much too risky. Better play safe and give the innocent version. Even to Gloria.

He was surprised to see Steve's car still in the driveway; perhaps he shouldn't have taken the ten minutes instruction so literally. It was too late to turn back now; anyone watching from the house would think it very suspicious, so although he hesitated in his progress up the drive, he carried on to the porch and rang the bell, desperately trying to think what to say if Steve answered.

But he didn't. She was there on the doorstep, wearing a housecoat, a frothy pink thing, her hair tied up with a matching ribbon and her feet bare. She looked temptingly vulnerable, as if she had just got out of bed.

"It's himself. Well, come in, I won't bite. Unless you're lucky."

George lurched forward, wondering whether he could embrace her but she stood aside as deftly as a matador, beckoned him in and closed the door behind him. It was only the second time he'd been inside the house and he'd forgotten how big and impressive and how very foreign the hall was: the pale colours, the marble, and the vivid paintings. He was disappointed when she led him past the staircase. They went instead to the back of the building, through a narrow doorway and downstairs into some kind of basement. The room was dark and when she put the light on he saw that the only window, which must face out into some basement yard, had a heavy blind drawn down.

The room was long and narrow, and furnished in black and purple. There was a thick carpet, a big mirror on the wall and a little table with a vase of artificial flowers. A curtain of glittery material was draped across the further end of the room, which Gloria swept aside to reveal a bed on some kind of low dais, a huge round bed, big enough thought George for six, made up with dark satiny sheets and a mass of pillows in bright jewel colours.

"This is our games room. We thought about a pool room but decided this was more fun."

George had a stab of jealousy as he imagined Gloria and Steve 'playing' together, on any day and at any time they liked.

He went over to the bed and hesitantly touched the bedcover with his hand; it was cool and silky. Then he saw there was a mirror on the wall behind the bed, and a big industrial lamp by the side. No, it wasn't industrial, it was like the lights they used on the stage; a spotlight.

She saw his interest. "They're photographic lights. Steve uses them for his hobby. Now, look up."

He looked up and saw himself looking down. They had a huge mirror on the ceiling. He'd heard about this sort of thing but he'd never actually seen one before. What kind of games did they play? What kind of games were there apart from jiggery-pokery from different angles? Fancy having this in a private house in Les Vardes! He wondered what the stolid Guernsey builders had thought when they refurbished the house after Mrs. Whatsit had died. Mind you, it was a flattering mirror, the glass gold tinted, which made him look more tanned.

Beside him in the mirror he saw the pink housecoat coming closer.

"So what happened last night? You managed to get yourself into trouble on the way back from the reservoir? I can't believe that. Not in Guernsey." She was standing very close and he could almost taste her familiar but exciting smell. He mumbled her name and reached out for her and encircled her pinkly-clad body. He looked up at the mirror and there they were, he with his arms reaching out towards her, she a blend of gold skin and pink froth. He caressed first her shoulder and then reached for her breasts under the housecoat but she moved his hand away.

"First things first, why don't you lie down and take your kit off Sonny Jim."

He was pleased he had on his favourite black and white-striped boxer shorts; he was still tall enough and still just about slim enough to look good in them. His pride was challenged a little as Gloria's long-nailed fingers eased them over his extremely white bottom, but he felt better again as he lay back on the satin cushions looking up at the reflection of his body, glowing against the dark fabric.

"Playtime!"

Gloria had turned on the spot. The transformation was remarkable. What was glowing before was now dazzling and brilliant. It was so bright that at first George could hardly see himself in the mirror, but he realised, with some satisfaction, that he and Gloria looked as if they were centre of a stage, about to act hero and heroine in a Technicolor fantasy.

Gloria sat on the side of the bed. She started stroking his body, a very agreeable sensation despite verging occasionally towards the ticklish. He began to relax.

"So what happened last night? Tell Gloria all about it."

"It's nothing really." George mumbled contentedly.

"So why did you say it was 'big' – and I quote," said Gloria a bit sharply.

"Just an excuse to see you....Mmm, that's lovely." He'd never had a proper massage before although he often thought of it. Somehow the act was always part of a banded offer; you could never get the massage without some really tacky-looking tart offering 'complete satisfaction'. There were times, like this, when a man just wanted to be stroked.

"Errghh." He'd spoken too soon. Gloria had begun to include more sensitive parts in her sweeping gestures. And again. And again. Nice.

"Well?"

All that was negative and puny and weak about him was being transformed by Gloria's warm hands. Feelings of grandeur and supremacy welled up in him like bedrock: strong, firm, unassailable. He was strength and manhood incarnate...

"You said something about an accident..."

Now the hands were homing in and getting faster and he was sailing before the wind.

"Last night, after I left you I forced someone off the road. Accidentally, of course." But it was too late, he'd told her too much, given her version three: definitely life imprisonment.

"You what?" The hands hesitated only fractionally. The voice had changed. She sounded impressed, "You did what?"

"Yes I caused an accident, not intentionally of course."

"Tell me." The hands moved more slowly.

His sense of grandeur had reached a plateau; he was free-wheeling, doing no work and gaining no speed although he could feel his heart gradually subsiding, grateful for the rest. There was work to be done, a big hill to climb but he was sure Gloria would help him to get to the top. He was safe in her hands. As if she could read his mind she looked up at his reflection in the mirror and winked. It was a slow and deliberate gesture, which reassured him that his secret was safe with her.

"Soon after you left, I was driving back up the hill when I was buzzed by a guy on a motorbike."

"What do you mean 'buzzed'?"

"You know, when they can't get past you so they get right on your arse and make a lot of noise. This bastard was flashing his headlight on and off, trying to blind me and get me off the road."

"So you stopped and gave him one?" Her hand went still.

"No, I thought about it and I would have done if it had gone on much longer."

"So what did you do?"

He was coming down off the plateau now, he was becoming George again, George who was perhaps saying more than he should.

"It was an accident really."

"Of course it was."

She understood. It was OK. He'd known it would be. "There was a tight corner coming up and he was pushing me from behind."

"Pushing?"

"I don't mean it literally of course. But he was coming up too close, riding right on my tail, turning his light on and off and hooting, revving up his machine – like they do. I couldn't stand it."

"So you came up to the corner…?"

"I could see it clearly so it was easy for me to get round. But he, he…" This was more difficult than he'd expected.

"What happened to him?"

Her warm hand on his thigh felt reassuring.

"Instead of going round the corner he went straight ahead." He was coming up to the difficult bit. He had to stop. He couldn't even look at himself in the ceiling.

Then Gloria's hand started again, gently, knowingly,

insistently.

"Don't tell me if you don't want to..."

She was working her hand now in a practised and rhythmic movement. Strict tempo. Like Edmundo Ross.

"-you know, don't you, that I think you're a real man?"

He felt some surprise at this. She rarely said anything affectionate. She must mean it.

"That's why I want to tell you. I know you'll understand. You're the only person..."

He was starting to climb the hill again, firmly and steadily, hand in hand with Gloria.

"...I stopped the car, got out and went back to see what had happened."

The hand stopped but the voice had become soft and cajoling "You were going to help him?"

"Not really, I just wanted to see what had happened."

The hand hadn't started again.

"He'd gone off the road straight into a field. It was dark so I couldn't see exactly what had happened. Just the lights of the bike somewhere out in the field, and the engine was still running. Mmmm.".

"So where was the driver?" Her voice was a little firmer.

"I don't know. I didn't hang around."

"What did you do?"

"I laughed."

"What?"

"It was nerves I think, but I had a laughing fit. I couldn't stop."

"What else did you do?"

Nothing really. I thought about wiping the wire down in case it had my prints on; I'm not sure if you can get prints off..."

"Why should you worry about prints?"

"I don't know. It just didn't seem to be a good idea to be associated with it. They might think I did it deliberately."

"It sounds like you were the victim. These kids can be devils.

They can make mincemeat out of younger men than you."

"Well, I might have engineered it."

"How could you have engineered it?" The hand had come back.

"I could have led him on a bit, gone faster than I should. I could have turned off my lights just before the turn so he couldn't see where to go."

"And did you? Did you do that?" Her hand started again.

He was starting up the hill again and breathing heavily. He closed his eyes, he must concentrate.

"Did you do that George? Did you try to get him off the road?"

"Oh that's good, don't stop – he shouldn't have made me angry."

"No, of course not, but did you try and get him off the road?"

He was getting there, if only she would keep it going for another minute or so. But no, dammit, her hand went still again.

"Did you try to make him have an accident? Did you try to kill him George? Is that what you did?"

"Yes all right, I did. I did. I wanted him to die."

Now he'd told her what she obviously wanted to hear, he hoped they could they get on with things. But Gloria stood back from the bed, looked up at the ceiling and said "It's a wrap." And then looked down at George and said briskly "The kid deserved whatever he got. Now don't you think about it any more."

"But can't we finish…"

"Eh, what's that? Is that someone I can hear upstairs? It's not Steve back early is it?"

George sprang up from the bed in alarm, all thoughts of further pleasure shrinking into non-existence. He started to clamber into his clothes wondering how he could ever explain what he was doing and how he could run with his trousers round his knees.

"Calm down. It's all right. There's nothing. Must be my nerves playing me tricks. But we'd better pack it in now. I don't know when Steve will be back and I would hate for him to find us here."

She turned off the lamp and smoothed down the bed covers while he finished dressing.

George, disappointed, looked at his watch, it was only half past eleven. Now wasn't the ideal time to discuss their little trip, but if not now then when?

"I wanted to talk to you about spending a weekend together. I want us to go away to a hotel. Maybe in London. You'd like that wouldn't you? Just the two of us. Go to a club, have a nice dinner somewhere, do a bit of shopping. What do you say?"

She stood, smiling, pursing her lips as if weighing up her response. "Sounds good, we could do the town together couldn't we?"

"Could you get away do you think?"

"Where there's a will there's a way."

"Next month perhaps? Could you get a couple of days off? It doesn't have to be a weekend."

"Let me check what we're doing. Steve's always got something on."

"Will you get back to me soon? Then I can make plans."

"I promise I'll get back to you soon. Now you'd better hop it before there's trouble."

He slipped guiltily out of the front door, tried but failed to walk quietly across the gravel and was soon back home and closing the door behind him. The car wasn't back and the house was silent; Eileen and Celia were still out. He felt in a positive mood. Gloria was right; he wouldn't think of the accident again.

He went up to his study and found a Hotel and Restaurant Guide for London. It was six years out of date but that shouldn't make any difference. He fancied the Basil Street Hotel; close to Harrods for a bit of shopping, and the park for maybe a walk before lunch. He leaned back in his chair, opened the book and soon found himself drifting off into a most pleasant doze, not really sleeping, more like a form of meditation. Images floated by of Gloria and himself hand in hand strolling round the food department at Harrods, feeding the squirrels in Kensington Gardens, buying lingerie for Gloria at Harvey Nichols, making love all night, having breakfast in bed. He wondered if the Basil had a Honeymoon Suite.

Chapter Twenty-Four
A letter from Amy

"For we are all, like swimmers in the sea
Poised on the top of a huge wave of fate..."
'Sohrab and Rustum' Matthew Arnold

After their lunch in town, Celia and Eileen went back to the house. Celia collected her overnight bag and said goodbye to George. He was looking more relaxed than in the morning and when it was time for Eileen to take her to the airport she was glad she could hug him with real affection.

Now she was sitting hunched up in the plane looking out of the window at the English Channel. She could see the white caps of the waves far below and felt the small plane being buffeted by a brisk wind as the island disappeared from sight. What a strange and unsettling visit it had been; she had gone to her parents for comfort and reassurance but come across a scene worthy of a Sunday tabloid. Her father was having an affair with a porn star, her mother seemed to be in the process of being seduced by a little man who looked like a monkey, and the neighbours were wanted by the police. It made her life in Camden Town, even when she and Margot had been at their most free-spirited, seem unimaginative and dull.

The affection between her mother and Ray was the most surprising. She was sure something was going on between them. Who would have imagined his being attracted to her in the first place? And who would have suspected that Eileen, always so conservative and puritanical, would respond to his approaches? He was an odd man, but intelligent enough and Celia liked his willingness to listen. He had treated both of them with real respect, unusual in a man of his generation. At first she had been suspicious of his good manners – the standing back at the door, the offering to light her cigarette, the insistence on buying their coffee – all very dated and bourgeois, but in retrospect she had to admit it was, for want of a better word, nice.

The sad fact was that she needed a bit of nice right now. As soon as they landed she would ring Jenny and suggest they have supper together. It wouldn't be wise to talk about her situation to anyone in her department; there would be an element there who would think it very amusing for the boss to have a crazy family. Now that Jenny had moved to Probation Services and was in a different building she was far enough away from Celia's staff to reduce the risk of gossip. She looked down on the disjointed line of freighters in the busy mid-Channel shipping lane, sighed, shifted her thigh as best she could away from the man next to her unsure if he was deliberately touching her, and reflected that life at the top was lonely.

"Yes, it's me, Jenny, but I'm not in. You know what to do, 'bye."

She half considered leaving a message, thought better of it and moved forward to the carousel to collect her bag. There was a family next to her: a pretty but dishevelled-looking thirty something mother, her handsome curly-haired partner and two children. The older boy, about eight, was holding his younger sister by the hand. She sprang forward when the carousel started moving and he pulled her back.

"No Sophie you mustn't touch it. It's dangerous, Mum told us. You've got to stand behind the yellow line."

He looked up and saw Celia watching him.

"She's only five you see so she doesn't know the rules."

"I'm not five. I'm five and three quarters."

The boy looked again at Celia, this time in a conspiratorial way, "Sorry Soph., that's right, I'd forgotten." Then, in a phrase obviously learned from his mother, "You're getting to be such a grown up girl. Would you like me to give you a piggy-back?"

As the train approached Waterloo and she looked out over the ragged lines of grey semis marching into London, she felt a sudden pang, a longing for a precocious but tender-hearted boy and a curly-haired five and three quarter year old little girl, someone to love, to give her a future. The mood soon passed, shaken out of her by the noise and bustle of the mainline station and the need to find the Northern Line and the tube for Camden Town. She hoisted her bag on her shoulder and plodded down the steps into the Underground. There were things to be done, papers to be read for the following day at work and food to be bought and prepared.

The desolation of the flat was still a shock: the book she'd left open on the kitchen table, the coffee cup and ashtray unwashed in the sink and the Busy Lizzie wilting in its pot on the windowsill. But first things first. There were five letters on the mat: three she could see immediately were junk, one was an electricity bill, but the fifth was written by hand. She set down the bag, put on the kettle and look hurriedly through the offers of cheap loans, bed linen sales and an easier way to pay her gas bills, saving the handwritten one until the coffee was made and she had lit a cigarette. She couldn't decipher the postmark although she could see it had been posted the previous day. The handwriting, in real blue ink, she tried it with a wet finger tip, slanted boldly to the right, the lines rising as if from excess energy. She opened it slowly, unfolding the two sheets of cream-laid paper. As she scanned the page she still could not identify the writer until she caught sight of the address – "Keyhaven Road, Milford-on-Sea." Amy.

"Dear Celia,

What a treat it was to have met you and to have spent the afternoon so very enjoyably together. I hope you don't mind my writing to you and I certainly don't wish you to see this as any kind of imposition on you to reply, or to maintain some kind of ongoing correspondence. I would not presume on your busy life.

However, I did want to say how much I enjoyed our conversation, as well as our expedition to the pub. I like to get out and about but the motivation isn't always there when I'm on my own; it always seems so much easier to stay at home. So I'm grateful that you came along and shook me out of my lethargy.

I know you won't be offended when I say that I felt, unusually for me, an almost maternal feeling of concern towards you – perhaps more accurately described as an old woman's recognition in you of herself at a younger age. So much of what you said, and perhaps left unsaid, reminded me of when I was a rebellious thirty year old. I wish then that I had had the courage of my convictions and not, for example, accepted a marriage that was so obviously wrong from the start.

Or, instead, that I had never experienced rebellious feelings. For then I would have settled uncomplainingly into the life expected of me. Instead I fell between two stools, neither satisfied for that which had been chosen for me, nor brave enough to throw it over and find my own future.

I am not sure why I feel that something of the same is happening to you, but I do recognise the same restlessness and sense of regret. If I am right, and you also see yourself in these words, then let me be agent provocateur and suggest that you learn from my example. Don't wait for your world; make it happen, the sooner the better. I wouldn't want you to be a lonely old woman living with a cat for company. I can cope with it; I'm what they call a tough old bird, but you, I can tell, are not. Embrace life while there is still time.

I do hope that you don't find these remarks too intrusive, but then, you can always choose to ignore my words, and I wouldn't be at all offended if you were to do just that.

I should always be very happy to hear from you, or see you

*here in Milford, with or without notice – and that I must admit
is a rare invitation from an old biddy like myself who enjoys her
privacy, so you should feel honoured!*
   Meanwhile, my very best wishes for your future,
   Sincerely and affectionately,
   Amy."

Celia took a deep last drag from her cigarette and as she
stubbed it out amongst the others left in the ashtray recognised
there was a lot to think about.

Chapter Twenty-Five
George versus Ray

"Slowly the poison the whole blood stream fills"
'Missing Dates'   William Empson

It was very early on Tuesday morning. He told himself he was, definitely, going down to the pools, but not yet. He lay alone in bed watching the fitful sunshine playing across the ceiling. It felt chilly. He turned his head towards the pillow next to him; it hadn't been used. Eileen had slept in the spare room again. He pulled back the summer weight duvet and looked at his bare legs. He hadn't known where his clean pyjamas were last night and Eileen hadn't been in a cooperative enough sort of mood for him to ask so he'd slept in his underpants. His legs looked good: straight muscled, tanned. But the belly was still too flabby; he grabbed a handful and gave it a good shake. A couple more months of the pools and Gloria should get that sorted. All in all he was in good nick and there was no reason why he shouldn't keep things that way for, say, at least another ten years. There were plenty of men who looked good in their seventies. Anyway Gloria would be in her fifties by then so she would past her peak as well. He hoped her breasts wouldn't sag. He looked at his watch again – time to go.

He decided to walk down to the pools that morning, and warm himself up a bit. Andrew and Don were already in the water; Ray was alone in the changing rooms and Bill and Kevin hadn't arrived.

"How's life?" asked George.

"Good, very good." Ray looked down, smiling enigmatically as he carefully folded his clothes.

"Getting enough then?" George was longing to be asked about his own sex life.

"Probably not as much as you!", Ray looked up and winked, "but then it's quality not quantity I'm after."

"Dream on." George had heard Celia use the phrase at the weekend and had been saving it for an appropriate moment.

"Dream on, nothing. I'm after someone like I told you and it's going to end in marriage. I've got that feeling."

"I thought she was already married?" George remembered Ray, for whatever reason, was chasing some middle-aged non-event.

"She is at the moment. But her stupid husband is having an affair and she doesn't like it, so I reckon I'm in with a chance."

"How do you know?" George was genuinely interested.

"She told me."

"How does she know?"

"How does any woman know? He probably wears his hair differently, uses too much aftershave, gets irritable if he's questioned... There are a million and one clues. And a woman always knows."

George took off his watch and laid it by his clothes. Did women always know? He hoped not. "Maybe he has his reasons."

"I'm not saying he doesn't, but I don't care about that. I can see my opportunity, and by the time the silly bugger has realised what he's losing, it'll be too late."

George followed Ray to the pool. The talk about adultery and the predatory nature of Ray's intentions had made him feel uneasy. Had he left a trail of clues for Eileen to follow? Was there anything he'd done or worn or said that she would notice was different? Not really, he thought. He'd joined the Vikings, and yes, he'd bought some new clothes. But his hair was the same and although he'd taken more care with his grooming it was highly unlikely that Eileen would notice; she didn't come near him anyway. Besides, she had never noticed any of his other affairs. He had always been very discreet; that had been one of his guiding principles.

Despite the sun, the morning was chilly with a brisk south easterly wind. The pool was choppy, and the water granite-grey. He had been intending to walk down the steps and gradually acclimatise himself but when Ray leaned over and slipped in headfirst at the deep end, George felt obliged, reluctantly, to do the same. He took a deep breath, screwed up his eyes and flopped, noisily, over the edge. No point in wasting a heroic gesture.

The water, still stone cold although it was mid-July, exploded about his head and ears and his heart thumped away as he surfaced, stunned and spluttering. He opened his eyes, blinking with the salt water, and saw that Ray was already halfway along the pool heading towards the sea end. Despite his better judgement – because there was no rational reason why he should consider Ray in any way a competitor, nor this a competitive situation – he followed in his wake, setting out with a good fast crawl, propelled by the cold. At the far end Ray turned and despite the turbulence of the water he must have noticed George coming after him head down and cleaving the water with serious intent, because he suddenly quickened his own stroke.

The next ten minutes saw a half-hearted challenge become an almost desperate race. If, initially, George had been proudly conscious of his longer stronger body and his ability in the water – for they all acknowledged that he knew what he was doing in the pool, even Andrew – his confidence this morning was misplaced. Ray, not normally a fast swimmer, today performed like a man inspired. It was as if he had a special power to subdue the grey water and create for himself a miraculously calm pathway along which he moved with a sustained and elegant crawl. George, fighting the elements as well as Ray's backwash, tried all his strokes in turn, shifting clumsily from sidestroke to butterfly and then back to a hurried and splashy crawl. Each time he looked across the troubled surface he saw the almost languid lift of Ray's arms and the foam from his trudging legs still well ahead and gaining. George motored on, making so much noise and taking up so much emotional room in the pool, that Bill and Andrew stopped what they were doing and turned to watch the pair.

It was Ray who decided when the race was over, and Ray who won. On the twelfth lap, as he approached the shallow end, he stood up and then swung himself up to sit jauntily on the edge, the water streaming from his small hard body and his nose and ears. He wiped his face with both hands and let out an audibly satisfied sigh as George swam nonchalantly over to the side instead of finishing the last lap and dragged himself up the steps as gracefully as his trembling legs would allow. He hung there on the handrail, his heart racing as he tried to catch his breath, carefully avoiding looking at the perky figure sitting on the concrete. Ray was small and stunted, but the bugger certainly had stamina. Neither man spoke.

Was it a sudden desire to compete or had Ray singled George out? If so, George could not fathom out why. Maybe it's some form of jealousy he thought to himself as he walked past Ray giving him a brief, tight smile and a nod. Jealousy about what though? Maybe of his height, his looks, and because he, George, was happily married, had a daughter and a proper family life. He'd be even more jealous if he knew about Gloria, he thought, and what we get up to. He towelled his hair vigorously and then rubbed his still-trembling legs as he changed at the far end of the room, keeping his distance from Ray. Whatever his problem was, George didn't want to know about it.

But Ray was persistent. "You strong in the arm? Your muscles look pretty good."

They were sitting in the sun on the café terrace, at one of the iron tables. The café wasn't open yet, but they'd all brought their flasks of tea. You're right thought George, I do have pretty impressive muscles for a man who has been behind a desk for most of my life. Just the luck of the genes again. He and Eileen had played a fair bit of tennis when they were younger. An image flashed through his mind of the shady path between the fir trees at the back of the tennis club and of Nita Fairbanks and her glorious thighs in her little white pleated skirt. What a summer that had been; his service had never been stronger.

"Come on then," Ray leaned forward, his right elbow on the table, hand open. George sat stock still, his right hand still curled around a plastic mug of tea.

"Well, come on," repeated Ray. "Let's see what you're made of." His arms were thin and ropey-looking but the dragon tattoo on his upper arm bulged over hard muscle.

Don cleared his throat and brought his chair in noisily closer to the table, "Coom on Andrew, coom and watch a pair of silly buggers fight to the death."

George withdrew his hand and flexed his fingers surreptitiously under the table. "You don't seriously want to arm wrestle do you? Not before breakfast, surely?"

"He's trying to back out of it the soft happ'orth. Trying to bloody creep away. Coom on George, get a grip of tha'self. Tha' can only lose. Unless, that is, Ray breaks tha' ruddy arm."

George looked into Ray's eyes. They were mean and small, still red from the salt water. Suddenly the last thing in the world that he wanted was to have another trial of strength with Ray. He tried a half laugh. "If you're that keen, Don, put your money where your mouth is."

"No," said Ray. "I'll take you first and deal with Don afterwards."

"The bloody cheek of the man." Don affected a look of wounded pride. "I'd rather play winner, Ray, if that's all the same with you."

"Queensberry Rules then," said Andrew as he moved away the flask and the mugs and then stood over them authoritatively.

"Ray put your elbow there, that's right. And George, put yours there. No, not at an angle, man; get yourself directly over your arm, that's better. Best of three, and you have to get the hand right down touching the tabletop. Start when I say one two three go."

There was no escape. George, heart thumping again, sat awkwardly over his right arm. His left hand, already sweating, gripped the tabletop. They clasped hands; Ray's was small, cool and dry. The flesh was soft but only superficially, like sanded wood. George suspected that his felt soft right the way through, and wimpishly sweaty. He hoped Ray couldn't feel his quickened pulse, or sense his fear. Fear? What was he fearful about – losing at a silly game?

"One two three go!"

Ray reacted quickly, putting a sudden burst of energy into his arm that nearly took George down. George only just managed to keep his arm from bending beyond the point of no return, but it was a near thing. He gritted his teeth, using his left hand to give him leverage. His longer arms gave him a natural advantage and with a rush of strength he managed to get Ray's hand over at a slight angle. The smaller man held gamely on for two, then three long minutes. Both of them were red in the face with teeth bared and the tendons of their necks were standing out with the strain.

"Stand by with the body bag." said Don. "One of them will pop their clogs if we're not careful."

Ray glanced over at Don as if considering a reply and George seized his opportunity; a second rush of adrenalin and there he was, his hand over Ray's on the table, victorious.

Ray rubbed his hand and arm ruefully.

"OK I'll give you that one. But it's best of three remember."

"Why don't we leave it there?" George was trembling inside and out "You've got nothing to prove. I'm bigger than you, that's all. And size matters in this game."

"Size always bloody matters!" Don slapped both his hands on

the table laughing.

"I want to beat you if I can." For all the serenity of his expression, there was an edge to Ray's voice and he set up his arm again, the small hard hand open in readiness. Reluctantly George sat down. He didn't want to do this but there seemed to be no way of backing down. Andrew hovered over them again making a few adjustments. They started again.

Ray stared coldly into George's eyes and held his gaze without blinking and they were both holding their breath to keep the strength within them. Thirty seconds, forty seconds they sat locked in combat, their arms shuddering. Then Ray suddenly exhaled as if he had to take another breath of air. George heard the sound, thought it was sign of submission, and for an immeasurably tiny instant relaxed his arm. Too late he realised his mistake; in the same nanosecond that he started to relax, Ray pushed with renewed vigour and he took George's hand down to the table top in one swift movement.

Don leapt up excitedly. "Small, but perfectly formed, by Christ! He's bloody done it. Well done man. Tha's as fit as a butcher's dog."

"Yup, well done." said George rubbing his hands together. He wanted to say that it wasn't fair, but to whom? While Andrew was, as he always was, impassively neutral, Don seemed to be on Ray's side. At that moment George realised that he didn't like Ray and Don was a bit of a pain as well. "Well that's that, one all. Well played." And he stood up again to go.

"Best of three," said Ray, his arm and hand in readiness again on the table.

George sighed impatiently, and sat down. This was all getting a bit silly. "Oh for God's sake! OK, let's make it quick. I've got things to do."

They leaned forward across the table again. George's arm and wrist ached and he could only hope that Ray was feeling the same. If that were so, he didn't show it. His face was impassive, the grey monkey eyes as bright as ever and focused steadily on George. They clasped hands and immediately went to the task full force. Within seconds Ray seemed to get a superhuman rush of strength and with a twisting motion that sent a shooting pain from George's wrist right up to his shoulder he bore down hard to the table taking George's hand with him.

"Argh! Shit!" George rubbed his arm "That bloody hurt."

Ray was sitting across the table smiling, "Don't dish out what you can't take yourself."

"What's that supposed to mean?" said George crossly, still massaging his arm.

"Here's Bill" said Don looking over George's shoulder, "he's a bit late for a swim."

But Bill wasn't carrying a sports bag and as he hurried over they could see that he looked worried. "Hi guys, I'm not stopping. Something awful has happened and I thought I'd let you know in case you see him. Kevin's son has died."

"Neil?" Ray stood up.

"What happened?" Andrew and Don spoke together.

"He was killed in a road accident on Sunday night. They didn't find the body until early yesterday morning. He was on his motorbike, took a corner wrong and crashed into a field."

"My God, poor old Kevin. Neil was only fifteen."

"Where did it happen?"

George was still sitting at the table and quiet, but with a terrible sinking feeling in his bowels he knew what Bill was going to say.

"St. Saviour's, up the road from the reservoir. The road bears sharp right but he drove straight on. Must not have seen the bend in the dark."

"What did he do, hit his head?"

"Worse than that, in fact pretty gruesome," Bill swallowed uneasily, "he rode through a wire fence and it cut his head off."

"Oh shit." Ray spoke, but all of them looked shocked. George felt his legs grow weak. He couldn't stand up even if he had wanted to.

"What time did it happen?" It was his voice but it didn't seem to belong to him.

"Sometime between ten and midnight they reckon. A local farmer found him the next morning. Pretty awful sight I should imagine. Apparently the farmer said he heard some noise the night before but hadn't taken much notice."

"What kind of noise?" George's throat was dry, he could hardly speak.

"He said it sounded like some youngsters, car noises and then laughter."

"Maybe it was Neil, maybe he was drunk?" George knew his voice sounded strange but surely, he thought, that would be natural in the circumstances.

"Apparently not; that was one of the first things they did, tested him for alcohol, but he was clean. No they can only think that he made a driver error, but they've got a whole team of men on the case. They've blocked the road off while they go over the ground, just in case there was someone else involved. Nasty business."

"Did anyone see anything?"

"Your guess is as good as mine at the moment. If they have found anything it will be in today's paper. Look, I've got to go, sorry to break up the party. Maybe see you Thursday, but I don't think we'll see Kevin for some time – obviously."

"Have you got his address?" asked Andrew, "I'd like to send him a letter."

Andrew and the others walked off to the changing room, leaving George still sitting at the table, his aching arm forgotten. He knew Neil; a tall lad for his age, nice open face, respectful – the sort of boy George would have liked for a son. He'd come to the pools a few mornings with his father, not to swim but to go running along the coastal path before school. After his swim Kevin would sit looking for Neil to come running down the steps and along the road. They got on well together, they were buddies. "My best friend, but don't tell Sheila." Kevin had said to George one day as Neil jogged towards them. What he couldn't understand was how the youth on Sunday night could have been the same person. The boy on the bike was a big, aggressive teenager, but Neil was just a kid, tall but skinny, not properly filled out yet. Was it possible that there were perhaps two boys killed that night near the reservoir? Of course it wasn't.

As he sat, drained of energy, unable to get up and uncertain of where to go if he did manage to get to his feet, he realised the irrevocable and dreadful nature of what had happened. If only he had known it was Kevin's son; it would all have been different. He would have waved at Neil and made a joke about dropping his car keys. And Neil would have said "Hello Mr. Buchanan. Everything all right?" and then have followed George respectfully up the hill until there was room to overtake. Then he would have waved and accelerated away, showing off to his father's friend. George would have been pleased to see him, would have remembered how he had felt at that age, and be glad that there was still youth and energy enough to keep the whole sad and sorry enterprise of life going on its way. Yes, that was how it would have happened if he had known it was Neil.

"Are you all right George? You look a bit shocked like." Don was looking at him in a kindly way. "Have you got your car? Do you want a lift?"

"No, thanks for the offer, but I'm going to walk back."

"Dreadful business eh? Dreadful. See you then. Take care."

George sat on alone for another half hour, until he had the strength and composure to make his way up the hill to home. As he slowly climbed the steps he muttered to himself "I didn't know, I'm not to blame, I didn't know, I'm not to blame..." Apart from convincing himself that he was not guilty, there was a second imperative and that was to make sure that he wasn't suspected. First thing was to look and behave as if he were innocent. He mustn't look too interested in the news, for example, nor show any particular emotions when, as would inevitably happen, Eileen wanted to talk about it. He walked carefully home keeping strictly to the paths rather than take the short cut across the grass, glad that the wind had dropped and the air was still; he couldn't cope with any wildness or extremes today. As he neared home he repeated the mantra that his department at Parson's and Green used at their motivation seminars "Everything is under control. I will succeed. Everything is under control. I will succeed..." only stopping when he walked up the driveway and into the house.

Chapter Twenty-Six
We must get rid of the tapes

"Oh what a tangled web we weave
When first we practise to deceive."
Sir Walter Scott

Eileen was in the kitchen reading the Guernsey Press. Damn, he'd wanted to get to the paper first and prevent her from seeing it. He took a quick glance and thought he saw on the front page a photograph of a field, with a police ribbon stretched across the entrance? He must find a way of looking at the paper soon but without arousing her suspicions.

"Had a nice swim?"

"A bit cold, but I managed twenty laps." He sat down heavily opposite her and watched her face as he spoke; her expression was softer this morning, as if some inner defence had been broken down, as if she wanted to communicate again.

"Tell you what though, my left leg is giving me hell this morning. I think it's the cold water, it feels as if I'm going to get cramp." He massaged the offending leg, composing his face into an expression of manfully-born pain. He hoped that this would prompt her to get up and make him a cup of tea during which time he could naturally lean over and have a look at the paper. No, she carried on reading. So he stopped, cocked his head on one side and looked up at her from his bending over position "Was that the post I just heard?"

"It's early if it is," said Eileen, but nevertheless went out to the hall to check.

George immediately laid his hand on the newspaper and pulled it across to his side of the table. The paper was open at Readers' Letters but she must have seen the front page. He turned to it now. "Youth in Shocking Accident" alongside a murky photograph of what he recognised as the entrance to his - to the field. There were half a dozen policemen, a dark shadow on the ground that might or might not have been the bike, pale ribbons of plastic stretched across the entrance and the caption "Police examine the scene of a fatal accident in St. Saviours." He started to read the article but Eileen came back into the room.

"I don't know what you heard, but it wasn't the post. I haven't finished reading that yet."

"Are you making a cup of tea?"

"I've just made one. I could top it up with hot water for you."

While she was on her feet he split the paper into two chunks, leaving the centre pages for her: "Do you mind if I have the sports section?"

And so they sat there on either side of the kitchen table, each bent over the paper but while Eileen was reading about prize day at Blanchelands College and the attractions of the forthcoming South Show, George was reading, with silent desperation, about death in a rural parish.

"Police are making a full enquiry over a fatal accident that took place on Sunday night. Neil Vaudin, aged 16, son of Kevin and Sheila Vaudin of "Greenlees", Rectory Hill, Castel, was killed in a bizarre motorbike accident that took place in a field near St. Saviour's Reservoir.

The full details of the injuries sustained by the victim have not yet been released but Alan Foulard, a local farmer, who found Neil's body lying near his bike at six thirty on Monday morning is said to have received medical treatment for shock at the Princess Elizabeth Hospital.

A statement released by the police last night confirmed that

Neil lost control of the bike as he took it round a corner on Rue du Moulin, at Neuf Chemin, St. Saviour's. He broke through a wire fence into a field belonging to Mr. Foulard, where bike and rider came to rest in the long grass. Police confirm that the injuries sustained by Neil Vaudin were of an unusual nature and it is for this reason that they are treating the incident as suspicious.

The accident is estimated to have taken place some time between the hours of eleven o'clock and twelve, midnight, last Sunday. Forensic testing has ruled out the possibility of drunk driving…"

George scanned the next few paragraphs until -

"No eye witnesses have come forward but a Mr. Thomas Eglington of Calais Road, St Martin, who was driving in the area around the time of the accident, claims to have seen a car parked near the field and believes he saw the figure of a man at the entrance to the field. (continued on Page 2)"

George turned the page with trembling fingers.

"Your tea's going cold."

He jumped at the sound of her voice.

" 'When I saw the man and then the car parked further up the lane, I didn't take much notice. I thought someone had stopped, you know maybe to answer a call of nature. Though I actually did say to my wife at the time he must have a weak bladder if he couldn't wait until he got home. I mean Sunday night – there's never any traffic. We were coming home from my parents' place so it would have been around half past eleven. I saw the car quite clearly in the headlights; I didn't catch the registration number but it was a small car, a Ford Focus or Fiesta, silver, definitely silver.'

Police are eager to hear from the driver of that car, even if he or she has no involvement with, or knowledge of, the accident. A search is taking place in the Motor Registration Office to identify all Focus and Fiesta owners on the island. To help us find this car more quickly please contact us if you own a

*light coloured/silver Ford Fiesta or Ford Focus, or if you know
someone else who does.*

*Meanwhile, the constables continue their inch by inch
examination of the field, including footprints and impressions
left by the tyres on the verge and around the entrance to the
field."*

George calculated rapidly. The island had a population of
about 60,000, of whom about a third must own either one or
two cars. How many would own a Ford – maybe 1,000? Of
those how many would own a Focus or Fiesta - maybe 200? Not
enough to keep the police occupied for more than a few days,
especially if everyone was busy grassing on their neighbours.

His next consideration was how many people knew they
owned a silver Focus? Gloria of course, but she knew the
whole story and wouldn't betray him anyway. The Vikings
may have noticed his car although maybe not in sufficient
detail to spontaneously identify it as a Focus. There were a
few acquaintances they had made, mostly in connection with
the Chamber of Commerce, who might have noticed and
remembered the car...but surely not many? Damn! At the
bottom of the article was a clear photograph, obviously taken
from a car magazine – of a silver Focus.

What to do about it? Several alternative strategies fluttered
through his mind: he could re-spray the car. He could even do it
himself in the garage if necessary. He could buy another car and
leave the Ford in the garage until the fuss all blew over, or take
the car over on the ferry to France and abandon it in some lay-
by? Dowse it in petrol and leave it to burn there, Or he could
push it over the cliff down near the dirt track on Pleinmont and
when they traced it back to him, claim that it had been stolen on
that Sunday evening.

"Have you seen this story about the accident near the
reservoir? They're looking for a driver with a car like ours."
Eileen's voice cut through his thoughts like a cold wind.

Here of course was the problem, sitting across the table from him. Eileen knew very well that they owned a silver Focus and all these scenarios depended on her cooperation and complicity, which meant she would have to know the full story of his involvement. No, not necessarily the full story; she mustn't know about the rendezvous with Gloria, but she could know that he drove down the road in St. Saviour's on his way home that evening, and had indeed stopped at that point in Rue du Moulin – either for a leak as the kind Mr. Eglington suggested, or maybe because he heard someone laughing in a field and went to investigate. Heard someone laughing while he was driving? Yes, it's a slow bend and it was a warm evening so he had had the window open. That didn't mean that he had anything to do with the accident or that he had seen the bike and body in the field. Did that seem feasible? If he were going to tell this half-true tale then he had to say it now, while Eileen was looking up at him across the table, waiting for his reply and probably wondering if she ought to repeat the question.

"They're not sure yet," his voice sounded unnatural to him but he forged on, pushing his way through the words, "whether it's a Focus or a Fiesta. It's only one man's claim, and if he can't tell the difference between a Focus and Fiesta, which are like chalk and cheese, then I'm not confident he can be sure about anything."

"You didn't go anywhere near there did you, when you went out to check out the engine?"

"I suppose I did go near the reservoir, but I certainly didn't see any accident."

"Well, I suppose we should ring the number and tell them." Eileen's voice was mild, disinterested, calm.

"We should. Quite right. I'll do it later. After I've had a shower. Give me the page where they've got which number to ring and I'll use the phone in the study."

He stood under the shower for a long time, letting the heat penetrate and loosen his muscles, and if it could, wash away his sins. He'd delayed the need to act for several hours; he'd think

315

what to do about the car later. But first there was a forensic job to do. He hid the newspaper page with the telephone contact on it under some papers on his desk. Eileen wouldn't dare to look there.

Later he crept out downstairs into the garden and drove the car quietly round the side of the garage where he couldn't be seen from the house and washed it down with a power hose, being extra careful to clear away the mud and the last few strands of grass from the underside. Finally he lifted the spare wheel from the boot and with some difficulty changed the near-side rear wheel; that might prevent whatever tyre tracks they found at the scene of the accident being traceable to the car. Later that day he would buy another three tyres and put them on and throw the old ones away, dispose of them one by one in different parts of the island. Hot and tired he stood looking at the car; it was, he hoped, free from anything that could trace it to the scene of the accident but not so shiny and polished that it would seem overly clean to an enquiring mind.

He walked into the kitchen, unexpectedly hungry for his lunch. It was one of his favourites; lamb chops, Jersey Royals and asparagus, and the half bottle of Sancerre left over from yesterday. Funny how food, and wine of course, had the capacity to soften the worst blows that life could deliver. George washed and carefully dried his oily hands and sat down at the table, with a hunger not just for the meat and veg. but for the comfort and deep familiar pleasures of a meal in his own home. They ate contentedly in near silence for half an hour; an island of tranquillity in a rough sea. Perhaps it was the contrast of inside versus out, like lying warm in bed listening to rain on the window, that emphasised this moment of sanctuary. For all its shortcomings, their marriage, he reflected, had become the one steady point in his life, and Eileen, slight and faded though she was, had turned out to be his rock, his fortress, his solid ground. For thirty minutes the rest of the world and its problems shrank round them until they were together in their isolation, shored up against what storms might come.

Eventually, as he poured the last of the wine into his glass – she shook her head when invited to share it – and sat back in his chair he saw her solemn face and realised the golden moment had passed.

"George, we've got a bit of a problem."

Her voice was grave and firm, and for the fourth time that day he felt his stomach lurch and gurgle noisily in complaint. The remnants of the Sancerre turned to acid in his mouth and he set down his glass in despair.

"What kind of problem?" His voice, he knew, sounded furtive.

Her face was drawn and the expression one of barely controlled fear; he didn't know whether to be frightened alongside or, if they were going to argue, pleased to see her in a potentially weak position.

"It's about those videos that Steve asked us to store in our garage." Her face relaxed slightly as if she was glad to have started. "I had to go to the garage the other day and, I know I shouldn't have, but I opened one of the parcels. They were videos, just as he said, but the titles looked odd. I began to worry about what sort of films they might be, what with the police having been round to his house and everything and, well, anyway I had a funny feeling about them so I opened one of the packets, well, three of them actually."

He was curious but he knew he must assert his authority, "You did what?" he said in a loud voice that usually unsettled her, "Those are Steve's private property. I said we'd look after them for him. You had absolutely no right to break into the garage and tamper with them."

"I didn't break into the garage. I had the spare key. The one from the drawer in the sideboard."

"I didn't mean it literally, you fool." That's right, there was a spare, how could he have forgotten? "I didn't mean you'd put your shoulder to the door, I just meant you shouldn't have gone in there and messed around with his stuff that we said we'd look after."

"That you said we'd look after. And I didn't mess around with his stuff. I wrapped them up again and put them back in the same place."

"What'll he say if he finds out?"

"I don't care if he does. Why should I?"

Sustained defiance this long from a normally weaker partner made him hesitate. "Even so, you said yourself – 'I know I shouldn't have…'"

"George this isn't an argument about which of us is right or wrong. I'm trying to tell you something. Those videos are bad, and it's dangerous for us to keep them here."

"You didn't look at one?"

"Two actually. Part of them, not the whole thing. And Celia watched the third one."

"Celia, you got Celia involved?" The whole world seemed to be slipping out of control into some mad free-for-all. "When was this?"

"When you were out on Sunday evening. I asked her to help me, for moral support, and in case Steve happened to see us. I know you feel loyal to him for whatever reason, but I don't trust him. And I don't trust Gloria either. They're not good people."

"I think you're wrong there but…"

"Those videos are terrible. Ugly. Pornographic."

Pornography? So that was why the police had been nosing around; Steve was in the porn business and had obviously overstepped some local legislative nicety. His gold chains and the deep tan, even next door's house itself with its lush bedroom colours, the bright lights and the lurid paintings, were suddenly explained.

"Gloria was in one of them."

"What do you mean?" What was Eileen up to? Was there a note of triumph in her voice?

"She was performing. You know, sexually."

He allowed the possibility that by 'performing' Eileen meant

318

that Gloria stripped off her clothes and did a few poses, but surely nothing more, dynamic?

"And that wasn't the worst thing. The last one, Celia said, was the worst - little boys. Pederancy."

"Pederasty." What was Gloria doing in that?

"She said it was really nasty. No wonder the police were round at their place. We must get that stuff out of our garage quickly."

"Get me the key. I'll have a look."

Half an hour later he was still in front of the screen wishing that he hadn't seen what he had seen. The evidence was undeniable; Steve was in a very dirty business and unwittingly George had become a partner in crime. That thug had corrupted Gloria as well, because there was no way that she would have done the things she did in those films of her own free will. The woman he had come to know and love could not have behaved like that. It was perhaps a trick with the camera, or maybe she was drugged and didn't know what was happening. Perhaps Steve had threatened her with violence. If so then he, George Buchanan, would go round and, and... and what? There was nothing he could do.

He sat with head in hands. The desperation of his situation had just come back with redoubled force; life had taken a disastrous and irrevocable turn and he couldn't see the way back. The room was quiet, apart from the clock. He had always thought of it previously, when life was normal, as a pleasant, reassuringly domestic sound but now its measured monotony seemed full of foreboding. It was eating up time, eating up his time. He would have to make some decisions and soon.

"Have you had a look at them?" Eileen came into the room and stood behind the settee.

He sat up and made one last attempt to defuse the afternoon. "They're certainly not pleasant viewing I agree, a bit tacky, but nothing more than you can see on television these days. I don't know if we really need to get upset about it all…" His voice tapered off as he recalled the soundtrack of the tape with the young boys. "You're right Ellie, we must get rid of them."

"Oh George, thank goodness you feel the same way. You see, I wasn't sure if you knew what was in them." The relief in her voice and the hand she placed on his shoulder, whether to console him or to connect with him, he didn't know, gave him a small spark of comfort. At least they were facing this part of his chaotic life together.

"Leave it to me, Ellie. I'll have a word with Steve, tell him that we need the garage for something else and would he move his stuff out."

"What if he says he has nowhere to put it?"

"I'll remind him he's got all that space in the basement."

"Which basement?"

He barely had the energy to cope with this reminder of his duplicity, but Eileen was thinking ahead: "You could tell him we need the space because we're getting another car."

"Not a bad idea." That would work well with his Plan B for how to get rid of the car. They could buy a new car and leave the Focus in the garage, and sell it when all this blew over.

"When will you speak to him?"

"Don't rush me. I've got to think about it a bit, choose my time."

Chapter Twenty-Seven
We need the space

"And dar'st thou then
to beard the lion in his den?"
Sir Walter Scott.

The very last thing he wanted to do was to go and confront a man who happened to be a criminal as well as the husband of his mistress. George knew he was vulnerable on both fronts and he needed to do some thinking about it 'out of the box' as those complacent creativity consultants were always telling him at Parson and Green. Into the box would be more like it with Steve unless he was careful. He went to get some Gaviscon for his stomach.

Half an hour later, feeling calmer and stronger he decided to see Steve that very afternoon; to strike while the iron was hot. Tell him he wanted the stuff off his premises. There was no need to give a reason; it was his garage after all. He might offer to help move the packages, but otherwise he'd stand firm and leave the problem with Steve.

All the same he didn't want to tell Eileen when he was going; he'd slip over when he felt primed and ready. As he made for the front door, Eileen was standing in the hallway.

"Are you going over to Steve's now?"

He wished she hadn't asked him. It destroyed his sense of being proactive, of having things under his control. Now that he'd been asked and had to do it, he'd been put on the back foot, pushed into a loser's role. Nevertheless he nodded, opened the front door briskly and walked down the drive whistling Colonel Bogey. But by the time he reached Steve's porch and rang the bell, he was trembling, with a visible juddering that he had seen before in game dogs and greyhounds ready for the off. It must be a protective device the body has in order to prepare for a fight he thought, suddenly fascinated by a long trail of ants bustling up and down the wall by the door. Fight or flight.

The door was flung open, widely, confidently, and there stood Steve in what looked like a new tracksuit and huge white trainers. How young and strong he looked today. "Wotcha mate, what can I do for you?" he said in a friendly voice with maybe a hint of impatience.

"Steve, how are you?" George had intended to come in with his request fast and to the point, but he'd forgotten his opening words. "Er, hope you are well. Haven't seen you for a bit.... we're thinking of getting a new…"

"Don't stand on the step, come in come in. I've got the cricket on. Aussies are winning – natch."

He bounced off along the hall and George had no option but to close the front door and follow him into the den. The big screen television was on.

"I say, that is a good picture." George took refuge in the booming colour and confusion while they both gazed at the screen.

"Sit down, sit down and grab yourself a tube." Steve nodded towards the cool box on the floor next to the couch. George chose a Foster's, snapped it open and there being no other chair, sat down alongside Steve. For the next ten minutes he sat in silence and comfortable appreciation of Rambaran's bowling and the cold lager. Perhaps he and Steve could deal with things as buddies; after all a man who liked cricket couldn't be all bad. He was rather disappointed when the broadcast ended and Steve turned down the volume.

"Great game. Great game. Gotta keep celebrating." Steve

handed George another Fosters, "Chuck the empties into the waste bin."

"Thanks, yes, great match. Eileen and I are thinking of getting another car."

"Worried about being identified with the scene of the crime?"

"What?" said George panicking, his mind whirling from one crisis to another. What was Steve referring to? Which crime? How many crimes had he committed? What were the things he could say to Steve, and which were the forbidden topics?

"You've got a silver Ford Focus haven't you? The same as the witness they want for that motor accident, the one in the paper where that poor sod was killed?"

"No. I mean yes, we have a Ford Focus. And I suppose you could call it silver."

"Can't think what else you'd call it unless gilt! Get it? Gilt, guilty?"

"Ha! Yes! Jolly funny. No, we have got a Ford Focus and obviously we're letting the Authorities know about it. But we're going to get another car. Not related to that incident in any way. In fact, we've been thinking about it for a long time; a car for Eileen, and that's why I came around."

"You want some advice? I know fuck all about those little saloon jobs. I drive off-roaders, always have. Goes with the image. I mean what would people say if they saw me wearing a car like yours? They'd think my dick had dropped off for a start. Only way I'd be able to get into it anyway. A man like me needs room. Gloria likes something big as well."

"I might let Eileen keep the Ford," George hurried to get off the subject of Gloria, "and I could get a four wheel drive. They look a lot of fun. But what I was going to ask..."

"Want a trial run? Sure, take her this afternoon if you want. I'm not possessive about my cars. My women yes; anyone caught messing around with Gloria would soon find themselves sorted," and here it seemed to George that Steve's voice had acquired a special emphasis, "not that she would keep anything secret from me anyway. You see I've got my ways and means of knowing. Yeah, I'm touchy about Gloria, but anyone can drive my car." Steve crushed the can in his hand and threw the corpse into the waste bin.

George's stomach was heaving as he summoned up all that was left of his courage.

"No I won't take her for a test drive thanks. The car I mean. Not Gloria of course!" He prayed that his reddening face would be thought a result of the lager, and as if to prove the connection he took another swig. "Although that's very kind. What I wanted to say was – you remember when we put all that stuff of yours into my garage? Well, I was wondering if you still needed the space?"

Steve gave him a big grin. "Yes, thanks mate, that would be good; I appreciate being able to keep the stuff there."

"No, I meant, if we are going to get another car, then we'll be needing the space."

There, he'd said it. George finished off the last of his lager, tilting the can a little further than he intended. A thin cold trickle of beer ran over his chin and inside his shirt right down to his navel.

"Oh yeah, I get you! But, look, you've got two garages. And you don't use either of them, do you? I see your car – the Focus – outside on the drive every day. So you've already got one spare." He was still smiling.

"Well, with a new car..." George knew he was weakening. Steve knew too.

"If you get an off-roader, that won't need to be kept indoors. They're tough, like me" Steve laughed and playfully but with some force punched George's upper arm. Then he made an elaborate gesture of looking at his watch. "Hey, is that the time? Sorry mate, I've got to go. It was good to see you." They both stood up and Steve put a heavy hand on George's shoulder and propelled him into and across the hall.

George walked slowly back to his house, still clutching the

empty beer can. He'd failed. Not my fault he thought. Steve's a dangerous guy and somehow he seemed to have got wind of him and Gloria. If so, how? He stood by his newly washed car for a few minutes, idly examining it and picking off an imaginary leaf while he pondered what to say to Eileen. He'd have to do what he always did, protect her from the truth while he gave himself more time to sort things out. The front door opened as he reached it; she had been waiting for him in the hall. For the first time he not only noticed her greying hair and the softening line of the jaw but felt some compassion. Even his chief adversary was getting old as well.

"You were so long. I was wondering whether to come over and see if you were all right."

"Don't be silly. It was fine. We had a couple of beers and watched the cricket. They've got a huge television. Plasma screen. Great definition."

"You had a beer with him, when you know what he gets up to?"

"Be reasonable. I've got to keep things friendly. Don't want him sending his heavies over. Anyway we were drinking it straight from the can."

"Is he going to move that stuff?"

"Y-eees. Yes. He's fine about it. He said just to give him a couple of weeks while he makes some space in his basement."

"A couple of weeks?"

"It could be earlier."

"Did you tell him we'd looked at them?"

"I didn't think that was a good idea, old thing. Told him we were getting another car as you suggested and that we needed the space. That way it could all be friendly and keeps us out of trouble."

"All right, but two weeks seems such a long time."

"You see, it will go in a flash", said George, not knowing that it would be the two longest weeks in his life.

Chapter Twenty-Eight
The Waiting Game

"I like the weather – when it's not raining
That is I like two months of every year"
'Italy Versus England'   Lord Byron

Continents have climates, islands have weather and very small islands like Guernsey have random meteorology. The two weeks that followed were the coldest and wettest on record for the time of year, with the low temperatures made worse by gale force winds streaming in from the Atlantic. August holidaymakers shivered as they sat in steamy cafes, skidded along the muddy coastal path or trailed around the more formal attractions: the Strawberry Farm, the Underground Hospital, the Little Chapel. Despite the lushness of field and garden, the island was bleak and hostile.

The place felt like a prison for George and not just because of the wind and rain. He no longer went to the Vikings, partly because he couldn't face the possibility of seeing Kevin again and because he didn't know how to react when the subject of Neil's death was raised by the others, although he was relieved and a little surprised to note that in the absence of any reminder of the accident, he found himself gradually forgetting the awfulness of it. It was as if he had convinced his inner voices that he was not guilty of any wrongdoing, and, moreover, was optimistic that in a few months he would have forgotten, not that it had ever happened, but that it was in any way linked to him: it was a sad event but somebody else's sad event, not his own. A tissue of time, like skin over an ulcer, was blunting the pain and erasing the memory.

No, a more potent reason for not going back to the Vikings was Ray's attitude towards him. His spiky competitiveness about what he still had no idea but it was obviously directed towards him, had spoiled the intimacy of the club, the sense of playfulness and of being welcome there as one of the boys. He had hoped that Ray would become a friend, but that no longer seemed an option. The only one he actively missed was Andrew, the group's unofficial leader: reliable, confident and kind. George would have liked to get to know Andrew better, would have liked to have had him as an older brother, would even have liked to have been Andrew: a man of steadfast character and integrity. Maybe when things were sorted and he could see his way more clearly he would get in contact with him again. Meanwhile, he explained his absence, first to the club and then to Eileen, by claiming a bout of arthritis, leaving it open as to if, or when, he might start swimming again.

He had also become reluctant to take the car out in public and used the rain as the reason for putting it away in the second garage. He had not, of course, reported ownership to the constables. It was their responsibility to find him; after all it was perfectly possible that he might not have seen the Guernsey Press that day: it wasn't as if it were obligatory reading, one of the conditions of living in a small community. To his relief Eileen seemed to have forgotten about the car, either that or she assumed he had contacted them and everything had been ticked off as all right.

Another reason for not leaving the house was Gloria. She hadn't contacted him since he'd been on his abortive mission to Steve's two weeks ago. His idea about the Basil Street Hotel and their weekend in London had faded into the very unlikely-to-happen category, in the company of his hopes that one day his hair would be restored to its natural colour, that newspaper print would be legible without the need for glasses and that he could recall his telephone number promptly when asked. Even if he and Gloria never went to London together, there was, surely, the possibility of finding private places here on the island, just as they had in the recent past? It was unfair of her to have stoked him up and then be mean with the coal. Although 'stoked up' was hardly how he would have described his state at the moment; his libido seemed at an all-time low. Maybe that was indirectly her doing as well. Perhaps it was natural that his desire should have diminished knowing now what sort of woman she was.

What kind of woman is that, he asked himself as he sat in the sitting room watching the rain being hurled against the window? After seeing her in flagrante in the video he wasn't quite sure how to classify her. Was she a victim? Or a willing participant, in which case 'slut' was probably the right word? Or 'tart' maybe? There didn't seem to be an acceptable word which could encompass all that she was and did.

There was another area of ambiguity, her motives with regard to him and the affair they were having, or used to have. As his desires dwindled his common sense grew. He knew he was no longer young, or particularly handsome, and probably he was nowhere as rich as Steve, so for goodness sake, why had she been so generous with her sexual favours? Was it a turn on for her to see him getting excited? He didn't think women were like that. Or did she like his style, his Englishness, his middle-class manners, his refinement compared with the brutish Steve? If she were that kind of woman, hankering after a bit of class, wanting to go up in the world, how could she do what she had obviously done? There was no sense to it.

He wondered what the old team at the office would have made of all this? Pearson and Fatty Hubbard in distribution would have turned their noses up. They had always struck him as a bit bloodless anyway. Randy Andy in accounts would have made no secret of his envy. He would have been both surprised and pleased that good old George was having it off with a porn queen. He imagined his team from marketing standing around the coffee machine talking about him with envy and admiration.

"Heard about Buchanan then?"

"What, have they asked him to come back?"

"No, Pearson saw him the other day coming out of the Basil Street Hotel with some red-haired totty on his arm; well-stacked, looked the part. Definitely not his wife, too young for a start."

"Someone said that he lives next door to a porn magnate over in Guernsey and they get into a bit of wife-swapping, parties round the pool, that sort of thing."

"Who would have believed it? George living the life! Some blokes get all the luck."

"He wasn't a bad-looking guy for his age if you come to think of it. And you know what they say, still waters run deep."

"Roll on retirement. Lucky Bastard."

George tried this aloud, as he looked out over the sodden garden.

"I'm a lucky bastard, a lucky, lucky bastard."

"Why?" Eileen had come in and was standing behind his chair. "Why are you?"

He jumped. "Why am I what?"

"You said 'Lucky, lucky bastard."

"I didn't say that."

"George, you did, I heard you."

"Don't tell me what I said. There must be something wrong with your ears. Why would I –"

He was interrupted by the door bell. Three long rings. George went into the hall and saw the outline of two heavy figures through the frosted glass. He slipped into the dining room and peered round the corner of the curtains. Damn and blast it was the constables. They rang again as he hurried back into the hall. Grabbing Eileen by the arm, he put his finger over his mouth in a theatrical gesture and then hissed "I'm not in; tell them anything you like to make them go away but whatever happens don't let them know I'm in."

As she went to the front door he ran silently up the stairs, only pausing at the far end of the landing to catch his breath and hear what happened when Eileen opened the door. Listening wasn't enough so he lowered himself into a crouching position behind the banisters, from where he could see but not be seen for as long as he kept back in the shadow.

"Good afternoon madam. Superintendent Nicholls and Sergeant Mahy, Guernsey Constabulary. Mrs. Buchanan is it? Sorry to bother you."

The Superintendent, a fair haired man in his fifties stepped forward almost coming over the threshold. His expression was both sympathetic and patronising. Don't worry, his face seemed to say, I've seen it all and whether you're innocent or guilty it's all the same to me. His younger colleague kept silent although his eyes were moving all the time, scanning first Eileen and then looking over her shoulder at the inside of the house. George moved back as carefully as he could and kept his face down.

"Yes, that's my name. What can I do for you?"

"It's really Mr. Buchanan we've come to see." The Superintendent smiled benevolently, as if wondering whether Eileen were old enough to be told the nature of his mission. He had good strong white Guernsey teeth - all that milk.

"I'm afraid he's not in."

"When do you expect him back?"

"Not until much later. He's up in Vale. At a friend's."

"Vale, I see. It might be some time then, before he's home." Was he being sarcastic? It was impossible to tell from his blunt, expressionless face.

"Do you want to come in?"

"Stupid cow Eileen", thought George, where he crouched on the landing with thumping heart and aching knees. "You stupid, stupid cow. Dear God don't let them in."

"Thank you, we won't come in now, but would you tell your husband that we came round to see if he had found the key to his garage and to have a little chat with him. It's just routine, eh? We could force the door and have a look now but we'd prefer him to be present."

"I think he has found the key, but I don't know where he's put it. I mean he's most likely to have it with him. I imagine so. I haven't got it, no..."

Nicholls inclined his head as he listened with professional patience. "Would you also tell him Mrs. Buchanan that we'll be back tomorrow morning and we will expect him to have the key by then?"

They strode with measured pace back to their car. Upstairs, George painfully pulled himself up by the balustrade into a standing position; as soon as he was able he staggered to the front bedroom and was just in time to see the tail end of the car as it swept round the corner and down the road. He sat down on the bed for a moment and massaged his legs back to life.

"George, they've gone. It's all right."

"Ssh! You never know, they could come back at any minute. I think I'll stay up here for a bit."

"I'll bring you up a cup of tea."

What now? George sat on the bed in the spare room trying to think his way out of the situation. The cup of tea went cold while he considered his options for getting rid of the videos before the following morning. He could burn everything down at the bottom of the garden. But would they stay alight in this rain and he wasn't sure they wouldn't just melt rather than burn? And how would he explain the plumes of black noxious smoke drifting through the neighbourhood: a failed barbecue?

What about dumping them somewhere? There were at least nine or ten carloads, maybe more, and he could probably just about do the job on his own if he worked all night. He could leave them in a field or on the cliff top; why not? One good reason why not was Steve. They belonged to him and he'd want them back. George had to keep them safe, unless he was prepared to run the risk of being at the sharp end of Steve's anger. Now, where was there a place on the island which would keep them dry and away from prying eyes? For the moment nothing came to mind. Even after he had been down to fetch the Perry's guide from the car and looked carefully at every page of the book he still couldn't remember having seen an obviously empty house or shed or old barn where he could store them for however long was necessary. He toyed with the idea of the bird hide but realised that it was far too small. Besides, what would happen when the first birders came to watch dotterels and found they couldn't even get inside the hut?

Eventually he was obliged to think along another tack. On the principle of a problem shared is a problem halved, he wondered whether maybe the best thing to do would be to go back to Steve, tell him what had happened and see how they could solve the problem together. This would mean giving Steve some hint that he, George, knew what sort of material it was, and that there might be serious repercussions for them both if it got into the wrong hands. If he could pitch it at the right sort of level Steve would realise that George knew what he was up to, but would at the same time be reassured that George was not going to blow the whistle on him. It was up to George to present himself as a man of the world, who could easily overlook a bit of sexual goings-on; he was after all a child of the sixties. It would be tricky but worth a try, in the circumstances. This time he would write out and rehearse what he wanted to say, so there could be no chance of things going wrong.

Several drafts later he wrote out his final script:

"Sorry Steve but a bit of a problem's come up. The wife happened to find a spare key for our garage and she picked out a couple of the videos that we're storing for you and do you know what? They're not blank. Not sure what exactly is on them but it looks like, how can I say it, adult material, if you understand me. Unfortunately the police came today and asked to see inside the garage. They said they were on some kind of routine search for 'illicit goods' – not sure what they mean. But

I didn't think it would be good for them to find the tapes so we told them we didn't have a key. We've managed to put them off for a while, but they're threatening to come back tomorrow and force the door.

Obviously it's not good news for either of us if they do that. So we need to find somewhere else now, tonight, to store them. I'll help you of course."

That, he felt, said everything that needed to be said without having to admit that he knew about the extreme nature of some of the films. For as long as he and Steve could discuss the tapes as if they were harmless, with no talk about criminality from either side, then it should be easy for him ultimately to disengage, to walk away from any knowledge of, or connection with, Steve and his goings-on.

Hanging over everything, of course, was the rather separate question of Gloria and whether George should disengage from her as well? He'd thought about this many times throughout the summer. At one level he suspected it would be the most sensible thing to do, and were a friend of his to ask for advice on the same subject, he would probably tell him to be wise, act his age and finish it, because only then would he be at peace with himself and be able to face the world without fear of retribution. In his own situation he could see what benefits would accrue if he finished with Gloria: there would be no need to hide things from Eileen and he would no longer be bound to keep the peace with Steve at all costs. His life would be an open book again, at least for as long as no-one turned back the pages.

He had to admit it would be a relief to be done with the subterfuge, the anxiety and even the physical hard work that was a necessary and integral part of the process. Because his sexual encounters with Gloria were hard work. His desire was still alive, just, but to express it these days seemed to be taking more from him than he had to give. Where once his body had been brimming over with surplus energy, that energy now seemed almost spent. The battery was nearly flat and a wise man would accept the inevitability of the decline; this was, after all, nature's way.

For a few minutes he thought about being that wise person, living a quiet untrammelled life, accepting what comes to every man sooner or later. Gloria would no longer exist as a luscious body but become just a memory, like all the other women he had wooed and won, safely stored away in his ageing brain.

Then he thought about never again stroking her skin or breathing in her foxy smell or seeing her smile; how could he turn his back on all that? He might as well be dead and buried. He had been dead before she came to live next door and saved him. She had shown him how to be part of life again. From her he had learned the lesson that to be a man no, to be a human being, he must be part of the game. Yet here he was telling himself to hang up his boots and look forward to a long life of being dead from the neck down.

"Bollocks!" he said out loud, "I'm in the game for as long as it lasts." He stood up from the bed and punched the air like a footballer scoring a goal. He was not dead yet, no, by Christ, not yet.

If real life has a way of standing on the sidelines occasionally, to allow a shot at goal, it always eventually returns to occupy the centre ground. So George, having given his vote for staying in some metaphorical game, now returned to worrying about what Steve might do to him if he knew of his wife's affair. He tried to comfort himself that even if Steve had his suspicions, he surely could have no proof? He and Gloria had been careful. Anyway who, at the moment, would suspect George of adultery? He must have aged about ten years in the weeks since the accident and in his current condition: muscles sliding back into flab, nerves making him jump at the sound of the microwave, he could hardly be seen as a risk to anyone. Besides, he and Gloria had done nothing for four weeks so surely any scent of their affair must have dissipated into thin air by now? No, he decided,

Steve knows nothing.

With this settled, things were looking brighter. His life was going to be all right again; he could feel it in his bones. First he would tell Eileen where he was going, and then he'd walk over to Steve to discuss things, man to man.

The heavy rain started again just as he walked out of the house.

Chapter Twenty-Nine
Betrayed

"The seas are quiet when the winds give o'er,
So calm are we when passions are no more."
Old Age   Edmund Waller.

Eileen watched him walk hurriedly away down the drive in the rain. What a state he was in! What a state they were both in! Where was the old and orderly life they were living before? Things had mostly been boring, and sometimes, when he was having his affairs, distressing, but at least it all felt real. Now that commonplace world had been replaced by an alien sort of fantasy and for the last four months they had been living another couple's life, with a script created for a completely different cast of characters.

She should have guessed that this stage of their lives would not be easy especially for George, even if he had been prepared when he left the company for the stripping away of the people and perks that had buttressed his working life. As far as she was aware, he had no unrealised ambitions and certainly no hobbies to fill the empty hole where his working life had been; his focus had always been the company for as long as she could remember. Silly of her not to have realised that without Parson and Green he was a man with a will but no way: a clockwork train that had come off the tracks, its little wheels still spinning, but its journey over.

She had not anticipated either how long it would take him to adjust to life without work; he'd been acting strangely ever since they came to the island; that was two and half years ago, and there were no signs of any improvement.

She felt for the bracelet around her wrist, the one that Doug had given, well, sold her back in May, and twisted it slowly round and round her wrist. If only things could go back to how they had been. And how was that, Eileen, little Miss Mouse? Not altogether satisfactory if one were honest. For years you have known that life is passing you by, that it has in fact already passed you by and left the remains, dry and brittle, stranded above the tide line. What have you done to fight back?

Not much she agreed, although it should be said in my favour that I've looked after George and Celia and kept the house and the garden.

Leave the dead to bury their dead.

Whose voice was that? It was the kind of thing Ray would come up with.

You know what I mean, come on face it, Eileen. You're still young enough to make a break, to do something with your life instead of watch it draining away with the dishwater.

The thought of Ray and how he would react to events had kept her going through these last weeks; and increasingly he was encouraging her to stand up for herself, put up a good fight against George.

Don't let him get away with it Eileen; you're too soft. He doesn't deserve you.

She and Ray had continued to meet at the computer centre, and even had lunch together afterwards; she explained it to George by saying she was taking extra lessons. After all, what did he know about computers?

It was still a pleasure to be with Ray, as it had been right from the start. He listened to her, offered her advice when she wanted it, and gave her what felt like unconditional friendship. It was Ray she talked to about the tapes and the problem with the police.

Any time you want to talk to me Eileen, you have my number.

Ring me night or day.

He was intelligent and wise and they laughed a lot. He was who she wanted to be with when George was in one of his states.

When you've had enough of it all, I'm here for you.

I must stay by George until we're over this business with the tapes and everything. Then I'll be able to think about the future.

Our future?

I can't say that, Ray.

But you love me don't you Eileen?

I'm not sure I know what love is any more, at least not the love between a man and a woman. I know my love for Celia; that just comes without effort. She's a part of me, like my hands or my eyes and I care for her as I care for my own body. Maybe more. But as for loving a man, being in love, that seems such a strange concept now that I'm older, almost absurd if I am honest. And if there's one thing I'm learning from you Ray is that the only way forward is through honesty. There, I expect you think I'm a prude?

Silence.

*

He had got wet just making his way round to Steve's and stood close to the door to keep out of the rain, while he rang the bell. There was no answer. Perhaps they were out and he'd have to abandon the attempt and come back later? He hoped so, but after waiting a couple of minutes he forced himself to ring again.

A figure appeared behind the decorative glass panel. George prepared himself with a deep inward breath. I must win and I can, I can, I can, he said to himself as the front door swung open. It was now or never.

"Gloria!"

'Gloria' indeed this afternoon. She had never looked more alluring. She was wearing the yellow dress that he had seen

her in from the belvedere on that very first day; surely there
had never been such a joyous colour, vibrant against her golden
skin. She looked edible.

"Well, if it isn't George! I was wondering when we might see
you." She seemed relaxed, as if she had been expecting him at
the house all along.

"Were you? I've been in a lot. You haven't rung." No, he
mustn't say things like that in Steve's house.

"Is that why you've come, to see me?" She put her head on
one side and gave a little smile.

"No, of course not, I mean I'm glad...." He was beginning to
get flustered, get on with it Buchanan. "I've come to see Steve.
Man to man. God, I've missed you." He reached out his hand
to touch her arm.

"Man to man eh?" she said, carefully evading his touch.
"You'd better come in before you shrink in all that rain."

He closed the door behind him and followed her down the
hall, conscious that he'd meant to go to the lavatory before he
left home, but forgotten. It wouldn't be right to ask to go here in
their house; he'd have to hold on.

She gestured towards the den, "The man to man's in there,"
she said, then shouted "Steve, visitor," before disappearing in
the direction of the kitchen. George was sorry but also relieved
to see her go; he would rather tackle this on his own, without
distractions. He stood on the threshold of the den trying to
remember his opening words: "Steve, there's been a bit of, I'm
sorry but er..."

It was too late, Steve was up and onto his feet and right next
to him.

"Glad you came; we were just going to ask you and your lady
wife over for drinks tonight. Gloria and I have got something
to celebrate."

"What's that?" George's mind was racing through some
possibilities: a business success of Steve's? Or they'd bought
a yacht? Or found a new house in a smarter part of the island

and would be leaving Les Vardes? Or could it be that Gloria was pregnant? He reflected on this for a moment while another part of his brain tried to retrieve his script. She was still young enough and if looks had anything to do with it she would produce lovely children. Another possibility loomed through the chaos of his brain. Could that baby be mine? They had used protection of course, and hadn't really done a proper job, but who knows, stranger things happen? He'd heard that some woman had even got pregnant from being in a municipal swimming pool, without actually touching a man and in a one-piece costume. So it could happen. Of course he would do the decent thing and marry her. Or maybe set her up with their son in a little house somewhere? Because it would be a son he was sure, Gloria wouldn't have girls. They'd have a tall golden haired son, good at games but with George's intellect and sophistication...

Steve was right in front of him, too close for comfort. "No, we don't want to tell you now, let's keep it as a surprise for this evening. You come on over at six thirty and we'll crack open a couple of bottles of Krug, all right mate?"

"Steve, it's very kind of you but there's something I want to talk to you about."

"What's your problem?"

"That's right, a bit of a problem's come up. It's about the garage. I'm sorry Steve but we must move that stuff out of my garage."

Steve's eyes narrowed and he looked mean, although the smile remained. George looked at his large, even teeth and wondered if they were natural or if he'd had implants. Australians often had bad teeth he knew, something to do with the lack of...

"I've told you already mate, sorry and all that, but it ain't convenient to shift them. You said I could keep them there, no problem and I ain't got nowhere else. Just leave it for a few weeks, eh?"

"The problem is the wife was looking in the garage for something and she happened to have a look at one of the videos. I mean I didn't know she was doing it, she only told me afterwards…"

"You been nosing round my stuff?" He brought his face even closer to George's, his expression cross but calm, with the carefree anger of a man who has no fear.

George felt his heart break into its familiar gallop, as if it wants to escape he thought, wishing he could leave with it. "It was Eileen, she needed to go into the garage for something and I'm afraid she had a look at one of them. Just out of curiosity – you know how women are. She told me about them and I had a look at one myself –"

"Bet you did!"

"- and I said I'd ask you to take them away."

"And what would you do, apart from shit in your pants if I tell you that I have no intention of taking them back?"

George smiled weakly. "For myself, you know, I don't mind that it's well, adult material. I mean whatever turns you on, one man's meat is another man's et cetera. But the police came round today, on some kind of routine search for illicit goods they said. Wanted to look in the garage. I told them we hadn't the key and they said they'd be back tomorrow and break in if necessary and have a look."

"Got a bit of a problem then aintcha?"

"What?"

"Wouldn't like to be in your shoes when they find that little load."

"You bastard!"

"Watch your language in this house mate." Steve wagged his finger in George's face. "Ladies present and all that. I'm telling you again, this is your problem and you're going to have to sort it."

"I'll tell the police they're yours."

"I'll deny the whole thing. And let me remind you that you said a while back that you told them no, you were not looking after anything for me. So who do you think they're going to

341

believe?"

"I'll tell them everything I know about you. I'll show them the tapes and when they see Gloria doing, er, acting in the film -"

Steve resumed his humourless smile "If you let them get at those tapes I'll tell a few people what I know about you."

"What do you mean?" The words came automatically although George had the feeling that he knew about what was to come.

"How would your wife like to know what her milk and water husband had been getting up to with my woman? Eh?"

"What do you mean?"

"I've watched you, you pathetic old bugger, right from the start your eyes stayed on her tits like it's feeding time down on the farm."

"Now look, of course I find her attractive, but I never, we never actually…"

"As far as Eileen is concerned I reckon she'll believe me when I say you've been jumping Gloria."

George moved back "It's only your word against mine."

"And mine, lover boy."

Her voice, immediately behind him, made him start. He half turned to see her; she looked just as relaxed and smiling as before.

"Gloria, you tell Steve that we have never ever – that we haven't – you know, ever had sex."

Gloria smiled enigmatically, "Well of course a lot depends on how you define 'having sex'. There are those that would say that what we've done isn't sex, at least not sex as we know it. Though that wasn't for lack of your trying. But I think others, and I'm sure that includes Eileen, would definitely call it sexual goings-on."

"What some would call sex, maybe," said George in a confused voice, turning back to look at Steve, who was standing with his arms folded, half smiling. "I'd call it flirting. I mean, Steve,

342

there's a world of difference between fancying someone and actually doing something. Of course I'm attracted to Gloria, I mean what man wouldn't be? But we never, you know, never actually -"

"Inhaled?" Gloria brushed past him and came into the room, "Give us a break Georgie. You were like a pig at a trough. You was naked, I was naked and we did things to each other, when we could find the wherewithal and you could remember what to do with it."

What was she doing? Walking right into trouble? To his surprise Steve was looking complacently down at her as she stood nestled by his side, as if what she was saying was fine by him.

"Now don't be unkind to the man, Glor, we can't all be equipped like Stevie."

George made a last ditch attempt at denial though he knew as soon as he opened his mouth that it sounded horribly false.

"Why are you saying this Gloria? It's not true Steve, believe me."

He edged backwards a little, planning how he would make his exit. Could he get to the front door and outside before Steve could catch him? Maybe if he threw something at Steve that would buy him a little time. But what? He felt in his jacket pocket and found nothing but a handkerchief and a packet of Extra Strong mints.

"Hope you're not pulling a gun on me? In my own house?" Steve asked in an amiable tone.

George hurriedly removed his hand and the mints fell to the floor. "I don't know why Gloria's saying what she's saying."

"Are you telling me she's lying? Now those are fighting words, mate." Steve put his fists up as if about to throw George a punch, although he was smiling all the while.

"Oh for Gawd's sake put him out of his misery Steve. He looks about ready to have a heart attack. Go on tell him. Steve knows all about us lover boy, every little detail, in living Technicolor."

George felt his insides sink, as if he'd just had all the blood taken out of his legs. He needed to reach out and hold on to the door frame to steady himself. Steve knew because she had told him.

"Why, Gloria?" Their secret, his miraculous sexual renewal, the romance of the midsummer night on Icart Point, the plans for the Basil Street Hotel – did Steve know it all. "Why?"

"Just look at yourself and ask me why again."

"But you did all those things, and said what you said to me."

"It was hardly mad passionate love, if that's what you're trying to say. Nothing personal mind and I've been with a lot worse, at least you were clean, but you're hardly my type, let alone my generation. You could say I was just doing you a favour Georgie Porgie, out of the kindness of my heart, being a good neighbour ..." she and Steve laughed, "...but that would be untrue. It was more an investment."

"Investment?"

"Yes, investment. I do hope one day you'll find someone who'll get rid of that habit you have of repeating whatever a body says; I found that really annoying. Worse than the hair in your ears or the way you handled my breasts like they were a jam jars that you couldn't open. It was an investment we made so that, come the day – well, like today for instance – Stevie and I would have something to trade with."

"It was all planned?"

"Forward planning – isn't that what you call it in business? Yes we planned it and you went right along with it."

George knew that the pain of what she had said had not yet hit him; that would come later, just as blood comes some seconds after the flesh has been cut. The pain and shame of what she said would well up when he was out of this terrible place and alone back in his own territory. At the moment all he felt was that a huge cloud had come down and blotted out his sun and that he was old and very tired.

Steve looked him almost sympathetically, "So I'll leave you

to sort out those tapes then. Put'em somewhere safe – there's a lot of money wrapped up in that little load. I'll hold you responsible for them."

George had almost forgotten about the tapes with the new and awful knowledge he had of Gloria's treachery. Now that Steve knew about - no, had engineered the affair, why should he bother about protecting him from the police?

"Responsible nothing. I'm going to tell the police that the tapes are nothing to do with me. They'll believe me when they know the whole story."

Had he left anything out of the equation? He thought not, but was troubled by Steve's smiling face. "Your choice mate, but ain't you forgetting something? If you tell the police, we'll tell your wife. About how you cheated on her."

Of course, Eileen, he'd forgotten about her. He stood there thinking furiously for a few minutes about how he could counter their accusations. Then suddenly his body sagged with fatigue and defeat. Oh sod it! Let them tell Eileen whatever they wanted to. She might not believe them, and even if she did she would probably see it, as he was now beginning to see it himself, as an old man's folly, something rather pathetic, the desperate scrabbling for a bit of action. Let Steve and Gloria do their worst; he was too tired to be blackmailed. Somehow he and Eileen would sort things out.

"Tell her what you like; it's up to you, I don't care any longer. But I am going to tell the police where those tapes come from. And that's my final word."

He turned and escaped quickly into the hall. He wanted to get home, partly to have a pee; his bladder was bursting. But Steve moved even more quickly and intercepted him on the way to the front door.

"Not so fast friend. There's something I'm going to show you first. You can decide afterwards if it's your final word."

"I'm really not interested in whatever you've got to show me," said George, attempting a bit of hauteur, and putting his hand firmly on the door handle. Steve knocked his arm away as if swatting a fly. It hurt.

"You will be."

George followed Steve meekly back into the sitting room, trying not to rub his arm. Steve closed the door behind them.

"Let's see the tape Glor."

She picked a tape from a pile by the fireplace, put it in the machine, then picked up the remote control and pressed 'play' with one delicate long-nailed finger. A bright and painfully clear picture sprang to life on the giant screen. It was a bird's eye view of a naked man lying against a dark background with a woman bent over him. George frowned, not sure of what he saw, until the camera zoomed in for a close up of the man's face, of his face, against the dark satin sheets of the bed in their games room.

"Last night after I left you I forced someone off the road."

The tape had been edited for what might be called the highlights.

"Instead of going round the corner he went straight ahead."

The bastards. There must have been a camera in the ceiling.

"You were going to help him?"

"No really. I just wanted to see what had happened."

"Did you try to kill him George? Is that what you did?"

"Yes all right I did. I did. I wanted him to die."

The figure that was undeniably George lay back on the bed with a satisfied smile.

Steve switched off the video and the bright image on the bed became a reflection of three figures in a room. The man who still occupied George's body but was increasingly unsure of who he was or how he would ever make sense of his life again, stood watching the blank screen with a sense of disbelief. He'd been totally out-manoeuvred. What a silly, incompetent and vain old fool he'd been. He'd lost everything.

Steve took out the tape.

"Not a pretty sight. Don't think we'll be asking you back for the sequel. But I guess you've got the message, right? Keep the constables off our necks and take care of that stuff in the garage or else the police and the TV and the radio and the press and your ever-loving wife will receive a little present. I've got copies for them all. And I'll have something extra special for you."

He lunged towards George, fists high, pretending to punch him in a series of jabs and a final left hook.

George felt a warm trickle coursing down his leg. One last indignity. He kept his knees together as he escaped awkwardly into the hall and lurched through the rain to the safety of home.

Chapter Thirty
A Hard Day's Night

"The best of men cannot suspend their fate.
The good die early and the bad die late."
Daniel Defoe

Eileen stood aside without speaking as George, pale-faced and moving oddly, came into the hall and clambered awkwardly up the stairs. He was obviously upset; now was not a good time to question him or even to offer a cup of tea, or something stronger. She went into the utility room and set up the ironing board. The warmth and mindlessness of the task should be soothing, but after one and a half shirts she could bear it no longer, switched off the iron and went into the kitchen, listening for any sounds from upstairs. Nothing; George must be upstairs in his study. She picked up the telephone and as gently as possible punched in the number.

'Hello this is Ray Meldon. I'm sorry I'm out. Please leave a message after the tone'.

"Ray. It's me, Eileen. Not sure why I'm ringing you really except the business with the tapes is getting very difficult here and I think George may be in danger. He seems very disturbed. Don't ring me back, not when he's here. I'll try you later. Goodbye."

She felt better for having made contact even if only with his recorded voice. Maybe when George was watching television she could slip up to the bedroom and make a call to Ray from there. George, of course, was unaware of Ray's existence; it had become too difficult to explain how he had come into her life and, most importantly, what he meant to her. She wasn't sure of that herself, but George needed someone like Ray this evening.

'Things fall apart, the centre cannot hold'...but where was the centre now? Everything seemed to be disintegrating, she thought; I'd better make us something to eat.

*

George climbed out of his damp soiled trousers, took off his shirt and underclothes and then stood for a long time in a hot shower. He decided not to think of Gloria and what she had done to him. That was a monumentally big topic for him to ponder over later, one that he would have to take out and examine all possible ways round until he could in some way tidy it up or at least explain it to himself. Now was not the time. Be practical he told himself; the most important thing is to decide where to hide the tapes. For he certainly had to do something, find somewhere to store them even if only for a couple of days.

After his shower he wrapped his biggest towel around him then sat on the lavatory seat and ran over in his mind all the places he knew on the island: Icart Point? Down near the reservoir? The old German trenches opposite Lihou Island? He realised with sinking heart that they were all rendezvous points he had known with Gloria; didn't he have a life before her?

What about the Vikings for example? Were there any opportunities in La Vallette? The Underground Museum? The lavatory that looks like a little house? The changing rooms of the pools themselves? He tried to visualise the main pool and imagined approaching it from the road. The entrance was on the right, and then there were rocks and a little headland on the left... Wait a minute, what about the cave near to the main pool? The one he'd come across that day when he had first met up with the Vikings, when he'd been walking round on the rocks. He remembered it as a deep narrow crack reaching

349

back into the granite cliff, a natural cave that over the years had been widened and lengthened by fishermen or smugglers. At one time they might have kept dinghies and lobster pots there, but all he had found when he poked around inside had been a few bits of rotting timber and rope. He should be able to reach it from the road by car. There was a narrow slipway of granite setts leading down from the pavement onto the foreshore and down into the sea itself at high tide. The cave was off to one side of the slipway, its entrance largely obscured from the roadway by a huge boulder. He could probably get the car down as far as the boulder; then all he'd need to do would be to haul the boxes around it and into the cave.

It was always possible that someone, maybe kids playing or nosy-minded ramblers would look around the cave, there were few places on the island that weren't known to everyone. He would have to store everything as far as possible to the back wall, one would need a torch to see it. The rain looked set for another day or two until the depression moved on so he doubted many people would be down there. It would at least give him time to find another more permanent place. Perhaps he could hire some kind of industrial storage unit up in St. Sampson's, or find a lock-up garage. If he rented a van he could transport everything in a couple of loads. Pay cash, use a false name, send the key over to Steve and be able to wash his hands of the whole affair. Perhaps.

It was a quarter to eight. He'd better get started right away and familiarise himself with the terrain before it got completely dark. He pulled out his most waterproof trousers, a Guernsey oiled-wool sweater, thick woollen socks and the new trainers, rejecting the idea of rubber boots as likely to be too slippery. He'd pick up his sailing jacket from the hall.

He decided to tell Eileen a near truth; that he and Steve were going to move the tapes down to a storage place near the pools, some place that Steve had found. Then he and Eileen could sit back and let the police tomorrow do all the searching they liked.

"Aren't you going to have anything to eat?" she had laid the table and there were smells that supper was ready. "What time will you be back?"

"Not sure Ellie. Probably after midnight. It will take a few trips to move everything. You have your supper and I'll eat when I come in."

"Where are you taking them?"

"Down near the pools, there's a sort of natural storage place, like a cave in the rocks down there."

"You'll be careful won't you? Remember he's a younger man. Let him do most of the lifting."

"Are you telling me I'm getting old?" He saw her uncertain expression, "It's all right, only joking. I can cope." Then uncharacteristically he kissed her on the cheek, "What a silly old game this is, eh?"

He was halfway down the hall before he thought he heard her call out, "Take care, darling."

*

He soon realised that it would take several hours to transport and stow all the tapes. He spent nearly an hour filling the car with the first load, experimenting by putting the boxes in different positions into the boot and body of the car. It was nine o'clock by the time he drove gingerly out of the drive, aware that because of the load he could not use the rear view mirror. He went slowly, but he hoped not so slowly as to attract attention, down onto the South Esplanade and along La Vallette until he pulled up alongside the main pool.

The wind had backed to the east and was coming in straight over the sea; it was cold. It was still not completely dark, there was enough light for him to check no-one was around before he locked the car and walked down towards the cave. The rain had almost stopped but he was right, the granite was wet and slippery underfoot. The sea itself was breaking as small waves over the bottom of the slipway about thirty yards away; he had no idea whether the tide was coming in or going out.

Things were more or less as he remembered them: the slipway, the boulder halfway down and the little branching path after the boulder turning back up to the cave.

He stumbled into the cave, bending his head to get under the overhanging rock at the entrance; there was a pungent smell of old seaweed and creosote. He flashed his torch around the walls and into the area at the back. There were a few bits of timber and some old rope netting near the entrance, and beyond that the cave opened out into a big empty chamber, with a roof that was at least eight foot high. There should be room for everything and it seemed dry enough. He moved the rope and wood to one side until he had a clear passage to the interior.

His only miscalculation was that the slipway itself was about six inches too narrow to take the width of the car. He'd have to manhandle each package out of the car, across the pavement and first down and then up into the cave. The job was going to take him the best part of the night.

Another problem was managing the torch; it was too difficult to carry along with the packages, and having dropped it twice he finally set it up on a flat-topped rock near the entrance, with the light pointing down on the path.

Stacking the packages into the back chamber of the cave also wasn't easy. The upward slope of the floor meant he had to scramble the last bit and he fell a couple of times on the uneven floor, thankful then for the protection of the thick sweater and his jacket.

By ten o'clock he had stacked the first load and he drove back up the hill to Les Vardes. There were lights on in the house and it looked warm and cosy; he would have liked to be there, sitting alongside Eileen, both them faintly bored, but safe and comfortable and together. Once this night was through, he would never ever complain again about the tedium of his uneventful, middle-aged existence. He was going to sit on the sidelines of life in future, and let the whole crazy parade go by without him. For a moment he was tempted to go in and ask Eileen for a sandwich and a cup of tea, but it was late and he had, he estimated, at least six or seven more loads to take.

The loading for the second trip was faster and within half an hour he was back near the cave. It had begun to rain; this would inevitably slow him down, and when he flashed the light around the cave he realised that he had stashed the packages too close to the entrance; he would have to move them back before he started on the second load. He worked as fast as he could to restack them and grew hot, despite the strengthening wind.

By now it was nearly half past eleven; perhaps he'd finish before daybreak.

As he came out of the cave and started back up the slipway he saw the lights of a car making its way slowly along La Vallette. He turned off his torch and stood in close to the boulder. It was probably someone out on a late night drive, who would go past the pools to the aquarium, turn around and then drive back towards town. But to his dismay the car came slowly to a halt just behind his. He could just make out that it was an old Peugeot. The headlights went off and he heard the handbrake being put on.

He felt the weight of the torch in his hand; it was heavy enough to do damage if need be. He tightened his hand and stood motionless in the rain for several minutes. Then above the sound of the wind and sea he heard muffled laughter and small shrieks of pleasure and the sound of the old car being rocked from side to side. A courting couple, that's all he needed.

He'd give them ten minutes, that should be enough in an uncomfortable car, and then reconsider his situation. Even as he made this decision he was surprised to hear a small wave breaking right behind him and a rush of water come up and over his feet. The sea was only inches away. While he had been working in the back of the cave, the infamous Guernsey tide had been coming in and it was now creeping, black and menacing, up the slipway towards him. What if the tide came as high as the cave? He went back into the cave and picked up some of the sand on the floor; it hadn't felt water in years. He was going to have to wade through the water to come around the boulder from the slipway. He'd collect his Wellingtons, slippery or not, on the next trip to the house, but he had to work quickly.

It didn't take much to get rid of the lovers. He simply stepped out from behind his car and flashed the light in on them. He saw pink skin, rumpled clothes and smudged mascara on a very young face. They were just youngsters. He turned off the light but it had done the job. There was a scream from inside the Peugeot, several expletives and the sound of seats being adjusted. The youth started up, did a noisy three point turn and gunned his way back to the South Esplanade. George stood for a few seconds, smiling, the flashlight dangling from his hand. He had a sudden remembrance of Icart Point and the pale midsummer night sky; it seemed a world away.

"Sorry kids", he murmured in the direction of the Peugeot as he started unloading his car, and just then he meant it.

*

Eileen had finished eating in the kitchen shortly after George had driven away from the house with his first load. She dished up his meal and left it under a cover in the warming section of the oven. Then, just as she had decided to watch the television in the sitting room she was startled by a tap on the window. Between the curtains in a shaft of light she could see a pair of eyes looking in at her.

"Who is it?" she said, her voice high and strained.

"It's me, Ray."

She opened the back door. He was wearing some kind of combat gear: camouflage trousers, a khaki jacket, and a balaclava.

"I got your message. I've come to see if you're all right."

Eileen hesitated; talking with Ray on the phone was one thing, having him here at the house, when at any moment George could be back, was another.

"The police came this morning to look in the garage but I told them I hadn't got the key. They're coming back tomorrow so George has gone to store all the packages somewhere safe tonight."

"You said you thought he was in danger?"

"He came back from Steve's looking very agitated as if he'd been threatened."

"What can I do?"

"I suppose I was hoping that somehow or another you could keep an eye on George. Make sure he's safe."

"Is it all right for me to come in for a moment? I'm getting soaked."

"Yes, of course, sorry." She stood back awkwardly from the kitchen door to let him in. "George has just left."

"I know, I saw him go; I've been hiding near the gate."

"I shouldn't think he'll be back for a bit."

"Where's he taking the stuff?"

"Somewhere down near the swimming pools, you know the open air pools in La Valette? Steve knows where there's a shed or something where he can store them for a bit."

"I only saw the one car and there was just George inside; I saw as he drove past me."

"That's odd. He said he was going to move everything with Steve."

"I'll check it out in a moment. I'll just thaw out a bit if you don't mind."

"Can I get you anything? I've got supper ready; George didn't have time to eat anything. If you're hungry, I mean...I can always cook something else for him when he comes in."

"Well, I wouldn't want to take another man's supper." Ray took off his jacket and the balaclava, and sat down at the kitchen table. "But it does smell good, and if it's no trouble..."

"It seems only fair seeing that you came over here to help us." Nevertheless she felt a sense of betrayal to have Ray in their kitchen sitting where George usually sat.

Ray ate George's supper and had just finished a second glass of wine when they heard the sound of the car on the drive. They both stood up smartly, looking at each other with guilty faces.

"Stay here," said Eileen, "while I see what's happening out of the front window. Be ready to leave quickly if you hear me open the front door."

She stood near the window in the dining room and watched George get out of the car. He was alone; there was no sign of Steve. When he hesitated and look towards the house she almost went to open the front door and welcome him in, but before she could move, he'd gone into the garage and started to load up the car again.

"He looks all right at the moment." Ray was standing behind her looking over her shoulder. He'd put his jacket on again and looked ready to leave. "Do you want me to stay here until he's finished?"

"No no, you've done enough. We'll be OK."

"I'll be on my way then. But remember, if you need me, just ring. Doesn't matter what time it is."

"I can't thank you enough."

"Repeat after me 'It doesn't matter what time it is'."

"Oh all right!" Eileen turned, smiling, "It doesn't matter what time it is."

"Ring me on the mobile, that'll reach me anytime, and anywhere I happen to be. Here's my card with the number on. Keep it safe. I'll let myself out by the back door and slip out when he's in the garage."

Eileen cleared up the plates in the kitchen, being careful to put away the second plate and glass, then mopped up Ray's muddy footprints from the kitchen floor and locked the back door.

"When lovely woman stoops to folly and paces her room

again alone, she strokes her hair with automatic hand and puts a record on the gramophone." Had she stooped to folly? She felt uneasy, disturbed by Ray's visit. It was not just the silly guilt at having given George's meal to another man, but something else, something about the way Ray had looked in on her through the kitchen window, and about his clothes - the camouflage jacket and the balaclava. They not only hinted at physical violence but seemed to reveal another aspect of Ray, something she had not seen before, a quality she couldn't define, something between competence and menace.

Chapter Thirty-One
Che Sera Sera

"When fate beckons monarchs must obey…"
John Dryden

It was midnight when George came into the house from his second run. The television was on and Eileen was asleep on the settee. Dripping water on the carpet, he looked down at her and, although he would have liked to tell how well he was doing, decided it was kinder to let her sleep.

In the kitchen he could smell shepherd's pie but there didn't seem to be any left for him and he was surprised to see only a couple of inches of wine left in the bottle though that would explain why Eileen was asleep. He cut himself a slice of bread, wrapped it round a piece of cheese and stuffed it in his mouth, washing it down with the remains of the wine. Then he changed his trainers for the Wellingtons, found a pair of old gloves for extra warmth and let himself out of the front door, locking it after him.

He had his third load in the car by twenty to one. He was making good time; he might have it all finished before it got light at five thirty.

"Bye Ellie," he said out loud as he drove away, "not long to go now."

A faint sense of optimism surfaced as he drove down the hill, the same feeling as had carried him through the worst days of Parson and Green's. 'Every day in every way I am getting better and better.' This is what they had taught the youngsters in the marketing team; it was old and hackneyed but, increasingly, as the years passed, he recognised that old and hackneyed was often the best.

He was about eighty yards from the slipway when he saw someone else had got to his place before him: there was a Transit van parked at right angles alongside the slipway and several people milling about in the headlights, which were pointing out to sea. His first thought was that the police had been watching him and had found the cache in the cave. He braked sharply, turned off engine and lights and let the car coast silently to the kerb. As his eyes adjusted to the dark he could make out four or five dark figures carrying stuff, running backwards and forwards up and down the slipway. It wasn't a police vehicle and the figures weren't in any kind of uniform, as far as he could tell. He wondered if perhaps Steve had suddenly decided to come down and help move the videos, but that was impossible; how would he have known where George was hiding them?

Anyway, he could see now that they weren't going to the cave but loading their bags into a dinghy pulled half out of the water onto the slipway. Even as he watched, one of the figures got in, the others pushed it away from the land and he heard the harsh sound of an outboard motor being started. As the dinghy moved across the water, further out in Havelet Bay he saw a red light come on and then flash one, two, three times.

Who were they? Smugglers? Surely in this day and age smuggling would be a more sophisticated activity than a matter of Transit vans and dinghies? And while it was common knowledge there was plenty of contraband coming into Guernsey – drugs being the most obvious – what on earth could they could they be taking out? Tomatoes?

He got out of the car, locked it, crossed the road and crept towards the people left on shore, staying well under what cover was provided by a stand of evergreen oaks. A few minutes later he heard the motor; the dinghy was on its way back and the loading process started all over again. Now he was closer he could see that there were four men and a woman. She wasn't carrying any of the loads but appeared to be standing guard with a flashlight, which was now directed up the road towards the South Esplanade.

"Fellas, someone's coming."

Her voice came to him across the night air like an arrow. It was Gloria.

"Fellas hold on, we've got company." The flashlight went off and the figures around the Transit van stood still.

Surely Gloria hadn't meant him? He stepped back further into the undergrowth just as he saw headlights, and heard a car coming down the road.

Instead of coming closer, the car stopped, right next to the Focus. He saw a figure silhouetted against the headlights walking quickly and purposively towards his car. Thank God he'd locked it. The figure raised what looked like a stick above his head and there was the hollow explosive sound of the windscreen being smashed accompanied by shouts and cries of angry jubilation. The figure jumped back into the car, the engine revved and the car drove past the pools, made a noisy turn in front of the Aquarium and careered back towards the Esplanade. As it passed the second time he saw it was the old Peugeot. The kids were getting their own back. Little bastards.

Two men from the Transit van ran over to his car and he heard them exclaim, presumably about the damage, and then run back.

"It's Buchanan's car." He heard the words quite clearly. It was Steve's voice. "The little shit must have followed us down here. The engine's still warm so he's still around somewhere."

George's first instinct was to run, although his head told him this was not necessary. It made perfect sense, surely, to make himself known, to go over and talk to them? After all he was only doing what had been agreed. But nevertheless he hesitated. There was an air of violence about the night and the atmosphere of a hunt, even in the way the two men stalked up the road towards his car, slowly scanning the roadside with their torches. The other two were exploring the road in the other direction, working their way down towards the Aquarium. It would only be a matter of minutes before they found him, and he guessed they were not going to be in a mood to discuss things rationally. They had become hunters and he was their prey. It was an easy equation that no longer required any decision to be made beyond finding an escape.

His first move was to back further into the undergrowth but he soon came into contact with a solid wall of rock behind him, much too smooth and high to climb his way out. Where else could he hide? Could he slip around the two men walking towards the Aquarium somehow, and escape up the Ozanne steps. He pictured himself panting his way up the steep flight while they, younger and no doubt stronger men, sprang up easily behind him, pulling him down onto the hard granite. What about the pools? Behind or, better still, in the changing rooms? They might not look in there and, besides, he knew his way around the place, even in the dark. He moved out of the bushes as quietly as he could and started to jog across the road, his rubber boots making only a very soft clopping sound. But she had heard.

"He's over here!" Her voice was as he'd never heard it before, harsh and angry, "He's gone into the pool entrance."

As he heard them running towards him he decided against the changing rooms; there was only one entrance and if they chose to look in there they would catch him like a rat in a trap. Far better to stay out in the open and give himself plenty of room for manoeuvre. In a curious mix of terror and elation he ran across the concrete surround of the pool to the far edge, to where the water was swilling in from the sea with an irregular heave and retreat. It was getting rough, he could see the gleam of foam as the water tumbled in over the edge spilling round his ankles and along the poolside. He crouched down at the far end, holding onto the iron railings trying to keep out of the water. They might not see him against the backdrop of the waves. His knees protested as he lowered himself, and he wasn't sure how long he could maintain his position. Nevertheless, he felt somehow protected by the roughness of the sea and had a sudden certainty that he was going to outwit them

The lights of their torches first moved erratically around the changing room area and were now being directed in broad sweeps across the pool. He crouched lower and pulled up his collar to hide the paleness of his face. Over the sound of the water he heard their voices again. Then the lights and the voices disappeared. He stayed there for a couple of minutes before he realised that they must have given up, perhaps deciding that on his own he was no threat to them. Just in time, he thought, as the pain in his knees was so great that either he stood up now or he would have to get down on all fours and crawl through the water back to the entrance.

"Come on you bastards," he said, half to his pursuers and half to his knees, "We're winning," and with a tremendous effort he pulled himself upright. He straightened his legs slowly, wincing at the pain, and then took his hands from the railing to rub his knees. It was at that precise moment that something hit him. It felt like someone with a stick hitting him smartly across the back of his knees. But it must have been a wave, at the vanguard of the incoming tide, slapping over the edge of the concrete and catching him off balance. Still wondering which of these was more likely, he staggered forward, righted himself, missed grabbing the handrail by a fraction of an inch, toppled forward again, his boots slipping on the wet concrete, and then fell, heavily, feet first, into the pool.

He was thinking, even before he hit the water, that it was a good job he was a strong swimmer, but that was before the blow to the head: a hard merciless thunk on the back of his skull, a one-sided encounter of man with concrete.

This took everything away from him: breath, vision, sense.

Almost everything. There was some small part, an ancient part of his brain that somehow remained on duty to help him survive. This tiny scrap of functioning knew that the cold water was bad, and that to struggle was good, so without his say-so his arms and legs struck out in the water and he rose to the surface just long enough to put his head above the surface and get a good lungful of air. The same part of his brain told him to hang on to this air, keep himself afloat while he tried to wake up, and get the frontal cortex operating again. He was beginning to realise what he was in was very cold and salty.

He opened his eyes. There was blackness with stars, lots of them that moved and swirled above him. A wave slid over his face and the stars went blurry. He let out his breath and took another quickly before his head went under the water. He knew he should be doing something but couldn't remember what it was so he lay back in the water, now buoyed up by the air trapped in his waterproof jacket which surrounded his head like a halo. Funnily enough it didn't seem so cold now. He was quite comfortable, all things considered, apart from his legs which seemed to be pulling him down as if they had found an escape at the bottom of the pool.

Then he thought he saw a pair of eyes as if someone were leaning over looking at him, their face close to his. All he could see were small bright eyes, not Eileen's, but the eyes of someone he knew. A good man, a friend. Things would be all right. Now he could close his eyes because he really did need to go indoors. And when he closed his eyes he found he was up in his study in the belvedere, looking down on the garden. Yes, there were Eileen and Celia, and some of his old mates from Parson and Green and that lovely secretary, what was her name? Who was that beautiful red-haired woman standing next to his mother? How nice of them all to be there, looking up at him, laughing and doing that thing with their arms, moving their arms, all smiling...

*

Eileen sat up on the settee; had she heard something? She looked at her watch. It was after one; she must have fallen asleep. No sound of George. She moved slowly and sleepily out to the hall and looked through the window. It was raining again. The car wasn't there; he must still be down at La Vallette. She wondered how far he had got with the tapes. Putting on her raincoat, she went out onto the front drive. The lights were on next door, lots of them. Gloria must be sitting up waiting for Steve to get back; or maybe they were both there letting George get on with things. She picked her way quietly down to the front gate and looked in at next door's drive. Their four-wheel drive was there, parked as usual close to the front door, but the house itself was ablaze with lights. The place looked ready for a party, although it was strangely silent.

She went back to their garage. The door was unlocked and she put the light on, heedless of whether next door noticed. Only about a quarter of the tapes had gone. There was a lot left to do. It was taking much longer than she'd expected. She stood for a few moments listening for the sound of the car. Maybe something had gone wrong. Should she ring Ray, ask him for his opinion, maybe even ask him to go down to the pools and check on what was happening? Whatever reservations she had about him were overcome by her need to speak to someone who knew what was happening.

Ray answered immediately.

"Eileen!" Even he sounded alarmed, jumpy. "No you haven't woken me. Are you all right?"

"Sorry. Just wanted to tell you that it's late and George isn't back yet. I've been out in the garage and he's still got more than half of the stuff to move."

A short silence. "Do you want me to go down and check the Vallette and see if I can find out what's happening? I can do that."

"Oh, no. I wouldn't want you to do that, but I just feel worried…you know there's no-one to ask."

"You worry too much. He's a man; he knows what he's doing. He'll be all right. Get some sleep, you need it."

"I expect you're right. I just wanted to get some reassurance I suppose. There's a lot of static on this line, are you outside? It almost sounds as if you're by the sea."

"That's Guernsey for you."

"I'd better say goodnight."

"Things will turn out fine, Eileen, trust me."

Chapter Thirty-Two
Andrew

"There is no joy but calm."
Alfred, Lord Tennyson.

A peaceful morning eventually emerged from the wet and windy night. The sea had retreated, leaving rocks and sand drying in the early sunshine, and although the sky was still misted with high cloud, it carried the promise of warmth. The water in the men's swimming pool was clear. It was easy to see right down to the bottom, where pebbles, a few shells and pale grains of sand were shifting and sifting lightly in the small to and fro of the waves.

Yesterday's high tide had thrown long strands of sea wrack around the edge of the pool and over the railings; they stirred in the light breeze, still oily and supple with salt water. Later the pool attendant would collect and throw them, stiff and drying, over the railings and back into the sea: dust to dust.

It wasn't a Viking day but Andrew had woken at his usual early hour; the morning was warm but he noticed the slanting autumnal quality of the light and the high cumulus of the passing depression; it was still only August but already the season was turning, like the leaves of the cherry trees in his garden and the ripening blackberries in the rough ground next to his house, which hadn't been picked these two years. The year was getting old and tired. He decided to go for a swim; for as long as it was his watch, he would report for duty.

He put on a tracksuit, warm from the airing cupboard, made the bed, folding up his pyjamas and placing them neatly under the pillow, set out the breakfast things for his return, left the house and jogged along the road to Clarence Battery and the Ozanne Steps.

He had always been a man of order and fixed habit and, increasingly these last few years, he was a man who needed solitude. He was disappointed then, to notice, out of the corner of his eye as he turned into the changing room, that there was someone already in the pool, over in the far corner at the deep end. It was proper to acknowledge whoever it was. He was a believer in manners, after all they were the glue that held the world together when kindness gave way, but to hell with it, this morning he needed to at least pretend that he had the place to himself. If it turned out to be someone he knew, he could always blame his cataracts.

He dived into the cold water, his mind relaxing as his muscles went into their practised routine but, despite himself, at the end of his second length, he stopped, aware that was something was wrong. The other swimmer hadn't moved, in fact Andrew wasn't even sure now that the bundle of red was another swimmer. It could be some kind of rubbish that had been blown into the pool during the night; it often happened during a gale. All the same there was something about the bundle that made him climb out and approach it with increasing urgency; he still might be in time to help.

There was no need to hurry. The moment when help might have kept death away, at least for a few more years, had passed several hours before. It was a body not a swimmer, a body half-submerged, face down in the water, the long legs with their rubber boots hanging like the giant limbs of some sea monster, the upper part enclosed in the folds of a red jacket that was just, but only just, keeping the grey head afloat.

Andrew knelt down and using a wave to help him, managed to roll the body over. The eyes were open and George's expression was one of repose, almost content, but his face was very white, as if bleached. Andrew towed him by his jacket down to the shallow end of the pool and by crouching down beside the body managed to pull it halfway up the steps, where they both rested for a while, George cradled like a son in the older man's arms.

He now noticed the blood; a slow thick stream was trickling down the steps and lazily spiralling in the salt water. He turned George's head with a tentative and gentle hand and saw the gaping wound half-hidden in the thickness of his greying hair.

After a while he went for help, leaving George propped up on the steps looking out over the ocean as if in silent contemplation.

Chapter Thirty-Three
Afterwards

Have you news of my boy Jack?
Not this tide..." Rudyard Kipling

They rang the doorbell at ten minutes to eight; Eileen was dressing after her bath and she waited a moment in case George was in the house somewhere and went to the door, but there was no sound from his room or from below. Then she remembered it must be the police. A dawn raid, she thought wryly. She could only hope that George had managed to clear everything out of the garage. She wished he were there. She brushed her hair quickly as she heard the bell ring for the third time – ask not for whom the bell tolls she said to herself as she went downstairs and opened the door.

There were three of them, two men and a woman. She recognised the older man as Superintendent Nichol, but the others were much younger, in their twenties, like big children in their uniforms, much too young to search for pornography. They stood there for several seconds, until Nichols removed his hat.

"Have you come to see the garage? My husband is out." Please God she thought make that garage empty.

"Mrs. Buchanan, May we come in. It's about your husband.''

Something very awful had happened. She could see it in their faces and now feel it in her gut. It was so awful that she could not ask what it was. Not on the door step and not right now. She

369

needed time. She led the way to the sitting room. This didn't seem to be the right place either. It all looked different. The settee was still wrinkled from where she had slept the previous evening but it wasn't the same, and neither was she. The bronze chrysanthemums had shed some petals. She wanted to pick them up, make things better. But instead she said the words "What's happened?"

"I'm afraid we've just found your husband..."

"Is he dead? You must tell me."

"Why do you say that?" It was the younger man, quick and keen.

Nichols raised his hand as if to silence him. "I'm very very sorry. Yes he is. He was found in the bathing pool down at La Vallette. A Mr. Andrew Melrose found him this morning..."

"What happened to him?"

"We're not sure. That's why we'd like your help. But his body was in the water. May we sit down?"

She sat on a hard chair, Nichols and the young woman sat on the settee; the younger constable took the armchair opposite her and leaned forward, holding his hat loosely, letting it hang between his knees. He was the first to break the silence.

"We'd like to know if your husband had any reason to think that he was in danger, Mrs. Buchanan? Did he have any enemies, would you say?"

His voice was touched by excitement.

"That's George's chair."

"Hurel, go and keep an eye on things outside. And keep an ear open for the radio." There was another silence while the younger man got up from George's chair and left the room.

Nichols turned to her, "It looks as if he drowned, fell into the pool by accident. But he's had some kind of knock on the head so we have to rule out any likelihood of foul play. So you see..."

"Are you sure he's – that he's not just stunned perhaps?"

"We're sure, I'm afraid. The doctor examined him an hour

ago."

"I want to see him. Can you take me to him?" George had such a well-shaped head. He'd always been proud of his profile, patrician, he'd say.

"Of course, but I need to know if you could tell me should we be looking for someone who might have a grudge against him? Do you know of anyone who might be disposed… to…well…"

"We've had problems with the people next door." The trembling had started. She felt very cold.

"That side? The Levinskys? Yes, well, our men had reason to go to their house earlier this morning and the place appears to have been vacated. They've left. In a hurry by the looks of things. Were you aware of that?"

"My husband was being forced by Steve, Mr. Levinsky, to store some video tapes for him in our garage. We didn't realise what kind of tapes they were. Of course you knew about those, that's why you came round here."

The trembling was almost out of control now; it was as if her body had nothing to keep it together. She kept her hands hidden in the sleeves of her jumper but the shaking was beginning to affect her voice. But there was no point now in trying to hold herself together; it really didn't matter. It was too late for anything to matter.

"We've had our eye on Mr. Levinsky for some time, for a number of reasons. If your husband was being pressured by him in some way why didn't he come and see us?"

"He was a foolish man in many ways. But I love him."

The young policewoman came over and put her arm round Eileen's shoulder. It didn't feel strange. The young woman had fine skin like Celia and smelled young and fresh.

"I must ring my daughter. She's in London."

"A couple more things Mrs. Buchanan and then we'll leave you in peace. Was your husband depressed at all recently?"

"He'd retired a couple of years ago and was at a bit of a loose end, but I think he was quite happy – do you mean suicide? Oh no. He wouldn't do that."

Had George been depressed? If so, had it been her fault? Was that what they were trying to say?

"Had he perhaps received any bad news recently?"

"Sorry I can't stop shaking." Had there been any bad news? She couldn't remember.

"Nothing to do with the family?"

Did he mean Celia living with that awful girl? George never knew the full story about that. She was glad that she had never told him.

"And you and he were...?"

"We're fine..." George hadn't known about Ray's feelings for her or that they met sometimes to talk, or that she liked Ray because he flattered her, made her feel younger. Had he?

"...We've been married for thirty-eight years."

"Do you know what he was doing down at the bathing pool last night?"

"Yes. I can tell you all about it. Let go of me please. I'm all right now."

"Seargant Falla, would you go and put the kettle on. You don't mind Mrs. Buchanan? I think we could all do with a cup of tea."

*

"Buchanan."

"Celia, it's me, Mummy."

Celia didn't like personal calls at work. It wasn't just the interruption of her chain of thought that she disliked – after all, she was primarily there for her subordinates, so interruptions were very much part of her remit – but the demand it made of her to switch from being impersonal professional to friend or lover, or in this case daughter.

"What is it Eileen? I've got a lot on at the moment."

"Something terrible has happened..."

"Sorry, hang on a mo. Julia take these over to the meeting and tell them I'll be there a.s.a.p. Sorry Eileen, what was it, I've got a meeting which should have started ten minutes ago?"

"…I'm sorry to interrupt you darling but I'm afraid something's happened to Daddy."

Oh God, what was he up to now?

"He hasn't run off with her has he?"

"No, it's, er, not that. I'm afraid he's died. He's dead. It happened last night."

Celia wasn't sure she had heard the words correctly. She wasn't sure if she knew what the words meant.

"How do you mean, dead?"

"He had some awful accident last night. The police have just been."

"What happened? The car?"

"No he drowned, fell into the swimming pool and hurt his head. They found him this morning. I'm going in to see him now."

"Oh Mum…"

Celia held tight to the edge of her desk. This was another new experience, a terrible experience and she had no answer for it.

"Mum, are you all right?" That was it, she had to be strong for them both.

"I don't know. It's all very sudden. I'm going to see him now at the hospital."

"Don't worry. I'm coming. I'll be over as quick as I can."

There was really no need to hurry. George would stay dead and their lives would change irrevocably no matter how long it took her to get to Guernsey.

*

Things, externally, moved rapidly after that. Sometimes it seemed to Eileen that decisions were being made in an almost indecent haste, as if people wanted to get George off their list of things to do. Her life, by contrast, had gone into slow motion and while everyone else seemed to want to get rid of George, put him into the past and 'move on', she needed desperately to stay in the present. As long as she could talk about him and the accident in the present tense, as if it were all still in the process of happening, the more likely it seemed that the situation might be reversible, that he would wake up in the mortuary, ask irritably where he was and demand to go home.

The memory came to her that after Kennedy's assassination in 1964 Jackie had seemed reluctant to change out of the pink costume she had been wearing that day, even though it was covered in her husband's blood. It was said she wanted that day, the last day when he was still alive, to last forever. Staying in the same clothes was one way to keep time from moving on. Eileen had not understood at the time how anyone could bear to keep the bloodied cloth next to her skin; now she did.

Despite all her wishes, a few days later she realised that this period of time in which George was still half-alive, as it were, when in her fancy he could return if they all willed it strongly enough, was racing backwards away from her, along with their years together as man and wife, their happiness, and all their many disappointments. Their past was slipping out of her grasp, retreating and unravelling at increasing speed. Gradually the excitement his death had generated died down; for other people the tragedy was becoming an incident, an incident to be sorted out and cleared away.

The young policemen ascribed to the case got on with their duties, sympathetically enough, but with the inevitable and unintended callousness of youth. To them it was the death of an old man who would have died in a few years anyway. It wasn't as important as if it had been a young person like themselves, someone with their lives in front of them.

The police focused on the practical details of the case. Hurel and Sergeant Falla collected the rest of the tapes from the garage and took them away in a van. They had also found the car keys in George's jacket and driven the Focus to the police station and removed all the remaining tapes from that. The fact that it was a silver Focus was noted down in relation to the accident with Neil Vaudin, but by some administrative oversight no-one examined the tyre tread pattern. So the car was struck off the list of potential suspect cars and returned to Eileen the next day. She rang the garage and they came and took it away on a tow-truck to replace the windscreen. The car was driveable but she asked them to collect it all the same. George had always been so proud of his driving; the car was a part of him in a silly kind of way. She didn't want to drive it herself, take away his pride.

She was relieved when the verdict at the coroner's court was accidental death by drowning. The case for suicide was rejected; Mr. Buchanan, a retired and comfortable-off man in good health and happily married had everything to live for. At sixty-three he was still in the late prime of his life.

It was also decided that there was no evidence of foul play. George Buchanan had no enemies, certainly no-one who would wish him dead. The Levinskys, who might have been suspected of wanting him silenced, appeared to have left the island a short time before Mr. Buchanan met with his accident. Although Steve Levinsky was wanted in connection with the importation and re-distribution of pornographic material, he had no record of violence. Besides, murders didn't happen in Guernsey.

At the autopsy it was established the blow to the head was consonant with the victim having accidentally struck his head on the concrete edge of the pool, either as he entered the water or shortly thereafter, perhaps by being slammed against the side of the pool by the waves. It was already on record as having been a very stormy night.

The police told Eileen not to worry about the pornography found on their property; no charges would be brought to bear. It was obvious that Mr. Buchanan had been involved against his volition, and that the Levinskys were the source of the problem. They searched Steve and Gloria's house on the day of the accident, collecting all the tapes that were strewn around

375

the various rooms and in the garage. These were sent in sealed packages to Scotland Yard where they were kept as a body of evidence to be used in the States versus Levinsky case, were the couple to be traced and brought to trial.

Neither the police nor Eileen ever realised that buried amongst these was a video of a middle-aged man talking nonsense about a boy on a motor bike. Twenty years later, when the case was finally closed, all the tapes were destroyed and George's betrayal by the woman he loved was lost for ever.

Nor were they aware of the tapes hidden in the cave by the pools, which have remained there to this day.

Chapter Thirty-Four
The Funeral

"I've a great fancy to see my own funeral afore I die"
Maria Edgeworth

In the silence of the now empty house Eileen's thoughts turned inwardly to herself and whatever future lay ahead. Celia's presence had offered some measure of comfort and solace and had helped her sort out what practicalities needed to be done, but she needed to go back to London for work after a few days and wouldn't be coming back until the day before the funeral.

She woke early the day after Celia had left and, sensing she would not be able to sleep again, pulled the curtains back on a grey, silent morning. She leaned out of the window to hear some signs of life: the birds, traffic, anything, but there were none. She stayed anyway, listening, sitting on the edge of the bed, grateful at least for the sensation of cool air on her bare arms. It was the first time in her life that she had been in a house properly on her own; although George had often been away on conferences and the like, she had always known that he would be coming back, so his absence was almost like time out, a little holiday. Now that he wasn't going to be coming back, not next week or next year or ever again, his absence was a different and deeply disturbing experience. What had been her home, cosy and welcoming, had become alien and indifferent to her needs. This morning it was throbbing with silence, as if waiting for something or someone to give it life. It would have to be someone other than herself, because she, Eileen, Celia's mother and George's wife had dissolved away. How insubstantial she had become and how little her existence mattered, either to the house or to herself. She had a sense of vertigo, of being poorly balanced on the edge of a cliff, looking down into nothingness.

Her face in the mirror was thin and purple-shadowed and her eyes ugly and still swollen from crying. There was a time, was it only a week ago, when she would have cared about the shadows and the puffy eyes; now the reflection was that of a stranger for whom she had no responsibility and in whom she had no interest.

Later, lying in a deep and very hot bath, she half listened to the seven o'clock news, as much for a sense of company as for any content. Strange that the world was going on about its business much as usual, and equally strange not to have the programme punctuated by odd comments and explosions from George: 'Damn nonsense!' 'Rubbish!' 'For God's sake, man, answer the bloody question!' He had been angry for much of his life. She never thought she would miss that, but she did.

The worst thing was that she not only wanted to tell him about his own death, but also needed his opinion and reassurance about what had taken place.

"George, something awful has happened. You've died. It was quite sudden; I don't think you could have known about it. Did you? You drowned in the swimming pool; no-one seems to know why.

It was terrible seeing you in the hospital. I touched your hand but it was cold – it didn't seem like yours any more, and I couldn't touch it again. Sorry. I hope you understand. But I combed your hair and made it tidy. It still looked as nice as ever. Are you all right? Is there something that I should be doing?"

Of course there was no George, and no guidance, not even an exasperated sigh. The completeness of the silence brought the tears again.

*

Then there was the funeral. It was a task that gave her something practical to think about, but even so she felt his absence in the planning of it. He had always taken on the role of head of the household with the ease of a natural leader, but she had not realised quite how much of their joint life had been planned, determined, organised and executed by him.

Now she needed him, not to open a bottle of wine, or change the light bulb, or fill in their tax forms or make the final decision about the colour of the curtains but, ironically, to help plan his own exit from the world. It was pathetic, really, that she hardly knew how to go about this without wanting his involvement.

He had never discussed with her what sort of a funeral he wanted, any more than she had told him her wishes. Death wasn't a subject they had talked about it; they still hadn't thought of themselves as old enough to die and, besides, it would have been embarrassing somehow, as if to speak about death would inevitably turn their minds to the totality of their life together, inviting judgment about how successful it had been, and if found wanting, inviting blame.

He hadn't liked the idea of cremation – so final – but as neither of them were churchgoers she was not sure beyond that what sort of service he would like, would have liked, nor even which hymns. Maybe someone should give a reading, but who? She would probably break down were she to try. When she felt stronger she would look in her poetry book and see what would be most appropriate and maybe Celia could read it.

She did know that George would have wanted to be sent off with a bit of a flourish; he would have seen this as a final endorsement of his success, so the more people who came, or who sent cards and flowers, the better. She went through his address book, the one he had always been rather secretive about and which he kept locked in his desk drawer, and worked her way through it systematically, giving information that he had died and the time and place of the funeral. She came across the names of several women whom she did not recognise, probably secretaries and liaisons. She only hesitated a minute or two. George had been a handsome man; he deserved to have his past victories acknowledged and, anyway, whatever had happened was well in the past, it no longer had the power to hurt. Let whoever wanted, come. It was only ever a bit of fun, Ellie!

In the same spirit of forgiveness she also sent letters to several of George's colleagues at Parson and Green, and when she found Doug's address wrote to him as well; he should at least know about his old friend, even if he couldn't be at the funeral.

Another indication of what a struggle life was going to be without George was when she tried to decide what he should wear when they laid him out in the chapel of rest. He had always been so fussy about his clothes; she felt ill-equipped to be the one to decide how he should present himself for eternity. After a couple of painful searches through his wardrobe, painful in the sense that on each occasion she was crying aloud with big racking sobs, she selected his best beige twill slacks, brown loafers, a good cream open-necked shirt and his dark blue blazer. She decided against a tie but included a handkerchief for the top pocket of the blazer; a chestnut coloured silk square with a fine cream spot. What was it they used to put on their party invitations back in the sixties? 'smart casual'. That would be George, smart casual, ready for anything.

She left his wedding ring on but she wasn't sure if he would have wanted to be buried wearing a watch. She had found his retirement watch in from his sock drawer and sat looking at it and its curious Latin inscription for some time before deciding that, yes, he would like to have that with him. He was always such a stickler for time and it would make him feel at home in, well, wherever he found himself. At the last moment she slipped a photograph into the blazer pocket. It was of the three of them on holiday in Devon in 1979, a happy two weeks and a rare occasion when everything seemed to have gone right.

She remembered they had asked some strangers to take the photograph, a couple who had seemed then to be quite elderly, though in truth they were younger than Eileen was now. More tears.

*

"......And now I die, and now I was but made;
My glass is full, and now my glass is run,
And now I live, and now my life is done."

Andrew's strong, gentle voice carried clearly across the congregation. He read well, with compassion and authority. Eileen had been surprised when he called round earlier in the week with flowers, late roses from his own garden, and pleased when he not only agreed to read aloud an elegy, but later proposed to include in it a poem, one that she recognised and had always admired for its rhythm and subtlety. Something about its shift between past and present suited the way she felt about George; their life together had been cut short and yet it still felt alive, much as they say an amputated limb still exists for the amputee. It was because of this mix up in the proper sequence of time that the funeral seemed premature; farewells were being said for someone who was, to her at least, so obviously still around.

Two of the other Vikings introduced themselves to Eileen before the service began – Don, and Kevin whose son had died in July – and sat near the front. Further back there were a few other locals, acquaintances rather than friends as such, whose presence was unexpected but welcome. It was a respectable turnout considering that George had not been a local man, and that they had only lived on the island for a couple of years. He would have been pleased with himself as well as with her. I must have done something right!

Also unexpected was the attendance of three of George's

old colleagues from Parson and Green. Eileen recognised one as the young marketing executive whom George had suspected of being the ringleader in the final rebellion against him. Nevertheless she smiled and nodded at them all and was genuinely glad they'd made the effort to be there. All that anger about careers seemed such a very long time ago. Anyway, old thing, you don't want to let them think they've won.

After his death and the first few days of total silence, during which Eileen felt abandoned, George had started speaking to her, not out loud of course, but very clearly, nonetheless. The first time was when by habit she'd asked his empty space at the kitchen table if he would like more tea. Just half a cup, he said, no more. She'd poured him some, being careful not to go over halfway. The second time had been when she went back to sleep in what had been their joint bedroom. Are you coming back to me Ellie? That's good, he said as she eased herself into her side of the bed. He liked things staying how they'd always been.

There were several other occasions when his voice and the very words that he had used when he had been more obviously alive intruded themselves into her brain, sometimes taking the place of her own vocabulary. His ideas and language invaded her and she found herself almost competing for the chance to be expressed. She was carrying his personality, giving it space, helping him continue living through her. He was her constant companion, even when there were other people, even now at his own funeral.

*

As they stood up to sing the last hymn Eileen turned and saw Ray sitting right at the back of the church. So he'd come then. She looked away quickly before he raised his head from his hymn sheet. She had contacted him on the morning when George had been found in the pool, from the need to speak to

someone familiar and more than that, a friend and ally.

"I'll come round now and do what I can," Ray said and true to his word had been there within the hour. If he had been hoping for some lovers' reunion, safe together at last after the impediment to love had been removed, that was not to happen. Something had been changed by George's death; for Eileen the little wisp of a dream that had sustained her, and made her believe some kind of romance was growing between her and Ray completely evaporated. When he stepped over the threshold that day, she quickly moved away from him, hoping he would not try to kiss her. She could think of nothing more inappropriate than the idea of their intimacy. He seemed to recognise what was happening because within seconds it was as if a veil had come down between them, making real connection impossible. As if by mutual agreement, his presence was clearly that of friend rather than suitor. Ray kept his distance and offered only practical help, volunteering to go to the airport for example and meet Celia's flight. Once he had delivered her, he went home refusing Eileen's unconvincing invitation to come in and stay a while. She hadn't seen him since that day.

"Eileen!"

She felt a big hand on her shoulder as they emerged from the dark church into the sunshine of the High Street. His voice, again, made its impact before she turned to confirm what she already knew.

"Doug!"

"I'm so sorry..."

In front of them all she allowed herself to be taken into his arms, big powerful arms which gave her a sense of comfort that came from long ago, when she and the world were young.

"It's so good of you to come; I never expected it."

"George was always a true friend. You have to be there for a friend."

Eileen could feel tears coming again, after she had so successfully fended them off throughout the service, and she was glad to turn to Celia, who was standing next to her, as a distraction.

"Celia, you remember Doug, don't you? Daddy's friend?"

Celia approached Doug at first cautiously and then to Eileen's surprise put her arms around him and said in a voice of uninhibited enthusiasm, "Uncle Doug! Of course I remember; you were always my favourite."

The two big bodies, instead of parting, stayed locked in their embrace for several seconds and then, as they released each other and smiled, each showing perfect teeth in their fine-skinned faces, Eileen experienced a long overdue revelation. It was something she had suspected for many years, but only now that George had gone and was no longer there to be hurt, could she let herself acknowledge the undeniable fact that Celia was not the legitimate offspring of her marriage, but a child of love, the product of a night of passion, the result of her wonderful foolish infatuation with Douglas Foster. This certainty, despite the improbability of the idea and the sadness of the day, produced a tiny and secret spark of joy.

*

There were only a few people left at the reception, it was too sunny a day to call it a 'wake', in Moore's Hotel. Ray and Celia were sitting in an alcove near a door onto the terrace, where Celia had just finished a cigarette. A lot was happening today; she wanted everyone to go so she could sort things out.

The funeral not only marked her father's death but was pushing her into a new stage of her life; with George gone she had joined the ranks of proper adults. Thirty-three. At long last childhood was coming to an end. The wider world seemed to be insisting that she play the grown ups' game but it was not a game she knew. Even the formalities and rituals of the funeral were an unfamiliar language. Earlier in the week, realising Eileen's anguish and her own changing role, she had assumed that she, Celia, would need to look after the funeral arrangements, make sure that everything ran smoothly and was satisfactorily concluded. In fact the reverse was true; and it was Eileen even now who moved amongst the guests with grace and poise, leaving Celia glad to hide in a corner with Ray.

"Who's that with your mother?"

"Uncle Doug? I haven't seen him in years."

"There's a family resemblance."

"He's not a real uncle, just an old friend of George – Dad's."

"Your mother seems to like him?"

Celia gave Ray a look askance; she had forgotten he had a soft touch for Eileen, though that idea now seemed unthinkable.

"Mm, yes she does. So do I."

"Big fella."

"You said it's the little fellas you have to watch."

"You remember then? Glad someone was on the ball."

"I'm definitely on the ball enough to see when someone's jealous."

"Are you now!" Ray paused as if considering whether to refute the idea. "And would that bother you?"

"I suppose not. Not if she wants things that way." Though Celia doubted that her mother did want Ray's advances. Rather, she seemed to need to be on her own.

"It's academic anyway." Ray must have read her thoughts. "It's you she needs at the moment, not a boyfriend. Are you going to stay around for a bit?"

"Another couple of days but after that it will be difficult. Not that I want to go back."

This was an understatement. Her existence in London had become a mess. The events of the summer had shattered the shape and boundaries of her life. From the time when she first met Margot through all that followed on from that: the weddings, Helena's death, Margot's desertion, the chaos of her parents' so-called retirement, until, finally, this, George's death; each event had evoked from her emotions she didn't know she had, emotions no-one had told her she would experience, which would demand new strategies for coping.

'Strategies for coping.' At work she had thought the phrase was relevant only to other people, inferior people suffering from an in-born incompetence and inadequacy. She had assumed herself to be more intelligent and gifted, more fortunate than those to whom she so readily gave advice. Now she knew differently. She had tried to adjust but it wasn't easy. She wasn't really coping at work or at home.

"Had enough?"

"Of work?" Celia reached for a cigarette, "Well, since you ask yes I have. I don't know why but it all seems so futile what I'm doing at the moment. Correction, trying to do. We've got more and more immigrants coming into Camden Town – well they can't help it I know, but there are tens of thousands of them and a lot of them have special needs and it's me who's supposed to be looking after them, and with fewer and fewer resources. The council has taken on more people, yes, but they only make more meetings and more work. End to end meetings where nothing gets done. It can get on your nerves."

"What about your private life?"

She was about to say 'that's private' but instead, to her surprise and relief, she starting crying; with big heaving sobs that shook her body. They seemed to come from nowhere and have a mind of their own as she couldn't stop them. Well then, he could think what he liked; she hadn't the energy to keep pretending any more.

"Sorry for asking."

Celia turned her face, now smeared with tears and mascara, towards Ray, "I'm so...so..."

She sniffed heavily; Ray passed her a handkerchief, and she wiped her eyes and blew her nose.

"Thanks. I'm so...so...I don't know why and it isn't fair but I'm so terribly lonely!"

She started sobbing again. Ray put his arm round her

shoulders. He felt strong to her, able to hold everything together.

"Let it all go. I understand. I understand. Believe me I do."

The sobs subsided. Gradually she became calm and straightened up. Ray took his arm away.

"Sorry that's not at all like me. I'm usually fine."

"You're going through a difficult time."

"Everything's changed this summer, and now with dad gone things will never be the same again."

"They won't. But you know you can change too."

"I wish I could."

Ray leaned forward and looked her eye to eye, almost as a hypnotist might send his volunteer into a trance. "Here's one way. Why don't you come and live over here? Get away from that bloody council and all the tossers living in the big city and come and live with a load of tossers on a small island. A lot of people come here, just like you, to lick their wounds and put two fingers up at the world. I did for a start. People who want a bit of time out. You could get a job here easy. You could make friends here easy. Needn't live with your mum if you don't want to. I'll help you find a place. It would do her good to have you around and it would do you good to make a break, have a new start, at least plan where you're going next."

"Me come to Guernsey? I don't think so Ray, thank you very much! Not after London."

"Think about it." His voice was gentle. "And if it's practical help you want, like developing a strategy for your future I can always give you some Coaching sessions."

"I've heard of that." The word 'strategy' perked her up. "What is it exactly?"

Something I'm good at – you'll see."

Chapter Thirty-Five
A year later. Ghana

"A poet could not be but gay In such a jocund company."
'Daffodils' W. Wordsworth.

"I wondad lonelee as a cloud, that floats on high on yonda hill when all at once I see a crowd, a host of golden daffodil." Samuel stood awkwardly while he recited, one leg twisted round the other, but his eyes, bright-brimming and triumphant, were focused confidently on Eileen.

"Good boy, well done Samuel." He was one of Eileen's best pupils. He couldn't have been more than seven, although this was guesswork as no-one in the village seemed to know their age, and he probably had no idea of what it all meant, but he'd recited it, from memory, accurately and with conviction. "That was very good indeed."

She glanced at her watch; four thirty already, she was ready to stop even if the children weren't. She couldn't get over how eager they were to listen and to learn; it was wonderful. Look at them now, still sitting patiently on the bare earth in a big semi circle around her, waiting for more words of wisdom and reluctant to go home.

She stood up, aware of a large damp patch on the back of her skirt. She still had not acclimatised to the heat and suspected she never would. She stood in front of the children swishing her skirt to make it dry faster, not that the children seemed to notice how much she sweated, but it was important to maintain standards, keep the flag flying. Now that sounded just like George. Funny how she had absorbed and now occasionally reiterated George-like phrases. Was it a mark of respect? Or plagiarism? Had she adopted part of his personality as a new facet of her own? It sometimes felt as if she had brought him out with her to West Africa.

She clapped her hands. "All right everybody, it's time to go home. Tomorrow we will have arithmetic and geography and then a spelling competition. But I am going to leave you with some homework. I want you to find out where rubber comes from. You can ask anyone you like, your mummies or daddies. Just see if you can find out, and tell me tomorrow in our geography lesson."

Half a dozen hands shot up, "Miss, Miss, I know about rubber, I can tell you now. No wait for tomorrow."

"No, Miss, me please I also know rubber, how they are makin' it! There are trees nearby."

"No, me Miss. Ask me. I can tell you."

They were getting quite agitated now, leaping up and down arms waving, shouting excitedly. Eileen wondered at their energy especially in the afternoon's humidity. The sweat was now trickling down her legs.

"That's lovely but we're going to stop now. Yes we are. Good afternoon children."

"Good afternoon Mis-sus Buch-an-an." But they still didn't leave. It was nice in the classroom, cool and comfortable under the thatched roof with the breeze from the river blowing through the window openings in the wall. They liked this old English lady with her funny voice and her stories. Besides, the sooner they got back home the sooner they would have to get down to household tasks: fetching water, fanning the fire for cooking, and looking after younger brothers and sisters. She shooed them out then with a last smile and 'goodbye', and stooped under the low doorway out into the sun. The children scattered in all directions but which way should she take back to her house?

It was four months, one week and six days since she had come to Bento and it still seemed strange, very strange to be there: in a village in the bush, twenty miles from any two storey houses, surfaced roads, pavements or even shops, let alone hotels or hospitals. There was no hot water, not that it really mattered in the heat, and only intermittent electricity supplied by the new generator which stood between the Chief's hut and her own proper bungalow. Originally the guest house for the local Colonial Administrator and other visiting VIPs, it was built of brick instead of mud, had a tin roof and the great luxury of a verandah. There was no air conditioning of course, but as soon as the generator was up and working she bought an electric fan, which she moved as needed between her kitchen and bedroom. After school she sat on the verandah in the breeze from the river, reading until just after sunset when the mosquitoes came out. They and the darkness drove her indoors to sit in front of the fan by an old storm lantern, which gave a good light but hissed and spluttered as if it were about to explode.

Once a fortnight she went to Accra by the local mammy taxi, ostensibly to collect and post mail. In addition to the mail she went shopping, checked out the Amity Bookshop and had a poolside lunch and a swim at one of the larger hotels. It was an extravagance but she didn't think she could survive without it.

The schoolroom environment had taken time to adjust to as well. On the day she arrived she had been exhausted by the two hour journey from Accra over the unmade laterite roads, and with every mile, as she lurched around in the back of the taxi with her Danish 'host' from Africa Teaching Aid, she had a growing sense of dread. This was a terrible mistake; she should have known better. She was too old for adventures, however well-intentioned.

She had expected conditions to be basic: stools instead of desks and chairs, old-fashioned blackboards and chalk, and probably a very restricted number of textbooks. When the village Chief – a stout imposing man in chintzy native dress – showed her the thatched rondavel with the mud floor and half a blackboard leaning against a few broken chairs, she was shocked. There were no stools, no desks, no paper and pencils, no maps and only three dog-eared text books, their bindings soft and rotted by the humidity. As she stood at the threshold of the school, she felt overwhelmed with guilt and misery. How foolish she'd been to think she could make a difference in this sort of setting.

"But how will I manage?" she turned to her host, her heart sinking.

Anders smiled enigmatically, shaking bleached dreadlocks back from his cherubic young face, "Don't worry, you'll be fine. You will soon learn the ropes. Now I must leave, otherwise we won't be back in Accra before night comes. The locals won't drive when it's dark."

"Eyesight problems?" She said, wondering if not being able to see in the dark was some ethnic difference that she had never been told about.

"No, bandits."

"Bandits?"

"They carry machetes and are not afraid to use them. So better for you to stay inside the village after six or seven. Don't get naughty and go for any romantic walks." The blue eyes were serious in the bland face. "I'll be back next week to check everything goes well for you. If you have any problems just ask Elijah to help you. He's the local Big Man, the Chief."

Elijah seemed pleased to be described thus and smiled broadly at her. "Yes I am. A Big Man."

For a brief moment Eileen considered climbing back into the taxi, which, despite the lack of suspension and the leaky exhaust pipe, now seemed like a limousine, and high-tailing it back to civilisation. Even the possibility of meeting bandits on the road in the company of a mad Dane seemed preferable to staying on in this bereft village. Courage failed her and she stayed silent while Anders jumped expertly into the car alongside the driver, shouted something which sounded like a warning about snakes, before they accelerated away in a cloud of red dust. She stood watching the car until it was lost to view.

"Eh heh!" Elijah coughed tactfully. "I can hear your mind madam. An' I know very well what you are t'inkin'. At this very moment you are t'inkin' dat dis job of mine in Africa is impossible."

"Not at all. No, I'm not. Well, yes, maybe I am. You're right. I think I have made a terrible mistake."

He smiled again, showing big and beautiful teeth despite his grizzled hair, "I'm thinking we will be fine. Hmm yes! God has sent you to be wit' us and the children here are very very smat and learn very very fast! Have no fear. Soon you will find William Shakespeare and Albert Einstein sittin' in this very hut. You will see! Eh – now you are laughing so I know you are feelin' better." It was true, she did.

*

The schoolroom had been built on the outskirts of the village and there were two routes she could choose to go home. She was still surprised at how readily she could use that word! She could go either through the village itself or by the path that followed the contour of the river.

She decided on the river walk in part because she couldn't face the village tonight. She felt pleasantly tired and wanted peace and quiet. To go through the village was to invite friendly but non-stop participation in community life. Even after four months the villagers still wanted to hear certain details of her life: where she was from, how many children she had, how many grandchildren, did she like Ghana, would she like a Ghanaian husband and so on and so forth until she had to shake her head, smile, give the elaborate farewell demanded by Bento culture and walk on. Over the weeks the villagers had become real friends but every now and again she needed to walk on her own.

The sun was getting low in the sky and cooler air was blowing in from over the water. The river was wide and slow moving and could be crossed by foot by the end of the dry season. Now at the beginning of the rainy season swift moving streams were beginning to swirl along the river bed leaving dwindling islands of sand. Close to the shore there were still small pools not yet absorbed into the main flow. It was here that the women did the laundry, standing knee deep, rubbing their clothes with big blocks of soap, then beating them clean on the smooth flat rocks.

It was also here that the villagers bathed, usually in the early morning and the evening, avoiding the heat of the day. Each group had their own area and tended to bathe at different times. The young men collected in a big pool out dangerously near the central current and they bathed in the evening making a lot of noise and spent much time mock-fighting and wrestling. The women and children went there in the afternoon and stayed near the shore. The older men confined themselves to the odd solitary dip in dignified isolation in the early morning, sometimes even before the mist had risen from the water's surface. They stayed close to the river bank, as if no longer needing the challenge of rough water.

Several times one of the women, Elijah's number one wife, called her over to join them, shouting to make herself heard over the rush of water. "Come, come and join us, Auntie. Make yourself to be cool."

She was a big, handsome woman with broad features and large slanting eyes, and she beckoned imperiously. Every time Eileen hesitated. She would have liked to stand in the cool water ideally with her clothes on so they could dry on her afterwards. That would be such a relief. But she sensed that it was not appropriate for an old woman, and there was no doubting her antiquity in the context of Bento, to be seen playing in the water. It might look undignified. Besides she felt shy. No, if she wanted to cool down then she had to rely on the puny shower in her bathroom, and a bottle of cold beer from the fridge. So she had waved and smiled at them but always shook her head and walked on.

*

She had become fond of the bungalow especially since she had organised several improvements. In pride of place was her desk, where she spent her evenings, reading, preparing lessons and writing letters back home. The desk had been made to her design by the village carpenter. It was roughly finished and she kept catching her paper on a snag in the wood but it served its purpose well enough. Besides it had been conceived and produced in two days a remarkable achievement she later realised, as everything else in the village seemed untouched by the press of time and things took however long they took.

She had also been responsible for the generator, paying for it with her own money and making a present of it to the village. It had taken two months to find anyone who could make it work but when it was finally operative it seemed to everyone in Bento, including Eileen, a miracle. Only the Chief's huts and her own house were connected and it wasn't long before a group of children came regularly after sundown to use the light that came from her window. They sat on her verandah for an hour or two, oblivious to the mosquitoes, and played games or read the books she had brought with her as teaching aids. She liked the sound of their voices, it was company. Later in the evening when they had gone off to bed she would sit by her radio twiddling the tuner while the World Service news came and went through a fog of static.

All in all she could look at her life and be amazed at the way she was coping. If only George could see me she thought, and she still had an inkling that perhaps he could, wouldn't he be surprised? Wouldn't he be proud to see me here in the middle of the jungle, perfectly happy? Because that was the most surprising thing about it; she was.

This evening as she approached the bungalow the Chief's youngest son ran over and gave her an envelope, with an airmail border. A letter from Celia. What a treat! She would save it until she had had her shower, taken a beer and some ground nuts from the refrigerator and was sitting comfortable and relaxed on the verandah.

While the tepid water trickled over her body she wondered if the letter would indeed have positive news and tried to anticipate what Celia would have to say about her new life. Because she, too, had taken a bold step. She had sold the lease on her flat in London, given in her notice at Camden Council and moved to Guernsey.

"It was Ray's suggestion" admitted Celia when she phoned to tell her mother of her plans. "I thought he was mad to start off with but then I thought Hell why not? Camden was getting old. I need a change."

Eileen had left for Africa before Celia came over permanently to Guernsey, so Ray offered to help her move into Les Vardes, find a job and generally settle in. True to his word he had somehow helped her find a job with the States Housing Committee, a position which Celia felt confident would showcase her bureaucratic skills.

In the months after George's death Ray had continued to be part of Eileen's life, just as he had hoped. They had not become physically or emotionally close, her choice not his. What she had suspected in the summer was confirmed by the passing of time. She didn't want to be someone's wife again, or even a companion. She didn't want what she began to feel was the tyranny of sharing minds, bodies and the other more mundane details of domestic life. She was looking for something new and bigger, and a way of being that was hers and hers alone. Ray, meanwhile, had recognised that with George's death the relationship with Eileen had taken a different direction and that his plan for their future had been rejected. If he was disappointed, he concealed it. He had learned to have patience, and now he simply watched and waited. So they remained friends...

Celia had been surprised. "I thought you two might have become an item by now? That Ray might have moved in?" She and Eileen were sitting together by the fire on Christmas Eve. It was the first time Celia had referred directly to the relationship since George had died.

"Ray has asked," Eileen explained carefully, "and I have considered it. He's a good man, with a good heart, though it's not always easy to see that. But what he has is not what I want now. I feel ready for something else altogether."

"He's quite attractive in his way. Physically I mean."

"Beauty lies in the eye of the beholder!"

"Oh no, I don't mean handsome as such."

"What do you mean then?"

But Celia hadn't an answer.

Two weeks after that conversation Eileen thought she might have found the something else. During a rather aimless session on the internet one morning she came across the Africa Teaching Aid website. *"Retired? Unemployed? Bored? Has life lost its meaning?"* read the copy. Yes, yes, yes and yes, thought Eileen. *"Come to Africa and do something valuable. Spend just six months teaching in villages in Africa. Give your skills to people who need them. Show your love. Start living again."*

Clever stuff. She sat looking for a long time at the pictures of mud huts, of women in bright clothes and of needy but beautiful children. That night she dreamed of Africa and installed herself within the picturesque scenery, a younger self in a long skirt, a Madonna-like figure walking slowly amongst groups of wide-eyed smiling children. When she woke, the decision was made to at least ring Africa Teaching Aid to see what they were about. Just a general enquiry, nothing binding.

"What about age?" she asked the friendly young man on the

switchboard. Are you sure I'm not too old?"

"You just can't be too old for Africa Mrs. Buchanan. The Africans respect age – it's not like England. Old people there have experience, wisdom, authority. Young people are unformed, all energy and no knowledge. Of course I'm assuming that you are in good health?"

"I'm fine thank you."

"Good, We need to replace someone in Ghana. The children of Bento don't have anyone. Could you be ready to go, say, in the first week of February?

"That soon? I'd need to – er, ask someone first. I'll call you back."

She looked out at the wet and windy January morning. Who was she trying to convince? There was no-one to ask. No-one to give or withhold permission. There was nothing to stop her from doing whatever she wanted to.

She thought about it for two days before giving her formal commitment.

"I'll miss you." Ray sat across the kitchen table looking at her

with a new respect.

"Celia will be here in two weeks. You can look after each other."

"I won't have had time to settle in properly before you leave!" Celia sounded faintly hysterical over the 'phone.

"Ray will look after you and you'll have the people at work. It's a friendly place. Anyway I'll be back by the end of July." Eileen was surprised at her own selfishness. She hadn't realised she could be so determined.

She had even managed at long last to tell Celia about Doug, putting things off until what she felt was an appropriate moment, on Boxing Day morning. Ever since she recognised that Doug must be Celia's natural father Eileen had felt guilty and joyful in turn, but eventually decided, it was an accident that had a miraculous and very positive outcome. She knew Doug had his faults and that he had probably never cared for her in the way that she loved him, but all that didn't matter. In a Strand Palace Hotel bedroom thirty three years ago they had created life, life which resulted in the existence of Celia – the person she cared about most in all the world.

That morning the weather was mild enough to go walking and as they sat on a bench at Icart overlooking Petit Bot Bay she felt the moment had come.

"I've something to tell you Celia. It's not an easy thing but I think it's time you knew."

Celia looked at her quizzically, eyes squinting in the sun.

"Years ago, when I was young and a bit foolish, I had an affair – well it was a fling really, just the one night, with a man I was in love with. I've never told anyone but now I feel I must. George is dead so this can't hurt him now." This was more difficult than she'd feared. "And you should know that I believe, am pretty sure in fact, that you are the result of that one night."

Celia carried on looking at her with the same expression.

"You understand what I'm trying to say, aren't you....?"

Silence.

"I know this must be a terrible – well, a shock for you…"

"You're telling me that George is not my real father?" Celia's voice was husky.

"No, I don't think he is – was."

Silence again, apart from the swish of the sea on the rocks below them and a plane overhead.

"Who is then?"

It was now or never. "Your Uncle Doug."

"Uncle Doug!" Disbelief. "You had an affair with Uncle Doug?"

"I thought I was in love with him. I was in love with him. I didn't plan to get pregnant, I didn't plan to sleep with him. It just sort of happened."

"Where was George?"

"At some conference or another. Harrogate I think. Doug had tickets for the theatre and his wife was away and so he asked me to go with him. And one thing led to another. It only happened the once."

"What makes you so sure?"

"The dates. In fact it could only be him. Daddy and I weren't very active at that time – it happens in marriages you know – so we were both surprised when I found out I was expecting, but I kept quiet and hoped for the best. I'm sorry. Maybe I should have told you before. But I wasn't sure until I saw the two of you together at Daddy's funeral. I knew then immediately – just the way you look and how you both use your hands – it was obvious."

A long silence while Celia reached for her cigarettes, lighted one and drew on it deeply, looking out to sea while she did so. "Funny thing, Ray said there was a family resemblance when he saw Doug at the funeral. I thought he was just being sort of polite." She looked down and scuffed the grass with her trainers. "Where does he live then, Uncle Doug?"

"Do you want to contact him? He doesn't know anything."

"I'm not sure. Maybe. I was just thinking I don't really know him. What sort of person is he?"

"Well, I liked him a lot."

"Obviously."

"He was the kind of man who makes a woman feel feminine, even beautiful. Protected. He never argued about anything or tried to prove a point. Always told me I looked nice – that was so important. He always had warm hands, and he was so lovely to cuddle. I just felt happy whenever I was with him. That was all there was to it."

Eileen wondered if she had done the right thing saying so much. At least George was not there to get upset.

"George never knew?"

"I don't think so, no."

"It's sad isn't it if he thought I was his flesh and blood all along."

"He loved you for who you are. You had two fathers."

"I'll think about it, seeing uncle Doug. Maybe later. It seems too soon now."

"I know what you mean."

*

Clean and cool and wearing a local tie-dye dress in orange and red, Eileen sat in her plastic chair on the verandah, put on her reading glasses and opened the letter.

Les Vardes,
St Peter Port.
Wednesday May 24th 2000.

Dear Eileen,

It's been such a long time since we've heard from you. I can't believe how slow the post is. And of course no email connection. They must be really struggling over there. How unfair it all is.

That's the capitalist system for you.

I hope the teaching is still going well. It sounds as if you're really enjoying it from your last letter. I'm glad the biros were a success with the kids. Never thought they wouldn't have paper! I'll send through ATA.

Hope the generator is working by now and that you've got electricity. Seems strange to think of you trying to get cool. It's wet and windy here at the moment. Don't worry. I've been keeping an eye on the garden and Mr. Perelle is keeping it neat and tidy.

Some big news. Ray and I have decided to be partners. I expect this is a bit of a surprise although I know you realised that I like him. I do, and he likes me, despite the age difference and everything. We've been seeing each other a lot since I came over, what with the Coaching sessions, and things have got more serious over the last few weeks. I didn't tell you before because I didn't know if it would last. But it really feels as if I've known him all my life and he says he feels the same. I hope you feel OK about it."

Eileen paused and took a deep breath – Celia and Ray! She put the letter down to let things sink in. She had noticed on several occasions how close they were, but only as friends, she'd never for a moment imagined that there was or even could be anything romantic about it. Partners! That was modern talk for lovers. Intimacy. Sex. Did she feel OK about it? No she did not. Ray was too old, it seemed wrong. Quite wrong such an old man when Celia was still just a girl.

She surprised herself by the strength of her reaction, and tried hard to look at the situation dispassionately. Ray was a family friend, reliable and decent. Intelligent too. A good companion. And from the point of view of providing for Celia there was enough money to look after them both. And at least he wasn't a woman! And George would have added 'Nor a bloody Marxist". Anyway, there was no mention of marriage so the situation wasn't irreversible. There was time for things to unwind just as they had with Margot. It was probably just a passing fancy: two intelligent adults getting together – what could be more natural? She turned back to the rest of the letter.

Even bigger news! I found out yesterday that I'm pregnant! It came as a bit of a shock. I'd been feeling sick on and off and when my period was five weeks late I thought it could only be one thing. I suppose it could have been a really early menopause but I've had it checked out and I am definitely going to have a baby. The doctor said I'm due in November so I must have conceived some time in March. Ray was really excited and insisted on opening a bottle of champagne when I told him although I said I couldn't take alcohol that wouldn't be fair to the foetus. So he drank the whole bottle himself apart from me having just a little sip which I thought wouldn't do any harm.

I'm pleased too although it has all come as a bit of a shock. I won't stop work of course but I am hoping they will give me the same maternity leave as I'd get on the mainland. Ray says not to worry about money. He's so looking forward to the baby and I think he hopes it will be a boy but of course I'm totally impartial. Gender is so irrelevant.

I wonder what George would have thought about it all, the baby and Ray and everything. I keep meaning to go to the cemetery and check his grave is tidy, but somehow with work and everything so busy here there just hasn't been time. I'll try and go next week.

How do you feel about becoming a grandmother!

Ray joins me in sending love and says he is writing separately.

All my – our love, and write soon!
Celia xxx

PS. You've got new neighbours by the way. A retired couple who seem very quiet."

Eileen sat for some time in the setting sun with the letter in her hand. Another shock, this time more profound and disturbing. Celia and Ray living together was one thing, but creating a family was altogether different: a huge step for them - and for her. After all, the baby would be her grandchild, her flesh and blood. Good news in principle but what she found disturbing and could not understand was how this had happened when she, Eileen, had not been there to see the relationship growing, to anticipate the pregnancy and give it her blessing? Surely Celia, at least, must realise how hurt she was at being left out, and then of only learning about it by letter? Their intimacy seemed almost like a conspiracy against her.

Yet even in her distress she had to admit that was ridiculous. Conspiracy? Celia and Ray were two lonely adults who were doing what they wanted, and it wasn't their fault that Eileen hadn't been there to learn about their relationship from the start. It was her decision to be five thousand miles away in a different continent.

She wished she could talk to George about it. He would have an opinion, be able to sort out her confused feelings. Use one of his tricks that he learned at Parson and Green. But there of course was the nub of the problem. George wasn't there. He was dead, and that was the real reason for her distress. What she felt about the pregnancy she realised was envy, not just about the baby but about the fact that Celia and Ray were starting their lives together and that they had each other and maybe many years ahead of them. She, on the other hand, had been suddenly left alone, at a time in her life when it was unlikely she would ever again have someone to care for or to care for her...

"For God's sake get a grip on yourself woman." It was George, loud and clear in her head. She hadn't heard from him in weeks. "Celia's having a baby. You're going to be a grandmother. That's what you've been wanting for years, isn't it? So what are you whingeing about?"

That much was true. She was going to be a grandmother. Celia was settling down with a man who would look after her and protect her. It was good news.

"You've always said that grandmothers get all the nice bits and miss out on the nappies. Well, here's your opportunity."

They would live close to each other on the island. Eileen could see the baby every day. And she could still come over to Ghana and teach her lovely children here. She would have the best of both worlds. Apart from the suddenness it was, really, just what she had wanted.

"Now you're thinking a bit more clearly Ellie. Go outside and find someone to celebrate with. Stop mooning around. Think positive."

He was right. She would find someone to tell. But who? Outside she stood on the verandah looking down the slope to the river bank. There were Elijah's wives standing in the river shallows. She could hear them talking and laughing as usual. They were all mothers and grandmothers several times over and would understand how she felt. They looked up as she came towards them. She stood on the bank and shouted to make herself heard over the sound of the river. The water was high that evening.

"I'm going to be a grandmother. I've just heard from my daughter. Isn't that wonderful?"

They smiled encouragingly but seemed not to have heard or perhaps didn't understand what she was saying.

"I'm going to be a grandmother!"

Still they looked blank behind the smiles. She'd need to get closer.

"Welcome, you are welcome, join us Eileen, come! I will hold you." Elijah's number one wife reached out her hand.

She hesitated for only a second. Kicking off her sandals she grasped the hand, and stepped carefully into the knee-deep water. The pull of the current was surprisingly strong but still holding hands she stood firm, laughing with them as the main river roiled and rushed and glinted past them on its way to the sea. It was cool and wonderful. She'd tell them her good news later.

Epilogue

Helena Amy Buchanan was born on 27th October 2000 in the Princess Elizabeth Hospital St Peter Port, Guernsey, weighing seven pounds five ounces. It was a trouble-free birth despite the age and weight of her first time mother.

Her parents, Celia and Ray, were besotted with her, of course, from the start. Celia stayed at home for six months after the birth then went back to working part-time as a civil servant for the Guernsey States even though Ray assured her that they had no need at all for her salary. Celia enjoys what she calls a balanced lifestyle: Ray and baby Helena for her nurturing side and the Department when she needs to express her skills at delegating.

Ray found he was cautiously but profoundly happy. He had attained his goal of a settled family life, and the reality of it far exceeded any hopes that he had kept with him on his long journey from the orphanage. You might expect him to feel a little guilty over the way he achieved his goal, but what did he do except let life and death take their course?

Helena has two grandparents: Eileen, her grandmother, lives half the year in Guernsey and the other half in Africa, and is amazingly young and active. She always has lots of exciting stories to tell her granddaughter and brings back funny presents from Ghana. She doesn't have a husband but is seeing the gentle 'uncle Andrew' who keeps her company when she is on the island. He writes poetry and she writes short stories and they go out for walks together along the cliff path. He doesn't swim so much or so far these days, but is still a member of the Vikings. They sometimes play bridge with the retired couple next door in Les Vardes, nice people from St Alban's.

Helena doesn't see her grandfather Doug who lives on the mainland - the big man Celia calls 'Dad' - quite so often, but when she's with him she's as good as gold, as if his mere physical presence is something essential to her wellbeing. Doug and Ray are in some kind of business together and spend a lot of time on the phone. Surprisingly, they get on well.

Helena's Godmother, Amy, lives on the mainland. She once made a trip to Guernsey, which she enjoyed, but she was glad to get back to her house and the cat. She sends her godchild books and her friend Celia long letters, which Celia keeps.

Steve or Gloria now live happily in Cyprus running their own hotel and spa. They are making enough money not to need to trade in soft or hard porn, although they occasionally have a photo-shoot with Gloria posing against the sky. While they have forgotten all about Guernsey the island authorities still have them in their records, a black mark against their names.

Helena is never told about them, nor about the beautiful but ageing Margot who disappeared amongst the crowds of North London but, eventually, surfaced as somebody's assistant's assistant in an animation studio in L.A..

She is told about her namesake, how Celia met her at the open-air theatre in Regent's Park and why she became an important part of Celia's life.

She has also heard a lot about her other grandfather. George is at peace under the turf near a big oak tree in the Foulon cemetery, dreaming of the life he led, and is all in all pleased with who he had been and what he achieved.

If he were alive again he would be glad to see that Eileen still keeps his study in the belvedere just as he left it. Sometimes she climbs up the steep stairs and sits at his desk looking out at the view of the sea, and imagines she can hear his voice in another part of the house, calling for her.

411